Brave Souls

By
Jacey K Dew

Content Information

Please visit the link below for a specific content information guide, leading to page numbers and brief nondescript summarizations should you decide to skip those pages.
https://jaceykdew.ca/books/content-warnings

Published by Crimson Notebook Publishing
crimsonnotebook.ca

This is a work of fiction. Names, characters, places, and incidents either are the product of the author's imagination or are used fictiously.

Hardback ISBN: 978-1-7387710-0-4
Paperback ISBN: 978-1-9992414-8-3
eBook ISBN: 978-1-9992414-9-0
Audio ISBN: 978-1-998486-03-8

To my wonderful children; Emily and Jeremy.

Your imaginations inspire me. I hope you continue your love for creating stories and fantasy.

I love you with all my heart.

A special thanks to Emily Dew (Age 7), who allowed me to use the Christmas song she wrote.

Santa Makes Our Wish Come True!

Snow, Snow a white blanket of snow.
Snow, Snow comes in the winter.
Snow, Snow comes on Christmas.

Oh, Oh, Oh, Oh.
All the decorations shimmer and shine.
Oh, Oh, Oh, Oh, Oh, Oh.

On Christmas night Santa brings all of us presents.
Santa goes all around the world giving us presents.

Oh, the tree ornaments shimmer and shine.

Santa makes our wish come true!
Santa makes our wish come true!

By Emily Dew

The Story So Far…

Alexa Brenner

Finds out her boyfriend (Darius) is a vampire when he kidnaps her niece (Rayleen) and takes Alexa to a farm (base of operations). He plans on leveraging Rayleen (even threatening her) to control Alexa (making her his vampire queen).

Sandra shows Alexa that supernaturals have been hidden since the 6th century, and many want to stop (extremists put into action a world takeover). Some, have gathered forces to take control of the world, including two of the Council (highest form of government) members; Seth (vampire – Nocturnal Council Leader) and Aalayah (fire elemental – Elemental Council Leader).

Former friends (now enemies of Darius) come to kidnap Alexa and turn her against Darius (to hurt him and destabilize his region) by showing her that he's on the wrong side (causing war, death, and destruction to take over the world). Miles (accidentally) gets captured and Darius forcing Alexa to hurt him, ensures that process.

Rayleen is rescued, but Alexa goes back and forth (rescued, Darius gets her back, but throws her downstairs to be eaten by hobgoblins because he finds her traitorous at the moment, then rescued again).

They make it to James' house (Magic Folk Council Leader) and start collecting people and land for a rebellion. Making friends with the dwarves in the Rocky Mountains (by tree nymph travelling) to get weapons and armour made.

The army finds them at James' and takes them to a school,

but sort out supernaturals to kill, so they get away from there and go back to the dwarves to collect the swords and armour.

They go check out a city nearby that seems to be doing well in the aftermath, but tensions blow up soon after they arrive. They collect the stuff and the dwarves and end up at the mall with a large base of people (allies – Nikki's group).

Darius attacks the mall to kidnap Rayleen and Alexa again, but Sandra has other plans. She kidnaps Nikki, suspecting she's from a long line of Dreamers (visions of the future in dreams).

This theory is why James says they have to go rescue her (no one wants the bad guys to have someone who can see the future in their ranks). They go to the farm and try to rescue Nikki. But, Rayleen is kidnapped instead. Sandra and Darius ride away with Rayleen and Nikki on the back of a dragon.

Alexa is a mess. They leave the farmhouse once they recover and collect themselves. Then bump into Jaiden in Red Deer.

Nikki Marshall

Skipping work to go to the mall with friends (at the insistence of Shawn - an elf who would have prior knowledge of something coming) on the exact wrong day (supernatural uprising) ends with them stuck inside a dollar store (having dodged doomsdayers on the road and supernaturals inside the mall, and collecting some people from the army store upstairs).

They scout out and secure the mall while finding people (including Tyler) and host a party at the end of the world. The atmosphere tenses eventually when rescue doesn't come and they can't agree on how to proceed.

Nikki and her friends go out to find their families but are found dead or missing. Finding no point in staying out, they go back to the safety of the mall.

Some want to continue partying under Tyler's lead, while others turn towards long-term survival. Nikki's friends group is split at the reveal that Shawn is an elf.

Nikki's group relocates to the theatre when Tyler's group ransacks the mall. Then, Nikki rescues some people from the hotel.

Kelly and Miles come. It's put to a vote to go to James's house or stay. The majority votes to stay at the mall. But, they agree to be allies.

Tyler's group attacks Nikki's and some are killed on both sides. They agree to split the mall and not enter each other's territory.

Kelly returns quickly as James' house was attacked and Nikki prepares for refuge and takes in a trickle of people from James' house.

Once James arrives, James plans for an eventual attack on the farm. Nikki saves Rayleen from Daniel (Alexa's new human boyfriend) after he violently rages toward her age-appropriate temper tantrum.

Darius attacks the mall, and Nikki is kidnapped on the back of a dragon. She's quickly rescued at the farm, and then kidnapped again, but this time Rayleen is kidnapped as well.

They land at a jail and are taken inside. Nikki is separated from Rayleen and tortured until she agrees to help them by telling them visions of the future (that she's going to have to make up).

Jaiden Kensington

Gets a vacation from her regular life when the world is attacked and spends a week alone and relaxing.

This ends when people break into her home. She decides to go to her (biological father's wife's mom's house) grandma's house because of a joke about everyone going there if the world ended and because she's also having visions of her sister (biological father's stepdaughter).

Gets to grandma's to find out a separate group is there and no family to be found. They have a set of werewolves captured and show her as proof of a demon takeover.

Jaiden separates from them on a walkabout, and find's her sister's ex-boyfriend, who brings her to his family farm (loads of his family/friends – pack of werewolves).

They rescue the werewolves and Jaiden finds out that the human group had killed her whole family (assumes Dominique is alive from visions and not seeing her in the pile of bodies). Jaiden decides to go back home and figure out the next steps.

Calli (succubi) takes her to a grocery store with a bunch of people. They are sent on a mission to the hospital and are attacked. Ostracized from the grocery store, they (along with Lucas) go south.

Calli brings them to Jerry's (bar/hotel/delivery service for supernaturals). They work for their worth. Jaiden saves some and herself from dying in an attack that she had a vision of.

Calli wakes Jaiden saying they have to leave (another attack). While running from an ogre, they run into Alexa's group. They travel further south then take refuge at a house.

Jaiden finds out the group is trying to rescue Nikki (who is also Dominique) through a poetry notebook Jaiden gifted to Dominique.

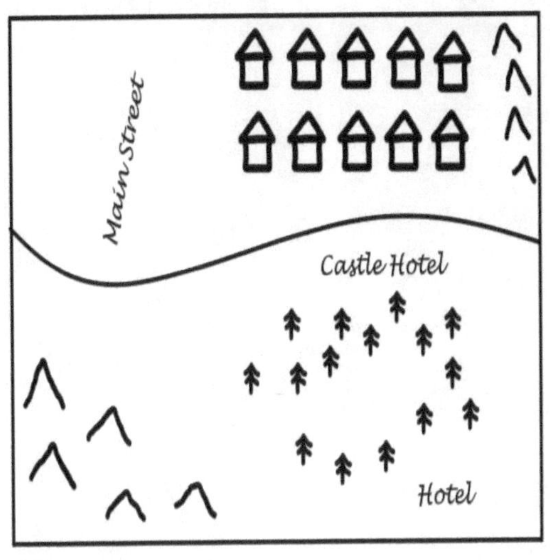

X
Jail

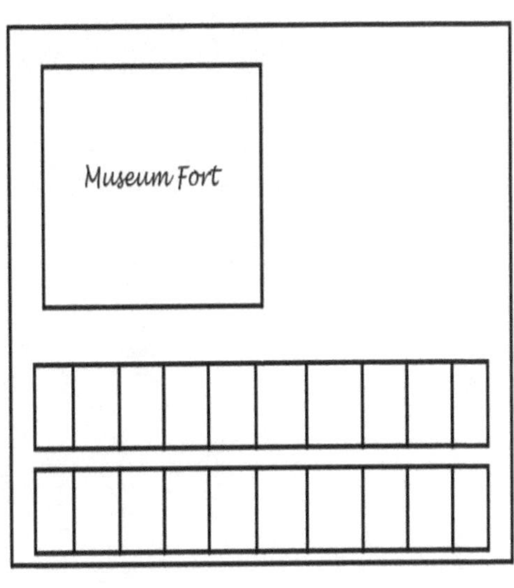

X

Fort MacLeod

Chapter 1

"It makes no sense. They decided to come with us fast; too fast." Daniel makes subtle accusations in his quiet comments. The same thought has crossed my mind a couple of times now. "Who are those people?"

The whole situation felt a little too convenient and scripted. Like convenient coincidences that happen in movies to purely just move the plot along. They threw themselves in front of our truck and talked with us for a minute before they were suddenly a part of our group.

We're supposed to be besties now; apparently. James immediately trusted them; integrated them into the group.

Though, I guess Jaiden knew some of us from school. I don't remember her. I don't remember seeing her at all. I don't remember her name. I don't think she was in any of my classes.

How does she know me?

Is it just because she paid attention to Darius and his group of friends? We were- they were part of the popular crowd.

Or, could she know Darius through the supernatural world? Could they be spies for Darius?

She seemed to know Daniel, Miles, and Kelly, while none of them seemed like they knew her. Her link to knowing them might be Darius.

An annoyed feminine voice starts to my right. She had gone unnoticed in the dark outside the glowing circle of the fire. "Let me put it this way, a King comes to you and asks you to join his group with no explanation; what would you do? Or, do you not even realize how important James is? He's magic folk royalty. Besides, isn't that basic nature? Something instinctual that people crave to be in large groups for protection?" There is a bite to Calli's voice.

I almost feel guilty for Daniel when Calli pipes up. He looks as surprised as I'm certain I look, yet not as bashful.

Welcome to the group. Now we're going to talk about you behind your backs, but still within earshot. Then, you're going to call us out for it.

All three newcomers had heard what he said. They've emerged from the dark one by two.

Her mention of magic folk royalty brings back memories from a couple of weeks ago. Memories forced into my head from Sandra's magic. I cringe at the memory of the itchy feeling magic. There were four people up on the stage, and James had been one of them. Seth had been another. I haven't seen the other two yet, but one was Ashlynn's sister; the fire elemental.

How long before the war did that gathering happen? Where did it happen?

Looking further back, I don't remember any of the guys going away for any long periods of time. Maybe it happened close to home? It would explain why so many important people were in and around our town. Maybe their headquarters are nearby.

The war started and I was immediately introduced to two Council leaders and two Elementals. Four people, apparently, very high up in demon society. It couldn't have been just a coincidence that all those important people were in the same area at the same time.

Daniel sputters and stumbles over some sounds. "That doesn't explain anything."

Calli rolls her eyes. She and the other two settle down in our circle around the fire. "Yes, it does. James is the Magic Folk's Council Representative. He is one of four people who rule all supernatural beings. He and Niklas, the Diurnal Council Representative, are against this aggressive revolution. They tried to stop all of this from happening. They are trying to restore peace. We want that too. Is that good enough for you, or do I have to explain it to you further?" Calli arches her eyebrow questioning him.

"So, what are you?" Brad asks her in a notion to save Daniel from further embarrassment. There is an undertone of distaste impossible to miss.

A shiver creeps up my spine. I pull my limbs closer to me. The wind has shifted and I no longer have the heat directed my way.

"I'm a succubus." Calli smiles at him; flashing her teeth. My knowledge of succubuses is they have sex with men and steal their souls. At least, that's how they're portrayed in movies.

"Are all of you succubuses-es?" He frowns. Visibly disgusted with the news.

"Succubi, if it's plural." Calli corrects him. "But no, they're both as human as humans can be." She waves her hand at Jaiden and Lucas.

"Why are humans travelling with a succubus?" Brad directs the question toward her companions.

"Food." Calli deadpans.

Lucas ignores Brad to glare at Calli, leaving Jaiden to answer. She looks up at him from the ground. "She's not eating our souls. We're friends."

"Did you know what she is?" Brad sneers.

Jaiden scrunches her eyebrows and shakes her head. "Yes, not that it matters."

"Of course it matters." Brad throws his hands up in the air.

Shawn sits looking at Brad with a blank face. His jawline tightens.

"No, it doesn't." Jaiden paces her words. A small space of time between each of the three words reminds me of how one might speak to a small child to get a point across. She continues at normal pacing. "What she is, what anyone is, doesn't have any bearing on how I think of them. Nor should it matter to anyone else.

Sure, it's interesting to know the ancestral background, cultural behaviour and nuances, or particulars, but no one should be judged on their species. Judge them as a person. Are they generally a good person; yes or no? That is what is important. And, if you want to be friends with them, it helps if your personalities get along or you have a couple common interests." Her words sound like jumbled babbling. Mixed trails of thought jammed together.

"You're naïve." Brad accuses her in his interruption. Her jaw drops slightly as her right eyebrow raises, and she looks deeply offended.

"You're a racist idiot." Calli's volume raises a couple of levels and deepens with her anger. "If more people thought like her we wouldn't be in this mess. Maybe if supernaturals felt like they had the option of revealing themselves without hate and backlash, or being killed or experimented on. Maybe, if we felt we would be accepted as more than second-class citizens and not treated like dangerous monsters. Maybe, we wouldn't have had to start a war to reveal ourselves."

"I'm not racist. I'm cautious." Brad's defence of himself falls short of being convincing.

"You're a racist. You're disgusted by me because you learned what I am. The first thing you said to me was 'what are you?' Then, you ask my friends if they knew; as if that would change their minds about me. You are a racist asshole." Calli points at him to further make her point.

"Well, if you're so goody-goody, what was the first thing you said to her?" Brad asks Jaiden. I can see he is trying to deflect the attention off him and to someone else now, but I don't think it'll work the way he thinks it will.

Luckily, Daniel got out of this conversation while he still could.

Even in the firelight, I can see a blush rise on her face. "I don't remember exactly." She looks at Calli for help.

Calli laughs a little. "Well, after you were done screaming, you grabbed your knife and told me to stay where I was." She looks back at Brad and addresses him. "But, to be fair, I broke into her room while she was sleeping. Once I explained what I was doing there, we kissed and made up. Now we're friends."

"So, if you didn't ask what she was, then how did you find out she was a succubus?" He asks smugly.

"That was part of her explaining what she was doing in my house and who she was," Jaiden explains.

Calli sighs. "I'm not a danger to any of you. I just need to eat souls sometimes in order to live. I only take a couple of years at a time, and never more than that from the same person. No one ever notices it. Souls outlive their bodies many times over. And, I don't take from souls close to expiring."

Her explanation raises more questions than answers, but most important of all is 'how do I know she hasn't already stolen part of my soul?' Or, it could be 'will she take some of my soul in the future?'

Brad, of course, is the first to voice his own question. "But, you could take more right?"

"I could. Some succubi will devour the entire soul; killing the person and their soul. I've never done that though, and I don't ever plan on doing that." At least, she sounds sincere about this part.

I have my doubts that she wouldn't ever eat a soul belonging to someone in our group. Demons are still demons after all. If she has to, I'm sure she wouldn't hesitate to take part of someone's soul. She says she needs it to live.

At this point, I'm quite sure her first target would be Brad, so at least I'd be safe on the first round.

"But, you could just take our souls if you wanted to." Brad gets to the point that I am sure is on everyone else's minds too.

"Just as easy as you could stab me while I sleep." She makes a good point. We don't have any reason to completely trust each other.

The fire pops and crackles loudly against the tense silence. Lit ash floats into the black sky. The chill is cut by the fire, but I squirm in my seat to work some of the cold out.

I didn't know that I would ever have to protect my soul from anything. Blood and heart I can understand. They are physical things I can see or visualize. Souls have never been more than a word in a few common phrases. Nothing tangible that science has ever proven the existence of.

"Okay, enough. No one's killing each other." Shawn tries to break the tension. I don't think it works, but for a moment he diverts the conversation. "Jaiden, you look familiar. Do I know you from somewhere? Have we met before?"

She looks him over and thinks for just a moment. "No, I don't think so." She shakes her head in the negative. Jaiden concludes. "Do you go to Leduc Composite High School?" Shawn shakes his head.

"You probably saw her picture somewhere. Jaiden and her rich dad are always in the newspaper because of charity events and business things. She even made the newspapers when she skipped some grades to get into high school; certified genius." Daniel spills some great secrets about the girl. It's a revelation; both about her and that Daniel does know of her.

All eyes turn to her. She stiffens. Daniel's reveal and the

newfound attention makes her visibly uncomfortable.

"You're rich and famous?" Her female companion didn't know this tidbit either. It must be extremely localized. Something, long-time locals are aware of.

Something that she hides and lies about by omission. Nothing she's said so far has led me to believe she's rich and famous. Though, with the apocalypse, she wouldn't be rich and famous anymore; I suppose.

"Her family owns half of Leduc," Lucas reveals.

Jaiden glares, for a moment, at Lucas. "My father was rich; not me. And, I wouldn't say famous. Just more, well known in certain fields as Mr. Kensington's daughter." She sounds like she's either in denial about it, or trying to distance herself from her privileged lifestyle.

"Wow. Rich, famous, a genius, you sure got beat with the lucky stick." Leah makes a motion like hitting with a stick.

Jaiden brushes her comment off. Typical rich girl. Does she even realize the hardships the rest of the world has to go through? She probably hasn't had to work a day in her life. She lives in her own bubble and can't possibly relate to any of us.

"What about you? We don't know anything about you?" Stephanie wags her finger back and forth between Calli and Lucas.

Lucas and Calli look at each other. A quick silent conversation passes between the two before Lucas starts first. "I've lived next door to Jaiden for a few years, but I used to live in Toronto. I collect fancy watches. Don't miss my job. Miss my car." He looks over at Jaiden, who looks away. I don't ask, but I know there must be a story there.

"I was passing through town when things happened. I don't really live anywhere. I just travel around." Calli reveals.

"And, steal people's souls." Stephanie elbows Brad in the side; a jab for a jab.

Calli brushes off his comment with a bit of a joking tone. "Mostly I go sightseeing and create websites for people. I freelance code. It pays my lifestyle well enough."

A throat clears. "Excuse me." James appears from the darkness. He catches all of our attention. "I will be taking my leave to obtain information about Nikki and Rayleen's whereabouts. You will all stay here until I return. I should only be a couple of days."

"Wait, I thought that's what we were doing?" Leah asks.

"I'll go with you." Miles stands up.

"I'm going by myself. It's safer and less conspicuous that way." I don't know if James heard the first question, or if he only chose to answer the one comment because Miles stood up. "I'm leaving. Don't kill each other before I get back." He waves once and walks into the dark.

"Bye." I wave despite his back already turned to me. There are a few echoes of "bye" from others around the fire. Miles and Kelly exchange glances after he sits back down.

People go quiet after James leaves. He broke the tension and stopped the direction the conversation was going in. No one seems confident in starting up another conversation at the risk of another lash-out.

I bide time by looking outwards. All I can see are the outlines of the fort surrounding us.

There is only one entrance and one exit that I know of, so I assume James left through there. Unless he has some special magical way to leave this place. He might have another tree he can travel through. He might fly a broom.

Do wizards actually fly brooms? With the numerous movie adaptations of how witches and wizards can travel, I'm sure some of them are probably true. There are probably some wizards in the writing rooms providing a hint of authenticity.

I look around. My eyes slowly adjust the longer I look away

from the glow of the flames. Four lookout towers are on the four corners of the tall log fencing. I can barely make out their silhouettes.

We had stopped for the night in Fort MacLeod. A three-hour trip had taken double that; delayed by empty fuel tanks.

Jaiden and Lucas had to ditch the motorcycles. Jaiden ditched hers at the old couple's house, but Lucas stubbornly hung onto his for longer. He drove it through freshly fallen snow and to the next town.

We drove through many towns and cities stopping along the way to get fuel. Which, as I found out, isn't as easy as it appears in the movies. We picked up a car along the way too.

It had been getting dark so we settled down at the historical village. The historical landmark and the actors working there had been a godsend to the locals, and us. They have been able to operate this section of the town as it would have a hundred years ago. They have survived off these skills, and they've helped many other people to survive off those skills.

People in the town opened their doors to displaced locals and visitors. The heritage site did the same, though much more able to accommodate larger groupings such as ours.

They didn't have too much damage or fighting here, but no power, gas and water still knocks a town out. They've managed to not just survive, but thrive.

There was one demon that had decided to attack the town, and the town's people captured her alive. They got the story out of her, threw her in jail and bunkered down for the last couple of weeks.

"Why did they take them?" Lucas' question gets my attention.

"She's Alexa's five-year-old niece," Kelly explains.

"Almost six. She's almost six years old." I announce before I can catch myself. It's a reflex from having a child that's too excited to grow up. She's been reminding me for a couple of months now that she's not just five years old; she's almost six. A few months from now she'll upgrade her age to six and a half. The extra half a year matters when you are that young.

"Why are we rescuing them?" Lucas' questions infuriate me. Heat fills my chest.

"We have to rescue them! Rayleen is my only family. I've raised her since she was a baby!" I can hear myself getting louder with each sentence.

As I'm about to continue and rip him a new one, he speaks and interrupts me. "Stop, stop! I didn't mean that we shouldn't rescue her." Lucas holds both of his hands up in defence. "I meant why are all of us rescuing them? Or do you have another group somewhere focusing on fighting back against the demons? Or do we expect a large battle to rescue them?"

I guess he wasn't trying to be rude.

"Nikki and Rayleen were taken by the leader of this district's rebellion. Darius leads over all of Alberta and also happens to be Alexa's ex-boyfriend. So obviously, he took Rayleen to get back at Alexa. We thought Nikki was a prophet, and maybe so did they. We find the girls, we find the leaders and we can take care of them. Once they're dead we shouldn't have much resistance to our own rebellion. Cut off the head of the snake so to speak." Kelly explains further.

This information is new to me. Is Kelly telling the truth? Had that been the plan since Rayleen was taken? I certainly hadn't heard anything about them planning on killing Darius; they can't. He doesn't have to die.

We just need to go and rescue Rayleen. I'll need to try to warn Darius so he isn't killed. I'm certainly angry at him, and he did try to kill me, but I do still love him. I can't let him be killed. He can change. He's just misguided on this.

I wonder if he would take me back. If I could avoid the fight, and get to Darius before the rest attack, I could get him and Rayleen to safety. He might take me back if I can prove that I'm loyal to him and always was. He'll turn me into a vampire, so I can protect her better.

If he knew the damage he was doing, he'd stop. If he knew there was another option, he'd take it. I know it. The beast he was pretending to be, is not who he really is. I think he might've gotten caught up in the moment.

Daniel catches my attention in my side view. I had forgotten about Daniel for a moment. He's nice to me, but he doesn't understand me. He was terrible to Rayleen.

We don't have as much history as Darius and I do. Darius spent hours and hours listening to my whole life story. Commiserated with me. He's the first person since my family died, to give me hope for a bright future. The only other person who loved me, other than Rayleen.

Yes, he's done some terrible things and he's kidnapped Rayleen, but I don't know how much of that is him. Sandra seemed more unhinged and also in lead. His temper could explain the rest. Or, good intentions with bad execution.

And, he saved Rayleen by kidnapping her the first time. He gave her to me. Maybe he's doing the same thing now. He saw she was potentially in danger, so he took her to keep her safe.

I honestly don't think Daniel will survive too much longer; maybe years, but he's human. The world has gone to the demons and you either need to join them or you will die.

I don't think this group will ever accomplish anything. Nothing can ever go back to the way it used to be, and the new pecking order places humans at the bottom.

Darius will turn me into a vampire, and we will turn Rayleen once she gets older. I can protect her until then; but only if I'm a vampire.

"How did Darius become the regional leader?" I don't think Jaiden directs the question at anyone in particular, but her gaze lands on Kelly near the end.

Instead, Miles answers. "Seth took an interest in Darius when he was brought before the council for his crimes against humans.

According to a treaty made between humans and supernaturals, it's a crime to turn any human into a supernatural and it's a crime for any human to be killed by a supernatural. Of course, it still happens, but it's typically hidden.

Darius was a human in Germany during World War II, and an unknown vampire turned him. Darius killed a bunch of humans to drink their blood. He was hunted down, captured, and taken to the Council for judging. He plead that he didn't know any better; complete ignorance to being a vampire, because the one who turned him, didn't show him another way.

Since Seth's sire was the Council Representative for nocturnal supernaturals, Darius was reconditioned under Seth. Seth went on to become the current Council Rep. Darius turned into Seth's right-hand man, so he of course got status in the revolution."

"So, then Shale went with Darius. And you, Kelly, and Alexa decided to fight on the other side." Jaiden surmises.

"Well, Alexa was with Darius at first, but they had a messy breakup and we had to rescue her." Kelly's joke jabs me the wrong way.

I tense. If they hadn't *rescued* me in the first place, Darius wouldn't have thought I betrayed him and broke up with me. I'd be a vampire by now. That thought hits me deep enough to pause everything for a moment.

It's their fault. All of this is their fault. Rayleen wouldn't be kidnapped if they had let us be. She would be with me, I would be a vampire, I would be with Darius, and we would be strong together. Safe together

I bite my tongue and take in a deep breath. My nails bite into the palms of my hands, and the cuts on my legs itch to be reopened.

"Were you at school when the attacks happened?" Miles asks Jaiden.

Jaiden pulls away wisps of hair that have fallen into her face. "Uh, I was in class, and the teacher ran in telling everyone to evacuate the building and go home. I had heard a rumour about a bomb threat as I was walking through the halls.

So, I went and grabbed some food from across the street and went home. I was up all night working on a project, so I fell asleep for a few hours. When I woke up and looked outside, I saw fire in multiple locations around the city. I figured I'd stay put until my family came back, or maybe the military. But, they never came."

"Maybe they just got trapped somewhere and couldn't get back to you." Stephanie offers.

"They're probably dead." Jaiden states.

"I'm sure they're alive and well. And, maybe, they just missed you. They would have thought you were at the school; maybe they went to find you there." Stephanie's optimism is bright against Jaiden's pessimism.

"I doubt it. If the person isn't in front of me, or I have tangible evidence they are alive, I'm assuming everyone I knew is dead." Jaiden's glum remark is a surprise to everyone. We all hold out hope that our loved ones are alive.

Calli voices our thoughts. "How can you say that?"

"Because that's war. That's how it works. Realistically speaking, people have to die, and it has to be someone. I'm not dead and you're all alive, so that means it was someone else." Only a small part of me sees where Jaiden is coming from. But, I wonder what she's been through to make her so cold-hearted.

"So that's it. You wouldn't search for family or friends." Brad looks at Jaiden with a smug grin.

"It would depend on the circumstance." With further goading from Brad's snort Jaiden continues. "Like, Nikki is probably alive and we're searching for her. They likely didn't take her away, just to kill her somewhere else.

But, I wouldn't go look for my stepmom or half-brother. I've had no sign of them since before the revolution and I'd have no idea where to start looking. I assume they're dead, and if not, they probably will be by the time the war is over. If they survive long enough for communication to be restored, then we might find each other again. But, I'm not risking my life chasing ghosts."

"So you didn't go looking for anyone?" Brad accuses.

"No, I did. After about a week alone, people broke into my house so I decided to drive to my grandma's house. There was a group there that let me stay for a couple of days, but I found out they had shot all the family members that had been there when they arrived and made a big pile with their bodies. So, I left." Jaiden's response sounds rehearsed. I wonder how many times she's had to tell it. How many times does one have to tell a story about their whole family dying, before they can rattle it off like they are reciting today's dinner special?

Her cold response creates an awkward silence. How should someone respond to her? 'I'm sorry' sounds right because she just mentioned that pretty much her whole family died, but she said it like it was nothing.

I itch to call her out for being a heartless bitch. I would be devastated if Rayleen died. Hell, I was a complete wreck for a year after my family's death. I can talk about it now, but couldn't at just a few weeks past.

"I lost my dad too. I came home and found him on the bed. His insides-" She trails off. Stephanie gulps for air, and tears gleam in the fire.

"You don't have to continue. I'm sorry, that must have been devastating. No one should have to go through that." Maybe she does have a heart after all.

Stephanie gets up from her seat and walks over to Jaiden. She practically sits on Calli's lap to sit beside Jaiden. Her arms wrap around Jaiden and she buries her head into Jaiden's neck. Jaiden looks surprised and uncomfortable for a split second before she returns the girl's hug.

Stephanie's sobs start soon after, and Jaiden rubs her back. She moves between rubbing her back and brushing her hair. I half expected Jaiden would push the girl away. She doesn't seem like the type of person to comfort another.

In the silence, I become eerily aware of exactly how quiet it is out here. There is no noise beyond the crackling fire and sobbing. There are only a handful of lantern and stove fires lightly lighting up rooms in the fort beyond the cloth placed for insulation.

It's still early, just after supper, but in the winter the sun sets at four. The black sky and cold air make me tired. I wonder when the days will start getting longer again.

What day is it? The winter solstice is on December twenty-first, and we shouldn't be too far away from that.

Did I miss Rayleen's birthday? "What day is it today?"

"Oh, I don't know. I haven't been counting the days." Daniel's voice makes me jump. I didn't realize I had spoken the question out loud.

There is a long pause. "I think it's December sixth," Jaiden mutters.

My heart sinks. "Are you sure?"

She thinks about it for a few agonizing moments longer. "Pretty sure," Jaiden utters.

Stephanie pulls herself away from Jaiden and wipes away all the liquid on her face. "I'm sorry."

"It's okay. Anytime." Jaiden turns to face me. "If I've got my calculations right, then it should be the sixth." She dazes off in thought for a moment. "Yeah, that should be right."

I missed Rayleen's birthday. I choke back a sob at the realization that not only did I miss her birthday, but she's also in captivity at the same time. I doubt anyone did anything special for her. I bet Rayleen knows her birthday passed. She's always doing her count down and an apocalypse isn't going to get in the way of that.

"Rayleen's birthday was yesterday." The words sound even more heartbreaking spoken out loud. I'm a horrible aunt. I stand up, painfully aware of my throbbing scabs. I don't want to be around people right now.

I know the way back to the room we'll be sleeping in. Without any words, I start retracing my steps back there. The further away from the fire I get, the colder I get. The more my legs itch and my hand twitches to scratch them.

The fire was set up close to the gift shop, and we are off in the side building. Our entire group has one room to share between ourselves and some other visitors. I don't know how all of us are going to fit in there to sleep all at once, but I'm sure it'll be warm from all the body heat.

Lost in my head, I don't realize Daniel is following me until he runs into me at the door.

"You didn't have to follow me. Go back to the fire." I insist to him. I don't want him to come with me. I'd rather be alone right now.

He holds the door open for me. I go inside. There is a bit more heat in here, but not much.

"You looked upset. I thought I'd cheer you up." He returns.

Despite my suggestion, he follows me. Daniel stomps his feet on the ground. I look down at my own feet. My shoes are covered in snow. I stomp my feet as I walk to get the extra snow off my shoes. No wonder my toes are frozen.

I walk through one room and into another. There is a fire going in the stove Taylor has open. She adds another log. The heat in here is more bearable.

"I missed Rayleen's birthday," I repeat. The words make it real.

"She'll forgive you. You can't control what happened. She's a smart kid and she knows that you are trying your hardest to get to her." Daniel tries to reassure me.

"Do you have a present for her?" Taylor asks. No, I shake my head. I didn't get her one yet. I always wait until the last minute because she always searches, and finds the presents I get her if I buy them ahead of time. "Why don't you think about grabbing something to give her? I'm sure she would enjoy a souvenir from this place. Then, when we rescue her, you can give her the present. It'll be great." She smiles. She makes it seem so simple.

"Yeah, maybe." I shrug.

Taylor leaves. I believe to give us some privacy.

Daniel wraps me gently in his arms and kisses my forehead. "I promise you, we'll find her soon."

"You're probably right. James said he will be back in a couple of days and he'll have information about where Rayleen is. She'll be back in my arms in three days." I affirm.

"Give or take a couple days." He says. I break the hug, and glare at him. Walking away, I plan quickly to just go to bed and sleep. I'm exhausted, and everyone is pissing me off. "Hey now. I didn't mean it like that. I was just meaning that James said he'd be back in two days, and we might need a day or more to travel. They had a dragon. What if they decided to fly to Saskatchewan, and we have to go by car? It might not be as simple as a walk-in and grab her. I'm just saying it might take a few days."

I lighten my glare and shake my head. There isn't any use in arguing about how many days it will take. I know that it might take longer than three days, but I want it to take as little time as possible. I want her in my arms now.

I miss her. My chest aches and I feel like I could cry at any moment. My face gets hot. I take in a deep breath and let it out slowly, but it doesn't help.

The more I think about her, the hotter my face feels. Tears flood my eyes until I blink and they fall down my cheeks.

I turn back around and seek comfort in Daniel. He immediately wraps his arms around me. "Are you crying?"

I don't answer.

The question is answered for him before I cry out. Perhaps, the wet drops or my shaking shoulders. He squeezes tighter and kisses the top of my head. Some of the emptiness I feel is filled by his comfort.

Chapter 2

Adjusting my position from my side to my back wakes me up to a sharp pain everywhere.

It hurts everywhere.

Ow!

Oww.

I groan. I'm broken. I'm sure those assholes broke every bone in my body.

I don't have to look to know there will be bruises of all colours covering my body.

I cut short a deep breath in a simultaneous coughing fit and side pain. Each cough hurts the same spot; everywhere.

I hug myself and curl up; ignoring the pain to do so. In hopes that this position will hurt just a little bit less.

Trying to stifle my cough only seems to help keep it going. Tears run freely from my closed eyes.

The coughing finally stops, but I refuse to move. I know moving will hurt more. My chest feels like it's being squeezed. I breathe shallowly; hoping I can avoid another coughing fit.

Not moving does much to control the pain, yet my body still aches and screeches at me. Cloth against skin feels sharp. Hair burns where it settles.

"Nikki?" My eyes open in a flash at the little voice against the dark wall. I barely see her as a dark shadow.

Shit. I forgot about her. Why did they put me back in the cell?

"Yes?" Talking hurts my dry scratchy throat. I swallow a few times; my jaw clicks the first two times. It realigns itself in a pop. There is a continuing pain that reaches from the back of my tongue down my throat with every swallow.

Left to right, front to back I move my lower jaw. A slight scraping sounds in my ears at the peak of each movement until everything realigns.

"Are you going to die?" She sounds scared. Her voice wavers and squeaks. I know she's worried about me. Or, at least, worried about being left alone in this place with these people.

Well shit. I don't really have a choice now; do I? My heart aches for her. "No." With children, I know, actions speak louder than words. I can tell her all I want that I'm not going to die here, but she'll never believe it; not until I can get up and prove it.

Every muscle I use, and some I don't, hurts when I get up from the bed. I don't know where the pain starts and ends; it's more about what hurts more or less.

My head whirls, and feels a bit faint. I close my eyes for a moment to stop my world from spinning. Putting pressure on my legs, I feel them intact. I sweep my hands down my arms, nothing feels out of place. Maybe, they didn't end up breaking bones.

I open my eyes, and pin them on Rayleen. Smiling through the pain, I nod and tell her, "See, I'll be okay." It seems to reassure her a little.

As my head clears, I assess my cell. It's chilly but dry. We are in a lightly coloured room. The only light comes in from a tiny barred window. It has two cots for two prisoners, a toilet, a sink, and two empty desks.

The room looks more like an insane asylum room than the typically thought-about cinder block jail cell.

The difference is in the cell bars as the one wall. An asylum wouldn't have one wall as a metal cage.

"You're alive." After a moment of confusion, I realize this male voice is coming from the cell bars. "Why don't you come over here and I'll make you forget all about your pain?"

He looks as skeezy as he sounds. He has wide eyes and a grease-stained t-shirt. He slicks his hand through his shiny brown hair.

"Fuck off." I bring my hand up to eye level and flip him off. The small pain from doing so is worth it.

"That's what I'm trying to do." I roll my eyes. That's what every horny sleaze ball says. "What do you say? I can make it worth your while. I have access to the lunch cart. Perhaps you'd like a bit of extra food tossed your way."

Does he really think he could buy me with food? What a loser.

"Not happening, so go away." I wave my hand at him and look the other way.

"What about you, sweetie?" I look back at him in confusion. His gaze is peering to the other side of the cell.

The only other person in this cell is a little girl.

I see red.

My blood pressure and rate rise enough that my heartbeat is all I can hear; for just a moment in time.

Charging him, I manage to grab onto his shirt and pull him hard into the jail bars. His head hits against the metal. One hand holds his jacket, and one hand beats his face repeatedly. I don't know what he is, but he certainly doesn't have much strength; his attempts at pulling backwards and away from me don't work.

I bash him hard against the bars again. "If I ever hear you say anything like that again, you will beg me to kill you. If you touch her, I will kill you. If you go near her, I will kill you. If you look like you are thinking disgusting things about her, I will kill you." I punctuate each threat by knocking him into the bars.

I don't get to continue threatening him because six other guards come to his rescue. I let go as they approach and back away to sit on the bed with Rayleen.

"Watch yourself girl. We can make your lives here a living Hell." This one pulls out a key from his pocket. His snarl promises he's going to harm us both when he gets his hands on us. I move myself to stand in front of Rayleen. Maybe I can hold them off for a little bit. Moving from muscle memory I get ready in a stance for the upcoming fight.

"Darius ordered you not to touch these two." Shale puts his hand on the man's chest. He presses hard enough to make him back up a couple of steps. Shale puts himself between all the guards and the cell door. They all give him a bit of room.

"She attacked me." The skeezy one whines. I roll my eyes.

"He deserved it," I claim in my defence.

"You obviously got too close. Open the door." Shale orders the one guard.

"No-"

Shale cuts him off before he can really argue. "Darius wants to speak to his prophet, and I'm going to watch the little girl. Either you can unlock the door, or I can. Unless, you want me to go talk to Darius about your insubordination and possible endangerment of his special guests." His voice threatens to harm the longer he talks.

The man looks at Shale blankly before slipping the key into the cell door. There is a click. The door swings open and Shale enters.

I don't trust him, but I think I can rely on him to keep us safe enough to deliver to Darius.

I stand up and put Rayleen in front of me. I might be able to shield her better and I can watch over her better in front of me.

Shale walks us out of the cell. I catch the eyes of the male I beat up. It's satisfying to see the bruising already appearing. A goose egg forming on his forehead.

Hopefully, I knocked some sense into him, or at least some fear; though I doubt it. Guys like that never change. He'll be a dirtbag for life.

The moment I look away, I feel a hand grasping my ass.

I don't have to see who the hand belongs to. In one movement I turn around and punch him in the face. The whole act echoes in pain through my whole body, but it's worth every bit of it.

I hiss at the sharp pain in my side and grab it for support. My knuckles sting from the impact.

He goes down. I think I knocked him out. He deserves it.

Others go to his side to aid him. One gives me a dirty look, while another looks thoroughly amused. I like to think that he's been waiting for someone to take the pervert out.

I turn back around and take hold of Rayleen's shoulders. Guiding her by her shoulders, I hurry our pace out through unlocked guards' doors. Just outside there is a glassed-in guard station illuminated by flashlights. There are no outside windows in here like in the cells.

Two desks take up practically half the room. One has one outdated computer and tower, the other has three screens. I think that one was a security camera display.

Shale goes through a desk and pulls out a pill bottle of pills. He hands it to me. I almost sigh in relief, but I remember my chest wouldn't go for it. Although, at some point, some of my muscles have stopped hurting so much; probably from a little bit of use or adrenaline.

"Thank you. Do you have anything to wash it down?" I don't

think I could dry swallow the pill with such a dry throat. My body registers all the pain as it drifts back to me.

He goes through a few more drawers before he finds a can of pop. He hands it to me.

I open the can first and set it on the counter before opening the pills. I pop two pills into my mouth and then swallow a few mouthfuls of pop. The pop feels weird against the pills, but it's not like I normally use a bubbly drink to wash down pills.

I drink about half of the pop with just the pills. I know I'm thirsty but I imagine Rayleen is too. Shale didn't pull out another can, so I don't think there is another. I hand Rayleen the half-full can. "Have the rest," I tell her.

"Thank you." She mutters quietly.

I can't help but feel for the girl. She's probably scarred for life already. She's already had enough happen to her, in the few days I've known her, that I would've been scared at her age. I would be in therapy for the rest of my life.

I can't imagine all that she's been through since the end of the world. A girl her age should still be innocent of everything bad in the world, not thrown right into the middle of a war.

"Why are you in here?" A booming voice comes from the entrance. I don't have to turn around to figure out that the voice belongs to Darius, but I do.

"We can't keep them in the cells anymore. The boys were threatening them." Shale calmly answers.

"Take her back. We're keeping them in the cell." He points to Rayleen when he says 'her.' I'm confused. Why wouldn't he take me back, then I remember Shale saying something about Darius wanting to see me. I guess it wasn't just an excuse.

"Alexa will never talk to you again if anything happens to Rayleen. That includes if anything happens to her psychologically. And, she just pissed off a bunch of people who I'm sure will be wanting their revenge. Do you want Rayleen dying; or your prophet?" Shale gestures to Rayleen and then me as he speaks about us.

"Then, they're your responsibility. If they escape, you're dead." He threatens Shale. "Watch her. You, come with me."

I hesitate for only a moment. I don't want to leave Rayleen with Shale, but I don't think my body will take another beating. Darius will easily overpower me if I try to resist.

He leads me to an interrogation room close by. There are two people in here; Sandra and a scared-looking roughed up woman. Her black and grey bun has many wisps out of place, and her green knit sweater has a few holes. Dirt is patched from head to toe.

The room is plain otherwise with just white walls, a table and three chairs. The only other notable thing is the mirror on the one wall.

"Doc, meet your patient." Sandra introduces.

"Hi, I'm Nikki." I introduce myself further.

"Hello, I'm Dr. Alderman. Were you in a fight?" She, Dr. Alderman, quickly flips on her professional doctor switch. Her fear disappears; or rather is buried deep below the surface.

"Not so much fight as much as they were beating the shit out of me to get me to comply," I tell her.

She looks briefly behind me and then looks away quickly. "Right, well I would like to look you over; if that's okay with you."

"You don't get a choice." Sandra looks impatient at our small talk and attempt at some slice of normalcy.

"Yes, thank you. I've been having some problems breathing." It's not like I am going to refuse an examination by a real doctor when offered. Neither of us appear to be here willingly, so we control this as much as we can; by pretending this is a normal doctor visit.

Might as well start where it hurts most, then move on from there. I walk over to her.

"I will need a stethoscope." She looks at Sandra expectantly, so I follow suit.

"You get the first aid kit." Sandra states.

Dr. Alderman tries to reason with her. "All jails have some sort of infirmary. Everything I need would be-"

Sandra cuts her off. "You get the first aid kit, or you get nothing; your choice." She won't budge.

Dr. Alderman takes a deep breath in and out. She turns her attention back to me; we focus on each other. "Have a seat." She motions to the chair. "Were you struck in the ribs at all?"

"Yes. They kicked me there multiple times." I sit down. From my position, I don't have many options on where I can look. My view is stuck on Sandra unless I twist my neck; which would hurt, I'm sure.

At a click, my curiosity turns my whole body to see Dr. Alderman open up the first aid kit. I'm not impressed with the items inside, and I'm sure she isn't as well. I see band aides, gauze, tape and some wipes.

Dr. Alderman pulls out the cardboard label that was on the lid. She fashions it into a tube. "Let's hope this will work well enough. Could you please hold still? I need to listen to your lungs."

She presses her ear to one end and the other side to my chest. She puts it down on a couple of places and asks me to breathe deeply. I resist the urge to cough, but a tickle in my throat makes me anyway.

Dr. Alderman says nothing as she pulls away. She lets me finish coughing.

We go over the rest of the places it hurts from there. I show her where it hurts, and she pokes around. There are a couple wounds she cleans and puts a band aide on. She checks my heartbeat and flashes a flashlight in my eyes. She doesn't say too much while she works.

After she completes her examination she tells me her diagnosis. "You should be just fine. Your worst injury is your rib. I don't think it's broken, but it may be bruised or fractured. You have some mucus in your lungs. Try staying more upright while you sleep. It will help clear the mucus away and help prevent coughing.

You'll need to take it easy for six weeks for your rib to heal properly. No more getting beaten up." She looks to Sandra and Darius to get the point across to them. "If you can find pain medication, take it as you need for the pain. Do you smoke?"

"Yes, when I can find smokes. I don't have any at the moment." I think about it for a moment. It's been a few days since I had a smoke. I've done this before, of my own will when trying to quit, and I had a nasty cough for a week. Could that be part of my problem? Maybe it's what is causing my cough.

"If you can hold out, I don't recommend smoking until you are healed. You could risk getting an infection. There isn't much else I can do for you without technology." She advises then admits.

Darius lets himself come further into the room. "Sandra will take you to your cell."

"Thank you," I tell her. I wish she didn't have to go back to a cell.

Sandra leaves with Dr. Alderman. Darius takes a seat on the other side of the interrogation table.

I'm glad to have the separation between us.

I'm also glad to be able to keep seated, though I do have to admit that some of the pains have eased. The meds must've kicked in.

"Don't think we won't torture you just because the doctor says so." Darius threatens weakly.

I don't want to do anything to risk getting beaten up again. I'm sure I'd die the next time. "I won't."

"Good. Tell me what I need to know." Darius gets to the point.

"About what?" I need him to reveal more specifics or I won't be able to fake this very well.

He hits his fist against the table. "You're going to start this shit already! Don't play dumb with me."

"I'm not playing dumb. I need to know what you need to know, so I don't tell you about a vision of someone wearing a hideous orange shirt while talking about how much it's snowing." I've spent a lot of time at the Tea House getting my future told, and I think I can fake my way through a reading with this guy.

I just need to ask questions, find out what he wants to know and answer them with vague details. I can do this. I take the edge out of my voice and tell him calmly. "I'm cooperating. I'll tell you the truth about anything you want to know."

He puts out his hand in front of me. He shakes it and looks at me like I'm supposed to hold it. Maybe that's how it works? I grasp his hand. "Are we safe here or is someone going to attack us?"

He pulls his hand away. Do psychics really get all the information they need from such a quick touch?

His first question triggers an idea. Could I work this to my advantage? I doubt Rayleen and I are safe here. We won't be able to escape a jail; they are built to keep people in. Maybe, I can convince him to go somewhere else.

"We're not safe here." I elaborate. "James and his group find us here and attack. They have about thirty people with them. They're too strong and kill almost everyone here. Some get away, but not you."

"Why should I believe you?" Darius ponders. I can't read him. His expression didn't change. I don't know if he is happy about the information or upset.

I need to go deeper. I need something that he will react to. Something that will make him change his mind about his fortress.

Shale had said Rayleen was important to Darius because of Alexa; I can work with that. "Because, Rayleen dies and I don't want her to die." He wouldn't want her to die either.

Sandra comes back into the room. "You're not a prophet. You lied to us."

Oh god, no, don't panic. She's trying to test me. She's smarter than Darius is, even though he's in charge. I know it will be harder to fool her.

I just have to remain confident and put my acting skills and cop-show knowledge to good use. "If you actually believed that, I would be dead."

"You're not a prophet. You can't see the future." She repeats.

"Yes, I am. Yes, I can." Maybe if I say it enough times I'll believe it. Part of being a good actress is being able to believe in your role so much, that it shows in how you play the part.

Now I just have to believe that.

"No, you're not. Don't lie to me. The little white blonde girl spilled your secrets. Jaiden. She gave you your poetry book." I'm sure my face pales as I process Sandra's words.

I panic. "Is she here? I want to see her." How could they have possibly gotten Jaiden? There's no way. But, how would they know about her otherwise? I feel sick at the thought of what they've likely done to her.

"So, she told the truth. You're useless. It was just a poetry book. You're not a Marshall by blood." Sandra sits down in the chair across from me. I can just imagine her giving a signal to

Darius to kill me if I don't say something immediately.

I still have to convince them that I'm a prophet so they keep me alive. "I'm not useless. I can see the future. How do you know she was telling the truth? I've only known Jaiden for a few months. She doesn't even know about my visions."

"You didn't deny it." She replies smugly. "You immediately asked for her. So she's more important to you than correcting a fact that decides whether you live or die."

"She's wrong about me not being able to see the future."

She snorts and shakes her head. "First I'm going to torture her. Then, I'm going to kill you." She and Darius exchange looks. He looks like he's about to advance on me.

"No, you're not, because I can see the future. I want to see Jaiden, first. Make sure she's still alive and well. If you hurt her, I won't tell you anything." I speak a bit louder; more assertively.

"Stop lying," Darius comments. "We're done."

I catch his eyes and speak directly to him. "I've already given you a prophecy. If you stay here, James and the others will come and they are going to kill you all." I try to switch the conversation from Sandra to Darius. Maybe, I can get him to tell me where Jaiden is. "Where's Jaiden?"

"She knows things about you that no one else does. She even gave you your yellow silk notebook." Sandra's statement, at least, proves it's my sister. "Who is she to you?" Sandra asks.

"Should we find her and kidnap her too?" Darius directs the question to Sandra.

"Darius!" Sandra hisses sharply.

I stop the smile before it appears. So, they don't know where she is and they don't have her. It was a bluff. But, how would they know about her?

"Her name is Jaiden Kensington, and we met this summer," I answer Sandra's question. "She gave me a notebook because she's friendly and gifts are her love language."

"That Jaiden?" Darius articulates thoughtfully; like he knows her from somewhere.

"You know her?" Sandra asks him, irritated. She's lost control of the interrogation and she knows it.

"Yeah, through school. Human family. Her mom died years ago and her dad owns Kensington Company, something or other. They own half of Leduc." He explains.

Sandra mulls it over for a moment before she turns back to me. "So why does Jaiden know so much about you that she figures she can decipher your vision poetry?"

"She's a genius. Skipped grades. Knows everything. She's probably just being cocky." I answer.

"So, if we kidnapped her and tortured her, you wouldn't care?" I know she's still trying to test me. I let my emotions run too much, and now I have to do damage control so they don't go after her.

"Why would I care? We've only known each other for a few months." We've actually only known each other for only three or four months; I think. That much is true. "She obviously had no issues being your informant."

"She's not the informant," Darius mumbles quietly, but I still hear him. My eyes flicking to him betray that I heard him.

"Darius!" Sandra hisses sharply. Darius is horrible at interrogations; bad for Sandra, but good for me.

"You have a spy. They're going to catch her." The *her* slips out. I hope it is either the right gender and it adds to my act or it was wrong and they ignore it. I think about correcting myself, but Sandra stands up abruptly.

She comes over to my side of the table and yanks me up by my arm. The movement hurts.

"Sandra, take her back to Shale," Darius orders her. She stops whatever she was about to do.

She wastes no time. I let her pull me. She drags me back to Shale and Rayleen. The little girl looks horrified as Sandra drags me in, but is relieved when she lets me go.

I expect Sandra to leave, but she goes through some drawers. She finds what she needs. A pen and a small notepad fly at me.

They hit my stomach and fall to the floor despite my efforts to catch them. The quick movement pierces my side with pain. I put my hand on the spot that hurts the most on my ribs.

"Write down all your prophecies. Everything you think is relevant. And, don't even think about coding it." She shouts then leaves; stomping on her way out.

I think I might have convinced her enough to let me live another day. I need to keep living.

I know I need to write convincing prophecies on the notepad; I wouldn't know how to code it if I needed to. Though, if they think my yellow notebook is my vision book, maybe they think my poems are coded visions.

"Are you okay?" Shale asks me. He looks a little concerned.

"Broken rib." I press my hand lightly against my side.

He hops off the counter quickly and rushes to me. He picks up the notepad and pen.

"Here." Shale grins a bit lopsided. "Do you need to sit? Or more pain meds?"

"I think I'll just sit thanks." I don't know what to think about Shale. He seems to be on the wrong side of the fight. He is nice to us, and seems to be protecting us; more than what is needed to keep us physically alive.

I sit down and watch Rayleen colour with Shale.

So, there's someone here that is on my side, and told me to pretend to be their fortune teller; unless I was hallucinating that. I don't know if they know I'm actually not psychic at all, but they might be somewhat convinced.

Shale seems too nice to be here. Maybe he supports the cause but doesn't agree with the hate humans thing. Maybe he's the guy on my side who told me to pretend. I could tell, maybe, if I heard him whisper.

Darius is an idiot, and I'm sure Sandra would've punched him out during the interrogation if she could. He's convinced I'm a prophet. He's the one in control, so that's what matters.

Sandra is smart. She should be leading this, but I'd be in a lot of trouble if she did. I don't think she fully believes me. I need to make some pretty convincing prophecies to convince her long enough until I can escape.

I need to work on an escape plan or take any chance to escape that I can.

Jaiden. I didn't think I'd hear her name again. Hope fills my chest and almost makes me dizzy.

She's alive. Maybe she's with our family too.

She has to be with James. How else would Sandra know about her blonde hair and her connection to my book? But for sure, she is with a spy and that could be very dangerous. Who could their spy be? I have no idea who she's actually with so it really could be anyone.

Unless they're lying and just found her name in the notebook. Maybe they were bluffing all along. But, the blonde hair? The Marshall family golden blonde hair; just like dad's.

The Marshall family is a strong line of prophets. Jaiden is a Marshall by blood. Is Jaiden a prophet? Is dad? Grandpa?

Why didn't they ever say anything? Or, is Sandra off her rocker? Maybe they've got the wrong Marshalls. It's a common last name and they can't all be prophets; could they?

Does mom know?

If Jaiden is a prophet, it would be very dangerous for her. I've already gotten a taste of what they are willing to do to get prophecies. I know I'm stronger than she is. She's so sweet; they'd break her by looking at her.

I have to talk to her.

I have to find her.

I have to protect her.

If she is a prophet, I can't let these people find out; ever. Which, might not be in my control.

She must be a prophet, right? It would be too much of a coincidence for her to have found James otherwise. Jaiden must be a prophet and trying to find me. That's the only reason I can think of.

Maybe I can try to give her signs that I'm alive. Leave her breadcrumbs to find us at the new place. Then again, if she can see the future then she could just have a vision to find me.

I shake my head.

There's no question about needing to find Jaiden when the only thing I need to question, right now, is what I'm going to write down for prophecies.

I open the notepad. There are a few used pages in the front. They contain scribbles of case notes. I rip them out and put them in the garbage under the desk.

The notepad now looks new. I open to the first page and think.

What do I write? I need a prophecy.

I start by writing down the prophecy I told Darius. I write it in just the basic details I told him. I don't want to get too detailed or I won't be able to keep all the lies straight.

The more general the prophecy the easier it might be to predict something that might actually happen.

The first big prophecy was easy and obvious, but I have no idea about any other prophecies.

I feel like I need something big to stand along with the first one. How can I match the jail getting attacked and Rayleen dying?

I sit and think.

Munching on the back of my pen as I desperately think of different scenarios. Anything that could possibly happen in the next few days.

Maybe I'm looking at this the wrong way.

I can't think of anything important that could happen here in the next couple of days, and I don't want to be here; trapped securely in jail.

What if I tell them I see us travelling to another site? I could say that it is now a vision from the day of the attack and we retreat to go elsewhere, but where is unclear. We're flying on the dragon.

If I could talk to Darius, I could then convince him that since we're supposed to go somewhere else anyway that we should leave now to avoid the attack. I need to convince him that the best thing is to avoid the attack altogether.

I'm brilliant.

The hardest part of all this might be getting Darius alone to talk long enough about my self-fulfilling prophecies.

Maybe, I could just ask Shale if he could grab just Darius so we could talk. Sometimes the simplest idea is the answer.

I think I might want to write down a few more prophecies before that. I still feel like I need a few smaller prophecies to really convince them of this prophet thing.

As good of a start as any, I write down the joke prophecy I had told Darius. A guy wearing an orange shirt while talking about the weather was genius at the time; sounds kind of dumb now. I don't even know if someone has an orange shirt, or why they'd be wearing a t-shirt with it so cold out.

Now I just need a few more small prophecies and I might be able to call it good.

Chapter 3

The zipper rumbles under my fingers as I unzip the bag. My arm aches from the movement. I might want to take it a bit easier for the afternoon.

It's been interesting learning as much as I can about how to do things the old ways. I've been helping everywhere I can, so I can learn as much as I can. We won't be here long, and there are many valuable skills we can learn from the people here.

Caroline showed me how to cut down a tree, and how to make firewood with an axe. Swinging the axe likely caused this ache in my arms. My back will feel the effects of it tomorrow.

The work is exhausting and repetitive. A proper stance helps avoid injury. It would be a horrible thing to place the axe blade through my foot or leg. An injury like that in the wrong place and wrong time could be deadly. Besides the extreme, it will also help avoid pulling a muscle or over-extending joints. A proper stance can also help with keeping up stamina over a longer period of time.

We set the wood aside to dry out; making for a better burn later. We crossed paths with Terry, who I then departed with to carry wood for a fire.

He started up the big fire with a lighter but was nice enough to show me a method to start a fire that I could do without any modern tools. Despite the act being known to me previously by hearsay, I was shown how to make a fire using a bow drill; with one successful attempt by me after a lot of effort.

Terry had made it look easy, but in practice, there is a lot of effort involved. Physical labour pushes the bow back and forth to turn the wood. The friction of wood moving on wood creates the fire, but this means that you have to be precise. Work and effort can be undone in an instant if either piece moves from its placement.

All that knowledge is stored for a possible later, for now, I'm secure in the ease of matches.

I pull out the food bag shoved haphazardly inside. After days of eating the food, there isn't much left. What is left, I don't know if it is still good for me to eat. I don't know how long jerky and dried fruit last, nor how to tell if it's gone bad; save for growing fuzz or a foul smell. I pop a morsel of dried apple into my mouth and start chewing the tough fruit; it seems fine. I haven't died yet, and no stomach pains.

I'm still weary of my tooth, but it hasn't fallen out or turned black. It's a little wiggly, but I think that may lessen as time passes. I'll just forevermore be careful not to use it. I wish there was a dentist I could talk to, but I doubt they would be able to do anything without technology.

As the remaining items near the bottom of the bag, a small zippered satchel shows itself. I hadn't noticed it. I don't think Lucas or Calli noticed it either the couple of times they've ruffled through this bag; they didn't say anything if they had.

I pull the small bag out. Running my hand along the outside, I feel a solid bulge inside.

Curious about the items inside, I open the bag and stick my hand inside. I probe at the two items but decide to pull out the paper object first.

The folded paper opens to reveal a birthday card. It's not my birthday. That was a month or so ago; whenever Halloween was. Opening the card up further, I quickly spot my name.

Jayden,

I'm sorry you had to leave so soon. It was unfair of them to make you think you had to leave. I doubt anyone would mess with Alpha Ken even if he had been caught harbouring a human.

It was a pleasure to meet you. You are one amazing person. I hope we'll get to reconnect soon.

Everyone has a birthday, so Happy Early or Belated Birthday!

I gave you a cell phone with my phone number in it, so message me whenever. You also have access to the internet, so you can research your heart out!

The phone works on solar power so when the battery runs low put it in the sun. Screen up.

Good luck finding Nikki. Try to remember to message John when you find her. He's really worried about her. I think he's still in love with her. Alpha Ken made him break up with her last summer after he heard the beginning rumblings of the revolution. He was worried John would choose to leave and be with Nikki at a time when he would need his Beta the most.

Please let me know if you're okay from time to time.

Stay safe,

Sara Kadiza

I fold up the letter and place it back in the pouch. I touch the phone but think twice about pulling it out.

I look around me at the people here. Some of them are supernatural beings and yet, I haven't seen a single person pull out a phone. It's certainly something noteworthy. People are addicted to their phones, so if someone had one, they would have pulled it out by now. The usefulness of the small brick would be too much to ignore.

There has to be a reason. They are all hiding one or don't have one. Until I figure it out, I resolve to keep this treasure a secret. Putting both hands in the larger bag I maneuver the phone up my sweater sleeve. The bag of jerky becomes an alibi for my hands in the bag.

Pulling out more jerky, I pop a piece in my mouth. The movements would seem to elude that was my goal the whole time; I hope.

I'm not too sure that I should let anyone know about my phone. Rules from the revolutionists seem to frown upon consorting with humans. I'd imagine if the wrong person finds out about the pack giving me the phone, or the necklace, there would be repercussions perhaps leading to their death.

I'd imagine the items would be safer with me, hidden on me. My bags could be lost, left behind, or gone through at any time. I don't trust these people. A few have had their hand in bullying me in the past. Some just rub me the wrong way. Though unintentional, Calli has shown she can't handle sensitive information. And Lucas, I'm not sure how he feels about supernaturals yet.

Making up my mind, I slide the phone into my hip pocket and cover it further when I pull down my sweater.

Anxious to get online, to get access to unlimited information once again, I excuse myself to do the most private thing one can do without suspicion. I go to the bathroom.

Using my shoes to lower the seat cover, I settle down. Palming my new phone, I press the power button on the side. It does nothing. For a moment I fear the battery to be dead until the logo brightly flashes on the screen.

A picture of a smiling Sara stares at me. She is surrounded by leaves and a tree with scant brown bark. Her hair is a little longer than when I had seen her, and white-rimmed sunglasses hang from her baby blue t-shirt. A v-neck is created by the sunglasses, but the wrinkles betray the natural form of the shirt neckline.

It takes me no time to figure out how to use the phone. It only takes me a couple of minutes to peruse the phone's files. The impression I get is that she gave me her phone to use. There are too many personal files and pictures on it for it to be an extra phone. She couldn't delete everything in a hurry. I do, however, find a contact with her name on it.

By my guess, I can surmise the morning I was leaving, she quickly scrawled the note and changed the contact information to someone else's number.

She wouldn't have had time to get a brand-new one.

I'm not too interested in the apps she has downloaded. As this is now my phone, I remove all her games from the main screens. The screens declutter in front of my eyes.

Finally, it's time for the pièce de résistance. I press the black internet logo. A black screen pops up with a white-outlined search box. Only a jiffy passes before a line of suggested searches order themselves below the box. It appears as though the internet works.

I ignore the suggestions and feel giddy as I type in 'werewolf pack rules'. Search.

Many links pop up, but I choose the first one labelled as much. It redirects to a brown-coloured website. The front page holds a world map, so as to break down the packs into groups by location. I click into North America, and then Canada. It further specifies province and district. Naturally clicking on the pack location information for the only pack I know; the links direct to information for the Kadiza Pack.

Current Pack Alpha Ken Kadiza leads one of three central Alberta region packs.

The Kadiza pack emigrated from France and settled in central Alberta in 1867. In 1918, the pack was split in three. The region split amongst the three surviving Kadiza siblings after the First World War.

I scroll down and skim the whole text. The website looks more like a family history site. I stop when I see the words 'werewolf trial'.

1573 Gilles Kadiza was accused of and convicted of being a werewolf in Dole, France. The Council decided against extraction and retribution due to circumstances at the time.

A werewolf trial was held after Gilles had been caught changing forms from lycanthrope to humanoid. He was immediately arrested and placed in the human court.

Fifty human witnesses came forth and accused him of devouring the raw flesh of his human victims. He was found guilty of crimes of lycanthropy and witchcraft and burned at the stake.

Gilles Kadiza was one of five true lycanthropes to die as such.

I back out of the website. Several questions I have derived from that text. I type 'werewolf trials' and press search.

Lycanthrope and witchcraft trials started in the 15th century after a lone werewolf and rogue witch tried to inform humans of supernatural existence. They were brought into the custody of the Council and punished by banishment. The damage had already been done.

Resurgence of human belief in werewolves and witchcraft also brought about fear. Humans started trying people as werewolves and witches; the latter of which was more prevalent and encompassing. Conviction often meant burning at the stake.

Often humans were the victims of the trials, though some magic folk and lycanthrope also lost their lives. Humans would often convict strategic victims, killers, and strange individuals. The trials would go on for many centuries.

I didn't know people were also convicted as werewolves. I had always heard of witch trials because of the Salem Witch Trials, but I had never heard of werewolf trials.

Though I suppose I shouldn't be surprised. There are many parts of Europe, and the world, where they believed more in the supernatural. I guess they were right all along.

I remember watching a documentary about vampires; where isolated towns in Bulgaria and Romania still practice digging up bodies to put stakes in them and eat their hearts or other superstitions to stop them; if there is reason to believe the person may be a vampire.

I search 'Salem witch trials' and press the search button. I click on the first link.

The Salem Witch Trials occurred between February 1692 and May 1693 in colonial Massachusetts. The hearings and prosecutions brought about the executions of twenty people (19 were hung, 1 died by peine forte et dure) and the death of five waiting in prison. All were human casualties of mass hysteria.

I raise my eyebrow at the last sentence; all were human casualties of mass hysteria. That figures. Of course, they were all human. It figures that we humans would conduct a witch hunt and execution only humans at a time when there was no concrete evidence that supernatural beings existed. It figures that we humans didn't manage to try a single witch in the most famous of our witch trials; not that it would have been right to do so.

The whole event is a product of our humanity. A product of the right circumstances birthing an extreme reaction. A product of scaremongering, extremism, and estrangement.

Three ideas when put together can be a very scary thing; a very dangerous thing. Unfortunately, sensationalism can cause people to gloss over how wrong the actions are. Guilt and understanding go hand in hand later.

I press on the linked 'peine forte et dure'. The literal translation should be 'sentence strong and tough' but I don't know exactly what it is.

Peine forte et dure (hard and forceful punishment) is a method of torture by placing heavy stones upon the person's chest until a confession is obtained or they die.

That sounds awful; though it's certainly not the worst torture method or device I've ever heard of. Though I suppose I'd still make any confession to save myself from being squashed to death. It's what makes confessions under torture so unreliable; most will confess to anything if it makes the overwhelming pain stop.

Unfortunately, for a lot of people, the torture techniques would kill them regardless. Many were meant to cause infections after removal; if the person survived the initial effects of the device itself. Many were intentionally covered in fecal matter to cause infections. No one cared much to clean the devices between victims either.

Torture devices like the peine forte et dure could cause irreparable damage and internal bleeding. You could confess and still die in the days after.

Torture procedures of the past were usually meant to extract the confession, while causing the person an unimaginably painful death.

That reminds me of the project I never got to present. Josef Mengele, the angel of death, and the deadly experiments he performed and oversaw. Unit 731's deadly experiments. Thousands of people were killed by unspeakable experiments; amputation, limbs sewn on, people sewn together, chemicals injected into eyes, intentional disease injection, chemicals injected, cold and heat exposure, cutting off blood supply to limbs, teeth removal, raped, pressure chambers, intentional pregnancy, pregnancy termination, premature baby dissection, buried alive, weapon testing, and no anesthesia during surgeries.

I go to the search engine and type in 'who performed horrific experiments in world wars'. I'm half tempted to see if humans or supernaturals orchestrated these atrocities, but I think I'd rather not know the answer to it.

Even though I know that I shouldn't ask questions I don't want the answers to, I have an inquisitive mind and don't like to purposely be ignorant of a subject just because I might be squeamish with the knowledge.

I've seen how dark answers to questions can truly be. I shudder as the Russian sleep deprivation experiment recount crosses my mind; I never should have read that. Sleep deprivation experiments have been run and can have horrible consequences and were run during World War II, but the events of that story never happened. It was only after I read it that I fact-checked it and found out it was just a story, but it's still insanely creepy.

All sides were guilty of atrocities against everyone; some more than others; at least from what information is available. As the famous saying goes, history is written by the victors. Victors don't want people to know all the horrible things they did. That's why they teach their children a very narrow view of everything.

It's only a few, who decide to do further research themselves, that learn a well-rounded view of history. The rest are blissfully ignorant that the war winners, the alleged good guys, also looted, raped, tortured, killed prisoners and civilians, and even beheaded people to show as trophies. Entire genocides are covered up and denounced.

Throw into the mix the existence of supernatural beings, and our entire world history is thrown into question.

Nevertheless, while it may be something to file in a good-to-know section of my memory, I don't want to view the horrific images that accompany the information nor do I want to let myself be consumed by the information again; at this moment.

I delete the words and search 'World Wars'. World War I comes up as the first option and World War II as the second option. I figure I might as well go in order.

I skim the page. The web page reads almost exactly like I would expect a page to read off the human web. I summarize the material in my head from what I skim through and remember.

World War I began on July 28, 1914, after Archduke Franz Ferdinand was assassinated. Austria-Hungary declared war on Serbia. Because of existing treaties Germany, Russia, Great Britain, and France were obligated to join the war. Canada joined in because of Great Britain. Italy, Japan, Ottoman Empire and Bulgaria also joined in. The United States joined in later after they had ships attacked. Italy switched sides. Russia dropped out when they had to deal with their civil revolution.

Many other countries were involved. They fought mainly in Europe. Trench warfare describes much of how the war was fought. There were over seventeen million deaths. Exhausted troops, influenza, diminishing soldiers, and mutinies lead to the Central Powers signing an armistice agreement to end the war. Germany, under the Treaty of Versailles, was severely punished for their role. Excessive punishment set the stage for World War II. The war ended on November 11, 1918.

All the basic information checks out the same as the human recordings. I guess it's not so different.

I click on the linked 'World War II' words and skim through the information.

World War II began officially on September 1, 1939, when Germany invaded Poland, but Japan was already at war with China since 1937. World War II is the deadliest conflict in human history with approximately fifty to eighty-five million fatalities. It directly involved over one hundred million people from thirty different countries.

Lines of civilians and soldiers were blurred in a state of total war; when countries put everything they had into the war.

The Holocaust was the genocide of Jews. People put in concentration camps were experimented on, gassed and their bodies burned, or they were put to work.

There were bombings on civilian populations and industrial centers. The atomic bombings of Hiroshima and Nagasaki. The war ended in 1945.

I'm not finding what I need so I word it differently; 'Supernatural roles in World Wars.'

'Supernatural Conscription in Human World Wars' is the first headline that catches my attention. I read the first paragraph.

Conscription started in the First World War as soldiers on all sides were running low. The decision was popular with some groups and criticized by others. Supernatural involvement in the first war was low until conscription per Council rulings highly recommending against the involvement of supernatural beings in human wars.

This lessened as the world wars grew and humans instituted conscription. It was then frowned upon for supernaturals to take high-level positions. The council ruled execution to any supernatural being that threatened the secret existence of supernaturals; on purpose or otherwise in war. This ruling carried over through the Second World War and was not lifted until 1991 with the end of the Cold War.

I backtrack and decide that I do need to know for the sake of knowledge and to take away ignorance. The acts committed were truly horrific, but I feel like I'm doing a disservice by not finding out. That, somehow, I'd be dishonouring the victims by not finding out.

I search 'Horrific experiments in world wars'. I click on the first link and skim the paragraph. It goes on to mention many different experiments; many of which I already know about from my project. It mentions that Mengele was a human, but doesn't mention anyone else by name.

The rest are written off as a mixture of mainly humans and a few supernaturals taking advantage of the situation. With the supernaturals eventually being convicted of war crimes for their roles and executed by the Council.

Humans can be truly awful people. That's not to say that supernatural beings can't be either, but for humans to do that to their own kind, is truly horrific. And, I don't know enough information about the supernatural beings, but I do assume they are like humans too. Some are good and some are bad. Ultimately, everyone acts in accordance with their soul and environment. You judge a person based on their individual actions.

In my scrolling, I pass into an 'Experiments on Supernaturals' section.

Through much of World War II an unknown vampire, who goes by Sir, ran a secret operation in many locations throughout Europe and Russia. He was indiscriminate in choosing his prisoners. He chose humans and supernatural beings of all races, gender, age, and species. An ample backdrop of war provided opportunity as people regularly went missing; no one caught onto him until one supernatural victim escaped and was able to contact the Council. His operation ran for only six months after that. Most of the information available is from the first-hand accounts of the only two people to survive Sir's experiments.

Sir took people to secluded or well-hidden areas to torture and experiment on. His favourite experiment was testing the process of changing a human to a vampire. He was also interested in the effects on new vampires, testing the limits of vampire powers, and understanding vampirism.

His methods were cruel. He would bring a human to various degrees of death before attempting to change them. Test the effects of vampirism on open wounds and recent amputations. Leave a changing human exposed to sunlight until they burned.

There is a picture of one of the survivors named Walter Ackermann. He looks very familiar. I click to expand the picture. Those stone-cold eyes are hard to forget. They're blue when not in a black-and-white photograph. Lengthen the blonde hair a bit and it's a spitting image of Darius.

Yesterday I was told, somewhat, about Darius' origin. They might not know the whole story, or could not think it's relevant; they could be protecting their friend.

I back out and click on the linked name. Another picture appears, and this time I'm certain it's Darius. The page doesn't go into much. It describes Walter as being a Nazi soldier taken as a prisoner. He was turned and tortured to test the extent of vampire regeneration. Walter was rescued when the Council's army came to rescue the prisoners. Sir set the place on fire to hide his escape. Walter was the only being to survive the fire.

Poor Darius had such a rough time. I can't imagine what he would have gone through. That's probably why the council made an exception and didn't execute him.

I need more sunshiny things to think about. I back out of the webpage. 'War of 500' catches my eye. I click the link.

The War of 500 started in Year 91 of Aelius-Arthur-Hypatius-Merlin Council Dating (500 AD Gregorian dating) and continued for six years. The war pitted humans against supernatural beings. Humans' high numbers and take no prisoners attitude contributed to their victory.

The war divided the Council as Arthur the Diurnal Representative and Merlin the Magic Representative chose to fight a battle of land in Britain and provide only local persons for the war effort.

The war ended with the Treaty of Evanesce and the end of Supernatural rule.

I skim-scroll through the rest of the page. The page is long and describes different parts of the war. I'm interested in reading it, and maybe if I had more time I would, but someone is bound to come looking for this bathroom eventually. There are so many questions that need to be answered first.

Two names stand out; Arthur and Merlin. I immediately assume it's talking about King Arthur and his wizard Merlin. King Arthur was supposed to have fought against the Saxons, or Germans, from North West Germany otherwise known as Saxony around that time, but historians never agreed on whether he was real or just made up legend from a conglomeration of multiple leaders. What was agreed upon was the romanticized stories were untrue to the time period. It was more likely he wore commoners' clothing over shiny armour and robes, and his castle was more probably a cave or villager house. Now he's a supernatural.

Merlin's story varied in origin. But, was regarded as more fiction than fact. He was a wizard, or he was blessed, or he was half human and half demon, and I'm sure there are more. Basically, the most popular version of him depicts a loyal wizard advisor to Arthur.

I quickly click on each of their links and read just enough to confirm that I am thinking of the correct people. Turns out King

Arthur was a half-elf. Human royalty on his father's side, and commoner light elf on his mom's side. Merlin was his best friend and, of course, a wizard.

I decide that I might as well find out the rest of the council members for that time. I click into Aelius. She is the fire elemental and a truly immortal being. Aelius was only one of many names she has gone by; or he has gone by. The page lists all the names to the current name, Aalayah.

Next, Hypatius. Flavius Hypatius was consular of west Rome in 500 AD. He was also an incubus. An incubus is the male version of a succubus; a being that requires consuming souls to live.

Their dating system is different than our modern one. It is helpful that they put the Gregorian dating in there for my reference. So year 91 of the Aelius-Arthur-Hypatius-Merlin Council dating is 500 AD. It reminds me of the consular dating the Romans did. Although that was just the names of the two consular for east and west, and their terms only lasted a year. So, year 91 of the ruling of those people in the council.

I back out of the page and search 'how long are council terms?' An immediate answer pops up stating each term is one hundred years. Short-term mortals choose successors for their inevitable death.

I search for 'The Council'.

The Council was formed in roughly 3500 BC as a way to govern supernatural beings in an organized manner. Originally, the four council positions were held solely by the four elemental siblings. This was changed in 909 BC to better fulfil the needs of the major groupings of beings while relieving the responsibilities of the elementals; Elemental, Diurnal, Nocturnal, then Magic in 912 BC.

The four elementals rotate the position between them. The other positions are chosen by all the current Council members from a group of candidates. The group of candidates are chosen by a mixture of two methods including nominations by previous and current Council members, and testing.

The system is designed so that anyone can be shortlisted to become a Council member, while the best person is chosen for the job. Unlike the human government, the Council is not run as a popularity contest. The people do not get a vote, as their feelings can get in the way of the greater good. The current Council members will deliberate on and with each candidate and must come to a minimum of three-to-one acceptance.

Each Council member is in charge of all beings in their grouping. Their word is the law. Immediate action is carried out once a Council member creates a law or orders a ruling.

Since the signing of the Treaty of Evanesce, a council representative's position has turned to the preservation of lives, and continual concealment of the existence of supernatural beings.

The Council could have its advantages, as well as some real faults in their system. It sounds like how they choose their leaders could be only slightly more inclusive than a monarchy system. They would need to have some systems in check for like if someone got out of hand and decided to attack the humans and take over the world; oh wait.

I smile at my small attempt at a joke.

Seriously though, if you do get the right person in the position a government system like this works. You see a need, and you can fix it immediately. You don't have to wait for a bill to make its way through the system; which could take months to years. You don't have to even make sure the ruling is popular with the people before you implement something that is for the greater good of all. That being said, it can also go really bad really fast if you get the wrong person in the position. There is a large margin for corruption with a system like this.

I scroll down. There is a long chart full of names going back to 909 BC of all the representatives for each century. At the bottom, there are four people; Aalayah, Niklas, Seth, and James.

They've only held their positions since Jan 1, 2009.

The natural ordering seems to be Elemental, Diurnal, Nocturnal, and Magic Folk, so I assume their positions respectively.

I already know Aalayah is the fire elemental, so I click on Niklas. He is a werewolf from Russia. Seth is a vampire whose origins are from Germany. Finally, I click on the person I'm most interested in knowing about; James.

James Ellesworn was born June 12, 1968, in San Francisco, California. He trained his magic with multiple private tutors. James started working for the council in 1999 as a Dispute Agent. He was a diligent worker with a high success record.

James was chosen as a candidate after completing the Prospective Council Member Test. In 2009, James was chosen as the Magic Representative.

In early 2009, James underwent a voluntary transfer of souls from previous Magic Council members.

I back out and search 'voluntary soul transfer council'. Many links pop up. I look for the first one that looks like an informative page rather than an account.

Magic Council members perform voluntary soul transfers to the newest council member at the beginning of their term. By transferring extra souls, and a piece of their own, the old council member can pass down residual memories from all previous representatives and extend their life to last the whole term.

The soul transfer ritual is a secret of high-ranking magic folk. It is considered dark magic and the practice is an executable offence. There are exceptions for soul transfers in the moments of natural death, and accidental cases, but these are treated by case.

The webpage isn't too informative, but it does make me wonder about how strict the Council is with punishments. It seems like every offence is solved by execution.

I don't believe that to be exactly true, but they may be strict because of the Treaty of Evanesce. I don't feel like reading a law book to find out all their laws and the repercussions at the moment.

I go back to the search home page. A thought occurs to me, if I can search for James maybe I can search for other people in the group. I may have a big issue in that, though since I don't know many people's last names.

Maybe, if I use a combination of name and location I might be able to find them. Or, I could just start by searching for people I do know.

Who do I know that is a supernatural being and I know their full name? John Kadiza is the first name to come to mind. I search for John Kadiza.

There's a Dr. John Kadiza in Toronto and a famous cyclist in the Netherlands. Also, a fencer in Portland, Oregon.

Finally, about five Johns down, I find something promising; John Kadiza profiles on SuperData. The detail below the link advises I can view profiles of beings with this name, and boasts that they are the largest social media site for supernaturals.

The social media site darkens the screen with a black background and brightens it up with white writing and red highlights.

I immediately realize something isn't quite right. A picture of the correct John is right at the top labelled as 'Pack'. I click on his profile because I don't want to lose his page. I realize that I must be logged into the site via Sara.

A new page loads with a larger version of the thumbnail photo. It practically takes up the entire screen. I try to scroll down, but it doesn't work. I try to scroll to the side and it flips to a new page. This page has information about him.

He was born on November 17th, 1992. Born and raised in Alberta Beach. Went to school at Onoway High School. Graduated in 2010. He is a werewolf and is the pack beta. He likes pizza and video games.

I flip to the next page. It's a photo stream. I scroll down and look at a few. They look like recent pictures from this last summer. In the one, they are building the bathhouse. I scroll to the side again. It's a message forum. It's been fairly active recently. There are posts from yesterday both to and from him.

While a lot of the world is in chaos, life goes on as normal for some people. There's a post to him from Fred Hansen inviting him for a hunt.

I scroll over again and find a friends list. It lists his pack first and then goes to a general friends list.

A knock on the bathroom door scares me. I shriek and drop the phone. I'm just barely able to get my foot under the phone. It drops onto my foot and slides quietly onto the floor.

"Sorry, I was just seeing if someone was in there." It sounds like Stephanie.

"That's okay. I'll be out in a minute." When my heartbeat returns to normal. I take a deep breath.

Picking the phone off the floor, I turn the screen off and place it securely in my pocket.

On second thought, I pull it back out. I turn the phone completely off; wouldn't want to drain the battery.

I leave the bathroom and give a sheepish smile to Stephanie. "All yours."

I return to my bag. I pull out a chunk of jerky and pop it into my mouth. I chew the tough meat. People talk around me, but I don't pay them any attention while I stare off into the distance and go over everything I just learned.

This phone could be a very powerful tool.

Chapter 4

A gift for Rayleen was a good idea.

In a town bustling with people, I'm finding it oddly hard to get one for her. Most places are closed down and locked. I'm sure the town's people wouldn't like it if we started breaking into stores and taking things.

Though, I have been tempted a couple times.

The air clouds in front of me from my deep sigh.

When we finally find an open place, I haven't been able to find anything there. The only thing we've accomplished is making a large list of *NO* as we've gone along. Gifts that she wouldn't like, or gifts that I'm sure she'd enjoy, but it doesn't work in some other way.

The stuffed animal was too big to cart everywhere. The doll had too many pieces. The ball is too awkward and big and could pop. Nothing that takes batteries.

Daniel and I have been searching for hours. We've walked up and down the road, and around the block.

The retro vibe of the street appears to be localized as a quaint gimmick to go along with the fort. Every brick and stone building looks like they haven't been changed in the last one hundred years. Stone colour distinguishes one shop from the next. Painted signs with capitalized letters boldly inform passersby of the establishment inside.

The whole street appears to be popped out of an old black-and-white picture and splashed with colour. Few modern cars that sprinkle the road appear out of place against their backdrop.

The crème coloured stone building catches my attention. Their white and blue sign reads *Queen's Hotel*. A smaller, hidden sign says *Tavern*.

I wish more bars were called Taverns. I feel like when you call a bar a tavern, it classes up the bar.

We cross the street. We didn't walk down that side on our last passing, but I did look. There wasn't anything there except the hotel, a bank, a few fashion stores, and some other things; nothing I think will be useful.

We pass building after building. Each store has a different look on the outside. They use a different style of brick or stone. There are a few stores we pass along the way that have planks of wood as siding.

"Wait!" We walk. "Wait!" The second calling gets my attention. I stop and turn around because the voice is coming closer to us. There's an old lady with white hair chasing us. "You baby." She is holding a necklace. She holds it out in front of me. Why is she showing me a necklace? "For baby."

"What?" I ask. Her accent is very thick, and she isn't saying much. What she's saying doesn't make much sense. I need her to say more so I can understand what she wants.

"Yaya!" A tall dark-haired man runs up to us. He says something to the old lady, and she talks back to him. I don't understand any of it. "My grandmother is giving you the necklace. She heard about you looking for a gift for your lost daughter. She says to wear the necklace while you search and give her the necklace once you find your little girl."

I take the necklace from the old woman. It's pretty. It's a light blue crystal wrapped in a brown string. The crystal is rough.

"Thank you," I speak slowly; unsure if she can understand.

The old woman speaks to the man again. He translates. "She says that the necklace is a macramé hemp wrapped light blue raw celestite stone necklace. It's for angels, and to calm and uplift spirits."

"Thank you. Rayleen will love it." I place the necklace around my neck.

I don't understand what he means about what the necklace is for; angels, calming and uplifting spirits. Is he suggesting the rock does things for people?

The old woman pats the top middle of her chest. She looks at the man and says something. "She says that you have to put the rock against your skin for it to work properly. You pull the two knots to tighten it."

I pull the necklace off to look for the knots. The old woman immediately locates both and shows me how to pull them. I put the necklace back on and tighten it until it's in the spot the old woman patted.

I thank both of them again. They part ways from us.

"We should have asked if she had another one. The colour compliments your eyes." Daniel declares before he gently guides my chin towards him. He kisses me gently but thoroughly. "Let's go back and find the others."

We walk the way we were headed. I use the hunter-green Empress Theatre sign as a reference point. I know the walkway back to the fort is right near the theatre. No matter where we walked along the old brick or stone front stores we could spot the bold sign.

Just passed the theatre and another building are two red brick columns holding a wooden sign. In between is the walkway back to the fort. It's a one-block walk, but the fort is right across the road at the end. We walk down the greyed log wall to the gift shop entrance.

It's a bit warmer in here than outside but not by much. We pass displays of things for sale or take as the situation would call for.

There are a lot of knick-knacks packed into this shop. There are books, carved animals, and beaded items. There are corny Mountie items like a teddy bear dressed in the traditional Mountie outfit. Everything here can be found in every typical Canadian souvenir shop.

We go out to the courtyard. I don't see anyone I want to hang out with.

Jaiden is busy with some people at the fire. They look like they're setting for supper. There's a pot over the fire.

I lead Daniel back to our room. Lucas, Stephanie, Shawn, and Calli are in here. They aren't exactly the crew I wanted to hang out with either. The others have to be somewhere. I didn't see them on our trip through the one road. They should be in one of these long buildings.

Daniel and I go through each room. We pass many people looking at the displays or just going about their own thing. Each room connects to another. We pass through a doctor's room and a horse room.

It's not until we find the small church that we find who were looking for. Brad, Kelly, Miles, Leah and Taylor sit in the room in a square.

"Hey lovebirds." Kelly chimes.

"Hey, what are you all doing in a church?" I ask.

Daniel and I take a seat on either side of the walkway. The benches are carved out of wood; just like practically everything else in this place. There's a cross at the front and a stand for the priest to speak at.

"We relocated after Jaiden suggested we help out." Kelly sneers.

"Doing what?" I ask knowing the answer has something to do with making supper.

"I don't know. Help the locals. She kept going in and out of the room, and every time she would look at us." Brad raises his eyebrow and pulls up his top lip after he finishes talking. I think he is mocking the expression she gave them.

"Like she was trying to shame us into helping her," Taylor adds.

"I think she gets off on it. Think about it, she wants kudos for helping people. She was just mad at us because we weren't kissing her ass and telling her how charitable and good she is. She is so obviously rich and famous, and those people are all the same." Brad lays everything out.

I couldn't say it better myself. Rich and famous people are all the same. They're always so fake. They do charitable things only for the attention or whatever else they can get from it. Behind closed doors, they always turn into another person altogether.

"She thinks she's better than all of us." I judge.

"She's all high and mighty," Taylor adds to my remark.

"What does she have to prove? We're guests. We don't have to do anything. James will be back soon and we'll be leaving." Daniel emphasizes with big gestures. "We deserve a vacation. We've been through so much. We've been through Hell, so we deserve to have this vacation before we get back to rescuing Rayleen."

"Sit back and relax, and let others do the work," Brad adds.

"She needs to lay back and let someone do the hard work. I'm sure she'd get pretty relaxed after that." Daniel's crude tone can't be missed. We all know exactly what he is referencing. She needs to get laid.

"Are you offering? I'm certain she wouldn't touch you with a ten-foot pole." Leah jabs at Daniel.

"You're right. I heard she's a lesbo." Daniel proclaims. "She's never dated anyone." I wonder how long he has known Jaiden. It's possible he's known her or of her for his whole schooling. Or, at least since junior high; when most people start dating.

"She's a prude." Kelly jeers. Jaiden comes off as uptight to me, so it wouldn't shock me if she was a prude.

"She probably thinks she's too good for us poor common folk." Taylor expresses.

"I'm Jaiden and I'm above slumming it with you people. I'm too good for talking to you. I'm too good to date you. I'm too good to screw you." Daniel mocks in a high voice.

"Oh but Jaiden wouldn't say screw, you know. She's too good for that." Taylor takes a jab back at Jaiden and Daniel.

Daniel misses it and continues with her train of thought. "She's too good for swearing."

Out of the corner of my eye, I catch Jaiden walking into the room. "Supper's done. Come get it when you're ready." She walks back out.

Laughs, giggles, and chuckles break out from most. I laugh.

"Do you think she heard us?" Taylor sounds a bit horrified.

"Might do her some good." Brad surmises.

"Knock her off her high horse," Daniel adds without missing a beat.

"We should go get supper before others take it all." Miles had been so quiet I almost forgot he was there.

He gets up and puts his hand out for Kelly. She takes it and they leave together. The rest of us follow after them. Daniel takes my hand when he catches up with me out the door.

It got dark in the few short minutes I was inside the church. We trudge through the snow to the fire and the growing lineup of people. There is a large pot at the end of the line.

"What do you think it is?" Daniel whispers in my ear.

"Soup. It's always soup." I tell him.

Soup is really common now. It has its advantages. It'll help keep us warm. They can water it down, so it's more filling.

"Great. Better not be as disgusting as the crap they made us at the school." Daniel pushes me forward gently. We shuffle forward.

No one mans anything. I grab my own bowl and pour the soup into it. I pick up a spoon and I'm free of the line.

It's a bit chilly out, and I can see the smoke rising out of the building we sleep in. I decide that I'll make my way inside; the others will probably follow after me. Daniel follows right behind me.

It'll be pitch black out soon. The darker it gets the colder it gets.

I can't wait for summer. This all would be so much easier if it was summer. We could sleep under the stars. We wouldn't have to worry about finding warmth and shelter. I don't want to have to worry about freezing to death while having to watch out for demons trying to kill me.

We enter the building and warmth brushes my cheeks. Someone kept the stoves going in here. It gets warmer as we make our way into the room we're staying in.

Jaiden, Lucas and Calli sit in their little triangle clique.

I sit down and get comfy on the only actual bed in the room. One by one, everyone from the church settles into the room. Others too, trickle in.

The broth tastes like nothing. There is some sort of red meat in this and some noodles. Not much else.

Conversations buzz through the room. We settle on a game of 'would you rather?' Ridiculousness follows.

I soon realize that our group is being the loudest when Jaiden breaks my concentration on what we are doing.

She gets up and collects empty dishes from around the room; as much as she can carry. Lucas takes a stack from her and leaves out the door. She continues picking up more dishes until she can't handle anymore. Then, she leaves to go outside.

"Would you rather be able to fly or read minds?" Taylor asks.

"Fly," I answer immediately. If you read minds you'd find out the deepest darkest secrets about everyone you know. You find out what they actually think about you. I'd rather not invade their privacy like that. I wait for other people to reply.

Daniel answers. "Fly."

Leah answers. "Read minds."

Miles answers. "Fly."

Kelly answers. "Read minds."

Brad answers. "Read minds."

"Fly. You could have the freedom to go anywhere. People who read minds tend to have to live alone in the woods." Calli answers. She joins our circle and then asks. "Would you rather be the smartest person in the world or the hottest person in the world?"

Kelly answers. "Hottest."

Daniel answers. "Hottest."

Taylor answers. "Smartest."

I answer. "Hottest"

Leah answers. "Hottest."

Miles answers. "Smartest"

Brad answers. "Smartest, then I would be able to figure out how to also be the hottest person in the world."

Complaints happen all around. "You can't do that." I protest. "The rules of the game are one or the other. You can't use one to get the other."

Others echo the same ruling.

"When I'm the smartest person in the world I can do whatever I want," Brad argues. He changes the subject with James' entrance. "Hey look, James is back."

"James!" Daniel exclaims his name as a greeting.

"Did you find Nikki?" Shawn asks quickly.

"And, Rayleen?" I'm hopeful.

"Yes, we'll leave tomorrow morning." He leaves back out of the room as quickly as he arrived. Why is he leaving? Why can't we leave now?

I move to get up and follow after him, but Daniel stops me. "We can't leave while it's pitch black out. James knows what he's doing. We'll leave first thing in the morning."

"Okay," I say, but I stare at the doorway.

I itch to leave. If James knows where Rayleen is we should be going after her immediately. Who knows how much time she has left?

I need to take my mind off this. The only way I'll get through waiting is alcohol, but I have no idea where we would get some. I don't remember passing by any liquor stores down the one street. There wasn't any liquor in the gift shop.

Maybe I could ask someone for the alcohol.

Hey, there was that hotel that had that tavern in it. I wonder if it would be open. It would, or should, be easy enough to find in the dark. But, they've probably closed and locked their doors by now.

People don't go out much when there are no street lights to light their way. It feels more dangerous out when you can only see a foot in front of you.

"Does my swearing bother you?" Brad's question gets my

attention. I look at him with confusion. His attention is off to the rest of the room. People have shifted. Some have disappeared. Then I notice Jaiden and Lucas returned. Jaiden shakes her head. "Does my swearing bother you, Miss Perfect? Or are you too good to answer my question?" Brad probes.

He's obviously picking up from the conversation from earlier.

"No." She objects.

"Do you ever swear? I mean you never talk." Daniel states.

"No, not really." Jaiden tries to look away and puts her head down. I think she's trying to end the conversation.

"Why? If you don't have a problem with swearing, why haven't I ever heard you swear?" Daniel asks.

I look at him, begging with my eyes to leave this conversation to die. He didn't have to join in, it encourages Brad.

Jaiden takes a moment to answer; long enough that I almost thought she was just going to ignore him. She turns her head to look at Daniel. "If you never hear me talk, why would you expect to hear me swear?" She pauses briefly. "I think of swearing as just another kind of vocabulary. You use different types of vocabulary depending on the person you're talking to and the situation."

"Oh, are you too good to swear?" Brad eggs her on.

"No. Swear words just aren't in my regular everyday vocabulary. I just use whatever words come to mind." Even with the lack of proper lighting in the room, and only fire light to go by, I can see her face going red. She must be embarrassed.

"Oh, I'm sorry. Little miss perfect is too perfect to use us commoner's language." Brad teases her.

"Let's just say there's a time and a place to call someone an imbecilic Oedipus complexian, and a time and a place to call them a stupid mother fucker." Jaiden gets up from her seat and makes her way out of the room.

"Awe, we were only joking around. Stay." Daniel offers her a seat with us; teasing her.

Jaiden pauses and turns in our direction. "I'm good. I was just taking a small break from cleaning up from supper. I have to go back anyways."

She leaves to go back outside. Something tells me that she's upset at all the torment we've been giving her.

"Miss Perfect couldn't wait to rub it in our faces. Oo. Work still needs to be done. Supper still needs to be cleaned up." Taylor mocks Jaiden's last words.

"Why are you being so mean to her?" Lucas asks.

"We're not being mean. This is how we always talk with her. It's a game we play." Daniel tries to defend himself and the rest of us. I never really paid that much attention to how Daniel interacted with Jaiden in school. "She knows we're joking."

"It doesn't sound like a game." Lucas counters.

"She brings it on herself." Brad defends. The excuse sounds lame, even to me.

"Grow up. She's a nice kid. Leave her alone." Lucas leaves.

"Oh, looks like someone's into the older men." As soon as he leaves and is out of earshot, Brad jokes. "You know what that means."

"What?" Taylor asks as if she doesn't know where this is going.

"Daddy issues," Brad explains.

"Calli, you not going to defend your friend?" Kelly asks.

Calli raises her eyebrow and sighs. "I've only known her for a few days. We don't really know each other more than acquaintances. Not enough that I would defend her against gossip I don't know is true or false."

"No loyalty for your new friend?" Leah inquires.

"I respect her enough not to bash her, but I don't know her well enough to defend her. It's none of my business, and you're going to say what you're going to say; no matter what I say, so there's no point." Calli reasons.

It's true. I've spent enough time on this side of the road to know that nothing can stop anyone determined to mess around with a person. And, Jaiden seems like an easy target.

I still have my dish from supper. Jaiden didn't take it with her, and I doubt she'll come back. I scoot off the bed and gather my dish. I pile Daniel's bowl and spoon into my own. The rest can take their own dishes. "I'll be right back."

"I'll come with you." Daniel offers.

"No thanks. It's just out there and I'll be back before you know it." I walk out the door and into the adjoining room. Then, I leave through the exit to the outside. It's cold. I'm going to need warmer clothes soon; we all are.

There is one light outside; besides the faint glow coming from the windows. The fire is going strong. A few dark figures are standing around the fire.

The short one, Jaiden I figure, is warming her hands by sticking them out closer to the fire. They're talking but in hushed tones. My crunchy footsteps give me away and they stop talking once they notice me coming.

When I come into the glow of the fire, Jaiden notices the dishes in my hands. She walks over to me. "I'll wash those for you." I hand her the dishes.

She takes them to a pot near the fire to rinse them off. They clang against the pot sides.

I take my eyes off her. The other two figures at the fire are James and Lucas. I stay to hear more from James. I need to know more about what he found out.

I walk closer, so I can stand in between the two.

"Where is Rayleen? Is she okay? Please, I need to know." I beg James. Tears immediately fall from my eyes and a lump forms in my throat. I can't say anything else.

"I don't know. The information I received was old. She was brought to an outpost at a jailhouse a few hours from here. She was okay when she arrived; both she and Nikki were alive and unharmed when they arrived. They had arrived the same day they were taken from the farmhouse. Darius ordered the guards not to harm them. I wasn't able to obtain any more information."

"That's it?" My voice carries the heartbreak in my chest. James nods and walks away.

A hand rubs my back. It's slightly comforting but not enough. The cold air freezes the tear tracks on my cheeks. I sob.

Jaiden comes from behind me. She hands me a cloth for my tears and goes back to rub my back.

"It's good news, isn't it? The fact that we know where they are and that Darius has ordered the people there not to harm them means realistically that both of them are alive." Jaiden suggests.

"How would you know? What if they're dead? What if they've been moved? We should go now. Why are we waiting?" I verbally attack her.

"I don't know. I don't know whether they are dead or alive. I don't know if they are going to be there or not. What I do know is that we should wait until morning; as James said. It's too dark out to go anywhere.

We were just talking about this right before you got here. We need to talk to the locals about gas or switching vehicles because we can't go as far as we need to with the little gas we have.

We can get on the road tomorrow morning. By the evening we should be at the jailhouse, we'll go in and find out immediately whether they are alive, dead, there or gone.

Until then, we can't do anything but hope for the best. We can't change whatever is going to happen and whatever has happened to both girls. A few hours, so we can make sure we get there safely, isn't going to change a thing." Jaiden's speech makes me feel a little better; enough to stop sobbing and new tears.

Maybe she's right on some level. I'd still like to get there as soon as possible. I need Rayleen. I need to find her. I'll do anything to find her. "But, what if something happens to her?"

"What if something happens to you?" I stop breathing for a second. I hadn't thought about that. "Let's say you leave now; in a rush to find Rayleen. You go search and find a vehicle in this cold and snow; in the black of night.

You miraculously find a vehicle that has enough gas to get you there. But wait, you veer off the road because in the dark you can't see where the road is. You roll into the ditch. You have to leave the vehicle there because you're stuck, but you can't see where you're going.

You wait for the morning, but you wait in the cold because you don't have enough gas to last that long or because snow is covering the tailpipe and the exhaust is coming into the car. Maybe you didn't realize that and you die of carbon monoxide poisoning.

You're near hypothermic. You get out of the car and start walking to the nearest town. You have frostbite killing your wet feet because you aren't in suitable footwear to walk through snow for long. Maybe you make it to town; maybe you pass out and die in the snow. Maybe you die because you get gangrene in your dead frostbitten feet.

Maybe you don't make it to the jail ever. You die and you can't ever rescue Rayleen. When we finally rescue her, we have to tell her you died recklessly trying to rescue her. Think about how heartbroken she will be. Would she grow up blaming herself? Undoubtedly, because everyone would. But most of all, she'd have to grow up without you because you couldn't wait a few hours until it was safe to leave."

Jaiden's words are heartbreaking. They are also sobering.

What if something happened to me? What if something happened to me and I couldn't rescue Rayleen? What if I die before I can rescue her?

She would be heartbroken. Her parents and grandparents went away on a trip and never came back. Now she's been taken from me. She doesn't deserve to have to go through losing me too. She doesn't deserve to have to go through more family not coming back for her.

She's too young to have been through what she's already had to go through. I won't add to it.

I have to rescue Rayleen, but I need to make sure I'm alive long enough to do so.

"Okay. I'll wait until morning, but we need to go get her as soon as we can." I insist.

"We will. We will do everything we can to rescue both of them as soon as possible." Jaiden reassures me. I wipe my face with the cloth she gave me.

I can't go back inside with the mess I know my face is. My eyes are surely puffy and red from my tears. Any makeup residue would be streaming down my cheeks or smudged around my eyes.

My eyelashes are freezing together so I walk closer to the fire. The heat quickly liquefies the ice on my face. I'm able to wipe the tears from my face, and hopefully any smeared makeup; though I'm not sure how much of that there is even left on my face at this point.

I blow my runny and stuffed-up nose. Putting the cloth in my pocket because I'm sure Jaiden wouldn't want it back.

I look at the fire. The flames are orange and yellow. Its

crackles are the only thing I can hear. It's like nothing exists around us.

I look up at the sky. The moon is just a sliver. It doesn't give off much light. I can't see anything outside the fort. It's like nothing exists around us.

There are more stars than I've ever seen up there. There are thousands of stars that I can see versus the hundreds I used to see in the city. I guess people are right when they say the stars are better in the country, and better when all the lights are turned off.

We all stay around the fire for a couple of minutes. I think my face should be back to normal or normal enough. I can blame any red cheeks on the cold.

If I stay much longer people will wonder where I am. I don't want to have anyone come looking for me.

From Jaiden's comforting, I feel a bit bad for making fun of her. I don't want anyone else coming back out here and harassing her; at least for the rest of the night. It'll be my repayment for her help.

"I'll see you all later. I'm going to go back inside." I let them know before I leave. They say their goodbyes.

When I leave the warmth of the fire, I find out how cold it really is. How did it get so cold out? My face freezes all over again. I tuck my fingers into my fists and cross my arms. All of me feels frozen.

I enter the building and start thawing out; slowly. It's not too warm in here either but it's above freezing. It's warm enough that I won't freeze to death.

People have settled down here. The room has been turned into a large bed. Blankets cover the floor, with people over some, and under others. More people settle around the stove than not. It's the warmest place in the room so I don't blame them. But, I do envy them at this moment. I could use the extra heat.

"Hey," I whisper to Daniel when I reach him and the others still at the bed. It looks like Calli, Miles, Shawn, Stephanie and Brad decided to go to bed. Daniel, Taylor, Kelly, and Leah acknowledge my return.

"What took so long?" Daniel asks.

"Oh, I was talking with James. He says that Rayleen is in a jail that they're using as an outpost. James said we'll head out first thing tomorrow morning and go rescue them." I tell them.

"Did you talk about anything else?" Kelly asks.

"No, not really. They did talk about having to get vehicles from the locals." I try to think of anything else that was said. I don't want to mention my crying or anything about that.

"Are you sure?" Kelly asks. "Nothing else happened?"

I don't get to answer. "Kelly." Leah cautions her. "Stop." Kelly goes to say something. "You already know exactly what happened." She explains to me, "we could partially hear; at least the shouting parts. Vampire hearing is better than human hearing."

Red embarrassment flushes my face. I didn't think their hearing was that good. That fire isn't too far from this room, but I didn't think anyone here would hear.

"We should just go to bed. Tomorrow will come the sooner you fall asleep." Daniel rescues me. He takes me up by my hand and pulls me over to a patch of blankets not taken up yet. We both remove our shoes. I remove my soaking wet socks.

Leah and Kelly leave the room while Taylor finds her own blanket.

Daniel pulls the blankets back for us to get inside. We settle in and get comfortable under the chilly covers.

He spoons against my back and wraps his arm around me. He kisses the side of my neck. "Good night, Babe."

I squeeze his arm and grasp his hand. "Good night."

Brave Souls

Despite the thoughts going on in my head, I drift off quickly.

Chapter 5

"Wake them up. We're leaving soon." Sandra's booming voice cuts through my dreams. Immediately, the irritation darkens my mood.

I swear, I just went to sleep. I closed my eyes in a blink, and now the most annoying voice in the world is telling me we need to be woken up.

I open my eyes to a dim light and two people standing in the doorway. Shale is receiving the order from an angry Sandra.

Doesn't anyone understand how important sleep is?

I pull away from Rayleen slowly; both for her to remain asleep and so I don't hurt my ribs. I roll backwards. The edge of the cot is right there. I put my feet on the ground and push myself to a seated position.

Sandra grabs the notebook I left on the counter and leaves. Shale and I look at each other. I put my finger up to my lips in a shushing motion.

My rib hurts with the movement of getting up. I can feel my lungs are heavy and my breathing is shallow. I walk to Shale and whisper to him. "Leave her sleeping as long as we can. I need to cough." My voice and throat feel rough. By the end of it, my breath feels caught in my heavy lungs.

He doesn't stop me as I leave the room. He does however

follow after me. Shale closes the door. As soon as he does, I take a deep breath in. This starts a tickle in my lungs and throat. One more deep breath in brings a strong and long coughing fit. I brace my arms against my ribs.

Mucus coughs up into my mouth so I spit it out against the wall beside me. When the coughing fit ends I wipe the tears from my cheeks and look back at Shale. "Sorry." I apologize. "The doctor said that'll happen after I sleep."

"That's going to suck. How long?" He appears like he genuinely sympathizes with my situation.

"A couple weeks—maybe? She said sleeping upright can help, but I don't know about you, but I can't sleep sitting up." I smile at him.

He shrugs. "I can sleep any way."

"Lucky Bastard," I call him. There is a pause. He doesn't seem like he's going to continue with that conversation, so I move on to another. A burning question in my mind needs to be answered in memory of my slumber. "So, why are we leaving?"

"Don't know. Sandra didn't say. She just gave me my orders. You two are leaving with Sandra and Darius. You're going to another hideout. I'm going to do preparations here, then follow after you." His response answers my question and a few others; while also bringing up more.

It seems those two have been busy talking since I left them. They took to heart my faked attack vision. I'm glad, because that means I won't have to do any more work on that front.

Hopefully, the next place is easier to escape from.

I yawn. I'm still so tired. "Do you know what time it is?"

"No, but the sun set a few hours ago." He reveals.

It's winter and that could mean anything. I think the sun sets at four, and a few hours could mean it's eight or it could be midnight; depending on his definition. "Great. Do you know how long we've been sleeping?"

He shrugs. "Maybe a couple hours."

"Does it matter?" Sandra appears out of the darkness.

"I don't know about you, but I need my sleep." I retort.

"I'm not happy about this either, but your vision's happening tomorrow and we don't want to be here." It only takes a moment to clue in, the fake vision about my rescue and the attack on the jail. It's amazing that I actually predicted something happening. And, it's happening tomorrow. I am both thrilled and upset. This could help cement their belief in me as a psychic. People are coming to rescue me, but they're going to be too late. People are coming to rescue me, but Sandra must've found out from her spy ahead of time. "We're leaving now. Is the brat up?"

"Not yet," I answer.

"Well?" She sweeps her hand out towards the door. I get her meaning; that I need to wake Rayleen now.

I walk into the room and to the cot. I stand over her for just a moment. Reaching out, I grab her shoulder and shake a little. "Rayleen, you need to wake up." She stirs a little and looks at me. "We're leaving." She closes her eyes, so I shake her again.

She wakes up enough to leave the cot. Goosebumps appear all over her visible skin. I take the blanket off the cot and wrap it around her. It's big enough that when we are travelling I should be able to wrap it around the both of us; at least if they decide to travel by dragon again.

Maybe, they have a vehicle somewhere. It would be nice; then we could put the heat on.

We emerge from the room and go to Sandra. She doesn't say anything but leads us out of the jail.

We pass by only one other person in the halls. They keep their head to the ground and stroll by us fast.

A blast of cold covers me when Sandra opens the door. It's

freezing. There is snow on the ground; about six inches high. Everything in sight is covered in the white stuff.

Darius waits impatiently holding the reins of a large dragon; the same one that brought us here. When he sees us he steers the dragon towards us.

We meet in the middle. He grabs Rayleen and jumps onto the dragon's back with her. He comes back down for me, and then for Sandra.

Darius leads the line, then Rayleen, me, and Sandra. The dragon straightens out its wings; the only warning before it takes off. It barely gives me time to grab a hold of Darius' shirt.

Rayleen is held on by the mere placement of my body before I put my other arm around her.

Cold air rushes passed all of us. It's a hard couple of seconds with my stomach in my throat until the dragon evens out and I'm able to relax my grips.

Sandra removes her hands from my shoulders. Rayleen relaxes between Darius and me. She didn't look like she had a chance to hold onto anything more than the blanket she has wrapped around her.

The blanket is wrapped around her in a way that it is stuck, and I don't feel comfortable enough to move her around to get it unstuck. I settle for tucking my fingers into a fold. There is a little heat there to make sure my fingers don't freeze stiff.

Some time goes by before I hear a peep from the little girl in front of me. It startles me as I thought she had fallen asleep.

"I'm cold." She whines.

I'm surprised her silence lasted this long. The blanket may have helped her stay warmer than the rest of us. But, she's also much tinier, so she'd get colder faster.

"I know. It's freezing." I can't think of anything else to say or do to help her; nothing that will help anyway.

"Darius, we need to stop in the next town. We need winter clothes." Sandra informs our driver.

"No," Darius responds quickly.

"We're stopping in the next town for coats." Sandra orders Darius.

"You can last till we get there." He insists.

"Fine, but they'll be popsicles by then." Sandra jokes seriously.

He doesn't say anything else, but I do notice his head moving to look around the ground below.

"Thank you," I say over my shoulder.

"Don't. None of us are dressed for this weather. I hate the cold." She mutters the last part. I hold back a retort; we aren't friends like that.

I hear skin rubbing against skin. A jolt of heat grabs at my cheeks and seeps down my neck to my body. Sandra's hot hands lay against my cheeks. The effects from her hands supply me with a bit of the heat I've lost.

Her hands recede. "Thank you." My gratitude is met with silence. She does the same for Rayleen.

We start descending a few minutes later. I don't know where we are, but I do recognize the unmistakable Sears sign.

Darius turns to grab Rayleen. Once she's in his arms he jumps off the dragon. "You have five minutes." He asserts as he places her on the ground.

He doesn't help the rest of us off. I throw my leg over and slide down the dragon's body to the ground. I almost lose my footing as I hit the ground, but I catch myself against the dragon. Sandra glides to the ground more gracefully than I did.

What little heat I had left from Sandra's magic and from my spot on the dragon fades fast. It chills me thoroughly.

The unmistakable sound of glass shattering draws my attention to the store's entrance. Darius is standing at the long frame of the window. He bats away any existing bits of glass that are stuck to the frame edges.

Darius takes a step into the dark store. Sandra goes after him. I take Rayleen's hand and follow. I pick Rayleen up to go over the glass. I look at the ground to try to make sure I don't step on anything that will go through my shoes.

When I lift my head there is a bright flickering light in Sandra's hand. Darius is nowhere in sight.

Sandra is stopped in front of the directional signs that tell you where to find the section you're looking for. I don't get a chance to figure out where the women's section is before Sandra has a direction in mind and instep.

She takes off at a quick pace. We rush to catch up. It seems like the women's section is at the back of the store. We walk a ways to get to it.

The coats take up a large section to themselves. Sandra doesn't have to instruct me to search for a coat; I quickly dig in. I don't want to find out how much patience she will have if I can't find our pair of coats fast enough.

There are so many coats here, but I know my brands. I know the North End jackets are winter jackets made for Canadian winters. I find a rack full of them and start looking for the thickest and warmest-looking ones in my size. Quickly, I find a black and grey jacket. I pull it on. I zipper up both zippers and almost immediately start feeling the difference with my body heat contained.

Not too far away, thanks to convenient product placement in-store layouts, I find snow pants, toques, scarves and mittens. I grab a set of cotton mittens and shove them into a zippered pocket. I put on one of each; black snow pants, a black toque, a patterned wool scarf, and insulated gloves.

"Did you see where the kids' section was? And, the boots?" I ask Sandra.

"I'll take you there in a minute." She waves me off. After she finds the accessories she needs, Sandra finally takes us away from this section and we go to the kids' section right on the other side of the aisle.

I set to work quickly finding Rayleen her own winter gear. It doesn't take long, but long enough for Sandra to huff about the time.

I hold back stating that Darius can suck it up and wait for us. My sharp tongue won't be appreciated right now.

We move on from there to our last stop; the boots aisles. My size eights are easy to find. There are many options to choose from, and I can quickly pinpoint the boots that look like they will stand up to the cold. On the other side, I squint to find Rayleen boots in her size.

There aren't much for options, but I finally find her decent enough boots.

We follow after Sandra and her glowing light, back to the entrance we came in. Darius stands at the dragon; holding the reins and waiting for our return.

He helps us all on the dragon's back. This time I notice straps on the saddle-type seat we're on. I brace myself on them for our ascent.

It's still so cold out, and the wind is sharp. There is a noticeable temperature difference. I no longer feel like my fingers are going stiff. Parts of me could be described as warm to the point of being toasty. Other parts, still exposed to the cold wind are still freezing.

I take advantage of the hood on the jacket and put it on. I draw the strings tight and hold them there with the clips. My scarf isn't doing much good bunched around my neck, so I pull it up to cover everything below my eyes.

I imagine Rayleen is cold just the same, so I adjust her winter clothes to do the same as mine. She leans against me when I finish. Her blanket isn't likely doing much now, but she still holds it right.

When I'm not freezing to death, the night is beautiful. The white ground sparkles from the little moonlight. The stars shine brightly. The sky is almost pure black with the sparkly exceptions.

Still, everything is eerily quiet and unmoving.

We are the only people around. Or, at least, it seems that way. There may be people in the houses or buildings hiding. I don't know how many demons there are and how many people they have killed.

Soft snores come from the bundled girl. I hold her tighter, and let her sleep. One of us should get some sleep.

There is nothing to do but think, sit, and wait for the destination.

My captors are not talkative people. They don't seem like friendly people. I can't imagine they would be up to having small talk.

I turn my eyes down to the ground. There isn't much to see. Nothing much changes, until in short bursts of time I see patches of dark ground not covered by snow. This gets more frequent as time goes by.

Just as slow as it left, the snow comes back.

Then I see mountains. White trees everywhere; surround us. Cities become infrequent, and the breaks in trees become lakes or roads.

Finally, emerging out of the white trees and mountains I see a castle.

I haven't seen this castle in two years. It's the Banff Springs Hotel. I went in once, years ago with my cousin, exploring. We pretended that we were guests of the hotel, so we could explore and ride the elevator. She showed me a spot up a stairway where, she claimed, a lady had spontaneously combusted. I didn't believe her at the time. Now I wonder if maybe the lady had been a vampire; they combust in the sun.

The dragon descends as we near the castle-like hotel. What a place to have a hideout.

We land softly. A whoosh of air brushes the sliver of face I have uncovered.

The jostle wakens Rayleen. She springs up from her spot against my chest. Had my arms not been holding her, she would have fallen with her balance off in her shock.

"It's okay. We're here." I tell her.

We're led off the dragon and into the castle. This place is roaring with life; a stark difference from the jail we were just at hours ago. People of many shapes, sizes and colours hurry through the halls.

Only half look human, but I know by now that they probably aren't human.

The lobby is as grand as I remember. The darkness causes shadows, but I can still make out the high ceilings, dark wood stations, and stone wall details. The grand stone staircase climbs to darkness. Their plants haven't fared well, and seem to be dead or dying; drooped over like they are.

One woman stops and gushes over Darius. Before she can say much, a manly voice calls Sandra's name. Sandra walks over to him near the grand stone staircase.

Darius pushes me in the same direction. I guide Rayleen that way.

I recognize this man from the house I was taken to. The man gives her a package, and then she takes off down the hall faster than I can follow. She quickly disappears in the crowd of people and dimly lit hall.

"I'll take you two to your room. Then Darius and Sandra will meet you in the conference room." I look behind me at Darius, but he isn't there anymore.

"Ram, can I go to the bathroom?" Rayleen asks innocently. I take note that they must have known each other in the past.

"There will be a bathroom in your room. You can go in there. We aren't too far from where you'll be staying." He explains.

Ram leads us to our room. He was right when he said it wasn't far off. He leads us up one floor of stairs, and into the first room there.

We go right into the room. Ram lights a candle and places it in the bathroom. The moment he leaves the smaller room Rayleen finds her way inside and shuts the door.

Ram points over to the window and starts walking over there. I follow after him. He opens up the curtains and points out the window to the right.

"That way is a highly guarded road. They have orders to kill anyone escaping on the spot." He points the other way. "That way loops around and goes up the mountain. There's nothing that way except hot springs and another hotel."

He points to the forest in front of us. "That is where we send prisoners for hunting. We have made the forest into a hunting ground. It's a game, if you will. The forest is filled with supernatural beings looking for lunch or some fun, and we've set traps. If you can manage to get through the forest alive, and to the road up there-" He points far up the mountain. "You get to go free. We'll even give you a ride to town and order no one touch you for a week."

He doesn't have to say the next part. I already know what he's leaving unsaid. "But, no one's made it out alive." I finish for him.

"You got it. I don't recommend you try to escape. It's a death sentence no matter what direction you choose. Stay here and you'll stay alive. Darius already has an order out that you are not to be touched. That order stands as long as you don't leave this hotel." Darius seems to want us alive; if he keeps giving those orders, I don't think I'll risk an escape; unless it's a sure thing.

The door to the bathroom opens. I hold my comment and look at the little girl rubbing her eyes.

"I'm tired." She announces needlessly.

I walk over to the bed and pull back the covers. "Take off your boots and go to sleep. There's a nice, comfy bed right here for you."

She doesn't take much convincing. The girl is practically falling asleep standing up. Rayleen kicks off her boots. She falls into the bed and passes right out. I pull the covers over her and adjust her position until she looks like she won't wake up with a kink in her neck.

I turn back to Ram and whisper. "We're going to sleep for a bit. It was a long ride here."

He shakes his head. "I'm afraid you'll have to wait for that. Sandra instructed me to bring you to the conference room when you were ready."

"And if I'm not ready until after I've slept?" I cross my arms; daring to be difficult.

Ram smiles big at my defiant question like I made a joke. He shakes his head. "Seems like you have a job to do first. I promise, you'll be back here before you know it, and you can sleep then."

I don't think I'll win this argument. As much as I would like to go to sleep now, I know Ram wouldn't let me. Or, Sandra or Darius would come to wake me themselves. They would probably wake Rayleen up at the same time.

"Let's go to this conference room then." I look at Rayleen, then back at Ram. "She'll be okay here, right?"

"Yes. I'll stay here and guard her." He promises.

"I thought you were going to bring me to the conference room," I question with a statement.

"Yes, well, I'm sure you're competent enough to find it on your own. Or, would you rather I find someone else to guard her and I'll escort you." He tries to accommodate me. Rayleen seemed comfortable with him, so he might be the best choice to watch her.

"No, it's fine. Where is it?" I ask. How hard can it be to find?

"Downstairs. Head right; there are conference rooms and ballrooms down that way. You're looking for Mount Stephen." He hands me a lit candle.

"Great. Thanks."

There isn't anything else to do or say, so I leave the room with the bathroom's lit candle. I go back down the stairs, and to the right. I pass many rooms, but I don't go through any doors until near the end. I wave the candlelight in front of the sign. It reads *Mount Stephen Hall*; that sounds right.

The room is huge. It truly looks like a room that belongs in a castle. There is a set of armour fixed to the wall. A candle-lit circular light suspends over a long wooden table and chairs with crests on their backrests. The floor, walls and arches are made of stone. The many windows give a beautiful mountain view.

The sunrise hasn't hit the valley yet, but the tips of the mountains are brightened. It's still dark down here.

It's so cold in this room. The stone and abundant windows don't hold in the heat as well as I would like.

I look to the opposite side of the table. Darius and Sandra both sit in the elegant chairs. The table is long enough that I feel comfortable sitting at the head seat closer to me, but it's not so far that I'm far away from the duo.

The seats are comfortable and soft. I feel like a queen sitting in such a throne-like chair.

"Explain your visions," Sandra instructs.

"Explain what?" I ask. I try to recall each detail of the visions I've told them so far. Sandra has my notebook in her hand. She must've been going through the book in preparation for a conversation with me.

"Tell us your visions. What have you seen?" Darius elaborates for her.

"Isn't that what the notebook was for?" I point the book out to make more of a point.

"The jail is going to be attacked. We moved locations. I'm not even going to get into the other useless bullshit you wrote down. We need more prophecies." Sandra closes the notebook and tosses it in my direction. It doesn't make it to me, so I leave it where it lands on the table.

"Alright." I trail off. It's all I can do to stall for time.

"Well?" She says impatiently.

"I can't think of anything." Slips out of my mouth.

"You must have a thousand visions, and you can't think of anything." Darius' voice is starting to deepen with anger and frustration.

"No, I can't," I say honestly. My mind is drawing a blank right now.

"We'll then I guess you need to have some new visions," Sandra says as she places a hand on Darius' shoulder.

"She touched us both on the ride over. She must have a thousand visions by now." Darius talks around me.

Sandra wrinkles her eyebrows together. "It doesn't work that way with her."

On the spot, I can't think of anything, so I throw Sandra's own words back at her to buy time. "I can't think of anything that isn't useless bullshit."

"Bullshit." She echoes, but her tone changes the meaning.

I restate. "The only visions I've had are of more useless bullshit; that you don't want to hear."

I sound strong and confident, but in my head, I trail off. I need new visions right now.

"Maybe that's a good thing," Darius suggests.

"How is it a good thing?" Sandra's anger is now directed at the male beside her.

"Maybe nothing significant is supposed to happen any time soon," Darius concludes. I like his point of view.

"Or she's lying to us and planning her escape." Sandra may still not be on my side. But, I don't completely disagree with her.

I try to ease her worries. I do plan on escaping, but not until I have a real opportunity. "Ram already explained the forest to me. I'm not planning on taking my chances out there. And, do you really think anyone will get passed those defences?"

"Sandra, just calm down. Can't you see she's trying to work with us? She's one of us now." Darius stands up from his seat and walks closer to me. He takes the seat to my left. "Sandra, go to the kitchen and grab a hot drink." He orders without even glancing in her direction. "Now!"

Sandra screeches her chair backwards, and storms off out of the room through a door opposite the one I came in.

Darius stares at me for longer than I'm comfortable with. "Can I help you with something?" I finally ask.

"I need to know about Alexa. Is she going to come for me?" The question feels off. Shouldn't he be asking if she'll come for Rayleen?

"She'll come," I tell him.

"Will she stay with me?" He responds.

"With you? Am I missing something?" He gives me a look. "I can't see the past," I explain to him. It's as good of an answer and an explanation as any.

"We were going to marry each other," Darius reveals.

"And, then what happened?" He doesn't respond. "You don't have to answer." Alexa appears to be a sore spot for Darius. "You kidnapped Rayleen. She'll come. She loves that little girl too much not to."

"But, will she stay?" He interrupts my trailing thought.

I'm stuck between spinning my tale of the future and what is reality. "It would take a lot of convincing. She has a boyfriend."

"Who?" He roars.

I try to think of his name, but I can't. Just the word 'asshole' comes to mind. "I don't remember his name, but he wasn't very nice to Rayleen." As I think about it more, I blurt out my thoughts. "I didn't see them together after that. I don't know if they are still together."

"Alexa wouldn't stay with him because he was mean to Rayleen?" What he says as a question doesn't sound like he was looking for a response so I stay quiet. "So, they aren't together?" He says with a hint of hope in his tone.

"I don't know. If they still are, they won't be together for long." I'll give him his hope.

"Would she still become my queen?" He asks. He's very focused on Alexa; almost to a state of obsession.

"Your queen?" The wording weirds me out.

"Will she turn into a vampire and help me rule?" His question reveals his intentions. Could this be why she left him in the first place?

"It's possible," I tell him, feeling guilty towards Alexa.

"Shouldn't you know?" He interrogates.

I panic. "It's complicated."

He slams his fist on the table. When he lifts up there is noticeable distress from the wood. Slivers of wood raise from where the piece broke from his strength. "How complicated could it be?"

"Very complicated, everything can be very complicated." I try to buy time, but my mind just circles back around to the word complicated. The whole situation is complicated, and I don't know how to keep this up. I don't know how long I can keep this up.

"Yes or no. Will Alexa become a vampire for me?" His eyes appear to darken and his body is visibly tense. He appears to be holding back his want to throttle me.

"Yes," I announce. I know it will calm him down to hear what he wants to be told. It's possible; it could happen. It could very well happen whether Alexa wants it or not.

Darius is strong. He's strong enough that Alexa wouldn't be able to fight him if she wanted to. I fear the next time they meet Alexa will become the next kidnap victim, and turned into a vampire. Her efforts to run away from him will mean nothing. He's going to get what he wants in the end.

"Will Alexa rule by my side?" He asks. The question is redundant by now.

I open my mouth to answer yes when a mug flies over his head and passed my side. Hot liquid pours out on its flight; over him, on me, the chairs, and the floor. The cup clinks and shatters on impact.

I stand in my surprise and fright. I wipe off the now cooled liquid from my cheek and neck, then from my coat. I need a towel, but I'm afraid to ask when I look at the furious woman.

Sandra raises her hands up in front of her face and opens her mouth; looking like she's about to take a bite out of an apple.

She pauses. She draws in a deep breath, closes her mouth, and brings down her hands. She turns and walks around the table.

Sandra glares at Darius as she sits in her previous spot. I can tell she wants to scream at him, but she's holding back. She closes her eyes and concentrates on breathing. Her face never loses its tension and anger.

"Sandra, take Nikki back to her room." Darius barks his order before he walks out of the room.

Sandra stands up quickly, and stomps my way; then passes by me. I follow after her.

Sandra obviously is still pissed at Darius, and I'd imagine she doesn't like doing Darius' errand of being my escort especially after he pissed her off. The question seems to be, what pissed her off?

The subject may lie in the person we were talking about; Alexa. Does Sandra have a problem with Alexa? Or, could it be Darius and his hang-up of Alexa?

Could Sandra have feelings for Darius?

Sandra hastily walks down the hall. She practically bounds up the stairs and leads me to my room. She opens the door enough for me to get in. As soon as I get partially inside she is running off somewhere else. I close the door and turn the lock.

I go into the bedroom portion of the room. Rayleen is right where I left her; only shifting a little from her position. Ram is sitting in a chair reading a book. We exchange glances.

My jacket is still wet from the spilled drink, so I wipe the jacket off with a towel in the bathroom.

When I leave the small room, I go out to the bed area.

Without saying a word, I take off my boots and crawl into the cold empty side of the large bed. My feet chill immediately. I wonder if maybe I should have kept my boots on, but can't find the strength to move.

Brave Souls

Now that I'm still and resting, my whole body aches.

One whole body pulsing with dull achy pain from head to toe.

Chapter 6

I wish I knew exactly where we are going. James said some correctional facility, but I have no idea where it is. I had never heard the town's name before and I didn't want to bother anyone by asking.

It hasn't been possible to pull out my phone to look either. The only clue I got was someone said northeast. Back up the way we came.

I'm trapped in the box of the truck with a bunch of people trying to stay warm. I'm trapped with a whirling head and nausea. The motion sickness is enough to take my mind off how cold I feel.

I'm really happy we had to ditch the motorcycles. They aren't practical for a Canadian winter. The snow only gets thicker the further north we go. I took for granted the amount of snow cleared by snow removal and the mere action of thousands of vehicles driving on the roads.

It's been snowing. I wonder how much snow Leduc got. It's further north, and should have gotten more than this. Would the roads even be travelable?

I am past the point of being able to pay attention to where we are going. My eyes are closed, and I'm sure those around me think I've fallen asleep. No one has tried to speak with me in a long while.

I wonder when my dream should be happening; maybe I was wrong. Or, we may have changed things. Dominique should be in Banff, but James said Nikki and Rayleen are in this jail northeast. Are Nikki and Dominique not one and the same? No, that's ridiculous. Why would a different Nikki have Dominique's notebook?

Nikki is close enough to be an obvious nickname for Dominique.

I was sure the place we were at was the Banff Springs Hotel. I was there at a convention with my father years ago. I explored all over that place; inside and out. There aren't any other castles in the mountains, at least that I know of, anywhere in Alberta.

Maybe, it wasn't in Alberta. Would we travel that far away? I guess it's always possible that we might travel anywhere, but I would assume we will stay in Alberta.

James mentioned it was old intel. Maybe the jail was just a stop in the road.

The truck slows. I open my eyes. They water a little from the sudden hit of cold air. My view is white. I close my eyes again and blink many times until the world goes to a tolerable brightness. There are trees, a field, and a lot of white. No distinguishable signs or buildings.

I close my eyes again.

There isn't any use in trying to see anything.

Another hour or so passes before the vehicle finally stops. I open my eyes slowly.

This is it; I think.

I pop my mitten hands out of my sleeves. The warmth collected quickly starts to disappear, but it settles at a manageable temperature. The reminder that I'll need better winter gear to survive winter, that we'll all need better gear to survive winter, pings in my mind's to do list.

At least the fort provided us with plenty of souvenir toques and mitts. They will do for now.

People are jumping up and stretching their sore muscles. I follow suit and look around me. There are woods to one side and a field to the other.

After a few minutes of confusion, people congregate around the open driver's door. The true pecking order of the group reveals itself when the arguments start. Everyone has their own idea about how we should go about rescuing Dominique and Rayleen.

James doesn't take complete charge like how I would have thought he would; a diplomatic approach I suppose. Four people are the most boisterous with their ideas, and they each have their backers.

Perhaps, this all should have been decided before we arrived. They're making too much noise.

I shake my head and roll my eyes. I back away from them and to the other side of the truck. I face the mostly obscured building. Scanning from top to bottom, I don't see any movement.

Does James know for sure that they are supposed here? No, it was old intel.

I watch and see nothing. There is so much of the building that is out of view. Maybe if I go closer I will see something.

Looking back at the group, I don't think they'll notice if I leave. They are probably going to argue for a few more minutes. I can be there and back in a minute or two.

I decide to leave. I jump off the side of the truck carefully. I jog to the tree line and then look back to my comrades; none of which have noticed me.

The trees give me cover from the front, and the wind is moving my scent away from the jail. I should just have to worry about sound, and possibly someone seeing me peeking out from behind a tree.

When my bright rad mitts catch view, I panic. It's like a bright neon sign giving away my location. Quickly removing my gloves and toque, I shove them in my pockets. The cold latches on, but it's better than being seen due to unnatural colouring.

I don't know what kind of supernatural beings are inside and out so this could end up being a fool's mission. I could be focusing on small details, when it wouldn't matter anyway.

I try to focus on my eyes and ears. Listening for any noises around me, and scanning all around me. It might be over-cautious, and I might look like a paranoid fool, but I do have a disadvantage in my ignorance of supernatural races and species. I recognize that. Then, there is the human disadvantage too.

As the entrance gets closer and more visible, I sit and watch. I focus on the doors.

When I don't see anything, I decide to loop around. Staying a few meters inside the tree line for cover as I make my way around the jail.

I'm taking longer than I had initially figured. They wouldn't leave without me, would they?

The building is large. It goes back a ways and then gives way to a fenced-in courtyard. Just as I pass the view of the corner edge of the building, I spy on four people having a heated conversation. Two are humanoid supernaturals, one looks like a large troll, and the fourth looks human on the top half, but has one oversized leg and foot as his bottom half. Each of them has a smoke in hand.

They are debating something. Their animosity doesn't seem to be towards each other, so I can only assume they are upset about something or with someone else.

I can't hear them here, but I think I could if I hide behind the corner.

It would be a risk. Their argument might cover my steps, and the smoke and wind might cover my smell. Someone could still see me.

If I go back, I might be able to catch a blind spot at the front corner and crouch under the windows. That would take time, and who knows when these guys might be done with their smoke break.

I double back out just out of their view. Approaching the tree line I sweep the area for potential lookouts, and when I don't see anyone I make a break for it as quickly and quietly as I can.

Taking my chance, I creep as close to the corner as possible. I lay my back against the wall. Double guessing myself, I pull my back away slightly to soundlessly sink low. I lean back against the wall.

I can hear them well enough from here. I miss the start of one's part of the conversation, but I certainly don't miss the end "fucking tyrant!"

"He's too worried about his humans. We should have just killed the bitch when we had the chance."

"And, why the Hell is he dragging around and protecting a child? Is it his?"

"He doesn't act like it's his."

"I heard it was his girlfriend's."

"Sandra doesn't have kids."

"No his girlfriend; a human."

"I thought he was dating Sandra."

"I thought Sandra was with Ram."

"I heard he had a human pet he was dating."

"I thought he ended that."

"I think the human thing is still a thing. Why else would he be keeping her kid safe?"

"That's the point, he wouldn't. We agreed to all or nothing. We had to give up all our humans. So, why are we taking orders from some putz that's in love with a human? Why does he get to keep his humans, when we couldn't?"

"There's always hypocrisy with those in charge."

"Why's he in charge anyway?"

"You know he's just going to turn her into a vampire. Human problem solved."

"He's just a face. They'll put anyone in charge that looks the part."

"He's just a face that could kill all our asses if he ever heard us talk like this. We should just leave. We'll come back tonight to witness the horror of all our comrades killed. Then we go to the hotel and tell them we are the only survivors. It was a tragedy. They came in and killed the rest. When we knew they'd kill us too, we hid so we could report back to them."

"That'll never work. We should stay and fight. If we die, then it'll be an honourable death."

"We should leave. Darius doesn't care about us. He left in the middle of the night with his girlfriend, the prophet and a human runt. He had every chance to take the rest of us with him, but he didn't. We need to fight back."

"He wanted to keep Banff all for himself. Have you ever been there? It's massive and extravagant. It's paradise compared to this shit hole."

That's all good enough for me. I have all the information I need that I can honestly say I could have deduced where they went and that they did leave this place for there. I don't have to hear anything else. I did the action to convince anyone watching that I could have obtained the information reasonably.

I stand up enough to crouch below the windows. I decide to go along the wall to the front corner. My back feels the strain near the end. I stand up at the corner's edge.

Peeking around the corner, I search for any sign of other people. I don't see anyone. No guards, and no one from the group. I run back into the tree line and don't slow down until I'm well hidden from the view of the jail.

It doesn't take much longer to get back to the truck. They are all still here and arguing about what to do.

It annoys me that these are the people I'm stuck with. How hard is it to make a simple strategic decision? Why doesn't someone take lead and simply tell everyone what they're going to do?

I was gone, for maybe, five minutes and managed to solve everyone's issue with a simple scouting mission that no one but me thought about.

They're letting their egos get in the way. There's too many people here that are trying to be in charge, and get heard. It's getting in the way of anything being done.

And James, he should do better as the actual person in charge. He should have stopped this after the first minute or so; after everyone had a change to put out their suggested action.

I approach the small crowd. "Excuse me." I voice. No one pays any attention so I say it louder. "Excuse me." Once again no one acknowledges that they heard me. "Hey!" I yell. When none of that is fruitful, I grab Leah's arm until she pays attention to me. "They aren't here. Darius left with them last night to go to the Banff Springs Hotel. They were tipped off that we were coming."

She looks at me for a moment until she processes everything I said. She turns her head back to the crowd. "Everyone SHUT UP! Jade has something to say!" Leah's booming voice surprises me but effectively gains everyone's attention.

I thank her in my head and then address everyone else with a repeat of my words to Leah. "They aren't here. Darius left with them last night to go to the Banff Springs Hotel. They were tipped off that we were coming."

"How do you know that?" This, and versions of it, are asked by multiple people at once.

"I went to the jail and eavesdropped on the guards' smoke break." I elucidate.

"That's one way to do it," Miles says smiling.

"James, are you sure there aren't any trees we could go by? Banff is really far from here." Daniel asks and complains.

"No." James doesn't elaborate. He already went through this all this before. The subject came up at both the elderly couples' house and the fort.

I did some supplemental research to complement James' minor explanation.

Wood nymphs can travel by the trees that are connected to them; as well as allow others they befriend to do the same. Essentially, all the trees that come from a singular plant are connected to the nymph. So, if you took a cutting off a tree and planted it, the nymph could connect to that tree and allow others to travel once big and strong enough.

James had a tree connected to a wood nymph at his house, but the tree was blown up. While helping James and a few others escape, the nymph sacrificed herself to ensure they were all safe by keeping the portal open as long as possible; dying as she was in that tree when it and she were killed.

Nymphs don't reveal themselves to just anyone and there is no other way to figure out if a tree is occupied or not; not that there are that many wood nymphs around anymore.

Once upon a time, there were thousands and thousands of nymphs; of all sorts.

Tree nymphs generally stuck to one specified area within the forest. They would occupy a hundred trees in the same area. This contributed to their annihilation because humans would come along and clear-cut the forest; leaving no tree standing. The nymphs of the forest would all die with nowhere to go.

There was a campaign to save the tree nymphs starting a couple of hundred years ago. Friends of nymphs would take seedlings or cuttings and plant them all over the world. This would ensure the nymph had somewhere to recede to if their other homes were being destroyed.

Back to the current issue, James only knew the one wood nymph so that mode of transportation is out of the question.

No, he can't just summon up another nymph.

"There has to be." Daniel insists.

"The only tree nymph I knew died. We take vehicles unless you have another idea." James reminds him.

"We can't leave yet," Brad announces.

"Why not?" Leah asks him deadpanning.

"What if they were lying or she heard wrong? We should go inside and investigate." Brad elaborates.

My blood pressure rises as he tries to talk around me. I speak up. "That means going inside and what, attacking everyone there until we figure out that maybe they were telling the truth. And, we just risked our lives and killed others because we wanted to make sure the guards weren't lying. Don't you think if the guards knew I was there they would have killed me or arrested me instead of making up a story so I could overhear and bring it back to you?"

"I'm not taking your word on it. We can't just go to Banff because you feel like the guards were telling the truth." I raise my eyebrow at his words.

"Were you there?" I ask him.

"No." He utters and purses his face in anger.

"No, you weren't. They were bashing Darius for dashing in the middle of the night and leaving them there to be killed by us. They said Sandra, Darius, the prophet and the human child went to the hotel in Banff.

They were talking about ditching the jail for our raid and then making up a story to tell Darius when they show up at the hotel alive." I change my tone. "They didn't know I was there. It's a ridiculous amount of detail to come up with just to fool the girl hiding around the corner."

"We should just leave. Why attack if no one we want is in there?" James tries to convince Brad to let it go.

"They could be lying." Brad insists.

"Then, how about you go and check it out for yourself," Leah suggests.

"Oh, this is ridiculous. I'll be back." Kelly then looks at me and directs her question at me. "Where were these guys?"

"Out at the back of the building; in the courtyard. There were four of them." I tell her.

Kelly runs quickly around the truck and disappears into the trees. I swear she ran so fast I could have blinked and she would have been gone.

If I can remember, I should look up comparable stats of a vampire versus a human in terms of speed and strength. Literature varies in its descriptions depending on the take each author took.

Kelly ran fast. Certainly much faster than I could ever hope to run, and if she's an average for a vampire I can see an issue arising for humans trying to fight them. A vampire's speed could win a fight every time. There would be no escaping or retreating because we couldn't hope to run fast enough.

"Should we go after her?" Miles asks.

"We don't know what she has planned. We could ruin whatever she's doing." James reasons.

"What if she needs help?" Miles asks.

"I suppose you should shut up then, so we could listen for a cry for help." Leah's voice gives away her irritation.

People stand around doing nothing or glancing over to the jail. I move and break the group up as others start shifting away from the group.

At the back of the truck, I grasp the wall and stretch my foot up to the bumper to use it as leverage to hoist myself into the box.

I sit on the side wall over the wheel and watch for Kelly's return. I'm not disappointed as she appears from the tree line. She runs towards us, and fluidly hops into the back of the truck.

"They're not here. We need to leave now." Her words spur people into action. Red and blue blood drops on her clothing alert me to a physical alternation probably ending the life of the guards out back.

Settling myself in a safer position on the floor near the cab, I take a deep breath. I feel bad that those guys died because people didn't believe me. I was, in a way, trying to avoid fighting and save more people from dying on both sides.

The dark irony finds its way to me that they would be the only ones to die when they were planning on running off so we wouldn't kill them.

The truck lurches forward when everyone is more or less in position. We have an easy getaway.

James turns the truck around in the right direction after we connect to the next road over.

I keep my eyes open as long as I can handle. The world pulling away from me screws up my head faster than when it passes front to back.

I close my eyes when it becomes too much. I feel nauseous.

"Are you okay?" Lucas asks.

I ignore him because maybe he will think I fell asleep. I don't need him concerned over something he can't do anything about.

"Jaiden, are you okay?" Stephanie asks this time.

I open my eyes to see everyone's eyes on me. Either, or both, Lucas and Stephanie's concerned question has brought everyone's attention on me.

I take a deep breath in and a short breath out. I smile as well as I can despite how gross I feel. "I'm fine. I just get motion sickness."

"Oh god, why didn't you say anything?" Stephanie exclaims.

"Who knocked you up?" Brad smirks.

"What?" I ask, dumbfounded at their accusations. "I'm not pregnant. It's motion sickness, not morning sickness."

"Are you sure?" Brad patronizes.

"Yes. I have motion sickness." I've had it for so long that I have a little script in my head to inform people. "It's when there is a disconnect between the movement I see and the vestibular system's sense of movement. Basically, it means my head feels like we're going one speed while my senses perceive another so it makes me dizzy and nauseous."

I close my eyes to end the conversation and go back to what I was doing.

Did they seriously think I'd be pregnant?

I'd have to have sex or have semen enter my vagina or have a fertilized egg implanted in me to possibly get pregnant. Seeing as none of those things have ever happened, it would be impossible. I'm only fifteen. Kids my age shouldn't even be having sex let alone getting pregnant.

I haven't even had my first kiss yet; if I don't count Calli's rude introduction.

Only a few minutes pass in silence before the truck stops. When the brightness fades I find myself in the middle of a parking lot. We're probably getting gas or switching vehicles.

James leaves the cab closing the door behind him. He instructs us to syphon gas from some vehicles while he goes and checks the store for supplies.

The group breaks into two parts; those searching for gas, and those gathering supplies. The ratio seems off to me. We only have one set of syphoning gear so realistically we only need maybe two people doing that.

When my head only feels the lingering effects of the ride here, I climb out of the truck.

I flutter around the closest vehicles, but I focus more on finding supplies left in the cars. People carry all sorts of supplies in their cars. Food, gum, water, blankets, jackets, and roadside emergency gear could all be found; possibly. I greatly lower my chances by not breaking into the cars to search the trunks.

The doors are locked on almost every vehicle I pass. Until, finally, I come to a white SUV. The doors are open so I let myself in.

They have some gum in the drink holders along with some change. It's useless as currency, but there are opportunities for the coins as metal objects. The door has a lighter in it. I pocket all of those.

The glove compartment has some driver's papers, but I leave those. Every other compartment is empty or has items of no value to me.

I move to the back. There's a sweater back here; too small for me. I check the floors and under the seats. Under the passenger seat, I see a gleam. Like a mosquito to light, I reach for the object. My hand encloses around a car key. It's a spare key.

With my hope up, I climb to the driver's seat and settle in. Sticking the key in place, I turn it. The white SUV roars to life.

I look at the gas tank. It's half full. If we could syphon enough gas for the two vehicles all of us could have a warm place to wait out the trip.

"Way to go little miss perfect. What's the gas like?" I jump at Brad's sudden voice and appearance. He doesn't wait for me to tell him. He takes the liberty of looking for himself. "Half full. Guys let's get some gas to fill this one up too." He shouts for the others to hear. "We'll take this one too. Turn it off so we can fill her up."

I follow his instructions. He takes the key from me as soon as I free it.

I'm left with nothing to do again. I figure the same people will take up the truck cab, so I claim my bag and put it in the trunk of the SUV. I'd like to keep it close to me, and I'd like to make it into the SUV. It'll be much warmer than risking the truck bed again. I don't stray too far from it.

The vehicles are filled with gas, people returned with minor supplies, and everyone was brought up to speed on the plan.

Brad, Stephanie, Taylor, Alexa, Daniel, Lucas and I all volunteer to pile into the SUV. The rest will fit snuggly into the cab of the truck.

Lucas pulls on my arm and practically drags me to the passenger seat. He opens the door and shoves me in. I look apologetically to my fellow travellers watching the spectacle. Lucas closes the door and then goes over to the people watching. He speaks with them, then Brad hands over the keys.

Lucas promptly gets in the driver's seat. "What was that all about?" I ask him.

"A friend of mine used to get motion sick. He said that the back seat was the worst place to be. The best was driving, but I figured you wouldn't want to drive. The next best place was the passenger front seat." He explains. His friend knew what he was talking about. It was nice of Lucas to remember that, and do this for me.

"Thank you," I tell him.

I look at the space behind me. There is plenty of room between my seat and the next. Quickly finding the right lever, I adjust my seat back at a slight angle. It'll make the trip more comfortable.

I buckle up. Lucas starts the engine, and the others all pile inside. There are four squished onto the back seat and Taylor finds a place on the floor.

Lucas starts driving once James moves the truck. The long game of following the leader begins.

We blast the heat in the beginning. We all need a little warming up. The warm air does wonders for the chill that has set roots in my bones. The heat makes my vision useless for a few minutes while my glasses are fogged up.

I close my eyes and settle in for the long ride. It's tiring doing nothing. It's tiring being motion sick for so much of the day; takes a huge toll on the body.

Soon enough I'm warm through and through. I savour the heat; so unlike me. I joke. For the moment, I'm content with it since I don't know how often I'll be thoroughly warm this winter. When we get to Banff, I should suggest we find a store that sells winter gear. Banff would probably have a greater variety and higher quality products than a big box store.

"Ah, wonderful." Stephanie hums. My sentiments exactly.

The motion sickness returns too soon. I need a good day to recover from the effects, then I wouldn't get sick so quickly.

"Know what I just noticed?" Daniel pauses. "Everyone here is human."

Each person in the car goes through a back-and-forth with Daniel. He says "right?" and I hear a "yes" in a different voice right after.

Daniel poses his question one more time. No one answers. "Jaiden?"

I don't answer. I pretend to sleep because with an introduction like that I can tell I want no part of this conversation. My plans involve sleeping or pretending to sleep.

Lucas tells them, "I think she fell asleep."

"It's the human SUV," Daniel concludes.

Brad gets passionate and excited "It is. How did we not notice that the first chance they got they separated from us?" I'm pretty sure we're the ones that voluntarily came into this vehicle. "It's us versus them. They've made that clear. Us humans need to stand up for each other and stick together."

There are a few things wrong with that, but I stop myself from scoffing at the last part. That's not exactly the tone he has been setting all along. How many times in the last few days have I caught him and others making fun of me, harassing me? Talking bad about me behind my back? It's not something I expect to change with this newfound comradery based on race.

There is a resounding "yes" around the SUV.

The people in this vehicle are racists. And, they're hypocrites. And, they're two-faced.

It could be argued that I acquiesce in my silence, but I'm not the type of person who has a voice. It's not worth the fight right now.

Besides, there's no point in arguing with people this passionate and ignorant about something. Whether they are right or wrong, they won't change their mind. It's idiocy and closemindedness at its finest. They are intolerant and racist.

"Once we get Rayleen and Nikki we should go find more of our own kind," Brad suggests.

"But, isn't Nikki a demon too?" Taylor reminds the group in the form of a question.

"Is she a demon or is she just a human that has visions of the future?" Brad answers her question with one of his own. Is he making exceptions on what qualifies as human or supernatural now?

His question poses some interesting questions. Visions are

obviously hereditary. But, because I have visions exactly how human am I? Does the fact that I'd have a sliver of supernatural blood in me, enough to give me the visions, mean that I'm a supernatural being? Not human, like I was raised.

Being human as described by a supernatural definition is a lack of being supernatural. I have visions, so that makes me supernatural by that definition.

But, if x amount of my past relatives over the last couple thousand years are all human, and my connection to supernatural beings could only be one fully supernatural being two thousand years ago, does that make me a supernatural?

In humans, people generally only take into account the past two hundred years or so; mostly because people don't know their ancestors going back further than that never mind going back thousands of years. Combined with genetic testing that can only really reveal a couple of hundred years of ancestry for a basic hundred dollar paid commercial test.

I don't know anything about my ancestry so that is out of the running.

Humans also determine the race of a person for their identity by what they look like. So it doesn't matter if you're white and Chinese, if you only look like one side people will tell you that's what you are.

Wouldn't matter if you are technically ten different cultural races either. So, I look human which would make me human.

But, many supernaturals appear completely human as well. They just have an ability that sets them apart.

Then there are the white supremacist groups that say one drop of blood of another group makes you not white. Meaning one drop of supernatural blood would make me a supernatural being. This would be whether or not I even had any supernatural abilities.

Or is that all completely wrong, and it's literally one race and just a matter of genetic switches on and off? Especially at least for the humanoid ones, especially if they can reproduce and have fertile children with each other.

It makes us one diverse species rather than different species.

It's generally recognized in one theory that every human on this planet came from Africa, from one being who mutated to a homo sapien approximately two hundred thousand years ago. Although I'm not sure how that fits in with knowing about supernaturals now. How is the human origin story there?

Or, how they may or may not be connected to other homo species?

Everyone who has blue eyes or has the recessive gene is connected to a common ancestor six thousand years ago; the first person to mutate blue eyes. But, no one includes that on their heritage list either.

When I get the chance, I should check to see if the supernatural internet has the same theory and if they have a complimentary version of a theory of evolution for supernatural beings.

I also read at one point that they estimate there were only one hundred million people in one hundred AD. There are now about seven billion people on the planet, well before the war, and where do people think all these people came from?

At some point, at multiple points, we are all related to each other. I don't doubt that at some point we all have supernatural blood in us too.

But, I digress.

It's all complicated.

I'm just going to go with my normal answer for my ancestral history; I'm a little bit of everything because I don't know anything.

I'm both a supernatural being and a human because they are

both a part of my ancestral history.

Unfortunately, society will require a check-one-box answer like it had before the revolution. I look human, so I'll be labelled as a human. Especially since I don't think I should tell people about my visions anymore. Not if people are getting kidnapped because of having visions.

I don't want to be a weapon of war.

For now, it seems, human is the safest answer; maybe. But, one day, I hope that it won't matter to anyone.

"It's not like she's physically different than any of us. She doesn't do anything freaky like drink blood or eat humans." Brad tries to defend Dominique. "She'll have to pick sides. If she picks human she can come with us, but if she picks supernaturals she's not welcome."

"I've had enough of fighting the supernaturals fight. It's their war, not ours. James isn't helping by provoking them. He himself is a supernatural and this whole war is just a huge fight between demons and the humans got in the way. We're food to them." Daniel cries enthusiastically.

I hate to play devil's advocate but I can understand why they had a revolution. They had to hide who they were. They were worse than second-class citizens because according to humans they didn't even exist.

They could have gone about it another way but maybe we weren't listening well enough. Or, maybe it was the execution threats from the Council. Everyone has a breaking point. Everyone comes from somewhere. Everyone has reasons for why they do something. You can't judge someone on their actions until you understand why they did it.

Intolerance and hate subside with empathy. Imagine yourself in their place. Born in their head. Raised as they were raised. Taught what they were taught. Been through all they've endured. Anyone would do the same. Understanding where they are coming from, whether agreeing to it or not, can mean all the difference.

But, you need to be able to have empathy; a rare trait in people these days.

"Who's dying? The humans. No one's killing the demons. They're all against us." Daniel argues.

I'm certain that isn't completely true.

"Life was great." Only because of circumstances Brad. Humans outnumbered supernaturals and rose in power, strength and numbers. We oppressed them. "We are the superior species. Look at how civilized our society was. The demons take over and it all goes to shit. We'll figure out how to beat them again."

Society makes geniuses feel like idiots in a sea full of idiots who this they're geniuses. Our schools breed ignorance and illusions of grandeur and failure. Once you get out, money talks or it's about who you know.

Mean rude small minded people rule the world, and nice people are deluded into thinking that they can make a difference and win. They win a small skirmish every once in a while, but never a battle and never the war, because of what the mean ones are willing to do to get what they want. A relatively small amount taken from the richest people on the planet could solve many of the world's problems if done the right way.

The food we throw away could end world hunger. But, we don't do anything significant to help.

We kill and hurt each other and no one cares, but the moment an animal gets hurt half the world rallies to have the person killed. An animal gets killed and we hunt the person who did it. We destroy their lively hood, their reputation and their life. We threaten them and their family and everyone who supports them.

People are being killed every day in the name of human constructs.

It is 2012, and not every single person on this earth has a basic standard of life, rights, and freedoms. Why? Because of physical attributes, history, religion, the difference in ideals and geographical locations.

What part of our society worked?

How could I expect any difference in how we treat supernatural beings when humans can't even treat their own with dignity?

"They're heathens. They aren't human. They're," Taylor struggles to find the right word, "less than."

Yes, because that kind of talk has only done well in the past.

It's never okay to talk about an intelligent race or species like they are less than human; less than anything. Humans have done this in the past, humans do it now, and humans always do it; I can't speak for the supernaturals but I do assume this does occur there as well.

"They're monsters. They can't get away with this." Lucas' voice finally chimes in beside me. He surprises me.

I notice the two silent figures in the back; Alexa and Stephanie. They haven't said a word. Maybe they don't feel the same way. Maybe they don't think they have a voice either.

Alexa was dating Darius; perhaps there are still feelings there? I don't know Stephanie's story, but she seemed a submissive type. She seemed genuinely friendly with the supernatural beings of the group, but that could mean nothing. Isn't she dating Brad?

The others certainly have wonderful poker faces in front of our travel companions.

"They are systematically killing humans. They have farms for humans where they hold you until they eat you. Their entire kind needs to be wiped out. Our ancestors should have taken care of it when they had the chance. Instead, they let them live and go into hiding. They're like cockroaches; they need to be squashed." Brad declares.

These people are making it harder and harder to want to be sympathetic and try to save their lives in the upcoming days. Maybe Daniel deserves to have his leg caught in a bear trap.

Chapter 7

It was such a relief to finally see the Banff Ave sign, and the *Welcome to Banff* sign last night.

The headlights on the SUV lit the words up beautifully. The whole sign was made as a simple log cabin image with a roof and all. *Welcome to Banff* and the equivalent in French were in white against the stained wood behind it.

I couldn't read the added signage board below, but it looked like a better version of those cheap black message boards that companies use.

My body ached from the long drive. The seat was non too comfortable on my butt and my lower back; both sore from sitting too long.

A small type of claustrophobia set in and I itched to stretch and wiggle. I yearned to be set free.

My stomach ached from missing supper since James decided to drive straight through to Banff. He assured us that it would be better if we made it before night fell, or it would be easier to see us.

The headlights could give our position away in the dark, but we needed them to see where we were going.

We still hadn't made it in time. The sun had set early in the mountains. The sliver of the moon gave only enough light to barely see our way without headlights.

It was a slow crawl but we made it to a hotel; literally the first building after turning off the highway. But, the snow made the road hard to see.

The place was deserted.

Not in the demons ran through the place type of deserted either. More like everyone up and left type of deserted. Though, maybe the demons were why they deserted the place.

Some breakfasts were left untouched on the tables. Occupied rooms had been left untouched by the cleaning crew. Beds sheets were left thrown open and belongings were left out.

Still, other rooms had been left untouched. These rooms had two sets of keys hanging behind the desk; deduced to be one set for the guest and one set for the hotel staff. The old lock and key system allowed us to get into all the rooms in the place.

Supper was provided to us by the hotel, as a load of nonperishable goods in the pantry; mostly canned fruit cocktails or beans. It was a feast nonetheless.

Tired from a long day of doing nothing, we all picked rooms and set off to bed.

I move away from the warm body behind my back. I roll over to look at Daniel. He looks peaceful. I can't resist swiping fallen hair from his face. If he was awake, the hair would have blocked his sight partially.

Daniel doesn't move an inch.

I'm fully awake, and ready to start my day.

I'm ready to go get Rayleen.

I turn on my back. Cold seeps to my back through the bed.

The light shines throughout the room from the light curtain layer. We hadn't figured to pull the blackout curtains in our tired haze. I can see a lot more than I could last night.

The room is rustic, with a wolf theme. Details in the room, down to the drawer handles, are in the image of a wolf. There is a glorious painted picture of a yellow-eyed wolf above the pillows.

The bed has a charming black and white tree print on the comforter.

There is a lot of wood in the room. Much of the furniture is wooden. The walls are lined with wood as decoration.

I work my way out of bed slowly and quietly. My feet touch cold wood, and I almost regret my decision from the cold that greets me.

The sun brightens the room, and I can see where we left our jackets and shoes. I'll need those immediately.

A rug over there that becomes my goal.

I touch my feet to the ground again and quietly run straight to my shoes. I grab them and finish my sprint to the rug. It's freezing and the shoes aren't much better, but I know it'll get better soon.

It encourages me to put my jacket on as quickly as possible. It's a bit cold from being on the floor all night, but there isn't anything I can do about it now. Maybe we should try to keep our jackets on during the night for the rest of the winter.

Gooseflesh raises and I shiver. The jacket and shoes don't warm up fast enough for my taste.

I jump up and down to get the blood flowing. I want to warm up, but I stop before I start sweating; that would just make me cooler.

The view catches my eye. I'm drawn to the balcony window. The mountainous rocks take over the sky from above the trees.

I didn't know mountains could be so big; though that seems obvious from their very description. I've never seen them in real life, and it's a bit different than pictures make them seem.

They're huge and rocky. There is a lot of green, grey and white. There isn't just one line of mountains, as I assume from the line on the map. Mountain top after mountain top overlaps each other as far as I can see.

Fallen trees, stripped of green foliage, lay against living trees. Rocks litter the ground beneath the snow, with tips and edges left uncovered.

It's beautiful here.

I just wish I could have seen it under better circumstances. It might've been nicer without the threats looming. Would have been better to have come here on a vacation with Rayleen, not a rescue mission.

After taking a moment to appreciate the view, I go to the bathroom. I leave the door open for the sunlight to filter in.

The mirror shows a bare face. None of my makeup remains. I wish for my makeup. I scour drawers for any piece of makeup even something that I can multi-purpose but come up with nothing. It's disappointing. I need makeup. I hate my face without it.

I'll have to keep an eye out for some.

I leave the bathroom and look at Daniel. He hasn't moved in the time since I left him. Other than his breathing, there is no movement there, so I leave the room.

I wouldn't want to wake him up.

It's darker in the hall as there isn't much natural light here. There is only one window down at the end of the hall that lets in any light.

I walk down the hall towards the lobby. I go around a corner.

One door is open. The sunlight draws me and my curiosity inside the room. There is some quiet banging around in here.

I cautiously enter.

Quickly, I let my guard down when I spot Jaiden and Calli

going through drawers.

The room had been occupied and there is evidence of their existence with their belongings. Two toothbrushes are left sitting beside the sink.

Other items are likely hiding in drawers and the closet. Anything, that is, that hasn't been found by the two tearing the room apart.

"Good morning." I greet them when they don't notice my existence on their own.

They turn around and greet me. "Good morning. How was your sleep?" Jaiden asks.

Jaiden in particular sounds too perky for how early I assume it is. She has to have been up for a long time, or she's a god-awful morning person.

"It was fine," I answer. "What are you looking for?"

"Anything useful," Calli explains. "Weapons, clothes, mitts, boots, jackets; anything that might help us this afternoon. It's cold, but we don't want to make too much noise. And, a pocket knife is always handy."

It's nothing that would be out of the ordinary for a hotel guest out in the mountains.

Well, maybe a pocket knife wouldn't be something I would expect to find. Though maybe it should be, because it's a huge camping and hiking tourist-centred city, maybe people would be more likely to bring pocket knives or utility knives.

"Okay." I stand here awkwardly for a moment. "Is anyone else up?"

"Kelly was out in the lobby," Jaiden informs me.

Kelly might be better company, and I don't want to go through rooms. I'd rather find out what the plan is for today. See how long it'll be until we leave to go rescue Rayleen. "Great, I will see you later."

I travel down the hall and to the lobby. Kelly stands at the doors, looking out through the clear window.

She turns around as soon as she notices me. I wave, and she greets me back.

"How are you?" I ask.

"Good," Kelly says. She leaves the conversation open to silence.

I walk up beside her and look out the doors. She wasn't looking at anything more exciting than trees and rocks.

"I saw Calli and Jaiden are up. Is anyone else awake yet?" I ask.

"James just left with Miles. They're meeting with someone to work out a plan for later." Kelly leaves me to sit down on the closest couch.

"Oh," I pause for a short moment. Who would they be meeting? "Did they say when they would be back?"

"No."

I walk over to sit on the other end of the couch; disappointed and suddenly angry. "So, we just wait here?"

"More or less." She answers.

"I don't understand why we couldn't have just gone to go get them now. What's this person going to say that we don't already know?" My voice rises naturally with my anger.

"We need to have a plan. We don't need another fiasco like the jail. This time, we won't have the chance to sit and talk. They're in a castle high up a mountain. There is one way in and out. We don't know how many people are there. We can't just go in unprepared. They aren't going to let us walk in and take them." Kelly tries to reason.

Some of her points seem logical, but I won't give up hope that we can solve this without bloodshed.

There has to be another way.

"But, what if we could?" Kelly just stares at me, so I continue. "I could go and ask to talk to Darius. He would let me take Rayleen."

"And, Nikki?" She reminds me about the other girl taken with Rayleen.

I honestly don't care about her. Why should I? It's not like I've known her for long.

"I could ask." I guess it wouldn't hurt; I add in my head. But, it certainly wouldn't be a deal breaker to leave her with them.

"Have you lost your mind?" She frowns at me.

What? "Excuse you?"

"Darius tried to kill you. He took your niece to get to you. He's not going to just let you walk in and leave with her because you ask nicely. He's after *you*." She gets louder as she goes on.

"He might," I mutter quietly. I haven't ruled out staying either, but I'm not going to tell her that.

"If you made it to the hotel without being killed on the spot, Darius will kill you." Her last four words are said to a point.

"He won't." He might not let me leave, but I don't think he would kill me. The hobgoblin basement memory appears to knock around my head. I shake it away. He had his reasons for doing that. It could have been Sandra's influence.

"Yes, he will. He'll kill you one way or another; sooner or later. As soon as he's done with you, or if Sandra says so. Or, if Seth tells him to get rid of you in exchange for more power or something." She insists. Her words strike a chord and further impresses that Sandra was why I was thrown in the basement. I already knew Seth was dangerous.

"You don't know that," I tell her. A little of my steam is gone from my fire.

"Yes, I do. He's done it before, so what is going to stop him from doing it again? We brought you back and you were practically dead. No one is going to save you, if you go running back to him again." Kelly knows what happened after I returned to the farm, and she's using that moment to hurt me on purpose.

"He wouldn't kill me," I say to convince her, but the statement is deflated.

"He wouldn't just kill you. He'd kill Rayleen too. Probably do it in front of you, and then kill you. Or, he might choose the other way around if Rayleen's pissed him off enough by now." Her words go too far.

I muster all the anger and hate I can into two words. "Fuck you."

"I can't talk to you. Stay here and wait for James to come back." Kelly stands up and disappears into the shadows down the hall towards her room.

Good riddance.

Our conversation leaves a bad taste in my mouth. Kelly doesn't understand our relationship.

If Darius was going to kill Rayleen he would have done so already, but he wouldn't because he loves me.

So what if he did take Rayleen to get to me, that means he wants to see me and wants to talk to me. Maybe he regrets the hobgoblin thing.

I could remind him of his feelings for me, and he would do this as a favour; our relationship pending on his answer. Use it to my advantage to get everything I want; then I can decide whether to leave him or not.

Kelly told me to wait here for James to return, but I'm not about to do her a favour. As far as I'm concerned, it was her job. And, merely only a suggestion for me to stick around and keep watch.

I will do what I want.

I walk towards the door. I stick right outside the doors.

It's colder out here than inside despite there not being any heat inside. The blocked wind is enough to make it warmer inside. Trapped body heat helps warm the place up slightly.

The white car is here still. I could find Lucas and ask him for the keys. Maybe he would give them to me. Then, I could drive to go see Darius. It shouldn't be too hard to find my way to the hotel.

Or, I could wait for James and Miles to return. They'd show me the way and help deliver me to Darius. At least then, I wouldn't have to worry about the demons killing me before I get to see Darius; like Kelly pointed out.

Kelly said they had just left. That means he still has to meet up with this person, have their conversation, and then come back. They're surely going to be a few hours.

But, what if Kelly is right? What if I don't even make it to see Darius? There are so many obstacles in my way if I go by myself. So many obstacles that would disappear, if I just wait for Miles and James.

Maybe, I should just wait for James to come back. We can go as a group, and I will just do my own thing once we get there. I can break off and go see Darius then.

Jaiden's words echo back to me. 'What if something happens to you?'

What if something happens to me?

I will wait.

A shiver runs me through. The cold pierces every inch of exposed skin to the bone. Any warmth collected since I got dressed is gone again.

I will wait somewhere warmer.

I go back inside the building. A shiver runs through me. Cupping my hands together, I blow a deep hot breath into them.

This helps warm them for a moment.

Settling back down on the couch just makes me antsy. Getting back up just makes me pace around the door.

Activity around this place is almost nothing. I don't hear much from the rooms, and I haven't seen anyone come to the lobby.

Kelly had said to stay here, but I don't want to stay in the lobby anymore. I'll stay in the building, but I'm not going to just sit here and do nothing.

Needing a distraction, I decide to find Jaiden and Calli. They were up, and looting rooms is bound to waste some time. It should help keep my mind off the time I'm going to have to wait. Maybe I can find something useful. Maybe I will scavenge some makeup.

I find them only one room over from where they were before.

This room has a woods theme. Leaves take the place of the drawer handles. Leaves and tree art adorn the walls. One leaf piece is welded out of metal and stands out against the wall.

The same bedspread in our room is on the bed in here. Their view from the windows is of trees and a pool. Their doors lead straight out to the pool. This location must be closer to the ground than our side; though we never walked up or down any stairs.

Their progress seems slow, but they might just be wasting time too.

"Hey, need any help?" I ask.

"Sure." Calli agrees before going back to opening and closing the drawers in the bathroom.

I don't know what they've already been through, so I just start at the entry closet. It's empty.

We go through the rooms one by one. One after the other we find out most of the rooms are decorated almost the same. One accent theme for each room is chosen. Wolf, bear, and leaves are repeated over and over.

We put all the items out on the bed; anything that might be useful. People can go through them easier once they get up.

I grab a couple of items for myself. My prize item is a small travel makeup bag. The bag has a few items in it and mostly a neutral-coloured pallet. But at this point, I'm not picky. Having any makeup is better than not having any at all.

After four rooms, I decide to duck out.

I open the door. There isn't any noise coming from the room. Maybe Daniel is still asleep. I continue into the room a bit more conscious of how quiet I should be.

I peek around the corner and spy his body still lying in bed; right where I left him. In all this time he hasn't woken up. He hasn't even shifted.

The excitement gets to me. I have a moment to put makeup on. The bathroom has enough light to do up my full face. It takes about fifteen minutes, but Daniel still isn't awake.

There's nothing to do but wait now.

I walk to the balcony and open the sliding glass door. The cold air rushes in. I close the door behind me.

Placing my hands on the railing I prop myself up and rest here for a minute. The railing freezes my hands too much so I remove them.

Staring out at the trees and mountains, I am reminded of their beauty. The sounds of nature are the only things I can hear. I feel like I could easily be in the middle of nowhere.

We are on the edge of, what should be a bustling tourist town. People should be everywhere, but I get the feeling that will be far from the truth.

The demons will have gone through and captured or killed everyone. If any managed to avoid the demons, they would be long gone into hiding and we probably won't see them at all.

The sliding door rolls open. Warm arms wrap around me, and lips go to my neck. They tickle their way sensually down towards my collarbone.

Turning around within the confines of his arms, I return his kisses.

Chapter 8

A ruckus outside our door beckons me. I open the door to a small crowd of people being led by our room. They don't pay me any attention as I watch the guards on either end corral them down the stairs and out of sight.

I know where they are going. This show has happened, at least, four times now.

I go to the window and look down. The same people are loaded into the back of a closed in truck bed that takes off down the road. These people will never return.

The guards that left in the cab of the truck, however, will return in a few hours. Sometimes others will join them, and other times the truck will go back and forth a few times with different people; not always with prisoners.

I assume they are all part of that forest game Ram told me about. So many prisoners have gone and none have returned. None have caused any sort of commotion around here like I would expect if one of them actually made it through.

The horrors that must be in the forest can only be imagined at this point.

There was a short story our teacher read us in high school about a person hunting a person for sport. Instead of a gun, the demons must use knives and claws and teeth. They must set people free and go hunt them down. The demon chases the human until they catch them and kill them.

The forest must be full of bodies. Or it could be remains and bones. I'm not sure what kinds of things the different demons eat on humans. The vampires have to drink blood, but they don't do anything with the rest of the body. There are probably other demons that eat the rest of the human body.

I look back to the desk that Rayleen is drawing at. She only has the hotel's notepad and one each of a black and blue pen. It's just about the only thing she can do to entertain herself in this place.

Ram had left while we were sleeping yesterday, and no one has felt the need to guard us since; not at least that I've noticed. I haven't tried to leave this room on my own, so there hasn't been any chance to find out if demons are secretly guarding us.

I didn't see anyone through the peephole when I gathered the courage to check.

Shale had come to get me for a meeting last night. His touch lingered on my hand extra long when we arrived, and then Sandra and Ram expected another reading.

That went about as well as the last one. Darius has an uncontrollable temper and obsession with Alexa, while Sandra has a nasty jealous streak over Alexa.

I did find out some information I could use. Shale had remained at the jail until well after the attack should have happened, yet it never had.

Sandra looked like she was about to pounce on me until Shale also revealed that guards had been killed outside.

They deduced I had been telling the truth about the slaughter at the jail, but something had interrupted what was supposed to happen.

They gave me enough fodder to give another attack prophecy. I mean, it's bound to happen. They had already thought that out for me. I just had to say yes to their theories and tell them that it looked like we had the upper hand in the battle.

They assume that it was James and his group that attacked at the jail. Somehow, they received information about where we were. Unfortunately, that also means that in my hurry to get out of the jail I thwarted their rescue attempt. I could be with them now if I hadn't said anything. Though, they also seemed to get intel from a spy that James was on his way anyway.

It isn't out of reach to assume that James and them will find me again. They found us once, they can do it again. I just have to buy time until then.

They sent me back to my room, by myself, while they figured things out. I couldn't convince them to let me sit in on the planning; that might be too suspicious.

With nothing else to do, I slept.

Doing nothing all day is tiring. I feel like having another nap now. I might as well because I am bored out of my mind. That would involve moving, however, and I am comfortable where I am.

I continue to stare outside. It's late enough in the morning that the sun shines over the mountains and lights up everything in the valley. Even with the extra height of the second floor, I can't see over the lightly snow-covered trees. My sight is limited to the immediate area.

Most of the road is clear of snow, but every other bit of ground is covered.

The comings and goings of the demons here are nothing exciting. No one seems like they are in a huge hurry. They calmly go in and out. They walk to and from the left and right. In and out of the hotel.

I wonder if the general person would even notice if I walked out the front door. I finish with a striking thought a moment later. Or, if I joined a group of prisoners on their way by my door.

The door opens behind me.

"Sandra wants to see you," Ram advises me. I pat Rayleen on the shoulder as I pass by her. I stop just in front of Ram and wait for him to move, but he doesn't. Seeing my questioning look he answers. "I'll keep Rayleen company until you get back."

"Thank you," I say.

It occurs to me that he's trusting me to go alone, but at the threat of Rayleen staying here. He knows I won't do anything to jeopardize her.

I pass by him and start on the trek to the fancy hall.

I take notice of everyone on my way there. I realize that I notice them a lot more than they notice me. None of them pass me a second place; not even a first glance from most of them.

The hall is as grand and breathtaking as the first time I entered. Each time another detail reveals itself to me of which I hadn't noticed before.

In the added light, I notice the sword and shields near the top of the walls. Each shield and sword match the other, though every set is different than the next. They line the columns on the second floor.

Sandra is the only person in here with me. Apparently, she wanted to speak with me alone. I can't help but think this will not go well.

She sits regally at the head of the table. Her hands are placed on her lap. She wears the same jacket we picked up at the store on the way here. Her nose is turned up at me.

"Sit." She orders. I stop dawdling and go sit in the seat at the opposite end of her. Sandra stares through me. An intimidation that won't work on me. She finally speaks. "They're here."

I wait for her to say something else. She looks at me to participate in a conversation she could very well just continue on with herself. I intentionally take the bait when she doesn't continue. "Who?"

"You know who." Sandra crosses her arms.

I can only assume she's talking about James and his crew. "Okay." I wait, but she doesn't say anything. I scour my brain for what to say next. Why is she talking so cryptically? "What do you want from me?"

"When are they planning their attack?" Sandra asks.

"I don't know," I respond dumbly.

"Why not?" Her voice hardens. There is an accusation within her question that I choose to ignore.

"I didn't figure out a date and time." The response sounds equally as dumb. But, I don't want to narrow it down to a specific date and time. There is too much risk for something to go wrong with the prediction

"Well, figure it out!" Sandra shouts.

"They're here already so it's going to happen soon. How much more do you need to know?" I ask.

"They're already here." A male voice half asks and half states. I turn to the quietened voice. Darius looks about ready to bolt out of the room from the couple meters he had made it inside without our noticing.

Sandra sneers. "Not here here. They are in the forest and I can see mountains. I didn't see how close they are to us, but I can bet you, they're going to be here soon." While she speaks she gets up from the head of the table to sit in the next chair over. From her position there she can easily see Darius and his approach. He comes up next to me.

I feel like Sandra was testing me again. She already knew they were here. She doesn't need a vision to tell her they'll attack soon. They are already on their way.

"Link to that girl and figure it out." Sandra glares sharply at Darius, looks at me, then forward. She closes her eyes and then sits still. She's statuesque. She looks like she's meditating in her spot.

I quickly realize that Sandra herself is the spy, or at least she is linked to a spy with my to-be rescuers. That may pose some issues when I get back to the group.

I'd like to figure out who the spy is before I tell anyone. But, I'll have to remember the clue Darius just revealed as the spy being a female. That sort of narrows down the suspects. I could also rule out Alexa since Darius is always asking how she's doing. If Sandra was linking to Alexa I would think Darius would be asking her despite her hatred for the girl. He'd say her name specifically.

I need to get rid of Sandra if I want to have a chance at being rescued. I need to cause a rift between her and Darius.

Maybe, he will do the work for me. They don't seem to be very couple cuddly right now. A lover's quarrel might be exactly what I need.

He is off put by the information he's already received. He's anxiously waiting for Sandra to come out of the trance. His body is rigid and tense. Darius clenches his fists and jaw.

"You're going to die," I whisper to Darius. "And, the killer will take your place." I look directly at Sandra hoping he gets the hint. She doesn't seem to have heard my statement or at least doesn't show it.

He doesn't respond right away. I don't think he heard me.

"Who?" His voice is gruff.

"I can't tell you that right now." I look back at Sandra. He can't be that stupid not to get the hint I'm laying down.

Sandra, on the other hand, seems off in another world. It can only help me if she can't hear anything I say. Her distraction can only help give me time to make Darius figure this out.

"Tell me." His voice is lowered in a growl. He side-eyes me.

I decide to tell him with a point at Sandra; with her eyes shut she wouldn't see me point at her.

Darius visibly takes in a deep breath as he glares daggers at Sandra. The new information will only help to cause a drift between them. If Darius thinks Sandra is out for his spot he'll keep her at a distance.

Sandra opens her eyes. "They aren't doing anything. They're just waiting in a restaurant; from the looks of it. I couldn't see anything. They weren't talking about anything important. But, I also didn't see James with them."

"Was Alexa with her?" Darius asks. His voice is rough and deep.

"Yes, she was curled up in Daniel's lap. They looked really comfy." Sandra shares too many details as if to hurt Darius. She's doing it on purpose too, and she knows how he'll react. She doesn't know that I've already set him on edge.

It works.

Darius rushes forward. He grabs a solid wooden chair and throws it in Sandra's direction. She ducks, and it misses her. The chair smashes to pieces as it hits part wall and part window. Glass shatters and flies out towards the balcony. Slivers of wood bounce back into the room from where it hit on the wall. I duck under the table.

From here, I can only see the barest glimpse of legs when they go in the spaces between the chairs and the table.

My heart is pounding.

Another loud bang sounds at the impact of another chair. The next bang echoes in my ears as the table above me shakes.

I shoot up from my spot. Darius throws bits of wood at the dodging Sandra. She's quick, but he's quicker. She's hit in the chest by a chunk of wood. Her body is thrown back like a rag doll.

Sandra hits the floor hard, and I see her head bounce. She rolls out of it on the second bounce.

Abandoning the objects he's throwing, Darius runs toward Sandra and tackles her.

He's going to kill Sandra.

A small part of me twitches to help her, but then I remember that this is what I need and want so I can get free.

Sandra somehow blasts him off of her. He flies up enough that she can free herself.

She picks up some of the broken-up wood and throws it at Darius. He tries to dodge but she bats her hand and the wood changes direction. He manages to barely dodge it.

Darius snarls and grabs a chair again. He throws it at Sandra who deflects it before it even touches her. I wonder how she's doing that; magic of course, but how?

Darius takes up another chair, but this time he looks at me. The chair flies through the air at me. I run to dodge it, but the chair changes direction suddenly and flies by me.

Sandra's hands are pushed out. Her magic pushed the chair far enough that it missed me.

This terrifying fight is out of hand. He's gone ballistic. I swear Darius' eyes have gone black.

I can't stay like this. I need to escape. That anger can't get a chance to be directed at me again. This distraction might be enough.

I run from the hall as crashes continue behind me, and back to my room.

"Darius is trying to kill Sandra!" I tell Ram as he looks at my surely frightened expression.

He dashes by me and disappears down the stairs. I close the door behind him; only slightly to leave the door jammed open a little. The heavy door stays where I put it.

Now to pull off the escape plan, I will need full cooperation from the other occupant in this room. How old is she? Can she read yet?

I take up a piece of paper and a blue pen, and write a little note telling her we're leaving soon and she needs to be quiet.

I hand her the note. She reads it and looks up at me. The little redhead nods and goes back to her drawing. Rayleen seems to understand. She doesn't seem to be affected at all by my outburst on my way inside the room. It strikes me as strange. She doesn't react at all to any of the information.

Staking out a position at the entry door, I wait and wait for a group to pass by. So far, they seem to bring a group by every couple of hours. I don't know if anyone came by when I was gone, so I don't know if I have to wait long.

The time passing lets me create a solid, part of a plan. We'll leave with the next group and go out into the forest. We'll escape capture, and stick as close to where they drop us off. When they leave we'll double back and escape on the road.

My feet are sore from standing in the same position for a long time. Shifting in place once more, I try to stretch my left foot while the right one takes all the pressure off my weight.

A familiar stomping of feet catches my attention. The ground vibrates a little.

I rush to Rayleen and grab her to a standing position. I take her hand and run back to the door. There is a knock into my back when she runs into me as I suddenly stop at the door.

I peek through the peephole; we need to time this right. Just as the guards at the rear pass by I open the door and shove us in line behind them.

We follow them down the stairs and go towards the door.

My heart beats strong and fast from the suspense. I try to keep my head down.

Temptation is too great to resist a few glances up and around me. People look our way, but never more than a passing second. They see the group as a whole, not for the individuals. They don't notice the two people tagging along in the back.

We make it outside and into the bright light. It's colder out here than it looked. I should have remembered to bundle ourselves better, but maybe we would have been out of place then.

I have my coat and boots, but I'm missing my snow pants, hat, gloves and scarf; they would have only added to my heat. There is no going back to the room now.

Rayleen just has her coat and boots on too. I should have thought a little bit more about our attire, but more so about hers. She's a little girl and has a lot less to her to keep her warm.

The guards' excitement is palatable. They practically throw each person into the back of the truck.

I shove Rayleen into the group first. Her inclusion is passed over easily because of her height. My opportunity comes when they lose their focus. I slip into the remaining couple of people and climb my way into the truck without making eye contact with anyone.

Pulling Rayleen into my lap, I gather her up in my arms. It's for comfort; both hers and mine.

The last person is piled inside and the door is shut. Guards situate themselves in the cab. The truck roars to life and lurches forward. I can hear boisterous laughter up front.

It's only about a two minute ride before the truck skids to a stop. The window between the cab and the back opens.

"We're going to make this brief because we're hungry. The door is going to open and you are going to run to the right; run to the left and we will kill you immediately. You will go right." He motions the direction for our added benefit. It helps because it's his right not our current right from the direction we're facing. "Into the forest where you will get a head start before we come after you.

If you can make it out to the other side, a road just a bit further up the mountain, you will be set free; yada yada. If you get captured you die. Watch out for other hunters and traps.

But, most of all, have fun. Because, remember people, this is a game." His closing of the window doesn't stop the cruel laughter from filtering into the back.

The back doors open and let in a rush of cool air. A couple of people make a break for it immediately. I set Rayleen on her feet, helping her get down and out right after I do. A few of the people huddle in a group. Hesitant to go into the forest alone.

There are trees on both sides of the road. We already look like we're in the middle of nowhere. I know, however, that town could be no more than a half hour summer's walk away from here.

I point Rayleen in the right direction. "Run," I tell her. I grasp her hand and let her set the speed for now. We run straight into the trees. Running side by side.

We run in a straight line; changing course only for obstacles in our way. I take the lead and pick up the pace a little. I pull her along to help her run faster than she ever could on her own.

In some frame of my mind, I watch the ground for dead bodies. I wouldn't want to step on anyone, nor would I like to expose Rayleen to a dead body.

Someone screams behind us. I feel Rayleen try to stop and look behind her. Feeling like that is a bad idea I tell her, "don't look back."

I feel a bit of a jerk in her hand. I don't know if she listened to me or not. I would hope not, but I also know that people don't tend to listen very well when you tell them not to look somewhere.

I try to pay attention to everything. I need to be able to turn us around and go back to the road at some point.

The cold air freezes my lungs. I'm huffing and puffing my way through this run. I'm not sure the doctor would count this as taking it easy.

I don't feel much pain right now, but I'm sure it's just from the adrenaline.

There is a scream; this time it comes from off in the distance somewhere.

Just when I can't take it anymore, I slow my speed. "Rayleen stop." An itch tickles my throat as I talk. The last word becomes almost nothing before I start coughing. I stop running and let go of the tiny hand to cover my mouth and hold my ribs.

But, Rayleen doesn't stop. The poor girl is so terrified that she just keeps running.

I try to yell after her but my coughing won't stop.

I settle for hacking up a lung while I try to run after her. Gasping for air, and choking it out again. My feet stumble from the force of my coughing. The last thing I want to do is lose her.

Through blurry tear filled eyes, I see her fly forward and down. "Rayleen!" I manage to croak out. A few more coughs and I can finally catch a clear breath.

Her cries get louder as I get closer. I look at the ground and see a rope had tripped her. It's now slack against the ground. A gleam to my left catches my attention. There is a blade, at my chest height, stuck in the tree.

Gazing at the blade, I try to wedge it out of the tree, but it doesn't budge. The tree clings to it.

This is a human trap. There's no reason for a hunter to set traps like this, so the demons must have set it. I wonder how many other traps are set out like this. Was that why those two people screamed? Had they been caught by a trap or a demon? I don't think I'll ever find out; not if I want to live. We should be more careful going forward, and we should keep going forward.

We should have stayed in the hotel room.

We'll get to the road. We have to be halfway there by now.

Deciding to abandon the useless weapon I walk over to help Rayleen and check her out.

I scan her over when she gets in my sight. The little girl is on her back and is holding her arm. Nothing else seems to be wrong. The blade must've missed her because of her height or because she tripped over the rope instead of just pressing on it.

I'd hate to think about what might have happened if I had continued running. I would have been the one to go through the trap; I would have set it off. And, because I'm a lot heavier and sure-footed than her, I wouldn't have tripped and the blade would have gone right through me.

I go to her side and pull her into a seated position. "Are you okay?" I kneel on the ground to get down to her level.

"No, my arm hurts." She sobs.

I pull back her sleeve as much as I can without jostling her much. I examine the arm as closely as I can without touching it. I can't see much at all, but the arm is straight and no bones are sticking out. It doesn't look swollen or bruised. There is no cut. It looks like a normal arm. "It doesn't look broken. Rayleen we need to keep running or the bad guys are going to catch us. They will hurt us if they catch us."

I don't give her a chance to disagree. I need to move this along, so I pull her up and start walking in the direction we were headed. This way may be safer now. I decided that we're going to try to find the road, and I hope it's the right decision.

Rayleen impressively pulls herself together quickly. Her tears dry up on her cheeks. She walks beside me.

We walk for a while. I frequently look behind me to see if we are being followed, but I never see anyone. Not a glimpse. I find it a bit weird that not one demon has followed us, and that not one person in the truck ran out in the same direction. Have they all been caught already? Did the guards forget about us; the two stowaways? Maybe they only release a certain number. Once they catch them, they'd have no reason to search longer.

There may be others lurking in the forest that could catch us along the way.

My ankle is encircled in pressure and is yanked out from beneath me. The top half of my back hits the ground and the air is forced out of my already abused lungs.

I gasp and sputter as the world is suddenly upside down. Spots appear in my vision.

I hear Rayleen panicking close to me. "It's okay. I'm okay." I reassure her. "We just need to get me down." A couple of coughs clear my throat.

My foot is stuck. I can't pull myself up to loosen the rope. Panic sets in for only a moment, and then I get an idea. I loosen the ties at the top of my boot. I kick and wiggle my foot. I thrash around like a worm on a hook.

The boot loosens just enough that my foot slips out and I fall to the ground. My butt and back sting from the impact, but all else is well.

The boot is too high to retrieve without a lot of time and work; neither are things we have a lot of. I choose to take my chances and leave it behind.

Hopefully, that rescue team is coming sooner rather than later. They have to be in town. We just have to make it there.

I'd hate to get frostbite in all of this.

The moment my foot hits the ground it is cold and wet. I don't know how long I'll be able to take this.

I usher Rayleen forward.

The ground in front of us doesn't look like it has any traps.

Now that we fell into two of them, we are both quite aware of their presence. They are harder to spot than I thought. With two so close together, it's a wonder we haven't seen another sooner.

I guide Rayleen around a depression in the snow that looks out of place to me.

How far away can that road be?

In the trees ahead, I see a break. There is a clearing.

I get excited and pick up my pace. Rayleen quickly does the same. We both quickly forget to watch the ground for more traps.

We break through the trees and into the clearing. It's just that; a clearing. There is no road here. It's an oval clearing in the trees.

It dampens my spirits a little, but we need to keep going. My foot is cold and wet, it'll start hurting soon. The frostbite will come after that. I regret not attempting to get my boot.

There is a wooden structure just ahead of us. It looks like the frame of a swing set. All it's missing is the swings.

As we near it, I see a rope on the ground and one wrapped around the top.

A chill gives me goosebumps as I realize that the structure probably has an evil purpose like typing up prisoners to torture and eat. I imagine a pile of wood would fit nicely under the structure. They could easily cook up whoever they caught right here.

The hairs stand up on the back of my neck. We leave the area quickly. I set up back to go into the forest on the other side.

Thud. Crunch.

Those noises didn't come from us but are too close for comfort.

Just as I glance to my left I see a large arm coming at me. Squeaking a scream I drop my body to the ground to avoid it. I bring my head up to look for the arm; ready to dodge it.

A large thing grabs Rayleen with his large arms. She screams loudly in fright and pain.

As my eyes are on her an impact knocks the back of my head. Face first into the cold snow keeps me from going unconscious by only the shock of temperature.

Cold drips down my face as I slowly raise my head; dazed from the hit.

A large hand grabs onto my unbooted foot. It drags me back through the trees to the clearing. I try and fail, to grab anything other than snow and grass. My hands scratch against the ground but I can't grip anything.

Kicking the hand earns me a tight squeeze that makes me feel like my ankle is going to snap.

Instead of trying to grab hold of something to stop our advance, I look for something to hit him with. Grasping around, I try to find anything that could help me.

There's nothing. Not even a twig to annoy him with. The snow won't clump together to form a ball.

Snow finds its cold way up my shirt and coat; it stings. My teeth start to chatter as I start to shiver.

My head feels hazy.

I forget my struggle for a moment to put my hand on the back of my head; it's wet. When I pull my hand away and look at it I don't see anything red. That might be a good sign. At least I'm not bleeding, so I shouldn't have to worry about a head injury.

The large demon drops Rayleen to pull me up to the wooden structure's top beam. He grabs at the rope on the top log to secure me in place.

I struggle to make it harder for him.

Rayleen stands up. I wave at her to run.

She doesn't. I wave at her again. Though she looks right at me, she doesn't run.

"Run," I say in more of a whisper than I had wanted.

She stays in place, frozen as she watches the demon tie me up on a string.

He thumps me once in the stomach for my struggles. It doesn't deter me, only makes me cough and wheeze. When he forces my limbs to comply, I know that he's won.

When the demon is done with me he grabs Rayleen and ties her up next to me. She gets to be upright as he ties the rope around her arms and body at chest height.

He looks at the two of us. He pokes at my exposed stomach.

He walks away. He just walks away, after ensuring we are stuck.

I watch as he walks right out of the clearing. My eyes go out of focus a few times. Shaking my head doesn't do anything to fix it.

Wiggling and struggling in my ropes, I realize this time will not be such an easy escape. I try to muscle my hands to my ankles but a sharp pain in my ribs stops my effort.

I shake it off and try again. Trying to pull myself up by climbing my body. My ribs scream. I stuff down coughs.

It gets me closer, but with my hands on the rope, I can't loosen it. Now would be a good time to have a knife on me.

In some part of my increasingly muddied mind, I think about climbing the rope to the top. If I could take pressure off the knotted rope I might be able to free myself.

I have no strength. My muscles won't hold me up enough to get close. When my muscles give out this time, the blood rushes to my head.

My vision goes white around the edges, then sparkles. My eyelids get heavy. I blink hard a couple of times. Each time gets harder to open again; until they no longer open.

Chapter 9

James guides our group through the trees leading to the hotel. The forest is quiet. They didn't think to have people guarding the dense woods. No one is around except for us.

It is as it should be.

James motions for us to stay here and rest a moment as we near the tree line.

The castle-like hotel is just as I remember it. Resting against the trunk of a tree, I look around for a sign of anyone here. There is dead calm.

Everything should be on schedule. I need things to happen the same; to a point. I need Shale to be in the same spot, I need him to give me the keys, and I need to go through the forest in the same spot.

My opportunity for change comes in the timing after we enter the forest. If I stop people from getting hurt and pick up the pace, we'll buy a bit of time for the rescue.

I'm shocked that no one's come outside to fight or capture us yet with the loud ruckus going on behind me. I doubt that they don't already know we're here. It would be hard not to.

I thought this is why we did planning so that we all knew what would be going on once we got here, but they can't seem to cooperate with one another. Some want to just rush on in since they can't see anyone, and others want to wait and see. Many more want to break off into groups and cover a larger area just like was in the plan.

Apparently, something changed once they actually saw this place. I'll stick with my plan and hope they stick to the vision.

The cold starts to get to me. My fingertips are starting to freeze. Cupping my hands together I exhale deeply into the hole I created; trapping the warmth for only a second. It feels nice. I stuff my hands into my coat pocket to try to preserve a bit of the heat. I need to start moving them around a bit more. The gloves are thin but they allow for maximum movement.

I'm happy I stole these winter boots so my feet are warm and dry.

James gives to silent order to cross the road. The order doesn't make much sense to me, but I follow along. Looking in all directions I make sure that no one can see me.

Well, at least from what I can see.

I cross the snow-covered road. And, go into the tree line on the other side. Trudging along, I try to go a bit deeper into the forest leaving the group just inside the tree line.

The thicker trees seem to keep some of the snow out. It's easier to walk now, allowing me to go at a slightly faster pace. The extra trees probably make me safer too, but it also makes it so that I can't see anyone as easily as I could before.

It's a trade-off I suppose.

Looking back to the group I see how far ahead I've gotten. I decide to go off on my own now; it seems right and I was alone in the hotel. We aren't getting anything accomplished here with their slow pace.

So far, no one seems to have noticed; typical.

Coming up to the tree line straight across from the entrance I look around for signs of anyone. Still, there is nothing. Where is everyone? I look back and I don't even see the people I came with.

Going a bit further up the road I figure that it will be easier to go unseen than making a beeline for the door from here.

Movement up the road comes towards me in a large black truck. I duck behind a stone wall to spy on the truck.

The back has a canopy on it. Strange for how large the truck is but I guess not unheard of. I recognize it from my dream. It's in the right spot.

I recognize Shale in the driver's seat. He looks to be the only one in there. He stops the truck after turning it around at the front door. He goes inside the building.

Deciding to go now, I run and jump across the road trying to jump in the ruts from the tires. Hopefully, no one will notice my footprints. I get to the wall and turn around to see if anyone is behind me. They're not.

On second thought, I've seen this before. Dominique isn't in the hotel anymore; she's gone into the forest. No one stopped me in the hotel or out. My footprints shouldn't matter much.

I get inside the building and go right. I can hear a commotion. They must've found the others. I don't care. I have to get to Shale.

The hallway is mostly dark, but I can make out many doors on each side of me. As I go past them, the numbers written on the doors get bigger, and bigger, and bigger. I know where I'm going. I know I'm heading in the right direction.

Shale steps into the hallway from a room; just as I was expecting. He is caught off guard, and I react quicker than the last time.

He is surprised as I push him up against the wall.

"I'm sorry." He apologizes to me.

"Where's Nikki?" I ask. The question comes easily as I

remember the dialogue in the dream, but one question eludes me; he answered to Dominique in the dream. I know he answered me correctly, so maybe she gave them her other name. Or he guessed who I meant. I don't have time to think about it.

"She's gone." He tells me. "Into the forest. She escaped an hour ago. They've probably already eaten her."

"Who?" I ask to push this along.

"The trolls, the goblins, vampires, take your pick of anything that's in the forest." He says.

I go over his useless response as he says it. "What direction did she go? Do you know?"

"Up the mountain. We have the south covered. Nothing and no one comes or goes that we don't know about. We would've seen her if she used the roads."

I let him go now and back away a bit.

It clicks in my head that if they have the south and roads covered, they might've known we were coming. Someone might've. So, they either let us come, or they had other plans. Or, someone was slacking at their job, and we really did have the element of surprise.

He goes for the keys in his pocket. The metal pieces clang against each other. He tosses the keys at me, underhand so I can easily catch them.

"Go down the road, and to the right. Not too far down, and park the truck. You might still see some of the people that are there. I just dropped off a load. She'll have gone that way. You'll find her in there. I wouldn't bet on her being alive though."

That dream was true; so far.

I run back down the hallway the way I came. Some people are fighting in the entry. More are fighting outside the doors and along the road. No one notices me; however, I noticed the truck to the left.

I sprint to the truck. I know the doors are unlocked, and jump in the driver's door. I leave it open, and Miles comes to the opening.

Ready to tell him what is going on, I spout it out before he gets a chance to say anything. "I know where Nikki and Rayleen are."

Consciously I change the name from the vision since I know that is what they know her as. There is no need to make it more confusing.

He shuts the door and runs around the front. I can hear him yelling at the others. He opens up the passenger door and climbs in scooting all the way over to me. It doesn't take long for another to pile in. I can feel the back of the truck hopping up, and down. The rest of the people are climbing into the back. After a couple of moments, someone hits the window signalling for us to leave.

I don't know how much time I'll have to change things, so I start the vehicle and drive away. It doesn't take me long to get up the hill and find the road I need to turn right on. About half a block down I see a couple of people just entering the tree line.

I stop the truck and get out.

People pile out of the truck while I scan the tree line. Blissfully ignorant people get out of the truck and walk across the road. I try to see if I can find the people who just left. Walking further and further down the road. I finally get a glimpse of someone familiar.

I move closer to the tree line. Walking a bit down the hill into the ditch. I know there are people right behind me. This is where I should be.

I concentrate on the group of five heading toward me. They are covered in blood. I'm still not sure how much is theirs, or how much is another's.

They disappear. A short scream from each of them sounds before being stopped and turned into gurgles. The people behind me start to run towards them. I throw out my arm and yell. "STOP! The forest is booby-trapped! We need to watch where we're going."

James yells at everyone. "Go back!" No, wait.

There are shouts and hollers coming up the road. As they round the corner I know it is part of the revolutionists catching up with us. There are a lot more of them than there are of us. I decide to take my risks with the forest. There isn't much of a choice. Either we can try to run down the road, face them, and fight, or go deeper into the forest; I don't think they'll follow us. They didn't last time.

I theoretically know the places not to step on this path. I know they will all follow me. Taking a deep breath I make a beeline into the forest; running past all the people coming out.

There are some shouts after me, but I ignore them and keep running. When I am too far into the forest to be stopped, and taken back I slow down. Turning around I see a bunch of angry faces, but none of the revolutionists have followed us this far.

I turn back to the direction I had been running in and continue walking. I may not know where I'm going but the path in the dream seems as good as any.

Retracing all the steps I took in the dream while paying attention to everyone around me, and the traps they're supposed to fall into.

My heart pounds and I have to concentrate on steadying my breath.

Then, right after, bear trap to my left. Daniel is heading right for it.

"Bear trap Daniel; right in front of you." I sound too calm. I point to it. I think that I'm just lucky that a shiny bit is sticking out or else I'm sure they would be wondering how I saw it.

He picks up a rock and tosses it into the trap. I jump as it sets off. "Thanks. That would have been bad." You have no idea.

We slightly veer to the right now. Tree after tree makes it a bit confusing. I hope that I am going the right way. Some areas make it easier to know that there must be something there. Blood splatters and blood pools give away some of the traps. There is something every twenty feet or so.

I walk in step beside James when we need to veer off to the right again. My slight angle moves us all in the direction we need to go in to hit the open field where they are at. Hopefully, they are there already. The clearing tree line is right ahead. I can see the structure and the girls hanging.

"Watch for the trap." I point.

I start running now and I can hear the rest doing the same. I know I'm not going to run into any traps. We have more time this time, but I doubt by much. It might just be enough though. As we get closer I can tell Dominique is unconscious.

I decide to cut Dominque down first, and Alexa does the same with Rayleen. I call her name, "Dominique," a couple of times to get her attention, but she doesn't wake.

Brad and Shawn help me cut her down safely. Brad braces Dominique as Shawn lifts me to cut the ropes around her legs.

Brad brings her to the ground, setting her on it. The other group has Rayleen down and Alexa and she are embracing.

Shawn touches Dominique's face. Only a moment later she's waking up. She jerks up and takes a blind swing. Shawn catches her hand and yells, "Nikki!"

She launches herself at Shawn to hug him. I hang back awkwardly. I don't think she noticed me. We don't have time for reunions anyway.

I take a step back from the group to examine the trees where the troll should be coming from. There isn't any sign of him yet. I don't think we have much time here.

I walk to James to tell him as much and move things along. "I'd hate to stop the reunion, but we should go before whoever tied them up comes back for them."

"You're right." He says to me. James goes to Rayleen first. She's up and is acting fine so he moves on to Dominique.

"Are you well enough to walk?" He asks her.

Brad helps Dominique up and keeps her steady. "My legs feel numb." She tells him as she tries to keep herself steady.

"They will for a bit. Can you walk?" James asks.

She tries to take a few steps. They look a little uneasy, but she manages. "Yeah, I'm okay. How's Rayleen?"

Miles reveals, "She'll be fine."

"Let's go then." I let James take the lead from here and I fall behind to the back of the group. My vision didn't go further than this so I'm as blind as everyone else.

I don't think they expect anyone to make it even this far. We walk at first. I'm sure it's to let Dominique get her legs back. James doesn't know that there is any real urgency other than the troll will be back some time.

We get through the tree line and in a little ways when I cringe at the sound of the troll roaring angrily. We were probably about two minutes ahead of the schedule in my dream. It was more than enough time to change things.

It doesn't take more than another ten minutes or so before we reach a break in the tree line. A slight raise in the snow tells me that there is a road there, and not one travelled on recently. James stops at the edge of the tree line. He waits for everyone to gather together.

"What way do we go?" He asks everyone. "Left should be another hotel, and to the right goes back into town."

"What's closer?" Miles asks.

James thinks for a quick moment, probably trying to gauge

where we are at. "The hotel is just down the road a little ways. The town is all the way down the mountain back where we came from."

Daniel goes up to stand with James. "I don't know about you all, but I'm freezing my ass off. We need to get somewhere warm fast. If this is the hotel I think it is, it also has a natural hot spring in it."

"Hotel." Multiple people echo his choice.

I'm not too sure that the hot spring pools would even be swimmable at this point, but whatever.

James nods and walks out onto the road. I'm sure it would be easier to go to the tree line but there is still always a risk of a booby trap going unnoticed, and who knows what's on the other side of the road. Who knows what's on the road even? I don't know, but it's better to stop going along this train of thought.

Both ideas seem like bad choices. They are too close and too predictable to evade Darius and his people for long.

We are lucky that the sun is out, though it's cold, it's not snowing and there isn't much wind. I'm sure we will all be hypothermic by the time we get there.

I look over to Dominique, noticing for the first time that she didn't prepare much to be out in this weather. And, she's missing a boot. How long has she been missing that? I hope she doesn't have frostbite. Maybe I should give her my boot.

We don't have much for extra supplies with us. I see Stephanie has a scarf. I go up to her. "Can I grab your scarf? Nikki doesn't have a boot on and she's going to lose her toes if we can't find something dry and warm to wrap her foot in."

Her eyes widen and she looks down at Dominique's foot. Stephanie forgets me instantly and goes over to tend to her foot.

I look for Rayleen because she's probably as ill-prepared for the cold. Alexa has tucked a jacket all around her like a blanket as she carries her.

The walk takes forever. I'm sure in part because of the cold. Leah runs ahead when the hotel comes into sight. She didn't say anything, so I'm not sure if she's just excited to get to the hotel, or possibly scouting out any enemies.

I almost don't care at this point. If we got captured by anyone, it would be welcome if we get to go somewhere warm.

I speed up almost automatically as we approach. When the rest of the group doesn't do the same, I slow my pace back down.

James opens the door and lets us pile in after him. The place isn't too much warmer than outside, but it is definitely dryer. Leah is still nowhere to be seen, but that's fine for me right now.

James sends most of the group off to find supplies. He leaves Dominique, Alexa, Rayleen, Shawn, Stephanie, and Brad in the lobby; mostly because three of them refused to leave Dominique's side and Alexa is focused on Rayleen.

He didn't instruct me to do anything, not directly at least.

Part of me wants to go over to Dominique, say hi and figure out how she's doing, but she has enough people surrounding her right now; trying to help her foot.

My focus is on getting a fire started. It'll help everyone. There is a fireplace in the lobby, something I'm sure they did to make the place more inviting to cold lodgers, something now that we will be able to use for warmth.

There is already a set of logs in there apparently, as James is able to go right up to the fireplace and immediately start the fire using his magic.

I go to the fire and stand down close to it. Sticking my hands in the air; the heat feels amazing. My fingers slightly burn. They don't take too kindly to being frozen for so long.

"What the fuck?" I hear Dominique shout. I turn to look at her and see she's looking straight at me. I guess she's processed who I am. She seems thoroughly both shocked and pissed off to see me. It's contrasted quickly when she tackle hugs me. I'm knocked off balance. We fumble steps while we try successfully not to fall to the ground. She seethes. "God, I didn't recognize you. Why didn't you say hi?"

I'm stuck on what to say. She pulls away a bit.

"So, she was telling the truth. You do know each other?" Brad asks as he comes up. I then notice that there are a lot of people staring and my cheeks go red from the attention and embarrassment. He still had doubts?

"Yep, she's really my sister. Surprise!" Dominique reveals to the group.

"Sister!?" "What?" Both questions echo through the crowd.

She glances at me with a hint of regret. Then puts her finger up to her lips in a shushing motion to everyone else. "You didn't tell them that part?" She asks me in a whisper. I shake my head.

Why would I? I don't want her to feel bad about it so I act nonchalant. "It didn't really come up." I shrug. She looks upset. Would that upset her? Did I offend her? Should I apologize? Or, is she upset at spilling the secret?

"And how was it supposed to come up? Hey Jaiden, this girl we're trying to rescue, is she related to you?" Brad mocks. "Why didn't you ever tell us you had a sister?"

"That's not a text conversation. We've only known for a few months." Dominique insists.

"How are you sisters?" Stephanie asks.

"It's complicated." I start explaining but I'm cut off. I'm thankful. I don't know how much I really want them to know. They seem like they are her friends, but they're certainly not mine.

"But, you're both complete opposites. Tall; short. Black hair; blonde hair. You're loud and outgoing; you're quiet and shy." Brad lists off.

"We know what we look like." Dominique glares at him. Her

voice powerful and screaming a tone for him to stop his line of speech.

"She looks exactly like your dad. Holy shit!" Brad exclaims. "He cheated on your mom! Do you have visions of the future too?"

I open my mouth to respond and provide all the information they are missing, since all of the secrets are coming out anyway, but Dominique cuts me off.

"No. And, shut up! She's adopted. She's not blood-related. She's not related to my dad, so she doesn't have visions." Dominique backtracks and shuts suspicion of my abilities down quickly. "You can't just go around accusing people of being prophets. Or are you forgetting that I was kidnapped because Sandra and Darius found out I can see the future?"

James suddenly comes up by my side. "I suggest you refrain from conversations about your relation further. The wrong people could have the same wrong assumptions and end up with her getting killed or worse." James looks around in authoritative warning, then settles between Dominique and me. "It's dangerous to be a prophet in war, and dangerous for those who could be used as leverage."

People return rather quickly; some looking a little green. James leaves us to go talk with each person who returns.

Unlike the hotel yesterday, this hotel wasn't abandoned by choice. Everyone left inside is dead. I assume others were eaten or kidnapped.

There was very little left in the pantry; barely enough to go around. I share what is left of my food for supper so people can trick their stomachs; I'm used to it.

It still isn't enough. We've eaten very well so far, but now we've run out and we'll need to be more creative if we can't find more.

I wonder how opposed this group will be to hunting.

Dominique is a vegetarian, but I don't know what her reasons were or if it's changed since the revolution.

I don't know if anyone else has special food preferences, or is against killing animals for any reason even if it's for food and supplies.

I have no idea myself how to skin and prepare a carcass, nor how to prepare other items; it's something I should look into the next time I'm alone.

I should also look into edible plants if there are any people opposed to eating meat still.

There is a commotion over with Rayleen and Alexa. Rayleen leaps out of a hug and holds up a necklace. "Put it on me!" She says with enthusiasm. Alexa affixes the necklace around the little girl's neck.

Rayleen excitedly hugs Alexa again. She kisses Alexa with a peck on the lips then turns to show Daniel her new necklace.

That was weird. Did she really just kiss Alexa on the lips? They must do that family kissing thing. That's weird and kind of disturbing. It feels creepy on many levels. We even didn't hug unless necessary. A kiss would be outrageous.

But, to each their own, I suppose.

I return back to the conversation at hand. Dominique is recalling her kidnapping.

I shift to a different seated position in the lounge chair.

"They beat me up pretty bad at first, but after I agreed to tell them visions they protected Rayleen and me from everyone," Dominique explains.

"How nice of them." Shawn's voice drips with sarcasm.

"They did mess up my ribs pretty bad though." She adds as an afterthought. "A doctor thought they might be been bruised or fractured."

"Did you want me to help fix them?" Shawn asks.

Dominique looks in wonder. "How would you do that?"

"Part of being me. I'm handy medically to examine and treat beings." He partially explains.

"Great, fix away. What do you need me to do?" She asks.

"Just sit there, and let me do things," Shawn instructs.

"Great." Dominique gives her permission and Shawn sets to work. He grabs her hand with both of his.

I had read up on elves and their abilities since we have two of them in our midst. If I remember correctly, there is a tradeoff or exchange that needs to happen for healing. For minor healing, a selfless elf may just take on the affliction for themselves. Major healing jobs require more beings, or life to take on the affliction, so the wound is spread out amongst them all. Or, some would take an animal to trade off the wound completely even if the animal would die.

"How bad are her ribs?" I ask.

"One fracture and there's bruising. I'll heal it right away." He seems to be willing to take on the problem himself. No one else seems to know the trade-off and he's not mentioning it.

"If you want, I can help." I hold out my hand over the arms of our seating.

"Thank you." Shawn takes my hand after a moment of hesitation. Immediately, I feel electricity in my hand. It travels to my ribs, where they start to feel tender.

"How would you help?" Dominique asks.

Shawn replies before I can. "Healing is a give and take. To heal you, I basically have to give the essence of the wound to someone while taking their healing properties to fix you." Dominique removes Shawn's hands and backs away in her seated position. "I wasn't done."

"You didn't tell me that you'd have to hurt yourself in order to heal me. You should have told me. I would've refused." Her voice lowers in her anger.

"Exactly why I didn't tell you. Your wounds are dangerous as is. They could put your life at risk. We're trading some bruising for you not to die the next time we have to run from a fight. It's not bad." Shawn speaks in a calm voice to try to calm her down.

Dominique frowns. "You should have told me."

Shawn shrugs. "You might have known. Somehow she knew."

"You know I wouldn't have known." She accuses.

"I don't know what you've been doing for the past couple of days. Someone might have told you." He offers up.

"Shawn." Dominique deadpans.

"Nikki." Shawn sing-songs. He smiles charmingly at the end.

Dominique huffs. "And, you." She points at me. "You shouldn't be taking on my broken ribs."

A lump clogs my chest. "I'm sorry. I just wanted to help." I look down at the floor. The apology shuts down any further berating she had planned.

"Why did you call her Dominique?" Stephanie redirects the conversation. "Earlier. When you were getting her down."

Dominique pauses glaring at Shawn and me to look sweetly at Stephanie. "Because that's my name."

"I always thought your name was Nikki," Stephanie says.

Dominique shrugs. "I've gone by Nikki for as long as I can remember, but a lot of my family still calls me Dominique. She met me around the family that calls me Dominique."

"What do you prefer?" I ask.

"Well, either. I mean. For the longest time, I hated my name and hated when people called me Dominique, but as I've gotten older I don't really care anymore. Call me what you want."

"I'm sticking with Nikki." Stephanie proclaims.

"I don't think I could call you Dominique. You've been Nikki for too long that Dominique doesn't suit you." Brad concludes his thoughts on the subject.

Dominique chuckles. "That's fine." She yawns. It starts a chain reaction among a few people in the room.

"Someone's tired." Shawn states.

I stop myself from adding a factoid about yawns to save myself any unwanted comments.

Yawning is commonly accepted as a response to our brain not getting enough oxygen rather than a direct symptom of being tired. When tired, you may not be breathing properly and therefore decrease the normal amount of oxygen in your brain. A lack of oxygen in your brain also reduces alertness and concentration; making you more tired. Your body induces a yawn to counteract this. A deep intake of air boosts oxygen levels. All this means that if you are yawning a lot, you need to fix your breathing. This will help to increase oxygen in your brain, help to raise your alertness and concentration, and stop you from yawning.

Stephanie yawns again. "I think we all are. It's been a long few days. We should head to bed. It's going to be an early morning anyway."

I follow the action of our little group. The others seem to be staying up.

We go to the makeshift beds by the fire. Sleeping in close quarters is good for body heat, but not all that comfortable for me. The heat wins, however.

A line of sorts forms to get people into their spots. I go beside Dominique, so I at least have one person to cuddle that I'm comfortable with.

She turns and hugs me.

A little voice in my head screams at her. Why are you hugging me again? I understand about when you first saw me and you were excited I was alive, but this is just going to sleep. We're not leaving each other and saying goodbye, and I don't think you want to manipulate me to do something.

Then it clicks. Her family are huggers and touchers. Each time we met there was a hug from each family member both on the way in and on the way out; someone was always touching me one way or another. This extends to so much more of daily life.

It's weird for me, but I will allow her to hug me as much as she wants if it makes her feel better.

"I'm really glad you're here." She proclaims mid-hug.

"It's no problem. I'm glad you're alive." I say back awkwardly. I shouldn't have said anything. She probably thought that was weird.

She lets go, crawls into bed and I do right after. Brad crawls in on my other side. I try not to think about it, but his presence itches even without touching me.

Exhausted, I drift off immediately.

The wet paint goes on easily. The deep bright red stands out against my pale skin. I steady my hand and stroke the brush again. Just a simple French tip is how I like my nail polish. It's a fairly easy thing to do with little practice.

Something I've perfected a long time ago after I figured out I didn't like getting my nails done at solons for events.

I glance up at the girls around me. They are all doing each other's nails. It's bonding and apparently so much easier. With the odd number I was to wait, but I decided to do my own.

They gush about how nice their nails are turning out, but I don't see anything special about them. It's just painted nails.

The warm spring breeze brushes against me.

"How do you get your lines so straight? I can't even do that

on someone else let alone myself with my good hand." Dominique gushes at my nails.

"It's not that hard. You just need a steady hand. It helps if you think about holding the nail polish brush with your bad hand still, and move your good hand to get the nail polish on the nail." I demonstrate.

Chapter 10

Being quiet doesn't work. Daniel and I are disturbing the sleep of the people near the fire. Rayleen has stirred a few times herself from the sound of our whispers.

I stand up, juggling Rayleen in my arms. Sauntering over to the bedding, I move over the top layers with my foot and place Rayleen within them. She stirs a little.

Shuffling over, I intend to lie down, but there is a hand on my back. Daniel is behind me. He points to the group splitting apart; some go to bed and others are going somewhere.

Sleep can wait for me. I'm not that tired anyway.

Ensuring Rayleen is properly covered in blankets, I kiss her goodbye. Daniel helps me up from my spot.

We quietly walk to the bar area and its pantry. Behind a no longer locked door is the mini-bar supplies; specifically the tiny bottles of alcohol.

I grab a can of pop and crack the top. I take a few sips out of it. Going to the shelves I find a bottle of spiced rum and pour the alcohol straight into the can. A learned trick from back in junior high has come in handy many times. There isn't always a cup to use, but there is usually a can of pop around.

My memory goes back to grade seven and learning this trick. After that I don't think I went a day without some alcohol in a pop can or some other drink for the rest of the school year.

None of my teachers ever noticed or caught me, but I was careful. Unlike Karl, who sat beside me for a while. He got piss ass drunk the day after he learned what I was doing, and he was suspended for a couple of days. He learned to do better after that, but he was always doing stupid things like that; all the boys were.

One time they brought chocolate ex-lax to school. They all took a piece as a game to see who could hold out the longest. I don't know who won, but the teachers figured that one out pretty fast too.

Before I can take a sip, Daniel is showing me a tiny bottle of rum I've never seen before. "Here try this one. It's very high quality rum. They only have a couple bottles."

"You sure?" I ask.

"Go ahead." He says. He pushes the bottle further in front of my face. I take the bottle from him and gulp down the liquid all in one shot. "Hey, you were supposed to share that."

"Oh, sorry." My cheeks enflame in red. Embarrassment quickly slips away and annoyance replaces it. He really should have said something if he only wanted me to take a sip. I was under the impression that the bottle was mine. Who shares a shot bottle of alcohol? It's only worth a gulp or two. "I thought you were giving it to me."

"To try, not to have."

I shrug. "You weren't specific enough." Besides, the rum wasn't that good. It has an awful buttery aftertaste.

I wash the taste away with my perfect drink within a can. Half the drink is gone in an instant.

"Let's grab a bunch and go out to the sitting area," Daniel suggests.

I sweep a couple shelves worth into my arms. A few fall and

smash against the ground. No use in cleaning that up. What fell on the floor can stay, and what splashed on my boots will wash away in the snow.

Kelly opens the door. I kick out my foot to catch it. I push myself into the way of the door and walk through the opening. Kelly goes and sits down at a table near the window. A little light is coming in from the moon, but not much.

I dump my stash into the middle of the rectangular table. The chair scratches as I pull it back and once more when I settle in.

The moonlight catches something shiny against the floor. The oddness of it catches my attention. I stare.

The darkness reveals a face looking back at me. Their dull eyes stare just off from where I sit. The face is miniature. The size tells me it belongs to a child.

My breath quickens with my heart. I can't help but imagine Rayleen's face on the body. Some part of me knows she is out in the lobby, but it's overrun by my lingering fear from her kidnapping.

The stuffy air is suddenly unbearable and choking. I need to go outside and get fresh air before I start freaking out and hyperventilating.

Running as fast as I can out of the room, and ultimately out of the place. I pass people sleeping in the lobby. No one takes any notice. I barely make a noise as I open the door and leave.

The cold air bites at my rapidly breathing lungs. Heated skin instantly freezes. Tears freeze into the corner of my eyes.

I take in one deep breath and purposely let it out slowly.

Snow is coming down quickly and is puffy. It looks like it's been snowing like this for a couple hours. The height of the snow on the ground is noticeably higher than when we arrived.

Wind brushes gently through my hair.

All of a sudden I feel exhausted. The weight of stress bearing down on me crept up until it finally hits me. My eyes shut. I take in a couple of deep breaths of cold air. Slowly things start returning to normal.

Finally, I think I am ready to go inside.

I open my eyes to a fright. Darius stands staring at me hungrily just three feet away. He looks a bit different; his eyes are darker. He feels different; more dangerous.

He closes the gap in a couple of steps. "Lexy."

"Darius." I return.

"Come with me." He holds out his hand for me to take.

I shake my head and don't reach out for him. "I can't."

"Is it because of your boyfriend?" He practically seethes in anger and jealousy.

"No. He's nothing to me; a rebound." I try to reassure him though I am uncertain of my feelings.

His hypnotic eyes drown my senses. Suddenly, I'm hot again. "Come back with me."

"Yes," I whisper in reactionary fear. In a deep crevice of my mind, a name shouts at me. Rayleen. "Rayleen. I can't leave without Rayleen."

His lip twitches and his nose flares in displeasure. "Then go get her."

"She's sleeping and surrounded by people in there. I can't." I pause and look away from his gaze. "I don't want to wake her right now. She needs her sleep, and I don't want to explain to everyone here. I don't want a fight. Please. Come back for us tomorrow night. We will be ready to go then."

He pulls my chin up. His hands are colder than the snow around us. "You will come back to me." My head screams 'yes'. The word almost falls from my lips. Pressure on the back of my head pulls me forward and his head drops to mine. Our lips touch gently at first. After a moment the kiss is rough and clashing.

Cold hands grasp at me.

Then he's detached and gone. I open my eyes. He's disappeared.

I scrunch my eyebrows in confusion. Where did he go?

"Kelly said you ran off. What happened?" Daniel asks with concern dripping in his voice and features.

I hesitate. A vision in my head flashes of the child's eyes in a dead stare. "I needed fresh air. I'm exhausted. I think I'm going to go to bed."

He comes closer. I avoid his grasp and look out into the woods. Fully aware, Darius could still be watching me and watching us. I can't run straight into Daniel's arms.

He gets a good look at my face. "Your lip is bleeding."

I bring my finger up to my lip and swipe it across. Liquid red streaks on my finger. The blood flows freely down my chin. Daniel hands me one of his gloves to help. I accept it and hold it to my lip.

He pulls the glove away and holds up snow to my lip. After a minute the blood stops.

I give him back the glove.

"Let's get inside before we freeze." Without any notice, he leans in and kisses me gently on my cheekbone.

I fully expect Daniel to be killed in front of me, but perhaps Darius has left.

Darius doesn't rush at us as we enter the building, and with the close of the door, I feel Daniel is safe.

The stark difference between the two men confuses my heart further.

Do I want to leave with Darius? Or, is it his hypnotizing charm? Could it be the threat of him?

Either way, I have a day to decide.

Daniel leads me over to Rayleen and pulls the covers back for me to lie inside. His caring chivalry is something I never expect from Darius. Darius takes care of me as a possession to be sheltered. He would keep me save.

I sigh.

The differences between the two men are bound to keep popping up for comparison.

I yawn. My exhaustion may be my only reprieve. Leaning my top half in closer to Rayleen I close my eyes and take a deep breath in. My lips gently graze the top of her head and hold their position for a few moments.

Ending the touch in a peck I pull away only slightly. A deep calm and serenity fills me. I can fall away into sleep in the comfort that Rayleen is alive and beside me.

Chapter 11

"Jaiden and I are going to go talk now. Alone." I watch as her face blanks.

She stutters, searching for something to say. "Okay?" Jaiden gets up.

Most everyone is in the lobby and the lounge. We need to find somewhere away from everyone. This place is huge, and there is going to be no issue finding somewhere to talk alone.

I take a flashlight with me and turn it on.

We need privacy for our conversation. I don't know how well any of these people can hear, so I don't know how far away we need to be.

In the spirit of exploring this mountainous hotel, I decide on where to go; to the top.

When Jaiden follows me, I lead her down a hall. I use the flashlight to light up the way, the doors and the signs.

A fair ways walk passes before we stumble upon a door leading to the stairs. It's unlocked.

The stairs are nothing fancy. They wind their way up to the top of the hotel. Their purpose is most likely to be for emergency exits.

On the fifth floor, we pass the body of someone that was

trying to escape but hadn't. There is a dark puddle around their neck. The cold is doing us a favour for our noses.

We climb further up; as far up as we can go on the stairs to the highest floor.

"Where are we going?" Jaiden breaks the silence. She sounds out of breath.

"You'll see." I don't sound much better. Stairs are killers and my ribs still ache.

It's colder up here than it is below. Whoever said hot air rises, never met this hotel.

The doors are further apart. There aren't as many rooms up top. You spend more for privacy.

We come to one of the doors and I figure this one is as good as any. I try the door knob. When it doesn't work, I decide to try plan 'B'.

Bracing myself, and finding a well-grounded position, I breathe and focus.

Focusing all my strength on a kick, I aim for right below the door knob. The door breaks and swings open. It bounces off the wall and comes back at me. All while, I lose my balance from the surprise and drop the flashlight. I catch myself before I fall to the ground.

I can't believe that worked.

"How often do you kick down doors?" Jaiden accusingly asks.

I can't help but laugh. "That was my first time. I wasn't expecting it to work."

She giggles too.

The room is glamorous and spacious. It's bigger than the apartment I grew up in.

The floors are dark wood, and the furniture is brown leather. The entire one wall is practically all window that looks out to a patio; beyond that a forest and mountain. It's still snowing out.

There are brown and white fur pillows and a blanket on the couch. I snatch the blanket to wrap it around myself.

We explore the rooms. Eventually, we make it into the bedroom. It is decorated in white and blue.

I pull back the comforter covers and climb in. What Jaiden does is her deal, but I'm getting comfortable and warm.

She looks awkward for a minute, but the potential warmth wins when I tell her, "I don't bite."

Once she gets comfortable I start. "Look, I don't want you to tell me if you can see the future. I need umm; what's that word?" My mind blanks but I feel like the right word is at the tip of my tongue.

"Plausible deniability," Jaiden immediately offers up the right words.

"Yes. I need plausible deniability. As far as anyone is concerned, I'm the prophet and you aren't. You can't tell anyone what you can do, or not do. You'd be kidnapped like I was, and we can't let that happen. It's too dangerous." I don't think she'd last being kidnapped, but I won't tell her that.

"Ok." She agrees. I think she's come to the same conclusion.

"And, we aren't sisters." But, people definitely heard that admission. "Or we are, but you're my sperm donor's kid. Not our dad's kid." I need to make sure we are on the same page despite my mess-up yesterday. I hadn't realized she might not have told people.

Even James pointed out how dangerous that could be yesterday.

"Sandra already suspects you mean something to me. I tried to throw her off that, I didn't know if it was you, but just in case you were you. And, then she said you were you." I talk in circles and I can see it's confusing Jaiden. "Sandra talked to me the one time about a little white blonde girl who knew me. They thought you might mean something to me. But, more important about that; they have a spy. Well, more like Sandra can link to someone that's in the group. It's a girl. I didn't get anything else."

She makes a hn noise. "Is there anything else that might tell us who it is? Like details that Sandra knew? We might be able to pinpoint or narrow down suspects if one person was gone while a conversation was happening."

"Good idea. Umm." I think back to the past few days and all my interactions with Sandra. "She said she knew I was lying to her about being a prophet because she knew I wasn't a Marshall by blood. Then she told me your name, and that you gave me the yellow notebook."

She interrupts me. "James has that by the way. If you want it back and I never told them you weren't a Marshall by blood. But, go on."

So, she was bluffing; this whole time. Was it just her suspicions? She saw Jaiden, through the spy, does she think Jaiden is a Marshall? And, that's why she was testing me?

"Darius knew you," I tell her.

Jaiden nods. "I went to school with them."

"Them?" I ask.

"Some of them; actually. I went to school with Darius, Alexa, Kelly, Miles, Daniel." She stops naming people, so I think she's done.

"What can you tell me about them?" I probe.

"Not much. We didn't hang out. They were popular. Darius, Miles, and Shale were on the football team."

"You know Shale, too?" I ask. She hadn't listed him with the others.

"Yeah. How-"

I cut off her question before she finishes asking it. "He was there too. He was the guard that helped protect me and Rayleen after I pissed the rest of the guards off.

Sandra knew about you guys attacking the jail before you were going to do it. They also knew about you being in Banff.

Sandra linked with the girl an hour or so before you came. She first mentioned that you were in the forest and she could see mountains but that was before the meeting then she linked while I was there and she said that you guys were in a restaurant and James wasn't with you.

And, Alexa was sitting in Daniel's lap." I try to remember any other detail, but nothing pops into my mind. "That's it."

"Okay, umm, well the last bit was when we were at the hotel on the outskirts of town. Right before we came here, we were gathered in their lobby slash restaurant. There were a few minutes when James stepped out to warm up the vehicles. We left right after."

"I think we can rule Alexa out," I tell her what I thought earlier. "Darius was always asking me about her, and Sandra talking about her in Daniel's lap is probably not coming from Alexa's eyes."

"Yeah, I think you're right. I don't think there's anything that really helps. What you told me, we were together almost all of the time so anyone could have been listening."

That's not helpful. "Damn, we'll we need to be careful."

"Definitely need to be careful. But, you said that they were linked together?"

"Yeah, Sandra went into a trance and could hear and see what was going on."

"How?" She asks.

I lean back to get more comfortable. "I don't know. Magic somehow. Darius and her fought and she was like, deflecting chairs without even touching them.

She's scary powerful. Sandra is more dangerous than anyone thinks. I tried messing with her and Darius while I was there but I don't think I did enough.

And, he's an idiot. I told him that she was going to kill him and take over his position and I really think she could do it. She's dangerous, and I'm more scared of her than of him."

"Maybe we could ask James. He might know how she does it. He should be warned too." Jaiden suggests.

"Yeah. So, how did you end up travelling with James?" I lighten the mood a little with my question.

"He tried running me over with a truck." She announces bluntly.

"What?" I ask. I need more of an explanation for the surprising statement.

"I was being chased and I ran out into the street and he almost ran me over. Calli knew of James because he's the Council Rep for the magic folk, so we decided to join up with them.

You know, safety in numbers.

But, then that night James was talking with a few people about rescuing Nikki the psychic who wrote down her visions in a code of poetry in her yellow notebook. And, I knew it was you."

"Wow, what a coincidence." It does seem like too much of a coincidence. Maybe she had a vision about it and made it happen.

"Tell me about it."

"So, what were you doing before that?" I ask.

"Oh, umm, so the revolution happened and I was at school. We were told to go home because there was a bomb threat, so I did. Then I had a nap. When I woke up I didn't know what was happening, but I saw smoke and fire everywhere. I stayed put." She trails off and hesitates. "Uh, until umm, about a week later when people broke in.”

“So you just lounged around the house for a week? I bet your dad enjoyed that.” I say sarcastically.

“He wasn’t there. I was waiting for anyone to return but no one came.” My heart breaks for her. She had to go through it alone. I reach over and hug her tightly. Jaiden loosens her grip after a second of hugging but I hang on for a few more seconds. “It’s fine. I’m fine. I enjoyed it. It was a good break from things. Umm, I went over to Lucas’ and stole his car to get away.”

“He wasn’t there?”

“No, I’ll get to that. Umm, I remembered the joke about the end of the world from your family. To grandma’s house we go.” Her mentioning it jogs my memory. I hadn’t even thought about that. My heart pounds. Maybe mom and dad went there. “So, I drove to your grandma’s house and a group of criminals had taken over the house.”

“Are they okay?” My heart sinks to my stomach.

“I didn’t see any family there. They said the house was empty when they got there. Missy was in the garage, and she protected me from them. They didn’t want to go anywhere near her. I was looking for a way to escape them because they took my keys and weren’t about to let me leave.”

“So how did you know they were criminals?”

“Stories they told me. They also had a couple of people they had kidnapped tied up. So I got their trust and they let me go on a hunt. I came across John; who says hi by the way.”

“John?” John Kadiza is the only John I could imagine that she’d run into out there; my ex. A pain hits my chest.

“Yeah, he recognized me, thank goodness, and helped me escape. But, we had to go back to attack the other people because the two people kidnapped were part of John’s pack.”

“Pack?” I hold back my second question.

"He's a werewolf, and so is the rest of his family. So the pack and I went and rescued the two people. No casualties on our side."

He's a werewolf? He let her put herself in danger. I interrupt her to be angry at John. "Wait, so John let you go?"

"No, I tagged along with other people. John didn't know I was there until he found me on the roof." Her nonchalance pulls my upset back onto her.

"Why were you on the roof?" I quickly ask her.

"I was shooting at the criminals because they were shooting at the pack."

"Jaiden!" I shout at her.

She jumps at my sudden outburst. "What?"

"You were shooting at people?" My voice rises increasingly in proportion to how distressed she's making me.

"Yeah, they were shooting at us first. I only killed a couple of them and wounded some others, but if I hadn't some of the pack would have been killed. Oh, and, the house burned down." My anger freezes instantly.

"What?" I peak my voice in the middle.

"Yeah, that was an accident. And, Missy died saving me." Each revelation is like a punch to my chest.

"What?" Eyes bulge. My heart breaks at the news. I take in a quick breath and let it out slowly.

"The leader cornered me and shot at me, but Missy jumped in the way." The way she states everything sounds like it didn't affect her at all.

"Jaiden!" I yell her name.

"I'm fine. That was it. That was the end and we went back to John's farm and ate and drank. And, I got a shower." Without meaning to she sounds braggy right at the point she says she got a shower. I envy that she was able to have a shower. I miss those.

I put focus on the shower as a tear falls. "A shower? God, I haven't had one of those in a while."

"I can tell." Jaiden scrunches up her nose in a sign of mock disgust.

We both share a bit of a laugh, and then I knock her arm. "Shut up. Why didn't you stay there?"

"Some people weren't willing to take the risk of being discovered with a human there. They would have been killed for committing treason. So, I decided to leave. I went back to my house.

Calli met me there. I met her. She woke me up after breaking into the house. We went to the Safeway where she had been. Lucas was there.

We went on a mission to check on some people at the hospital but they were dead. And, the group back at Safeway didn't want to take us back."

"Why?"

"I'm not sure exactly. I think maybe they thought we were turned into demons and were scared of us. So we went south to Red Deer and to a bar. Calli had a friend down there that gave us a room and let us work to stay by doing deliveries."

"What kind of deliveries?" I start to wonder if she'll get tired of my interruptions and questions.

"Food and drinks. I don't know what else. I never looked in the packs. But, it was fun. I met a few interesting people and learned a few things. It was cool, but then a rival tried killing everyone inside. We had to leave and that's when we ran into James' group. We hopped around a few places and stayed a few nights at Fort McLeod.

James went off to find out information on you and Rayleen.

When he came back he knew you were at the jail, so we went there in the morning. We figured out quickly that you had moved on to Banff and went right there.

What about you? How'd you end up kidnapped?"

I tuck away my questions to answer hers. "I mean, I was at the mall. We drank and had fun. Then, we disagreed on how to handle things so we split off into two groups. Tyler's group still wanted to drink and party, but we wanted to survive.

They attacked us then James' group came to stay with us. But then the mall was attacked by Darius and Sandra and I was kidnapped.

Then James attacked the farm, rescued me briefly but I was kidnapped again and taken to the jail. And, you pretty much know the rest from there."

"And you're okay, right?" She asks concerned.

"Yeah, why?"

"You were kidnapped." Jaiden points out the obvious.

"They beat me up a little, but not too bad." I brush off.

"They broke your ribs."

"Bruised my ribs." I correct her.

"And Shawn said one was fractured." She recalls.

"It is."

"Have you seen your face?" Jaiden asks.

"Not really." That's not true. I saw my face in the darkened mirror of the hotel room. I was hoping it wasn't as bad as that made it appear.

"Is the rest of you just as bruised?"

Thinking back on my torture I remember the person who spoke. "So, something weird happened after I was beaten. Someone told me to fake being their prophet so that I would live."

"That is weird."

"I have no idea who they were. I think it was a guy, but I don't know anything else."

"So, someone there was trying to sabotage Darius and Sandra." She points out.

"That's what it seems like. Some of them, I could tell belonged there, but some didn't. Shale helped us out a few times. I don't know why he was there. He was too nice."

"He was friends with Darius beforehand. He probably went to that side for loyalty's sake. He could also be how James has been getting information. He might be our spy.

Hey, look. It's stopped snowing." Jaiden points to the window.

I look to make sure. "Maybe James will let us leave now."

"You don't like James much do you?" Jaiden caught the slight tone I had brushed on James' name. She's observant.

"He's fine. But, I don't agree with staying here for so long. We're asking to be attacked. The snow wasn't falling that badly; we could've left this morning."

"Yeah, I agree. This hotel was a pretty senseless place to go, but he's set up as the leader so he's got the final say.

Eh, really though, the group as a whole doesn't seem to do well with decisions. At the jail and the hotel, they all spent so much time arguing about what had to be done. You saw them this morning.

And, James didn't take the reins until he ended things. We're supposed to respect his decisions because of his position, so that's just what we have to do."

"I don't have to like it." I cross my arms for effect.

"And you don't have to."

"I won't." I punctuate my stubbornness. "But, we should go."

"Ok."

We leave the bed and go on the long trek down to the lobby.

"James, the snow's stopped," I call out. People come alive at my words. They get up and grab their bags. James doesn't have to order us to leave, my words just jumpstarted that. "We should get going before they come to attack us."

Jaiden and I grab our new supplies.

In a rush, everyone else grabs their supplies and sets to go. We leave the building.

White. Blinding white as far as I can see. Only shadows help distinguish objects and the odd bit of green of the pine trees. The sun is bright and high in the sky. It makes the snow twinkle and sparkle. All in all, it's disorientating and hurts my eyes.

There was a blizzard in the night and early morning. A thick blanket of snow has engulfed the whole mountain.

I was disappointed when we weren't able to leave first thing. I want to get as far away from this place as fast as possible. There is too much risk that they will come back to collect me.

The only thing that saved me from walking out the door earlier was James' argument that if we're stuck so are they.

But, the blizzard has stopped now, and we are leaving.

I'm one of the first people out the door and on our way. James leads, and I walk beside him. The deep snow creates resistance. My feet are unsteady and I feel like they'll fly out from underneath me at any misstep.

We seem to go straight for a long time. I look behind me to gauge our distance from the hotel. I can't see it, nor do I see Jaiden.

It takes a second glance at the people trailing behind me to recognize Jaiden's jacket. Jaiden's head has all but disappeared. Her scarf is wrapped right around her head; I'm not even sure how she can see.

I slow down until I am beside her. "Can you see?"

"Enough." She shrugs.

"Are you cold?" I ask.

"It helps with that too, but no I'm good. It's too bright for me. My eyes were hurting. I don't want to get snow blindness, and this will help with that." Jaiden explains but I don't quite understand.

"Snow blindness?" I ask.

"It's basically when you get a sunburn on your eye because the sun is reflecting off the snow and right into your unprotected eyes. The burn to your cornea causes you to go temporarily blind." She clarifies.

"That's a thing?" Her description makes me concerned about my eyesight. I was just thinking about how blinding white the snow is.

"Yeah."

"So what, do I need to wrap a scarf around my head?" I reach for my scarf.

"Yes and no." I stop. "Sunglasses would work too; if you have them. We don't have sun goggles so I improvised with the scarf. The idea is to lessen the amount of sun that has access to your eyes. Cover most of your eyes with something. All you need is a little slit to see."

"God Jaiden, you're so white you can get a sunburn in the middle of winter." Brad jokes. I'm suddenly aware that everyone is listening to us when the rest laugh and chuckle.

"Technically anyone can," Jaiden mumbles under her breath. I don't think anyone else heard her.

"I thought you never went outside. How would you know about snow blindness?" Daniel ponders.

"It was a tidbit in the Native American studies we did in elementary grades. Indigenous people would make snow goggles to reduce the chance of snow blindness. They made it out of different materials, depending on what they had handy, but it was basically a rectangle that went over both eyes." She holds her fingers up to her face to demonstrate the rectangle. "A slit was cut over each eye so they could see." She draws a horizontal line right over her eyes. "Sometimes soot was also used to reduce glare."

"We never learned anything like that," Alexa says. Come to think of it, I don't remember being told anything like that.

"Maybe you weren't paying attention." Daniel nudges her.

"That does sound like me." She laughs. It sounds like me too. I was never interested in the learning part of school.

The whiteness of everything is bothering my eyes. I decide to repurpose the scarf to help immediately. I stop so I can unravel it around my neck, and try to wrap it around my head.

Soon everyone tries to make something work like the snow goggles Jaiden explained. She helps a few people out with their headgear. Eventually, someone brings out a knife so they can cut fabric to fit like a headband. Some people look like Zorro wannabes.

When everyone is set, we continue down the mountain. The scarf does help, but everything is still so white. I don't know how James knows where we're supposed to be going. The scarf blocks out a lot of the view.

It feels like forever passes until I catch a glimpse of the town. Every inch of my body is frozen. I'm sure I'm going to lose my toes; these boots are worse than my other ones.

There are two vehicles parked on the side of the road. James leads us to them. As we get closer all of us can see that the vehicles' hoods are open more than they should be.

Brad opens the hood fully on a white SUV. The battery is removed. The other one is checked with its opened lid and the result is the same. Someone tampered with the vehicles so we would be stuck here.

Someone checks the back. "All our shit is gone." They slam the door.

People worry together.

"Now what?"

"How are we going to get out of here now?"

"I have an aunt and uncle that live here. We could see if they are here and could help." I shout so everyone can hear. The group quietens down.

"We will go into town for supplies and vehicles. If you want to take a few people to see your aunt and uncle I won't stop you, but wait until we can establish a base so you won't lose us." I nod to agree. It sounds fair enough. "I take it you know about the town."

"A little," I admit.

"More than I know. Where would you think would help us the most?" James inquires.

I think about it for a moment. "Well, there's not much to the town. A lot of the shopping district is down that way." I point across the bridge and straight. "There are a couple malls that way about five or ten minutes walk. I mainly went there and to tourist sites when I came here."

The last time I was out here and really exploring around the town, was when I was fourteen. As my aunt put it, I am old enough to explore by myself but not old enough to explore by myself for more than two hours at a time. This meant I could explore but I had to stay close to the house.

"My aunt and uncle live just on Buffalo Street about five minutes walk that way. They run a bed and breakfast and will probably have everything we need."

"We'll go straight until we find something useful then to the malls." James evades the parts about my aunt and uncle.

It's only a couple of minutes out of the way once we get across the bridge. It'll be further if we go all the way down to the malls.

We cross the frozen Bow River.

I look to my left at the Museum. I spent a bit of time in there each time I came to Banff. Mainly, just to come to see their mermaid skeleton. Back then, I assumed it was a hoax, but now I wonder if it could be a real mermaid skeleton.

When we cross Buffalo Street, I look longingly down the road. Their house is just a couple minutes' walk from here. I should just run for it now. But, I don't. I'll go there later.

We continue walking down the middle of the road. I point out the sports goods store to James. "Sports store is going to be as good as it's going to get close by."

"Let's break into the sporting goods store." He orders everyone. Leah breaks ahead of the group. She walks up to the window and smashes it in a single punch. She kicks out any remaining glass against the bottom and sides.

Once inside, she turns and pulls down the scarf off her face. A wolfish grin tells me she thoroughly enjoyed that.

The grin drops for a moment when James walks up to the entry door and opens it easily. It had been unlocked and it wasn't necessary to break the window.

Most people stomp through the shop like kids at a candy store. Jaiden, now scarf-less, hangs back and doesn't touch a thing.

I set to work quickly grabbing a better winter outfit for myself, then grab a set for her; only the best.

"I guessed your sizes. Try them on." I tell her.

She looks like she's about to protest but she says, "thanks." She covers herself head to toe in the new winter gear. It's a small upgrade for me, but a huge upgrade for her.

Jaiden goes to the counter and pulls out some sunglasses until she finds one she likes.

Jaiden hands the glasses to me. They are white and have padding all around on the inside. The material looks like what would be used on goggles, but they are attached to the sunglasses.

"What about you?" I ask. I put them on.

"Glasses." She taps the side to emphasize. "I have to wear them or the world's a blur. They don't look like they have any prescription ones here. I can just keep using the scarf."

"Nikki, did you want to check on your Aunt and Uncle now? We will be here for a little while. I do expect you to be back within a half hour." James says in passing. He already knows I'll say yes. This feels more like he's permitting me to go.

"Do you want to come with me?" I ask Jaiden.

"Sure." Jaiden agrees.

I walk over to Stephanie and Shawn. "I'm going to my aunt's. Do either of you want to come with me?"

"Yes." Shawn quickly says.

I look at Stephanie, but she looks hesitant. "I don't really want to go." She looks at Shawn expecting him to withdraw his offer. "I don't really want to stay here alone."

What about Brad? Or, did something happen while I was gone? They haven't been particularly couple-like. I wonder if they are having a bit of a tiff again. This could still be from what happened at the mall.

If they haven't made up by now, I wonder if they're even still together. They've had their spats in the past, but nothing that lasted longer than a week.

Brad seemed to have come to his senses about Shawn, but maybe his reaction changed how Steph sees him.

If I'm completely honest, it's changed how I see him. And, I don't think it's ever going to be the same again. That nagging feeling in the back of a memory.

I'm about to let Shawn off the hook when Brad comes up and interrupts. "I'll stay with her. You guys go." Brad places his arm around Steph's shoulders, and pulls her body into his. Steph stiffens her smile.

"Okay?" I ask Shawn.

"Okay." He says back. I don't think he catches the awkwardness of what's happening in front of us.

"We'll see you later." I wave for good measure at Brad and Steph.

She doesn't give me a look to rescue her, so I turn to leave.

Jaiden is following close to me, so I don't have to collect her. The three of us leave the store. Backtracking the way back to Buffalo Street then turning left. We quickly enter residential housing.

It's all old houses down this way. I remember my uncle boasting that their house was around a hundred years old.

I recognize the old wooden house as soon as I see it. I open the iron gate and let myself into the front yard. Going to the old tree, I search for the little hole that contains the spare key. Three-quarters the way up and facing the front room window, I find the hole and the key inside. Shawn is right behind me when I turn around.

Jaiden waits on the front porch. I forgot to mention that we were going around the back. "Back door." I point towards the gate.

Shawn and I push hard against the snow heavy wooden gate. I lead them through the opening and around the house. The spare key is for the back door. They have the locks different on the different ends of the house because of the bed and breakfast.

I unlock the door and let myself in.

"Auntie? Uncle? Bow?" I call out each name and leave a space in between. I don't think they are home or Bow would have been right on me.

"Who's Bow?" Jaiden asks.

"A German Shepherd. She's friendly, but a guard dog. So don't be threatening, call her name, and let her sniff you." I instruct.

I have no idea if any of that will help. My aunt and uncle introduced me to her and I just had to let her sniff me. Might be because they introduced me.

We walk from the sun room entry into the kitchen. I open the curtains in here. Light shines into the room.

There is a note on the fridge in my aunt's shaky handwriting. 'Gone to the shack,' is all it says.

I know where they are, and I know they are alive.

"Anyone want to go on a mountain hike?" I ask.

"What?" Jaiden shouts from the dining room. She comes back into the kitchen.

"They left a note. I know where they are, and I know they're alive." I tell them. "So, let's go."

"We can't. James gave us a half hour." Jaiden reminds me of James' deadline.

"I don't care. I'm going to find them." I let her know.

"Let's go back to the store and talk to James. I'm sure he'll be fine with us going to find them. It's only a few more minutes." Jaiden lets me know her position. She's not willing to go against James' words it seems. "You'll need more supplies to hike up a mountain."

"We talk to James, and then we will go find my aunt and uncle. I don't care if he agrees or not." I tell her.

"Of course," Jaiden just nods. Her cheeks are flushed red.

"Well then, let's go." I usher her out of the house.

I lock up behind us and place the key back into the tree hole.

We follow our footsteps back to the store.

It takes less time to go back than it did on the way there.

There is now a truck parked out front. Looks like someone was able to start it; maybe they found parts.

People are still going about their shopping trip and now loading some things into the back of the truck.

I spot James at the counter with the register. "They're alive. They left a message, so I'm going to go get them."

"How long would that take?" His tone suggests he's humouring me for the moment.

"I don't know." I don't remember how long it took to get there and that was in the summer. I haven't been there in years. "A few hours to go there and back."

He shakes his head. "We need to leave before nightfall. You would never make it back in time."

"Where do you need to go?" Leah asks as she walks through the windowless window.

"It's up a mountain," I say.

"I could get you there faster." She offers.

"I don't think that would work. My uncle uses stone markings along the path to show the way, and I don't remember exactly where it is. It was hard enough looking for them in the grass. Most of them will be covered in the snow." I admit.

I don't think I could figure out where they are if I can't find those markings.

"Do you remember anything about where it is? I could run you up high and we could work from there." She suggests another way.

"There's one place where the mountain is steep and there aren't any trees there." My cousin fell down quite a ways there.

We had to help him get back down from there. "If we could find that, then the cabin isn't too far off from that."

"We find that and start from there. We could go and try to find it. It would be faster and we could limit ourselves to an hour." Leah tries to make her case with James.

"Alright." He gives in. I'm joyful and thankful.

"Thank you," I say; more to Leah than James.

I rush us outside and turn the corner of the building entrance.

Standing on the road is a large red dragon. It looks like the one that dropped me off at the hotel. This time, there is no saddle and no riders.

It huffs and smoke comes out of its nostrils. There is a hard yank on my arm before I fly through the broken window and into the shop. The rushing world stops as I'm steadied by Kelly.

She sets me down. I quickly utter my thanks.

I rush to look back out the window and see the equipment in the back of the truck and the cab is on fire.

If the movies have taught me anything it's that the truck is going to blow any moment.

There is no fighting a fire-breathing dragon.

I hear from someone that there is no way out. I don't know if they mean the shop, or if they are talking about Banff in general.

Jaiden rushes for the entrance. She peeks around the corner at the broken window. She steps through the window.

Nothing is happening, but I panic a little with her out there. I can assume she plans to run by the dragon. It's the best plan we've got.

My feet move faster than I thought they could. Jumping through the window, and grabbing onto Jaiden's jacket. I pull her with me whether she's ready or not.

I feel her boots scrape as she stumbles but she comes with me easily after that. I keep hold of her jacket to pace her faster. Over my shoulder, I can see the dragon start chasing after us.

Something stops it; someone else catches its attention. Other people run out of the building and in different directions after that.

I run between two buildings. I pull Jaiden around the whole building. Other people ran straight through the street.

As we get through the other side, the dragon runs passed us; chasing Alexa and Rayleen. That must be its plan. Darius sent it off to get them; like a search dog. But, is it trying to take them or kill them?

Letting go of Jaiden, I run after the dragon. I hit its tail as I run by it. The skin is tough and my hand hurts from the impact.

The dragon circles around with a deep bellow. It sees me as the new target. I run between two cars on the other side of the street. I hear a hiss. I duck down to the ground.

Immense heat surrounds me. The unmistakable bang of an explosion reaches my ears. I expect to be burned alive, but I realize it was the truck finally going; the noise was further away.

I run out away from the car. It's only a matter of moments before these two could be exploding as well.

I hear shouting around the flames. "Hey! Come here you fat flying lizard!"

Bang! Bang! Two shots ring in my ears from a gun.

The dragon roars as it sharply turns around.

It chases after Lucas this time. He drops the hunting gun he had shot off.

Kelly runs and jumps onto the beast's back. Like a surprised horse, it tries to buck her off. I take the distraction to run out down the street.

The separated groups come together as they dash into the mall.

I follow after them.

I look for Jaiden, but I don't see her amongst the group.

Kelly and Lucas are still gone too. I don't see anyone else missing.

I wring my hands as I wait.

The wait kills me as much as the unknown. I try to go to leave but the dragon is waiting and crashes into the door. It snaps at the glass. I back far away.

There has to be another way out.

I dash to the other end of the mall. There is another set of doors here. I leave through them only to be confronted by the dragon again. It spots me and charges. I get to the doors in time not to be roasted.

And, I didn't see Jaiden.

This dragon is intent on making us its prey. Maybe it was sent after me too.

I rejoin the group on the other side and pace back and forth. I should go out there and find Jaiden.

It's too long before the door opens from the outside. Kelly walks in. "Dragon's gone." She informs us. Jaiden walks through the door next. My heart practically sighs in relief. I run up and hug her tightly. "Thanks to the dragon whisperer."

I release the hug to see Kelly talking about Jaiden.

I look back inquisitively at Jaiden but she just shrugs. I'll ask her about it later.

"She just told it to go home and it did." Kelly elaborates.

"We'll need to stay somewhere for the night," James moves on quickly.

"My aunt and uncle's place is a bed and breakfast. It's got a wood stove and plenty of beds and blankets. And, we don't even have to break in." Somewhere homey for the night would be a nice change; comforting for the soul.

"Lead the way," James says.

I search the skies for the dragon along the way. Who knows when it might come back?

Chapter 12

The snow looks untouched. It should hopefully be clean.

Sweeping the pot down to the ground, I gather enough snow to fill it. I press to compress the snow and leave less space for air. I do this until I am satisfied I will have enough water for a three-quarter filled pot.

I go to the spruce tree next. Painstakingly, I pull the needles off the branches.

My fingers are frozen by the end and I don't have much dexterity left. I look into the pot at the pile of needles and decide that there is enough there. I'll break the needles up to help release the essence.

I'm chilled to the bone and excited about the tea. Tea is great for warming from the inside out.

I make my way to the back of the house and inside into the kitchen. People have gathered around an old gas lamp. To me, it looks like a lamp people would have commonly used fifty years ago or more; I imagine an early days train conductor using it to light his way.

The fire is going strong in the wood stove. I put the pot on the top with the handle hanging over the edge to try to keep it as cool as possible.

Gathering the spruce needles, I leave them on the counter as I search for a knife. There is a wooden knife block on the counter near their modern electrical stove. I pull out a paring knife and chop the needles around a little.

After I'm satisfied that each needle should be cut at least once, I leave them to rest for a moment.

The snow melts, while I look for a spoon in one of the drawers. There are only three of them, and I find what I need in the second one; along with two steeper balls. I grab the wooden spoon and stir the pot.

I pinch the needles and place them inside the balls. They don't have any handy chains on them so I just plop them into the pot.

This will be a long process. First, the snow melts, and then it starts to boil. Finally, the colour, nutrients, and flavour leaches into the water.

I take the pot off the top of the old wood stove. The pine needle tea should be ready now.

When I think the tea should be done I use a soup ladle to fish out the tea-steeping balls. I place them on a paper towel on the counter. I should be able to reuse the needles for one more tea batch.

The handle of the pot is piping hot. Using an oven mitt on the handle, I bring the pot over to the table. I pour the tea into coffee mugs as neatly as I can. The first couple of pours leave drop puddles on the table, but I cleanly pour after that.

"And, you're sure this is safe to drink?" Brad looks at the tea I serve with disgust.

"Yes," I say.

"You're positive?" He asks staring at the liquid in his cup.

"Yes," I state with a little irritation leaking into my voice.

His head dips down and he sniffs at the liquid. "But-"

I interrupt him. "Spruce needle tea has been consumed for centuries; thousands of years."

"You're making that up." Daniel accuses me.

"How did you know about the tea?" Dominique asks me.

"Jacques Cartier and his men got their ships stuck for five months. They began to come down with a disease, scurvy, and many died. The Native Americans treated them from a tree they called Annedda. There is a dispute as to exactly which tree it was, but one of the guesses is the spruce tree.

My teacher told this joke about how the European settlers would come to America, and die from scurvy. The cure of which, was right outside their door in the form of pine needles. The trees that you can find everywhere, can be made into a tea that is high in vitamin c.

We even made some at the time. It tasted fine, and it didn't kill me. People can develop scurvy in as little as one month, so drink up." I explain the information I know as correctly as I remember it.

"That's not a very funny joke." Brad finally looks up at me. He shakes his head.

"More, funny ironic. Like how B12 is most typically naturally found in meat, dairy, eggs, and fish, so a lot of vegans and vegetarians who don't properly manage their nutrition with supplements or fortified food, or nutritional yeast, end up B12 deficient. On the light side of this, it can cause tiredness. On the extreme side brain damage and psychosis. Actually, we should make sure we're getting all our nutritional requirements. There are downsides to deficiencies across the board, and we are lacking variety." I explain.

"Why do you always sound like a textbook?" Daniel asks. I choose not to answer him as my chest pangs. I shrug. It's not the first time people have made that comparison, usually they mean it as an insult.

"And, you're sure it's not going to poison us." I stop myself from saying an exasperated 'seriously', and just raise my eyebrow at Brad instead. Fine, die of scurvy. I don't care.

"Just listen to the walking talking encyclopedia and drink the tea." Calli takes over and defends me. She takes a sip of the scalding drink. "It's good."

"But-" Brad interjects.

"Drink it," Dominique commands while cutting him off.

"I'll burn my tongue." Brad must just be purposely trying to be difficult by this point.

"Well, wait for it to cool first." I add 'obviously' in my head.

I blow on my tea to cool it down. I know it'll be about fifteen minutes before it'll be cool enough for me to drink without burning my tongue. I've always preferred lukewarm or cold tea for that very reason. I always burn my tongue otherwise. I had to boil it to get rid of bacteria.

The conversation moves on from there.

I look around, not interested in conversing. It's pretty dark in here. The gas lamp and wood stove do a good enough job to light up the room so we can see everything beyond the table in dim light.

There is a very old country feel here. Wooden cabinets are in the one-man kitchen. The kitchen portion of this combination room is so tiny that a person can stand in one place and reach practically everything.

There is rooster paraphernalia everywhere. Someone must've had a love for roosters; Nikki's aunt I'm betting. There are rooster pictures, tin rooster figurines, a rooster clock, a rooster cookie jar, and rooster pillows. I even saw a rooster bobble head.

Overhead is an old stained glass lampshade. I imagine it would make lovely colours on the walls when the bulb is turned on. As is, the gas lamp light refracts off the glass. There are bits of blue and red that I can be picked out against the wall and ceiling.

The tea warms me from the inside out. I enjoy it straight, but I notice a few people drowning it in sugar. It has a bitter earthy taste like many teas do.

I'm not surprised to find out that most of the people here are coffee drinkers and not tea drinkers.

"Let's go into the living room. It'll be more comfortable in there." Dominique suggests as she places a hand briefly on my arm. I'm happy about the suggestion.

My legs are falling asleep from sitting in this booth. My legs dangle over the ledge and I'm not tall enough to reach the ground. The wood lining the edge is cutting off circulation.

She leads the way around into the living room on the other side of the house.

The room looks like every grandparents' living room. They have the brown floral-designed couch, with end tables on both sides. There is a couple of, now-dead, plants. An old TV is stuffed into one of those tall skinny cabinets. Knickknacks are everywhere.

Photos of the family are up behind the couch. Dominique and her parents are in one of them. They are arm in arm, standing knee-deep in a lake. Giant true grins on their faces.

They must've been out on a vacation here some years ago. Dominique looks a fair bit younger; maybe a preteen age.

I glance through the other pictures, but I don't know anyone else in them.

A glass chess table triggers a vision memory.

I look at the people in the room. The two playing chess have the room captivated into silence. We watch for a while.

I yawn. I'm tired and should go to bed.

I stand up. "Excuse me. I'm going to go to bed. I'll see you all in the morning."

"Good night, Jaiden." And variations of that are said by each

person.

I round the corner. The stairs are old and creaky. My toe catches the edge of the abnormally high step causing me to stumble. I've already shut down my mind in exhaustion but this jolt quickens my heartbeat and races my mind. At the top, I go to the right of my designated room.

Alexa is in here. It takes my head a moment to figure out and process that if Alexa is in here that this isn't my room.

Caught red-handed Alexa looks guilty. She cries "go away." Darius disappears out the window.

"Uh. Yeah, I think we need to talk." I go sit on the bed.

I don't remember much of what I said after that, but I remember it was a long speech about love and that she can do better than Darius.

Alexa catches my attention quickly. I watch her suspiciously. At some point tonight she's going to meet with Darius.

I'll be watching two people play chess, and after I yawn, I go to bed. Stepping into the wrong room, I find Alexa at the window with Darius.

The dream wasn't threatening, but I'm sure to be on my guard. I feel like I should follow the dream.

There could be bad consequences if I don't interrupt them; there could be bad consequences if I do interrupt them. This one, I think, I'll just let happen.

I go back to the kitchen with my tea cup on the premise of filling it back up. I need to stay alert and awake.

There is a knife block on the counter. I select a small sturdy sharp knife; sure to stand up to a stabbing, yet small enough to be hidden. I leave to just outside the kitchen.

Cutting a slit in my boot. I shove the knife in between the two layers. It won't stab me and I have a weapon on me at all times. It covers nicely with my snow pant leg.

"What are you doing?" I jump sky high, and my heart races from the fright, but I recover quickly since I recognize Dominique's voice.

"Nothing." I remember now, that I was supposed to be following her.

She pulls out something from her pocket and walks closer. Dominique skillfully opens the Swiss Army knife to show me the blade, and then puts it back in position and away in her pocket.

"We should get you something better." She proposes. An utility knife would be better. "Do you want to see something?"

"Sure," I tell her.

"Leave the tea here." She tells me. I put the tea on a side table and declare it abandoned in my head.

She grabs a flashlight out of a kitchen cabinet drawer and goes through the closed door on the left-hand side of the bench. Apparently, we are going somewhere else.

I follow quickly after her. She takes a sharp left and opens the door to a basement. The wooden stairs creek under our weight. I can't shake the feeling that the old stairs will give away and we'll fall to the concrete floor below.

The feeling ends when the stairs end. Dominique reveals a room to the immediate left by opening the door. She lets me go in first by the small amount of light in her possession.

This feels like one of two things; one the more likely. She's either bringing me here to kill me, or she needs to talk again.

I've gone over our conversation this morning a few times already. I said too much. She told me everything she learned and observed while in captivity. There are key strategies that can be made from the information. Troubling facts also were revealed.

We agree that Sandra is more dangerous than anyone thinks, and Darius is an idiot. But, that can also make him more dangerous in a different way.

She doesn't see the future and she doesn't want to know for sure about my abilities, an unspoken agreement was brought between us that we would protect that information. It's just like James had said, it is very dangerous to be a prophet. They already think she's the one, so we'll keep it that way.

I can't see much until she lights things up. The room is small, made smaller by a couple feet on every wall. A table was built and an elaborate landscape was built on top of it. From halfway up the wall to the ceiling and beyond, is a tiny-scale train world.

"My uncle collects trains and built everything in this room. His grandfather worked on a train, and he had grown up with a love for them.

He has trains in here that are worth a fortune. There are trains from different places in the world and date back to when he was a kid." She passes me and laughs once. "I've only ever been allowed in here when he's brought me, and I was never allowed to touch anything."

"I promise I won't touch," I tell her.

He has his own town made out on the table in a boxy 'U' shape around the room. Train tracks weave through the town and into the mountain. The walls are painted to match as a background supplementing the scenery.

Above that is the painted sky with clouds on the ceiling. A single row of shelving on every wall near the top houses the many train cars on display. Some look brand new and others are rusted with age and humidity.

There are too many details to account for so I zero in on one small section of the town.

The amount of detail that had gone into this setup had to take many hours over many years. I couldn't imagine how long this all took him.

A log mill has every detail I would imagine a real one to have.

Tiny workers make the whole place work. They create a paused world.

A log hauling truck is partially loaded. A pile of logs is ready to be loaded up. Logs lay where they had been cut and stripped of their branches and bark. One log has two workers on each side mid-saw with their two-person saw.

A dried water bed nearby has tiny fish sticking up and may be filled with water from time to time.

The train tracks loop on the outskirts of the pond and there is one behind the log mill building too.

We both spend time looking through the town. I'm amazed by the little details and the scene as a whole.

The people even have painted expressions to match their mood. Street signs have legible names.

A mine on the side of the mountain looks like a working mine site, and I wouldn't doubt if he used real dirt and rock.

Anyone looking at this can see the hours, dedication, and passion that went into building all of this.

After a time Dominique suggests, "we should go. I don't really want anyone else coming down here. Sorry."

I'm touched. "We've been gone long enough. I understand. No worries. Thank you for showing me this. It's amazing."

We close the doors behind us as we return up the stairs and return to the living room.

Alexa seems antsy. She looks longingly out the window. I think she is expecting Darius to show up now that its dark out. If she is, that means they spoke at some point and planned to meet up. Could that be why we haven't been attacked yet? That would make sense.

Maybe Dominique is wrong. Maybe Alexa is the spy. Darius and Sandra certainly had access to her.

That reminds me, that I was going to research magic and

linking. I still need to find alone time to do that.

James strikes up a match against Dominique. She learnt from her uncle. She shows a piece that she had broken as a kid, and it had been glued back together.

Alexa excuses herself. She takes Rayleen upstairs to tuck her into bed. I go on edge. This should be it.

A couple of minutes later, I'm surprised when she returns.

"Jaiden, would you like to play?" Dominique asks. She brings my attention back.

"I've never played chess," I tell her.

"What?" She's astonished. "How have you never played chess?"

"Easy, generally speaking, chess is a two-player game," I state. It speaks to a sad big truth about a lot of my life so far.

"Yeah, and?" I shake my head a little and raise my eyebrows in a motion to get her to think a little bit more about what I said. When she finally gets the hint she lets out a soft "oh."

"Would you like to learn?" James asks.

"Sure," I say.

"We'll set up and you can grab in a practice round while I coach you." He suggests.

I shake my head and offer another solution. "If you want to play with someone else for a round and just explain things, I should catch on well enough. Maybe I'll play the round after that."

"Very well." He agrees.

James and Miles set up the board for another round. In the intermission, the room empties a little. Dominique goes back to her friends in the other room at their insistence. Alexa leaves too.

"Alright, these are your pawns. They move two squares on the first round and one square after that. They can only go up, left or right; never backward.

Rooks can go any number of squares up, down, left or right. Knights go in a 'L' shape. Two squares and one square. Bishops go diagonal any square amount. The queen can go any amount of squares in any direction. And the King can move one square in any direction.

If your King is threatened it's 'check'. If your King is taken it is 'checkmate'." James quickly explains. Most of it goes in one ear and out the other.

His words refresh old knowledge from an old Google search. I understand the theory around the game, but I haven't actually played. I need to understand more about the strategy.

A round goes by before they switch me in to play against Miles, while James coaches over my shoulder.

I figure out pretty quickly that some of the game is about sacrifice. If I sacrifice my pawn in the right place, I can take the piece he took my pawn out with. Obviously, there is a hierarchy to the sacrifice.

The game doesn't last long. I thought I was doing well, but suddenly he calls checkmate. Between my pieces and his queen and rook, my king has nowhere to go.

I have no idea how it happened and where I went wrong. I wish this was checkers; I never lose at checkers.

I sit back for another round. Quickly, I realize things are aligning in place for my vision. I yawn, and then excuse myself for bed.

I go up the stairs. One thing I make sure to do is to watch my step. This time I don't stumble on the obnoxiously tall stairs. There are four bedrooms up here. I need to go into the first one on the right to catch Alexa.

I walk into the room.

Darius is hanging in the window.

I surprise both of them. Alexa looks guilty.

Rayleen is asleep in bed. I hadn't noticed her in the dream. I can't recall her in the dream at all.

Did I change things?

Or, did I just not notice before?

Alexa cries "get out." She looks at me so I'm not sure if she's talking to me or Darius but Darius takes it to mean him just like in the dream. He jumps out the window.

Alexa's look suggests she was talking to me and not Darius. She increasingly gets upset by his departure.

I know the background of her and Darius. It was a toxic relationship, though I'm sure neither of them would admit to it. Darius was toxic to most, so it isn't a surprise how he turned out.

"What was he doing here?" I ask. It sounds hostile as soon as I say it. I should have gone with what I said in the dream. Too late now.

"Nothing." She crosses her arms; closing herself up mentally.

"Obviously it wasn't nothing. He was here to see you? Or, was he going to start an attack?" I need to know.

She's hurt by him and mad at me. "I was going to leave with him."

"Why?"

"I love him," Alexa tells me.

Her words don't surprise me. Every girl in high school says they are madly in love with their boyfriend; even if they had only dated for a day. It disgusts me. "Do you? Does he love you?"

"Yeah." She insists.

"Of course he does," I say sarcastically. "But aren't you with Daniel? Dominique said Darius is dating Sandra."

"They broke up. He made a mistake with me, so he broke it off with her. He said he was sorry for everything. No one's attacking us for my sake." She leans against the open window. The cold comes in. I can feel it from here.

I walk closer to her. Reaching behind her I close the window. There is no point in losing whatever heat we do have. I quieten my voice now that I'm closer to Rayleen. "And, that suddenly makes everything all better. Did you lead him here?"

Alexa hesitates. "He's been watching me." There is more to that story. She's too bad at this to hide her nervousness.

"Should we expect to be attacked in the middle of the night? It's dangerous for us all that he knows where we are."

"He promised he wouldn't harm the group." She shakes her head. Alexa looks everywhere but at me.

"That's what he told you?" I rub my hands together to rub heat back into them.

Alexa finally looks me in the face. "Yes. He was telling the truth, I could tell."

"Okay, so let me see if I have this right. Darius has been watching us all day so he could come pick you up and take you with him and you were going to live happily ever after." I can't help but patronize her.

"Rayleen was going too." She smiles. She didn't comprehend that I was being condescending.

"Of course she was. Not that you were going to give her a choice. And, after he took you back to the castle he would come back to kill all of us. You would be fine with that."

"He wouldn't." Alexa denies.

"He would. And, you were expecting Sandra to be okay with him dumping her to go back with you." I poke little holes in all of her points.

"He didn't love her. He loves me, and he's going to make me a vampire, so I can protect Rayleen better." She sounds like she's trying to convince me and herself now. "I need you to leave now."

"We need to talk." I haven't made the love speech yet. I shouldn't have changed the script.

I shouldn't have started off as sharp as I did.

"No, we don't. Get the fuck out of my room." Alexa walks forward with her hands out, intending to make me leave.

I leave the room and close the door behind me. If the speech I was supposed to make, made any impact, I may have just messed things up.

I'll try to talk with her tomorrow when she's not on the defensive.

I stand in the little room at the top of the stairs. I can see light from the lamp in the living room.

I'm torn between what I should do now. I can go to bed and hope nothing happens for the rest of the night, or I can go downstairs and tell James what transpired.

I know what seems right for the group as a whole. I should go tell James. Alexa will look bad, and I'll probably ruin that friendship forever, but I can't rule out the chance we will be attacked tonight. I don't want blood on my hands.

I quietly hike the steep stairs down to the living room.

I interrupt the chess match. "James, can I talk to you alone?"

He looks at me surprised by my sudden appearance. Everyone looks confused. "Yes."

James gets up and I lead him into the sunroom.

I blurt everything out as soon as he closes the door. "He's gone now, but Darius was in Alexa's room. She was going to run off with him and take Rayleen with them. Darius was apparently watching us all day. Alexa says he promised not to attack us while she's with us, but I'm not too sure about if she leaves with him. He might be back, even tonight."

I feel out of breath. My heart is beating with anxiety.

"Alexa is a liability as long as she's involved with Darius. I'll need to prepare for a possible attack tonight. We'll leave Banff tomorrow morning. We'll need to hide our movements as much as possible. You need to sleep."

"Okay." I can't help but think that Dominique isn't going to like that very much. She's intent on finding her aunt and uncle. Hopefully, they aren't dead.

The dead family is something I should talk to Dominique about. I feel she has a right to know that most of her close family is dead. Her parents are dead. But, if I don't then she can still hope that they are out there somewhere.

Is it too late to tell her?

Should I have told her back when we first rescued her?

Back at the hotel?

Would she be mad if I told her now?

He guides me out of the sunroom and to the stairs. "Pleasant dreams."

"Goodnight," I say.

I climb the creaking stairs.

I still need to do some research, but I'll make it quick. The bathroom up here is supposed to be straight ahead. It's a closed door.

As quietly as possible, I turn the knob and open the door. It whines. I reach down and feel the counter surface top.

The bathroom is dark; darker when I close the door.

I unleash the phone from the zippered pocket of my sweater. A bright light brightens the whole room. It's going to be a problem.

I grab the towel off the rack and place it at the bottom of the door; it should block most of the light from the cracks.

All the crinkling of my jacket and pants makes me very aware of every movement.

I lower the toilet lid and sit down. Searching on my phone the question burning me about Sandra's spy; magic linking.

I have no other way that I can word it, so I press enter. Clicking the first link that seems right, I am brought to a page of dark magic.

It explains that magic folk can use their magic to meld with a person. It's part of the dark magic that is frowned upon in the modern world.

They use a potion to connect with a portion of a person or a whole person in extreme cases.

The blood of the spell user is required to be exchanged, along with the potion. A wound is created on the spy where they wish to meld. The blood potion is exchanged to the opposite person through the wound.

The wound takes a fraction of the time to heal. Going forward magic users can use the link to see, feel, touch, taste, or hear what the other is experiencing.

It is undetectable if unaware of what is going on. Humans never seem to detect when the meld is happening. So the spy may be completely unaware of any of this; which is my bet.

Dominique mentioned that Sandra was both able to see and hear what was going on, so I'll need to ask around to who was injured in both by Sandra.

The link is temporary; which is good for us.

The magic lasts as long as enough of the blood is alive in its regular life cycle. Which varies, but the expectation of the longevity of the magic is a month. Up to a one hundred and twenty-day life cycle of blood.

It mentions that there were experiments done on humans that resulted in complete control of said human through the meld when enough magic and blood was injected directly into their veins.

I yawn. I'm exhausted.

My eyes are strained from reading a bright phone in the dark. I look at the battery, and it's only at thirty-two percent. I should figure out a way to charge it tomorrow.

The instructions said to leave it out in the sun, but that's hard to do when you're hiding it from others.

At the last minute, I remember to text John and Sara. She had requested I let her know I am alive, and to message John when I found Dominique.

Alive and safe. Thanks for the phone. It's really helped me out. Saved Dominique in Banff. She's alive and well. I send the message to Sara, and then open another message conversation for John.

Found her. Rescued her and she's healthy and safe. We're in Banff. Hoping to find somewhere warmer tomorrow. I read and reread the message over. I think about rewording it, adding more, or simplifying it. I end up pressing send just to save my battery.

I turn the phone off, place the towel back on the rack, and leave the room.

My eyes readjust to the darkness.

This time, I go to the second room on the right side of the stairs. I crawl into bed in the small spot available on the very edge.

Very aware that I might fall off sometime during the night, I lay my arm pointed at the edge; it mostly lays in midair. There isn't anything else I can do unless I wake up everyone in the bed to move over.

Lying awake, listening to creeks and groans and snores, until my eyes finally shut in exhaustion.

Chapter 13

I'm a groggy grump compared to the sunshiny little girl begging me to start the day. I feel hungover after such a restless sleep.

I look over to the window to gauge the time, which is impossible with how dark it is out there. With how late it's getting into December, it could be sometime through the night, or it could be seven in the morning.

I missed my window of opportunity to leave with Darius last night. Expecting him to return, I left the window unlocked and cracked. I waited for him to come back for hours, but he never showed.

Eventually, I decided to fall asleep. I left the window open; just in case he came back. I figured he might wake us when he returned, so we could go with him.

He didn't come back for us; part of me hurts from this. Then, I remember why he didn't take us in the first place; Jaiden.

Jaiden burst into my room and interrupted us. She made Darius leave.

And, I bet she told everyone. It would explain why Darius didn't come back. Why no one else came back into this room last night, despite the lack of room and bed space.

I told her we're safe from him. But, it would be just like her to tell everyone else just so I couldn't leave.

Rayleen told me that Darius made sure she was safe. He warned everyone not to hurt her. It proves that he's still good; he's still the man I know and love.

He took Rayleen to keep her safe for me. Sandra got in his head to make him hurt me; maybe she controlled him to do it.

I'm so pissed off that tears flood my eyes. A deep breath in settles them without making them fall.

I take a deep breath. I might be too irritated and a little over emotional from the lack of sleep.

Rayleen pulls me up and out of the bed. "Come on. I'm hungry. I want to go downstairs and eat breakfast."

A groan comes from the bed. It scares me in surprise. Daniel snuck into the bed at some point. He doesn't wake.

In my head, I let out a cry of frustration. Out loud I groan just a little. "Okay, okay. I'm up." I whisper.

I let her drag me out of the room and down the stairs. She thunders down them as loud as she can. We go through the door to the kitchen to take the shorter path.

"Good morning, Rayleen. How are you this morning?" Nikki asks her in a sing-song between the counter and stove.

"Good." Rayleen answers.

"Morning." Leah grinds out as she knocks into me in passing.

There is a noticeable difference in greetings. Rayleen is greeted with joy and smiles, while I get something made out of courtesy and a shove.

Jaiden isn't here but if she was I'm sure there would be a guilty look on her face. Even though there are only a few people in here I can tell it on their faces; in their stares.

They know. They all know. And, I know she told them.

That Bitch.

It was supposed to be between us. She had no right to tell them about Darius. He didn't do anything wrong. I didn't do anything wrong. What does it matter to any of these people if I go off with him?

I'd punch her smirk off her face if she were here.

Nikki hands me a cup of the disgusting tea. "Thank you."

I sit down next to Rayleen. She has a cup of tea too.

I stare at the steam coming off the hot liquid. I'll wait for it to cool then hold my nose while I chug it.

Rayleen told me last night they were fed better under Darius' care. There is plenty of food at the hotel.

Rayleen needs better food to grow.

"You're just going to sit there and act like nothing happened?" Kelly outbursts so loud the whole house is bound to have heard.

"Do you have a problem, Kelly?" I ask.

"Yes, I do; with you. You've gone too far. You put us all in danger. What the fuck were you thinking?" Kelly gains volume with each sentence.

"Kelly shut up. I think she knows." Nikki comes to my defence.

"No, she's right. They could have attacked us." Brad shouts at Nikki.

They don't get it. None of them do. "But, they didn't. Darius said he wouldn't kill any of you. No one's in danger." I speak to my own defence.

"Of course, we're in danger; you ditz." Brad turns his ire toward me.

I roll my eyes and shake my head. "You don't get it."

"Oh? We don't? Then explain it to me because I just see a love-sick idiot trading us for a vampire fuck." Brad sneers.

My jar unhinges slightly. What?

"I don't care about why she did it. What I care about is what she plans on doing now." Shawn calms Brad down a little.

"And, I don't care what she plans on doing. I've had enough of her bullshit. She needs to go. Let her go to Darius and stay there. I'm done dealing with her." Kelly stands up to emphasize her words.

"She doesn't have to go." Nikki defends.

"She does." Kelly insists.

"She's going to get us killed," Brad shouts.

"We can't just kick her out," Shawn says.

"Of course we can." Leah counters.

"Darius will take her. It's not like we're kicking her out in the middle of the ocean to be eaten by sharks." Kelly asserts.

"That's exactly what you'd be doing." Nikki reasons. "And, there'd be no reason for Darius to not attack us once she's gone."

They're all yelling at each other quickly. Lines and sides are being drawn, but this is about what I want, and after this display, my mind is made up.

"Rayleen and I are leaving," I announce.

We can't stay here anymore; not with what they think of me. They want me gone. Darius wants me with him. It'll be safer with him. I'll be stronger with him.

"You can't be serious? You're going to take Rayleen back there?" Nikki turns on me.

"Yes. It's my decision." I remind her. I'm grateful she looked after Rayleen while kidnapped, but she needs to remember her place and mine.

"She's staying here!" Her volume reaches levels not previously reached.

"She's going with me! I'm her family!" We have nothing to bring with us; only what we have on us. "We're leaving," I tell Rayleen quietly.

It's just now that I get a good look at her. She looks terrified, and tears waterfall down her face. The fighting has made her scared.

I pick her up. I'll carry her all the way there, if I have to.

No one stops me physically, but I heard shouts after me.

Someone yells out for James.

Nothing they do will help them; I've made up my mind.

Rayleen sobs against my neck. Her little body vibrates against mine. Anger boils inside my chest. I would hurt the people that did this, if I could.

I'll get Darius to turn me into a vampire as soon as possible. I'll be stronger and no one can push me around anymore. They'll fear me as a vampire.

I'll be able to protect Rayleen from everything once I'm a vampire.

We won't have to worry about someone hurting her anymore. I won't have to worry about anyone taking her away from me.

I'll be able to do everything easier and better with super strength, super speed, and super senses.

The way back is clear in my memory; not that it's a hard route to follow. Straight to the bridge, cross it, and go up the road. If I get lost, there are clear footprints in the snow.

The hotel is clear from the road. I turn away from the footprints to go down a snow-covered road toward the Banff Springs Hotel.

There are a few people down this way. They are on the road going to and from the hotel. The closer we get the more we can see.

It doesn't take long for someone to notice us and decide that we don't belong. A tall girl with short spikey hair confronts us.

"Take me to Darius!" I demand.

She raises her eyebrow. "He's not here sweetheart."

My heart sinks. I hold in my panic.

"Where is he?" I ask.

"He left last night. Said he'd be back. He's not back." Her answer has me wondering.

When Jaiden told the others about Darius, did they do something about it? Did they go out to hunt him down?

No, they would have said something. Bragged about killing him. Or, at least let me know before coming here.

I think they would have the decency to let me know.

"I want to talk to Sandra." I petition as a second choice. I don't think she'll want to see me, but I might have better chances with her than some random demons who don't know us.

They might make us prisoners.

Another shorter girl shows up. She makes a display out of smelling in our direction, then turns up her nose. "Like she'd talk to a human." The spiky-haired girl tenses.

"Darius will be pissed if you hurt me." Sensing an attack I decide to warn them.

They both laugh. The shorter one responds. "Darius won't care."

"He loves me." I defend myself. They laugh. "You don't know who I am. I'm Alexa. I'm his girlfriend." They only laugh harder.

"This one has a sense of humour." The spiky-haired one says. Her fist quickly comes up and stings me in the cheekbone.

"Enough. Let's just take her back." The short one holds back another punch from her friend.

"I plan on it." She grinds out.

"Now. Unharmed. What if she's telling the truth? That she's Alexa." The shorter one has some sense.

Spiky hair thinks about it for a moment. "After you, your highness." She points the way then bows. I know it's all a show, but at least it gets me what I want.

The top of her head moves. A divot appears and then grows. Her head divides in half. It grows and reshapes as fast as it splits. The divide continues down her body.

She undresses in front of us to allow for the divide. Her head is fully formed and reformed into identical heads.

The two bodies fully part. As they each continue to form the other half, they dress in practiced movements from the original clothes and another set pulled out of a small pack.

My eyes refuse to avert through the process as gross and weird of a display it is.

"You can leave. We've got this." Both versions of the spiky-haired girl say in unison to the short girl. She hesitates only for a moment before running off. They turn to Rayleen and me. "Let's go."

They move together, but separate. One grabs me by the shoulder, on each side.

The two girls guide us to the hotel and inside. Eyes turn to us. A familiar face turns our way when he notices people's distraction. Relief floods me.

He quickly comes over to us. "Let them go." Ram orders the girls. A smug smile carves onto my face. They leave like they are dismissed. "What are you doing here?"

"We came to see Darius," I announce.

"Well, let's go see if he's returned." Ram turns and walks away from us.

I usher Rayleen after him.

Light orbs light our way through a stone and wood lobby. We go up stone stairs deeper into the hotel. The grandness of the hotel makes me wish to go back and visit this place before all this began.

We go down the stairs on the other side. Ram leads us into a large lounge area.

Sandra sits behind the bar. She's pouring herself a drink.

"Why is she here?" Her voice slurs slightly.

"She came to see Darius."

"He's not here. He was supposed to be collecting her. Didn't you hear? We've broken up. I bet you're ecstatic. Now you get to be in charge." Sandra talks around me.

All the wildness from her at the farm comes back to me. As the woman left, she is scorned. As the women left for, I am weary. "Put them in a room. Something in the penthouse will be suitable, or would she need more?"

Ram pulls on my arm to start me on the way out of the room. "That will do fine." He tells her. We turn to leave.

A glass breaks behind me. I jump. I pull Rayleen to the front of me. I put myself between her and Sandra.

Ram leads us to the stairs. We go up as far as we can. There is a hall and more stairs. We follow the stairs as far as it goes up. Glancing through a window shows me exactly how far up we are. The people below are ants.

Ram lets us into a large suite.

"Stay here. Make yourself comfortable. I'll come to retrieve you when Darius shows up." Ram's instructions sound nicer than reality.

"Could we get something to eat? We left without eating breakfast." I hold back from rambling about the chaos that was this morning.

"There might be something in the cabinets and mini fridge. I will try to rustle up some food for you both." He smiles briefly and leaves us in the room.

The question of Darius' whereabouts plagues me as I search everywhere for food and drinks. I come up with two bed chocolates, a coffee mix, tea bags, six waters, a couple of mini bottles of alcohol, and pretzels.

I lay our feast out on the coffee table to pick at. I give Rayleen the chocolates and pretzels. She's hungry and I can wait for Ram to return.

I have an adult liquid breakfast that goes straight to my head. The fuzziness feels nice and helps the time tick by.

Rayleen and I pass the time.

With no clock, the only tell of time is how bright it is, or how dark it is.

No clock both makes time seem like it's going slower and faster than it might actually be passing.

No clock means our stomachs have no sense of when a meal should be consumed, only knowing that it is empty and food should be filling it.

I get the idea to look into the hall. Ram should be coming back with our food. There's nothing to do but wait, and he's taking an absurdly long time.

A crack is enough to alert guards outside. "Close the door." A deep voice booms.

I slam the door in my shock.

When I gather my wits together I peek through the eye hole. Two people on the other side of the hall are visible. I know the person who talked was closer to me than that. There have to be at least three people out there guarding us.

I slide the lock soundlessly into a locked position. No idea if it will hold back those on the other side, but there is a little security in the lock.

There's trepidation and anxiety building inside me. Darius isn't here and Sandra is shutting us up in the tower.

I think we've just become prisoners.

Where the Hell is he?

Chapter 14

"James left." I watch the faces fall in surprise; except Miles who already knew. The only other person keeping her poker face is Jaiden and her forever smile.

People freeze in their positions in the living room. The information kicks each of them still. The information has to be a surprise, more so than Alexa and Rayleen walking out earlier.

As a leader, James would be expected to stay and lead. But, James also has other duties; or so he says. He claims he has duties to a council and his people; that no longer exist in my mind.

I think he's given up on us. Given up on using Alexa to get to Darius. Given up on hoping we're the group that's going to be able to kill Darius.

He knows I'm not a danger; he's likely guessed I don't have visions. I'm not dangerous if I get captured again. My worth to him is gone. They don't know about Jaiden, so they'd just kill her.

No one says anything for a bit. I let them sit and have the information sink in.

Jaiden sits at the window with a book in hand. Barely glancing up at me through the top edge of the paper. I know I have her attention as we meet eyes briefly when I look at her.

Miles and Kelly paused in their chess game with Miles' hand on his knight hovering over a space filled with a pawn.

Taylor's mouth hangs open in her spot on the couch.

Shawn sputters tea after choking a bit. The hot liquid rolls down his chin and onto his jacket. He wipes the mess up with his sleeve.

Brad and Stephanie look up from their intimate cuddle on the other end of the couch; both look in shock. It crosses my mind that they must've mended things between them.

It had been a bit rocky at the mall and since. Maybe leaving them alone together yesterday helped fix what was broken.

Leah raises her eyebrow in question. She stands aimlessly in the area connecting the dining room and the living room.

"Is this what happens when I sleep in?" Daniel jokes soberly. Within his joke, there is the pain of being left. When he woke up and made his way downstairs Alexa and Rayleen were already gone.

Leah broke the news to him bluntly.

His face had twisted in sorrow. Daniel had turned and left immediately. No one went after him so to leave him to greave the end of his relationship alone.

It's bad enough to go through a breakup, more so if they break up with you, and absolutely heartbreaking betrayal if they leave you for another person.

I can't imagine how it would feel if they left you for an enemy.

"What happened?" Stephanie asks over the tense air left by Daniel.

"James." I pause. "James said he had important things to do elsewhere and left."

"When is he coming back?" Taylor asks. I don't know.

"He isn't," Kelly tells her.

"Are we supposed to meet him somewhere?" Taylors asks.

"No," Kelly says. "What Nikki is trying to say is that James left us and he's not coming back, and we shouldn't expect to see him for a long time; if ever again."

"He'll come back," Miles swears. I wonder if they had a conversation about it. That could be why he sounds so confident. "He needs us to help fight in larger battles, but he has bigger things to do right now than lead us around. He'll contact us when he needs us again. We just don't know when. We just need to keep up the good fight while he's gone."

In other words, James has left and we are free to do what we want. At least, that's how I interpret it. "This means, I'm going up the mountain to get my aunt and uncle then we're out of here to go somewhere warmer."

"Where are they?" Brad asks.

"Up a mountain," I tell him and everyone else vaguely. Everyone is in this room; I have to assume this includes the spy. I have to assume Sandra could be watching at any time.

"You want us to hike up a mountain?" Daniel asks.

"To find her Aunt and Uncle in a cabin, that she doesn't remember where it is," Leah adds.

"That sounds awful. I'm staying here." Daniel crosses his arms.

There are grumbles and words from almost everyone to that feeling and idea.

I purse my lips. "I'm not telling you to go. I'm telling you that I'm going. You can all stay here and I'll go by myself. If anyone does want to go with me they are welcome to join. I could use the company."

No one volunteers to go. I expected Leah to speak up because of her last offer, but she stays quiet.

Jaiden finally speaks up. "I'll go."

I smile. Somehow, I knew she wouldn't let me go by myself.

"Great, go pack whatever you think you'll need for a few hours of hiking and we'll go." She hesitates for a moment before getting up and running around the house for supplies.

I think I surprised her with the suddenness of our to-be departure.

I had an opportunity to pack a little earlier, and as soon as I was told James would leave I decided what I'd be doing.

"So, what are we supposed to do?" Steph asks.

"Whatever you want. Just be here for us when we come back." I tell her. There is nothing for them to do but survive the next few hours. I don't think it will be too hard; as long as Darius doesn't come back to attack them.

Between blindly hiking up a mountain for a cabin, and staying at the house in a location known to dangerous demons, I believe the first option is safer.

Jaiden comes down with a backpack on, and a few more bits of winter clothing and accessories. She looks ready to survive a week on the mountain, not a few hours.

For a moment, I second guess myself and my measly packing. I have my knife and all the clothes on me; we shouldn't need more than that. But, if she's going to carry all that stuff, I won't stop her.

"Alright, we'll see you all later." I wave and smile at the crowd resuming their activities.

"Have a great day. Bye." Jaiden cheerfully extends a goodbye to everyone at once.

We leave out the back. A noticeable temperature drop greets me. It's a bit of a surprise that the house holds enough heat to make a difference. The bright lights hurt my eyes. Grabbing my sunglasses, I put the lenses over my eyes. The pain immediately subsides and I can handle the light.

I know the mountain; it's the one the town is essentially wrapped around. We took a car to get to the trail before and it took less than five minutes. As a walk in the snow, I expect it to take about twenty minutes.

Jaiden has a bare face open to the snow and cold. She has to notice; I'd think. "Are you going to put your scarf over your face? You know; snow blindness." She doesn't say or do anything. Her head must be in the clouds.

Jaiden's always in her head thinking about something. She shuts the world out and retreats into her own thoughts. I had thought it was a genius thing; everyone always says geniuses are eccentric. It could have been a quirk special to her. But, now I wonder what else is going on in there. I'm certain she's a prophet. It makes a few things make sense in hindsight.

"Jaiden!" Her head snaps to me. I repeat what I had said. "Are you going to put your scarf over your face? You know; snow blindness."

"No, I'm good. There's enough contrast that I think I'll be fine; for now. The sun isn't too bright yet." She tells me. Jaiden is right. It's not pure white everywhere like the road by the hotel. Wind has brushed some of the snow away from the trees. The houses provide contrast.

I muse along the road as we walk by signs that say Buffalo Street, Otter Street, Grizzly Street, and Wolverine Street. Personally, I think I like the theme for street names much better than numbers and letters like you see in Edmonton.

We cut out much of the walk by going straight through the trees on a crude path made by many doing the same before us. A wooden sign says it's the St. Julien Trailhead.

We come out on a snow-covered road across the street from the Tunnel Mountain Road Trail. Peculiarly, there are a few vehicles here abandoned.

We walk in silence, but strangely it is a comfortable silence.

I have no way to tell if it had been snowing here before the demons took over, but I would think so. I would think the mountains would get snow before other areas of the province.

I stare into the windows of the vehicles as we pass. Not one looks like they are in any people or objects left in any of them. They were abandoned and everything in them was removed. I assume taken by their owners since the doors look locked and none of the windows seem broken.

We start on the path.

The path is almost intuitive. The snow has landed on the mostly flattened trail. It's easy to see the trail grooves compared to the rest of the uncarved mountain.

In heavier treed areas, there is less snow than the path out in the open. Some of the paths are untouched by snow.

Snow doesn't fall from the sky but still manages to time well enough to drop on my head in large mounds from what falls from the trees above.

Jaiden goes down head first in the corner of my eye. Her hands go down into the wet snow. "Are you okay?" I ask urgently.

She seethes and gets herself upright. "Yeah, I'm so clumsy sometimes."

Jaiden removes her mitts and puts them in her pocket. "What are you doing?" I ask. Her hands are going to freeze off in this cold weather.

"Wet gloves will freeze my hands faster than cold air. I'll just tuck my hands into my sleeves." She demonstrates.

"Okay." I'll take her word for it. She sounds like she knows what she's talking about; she always knows what she's talking about. "So, that's crazy about James leaving us like that, right?' She makes a 'hn' noise. "What?"

"I'm not really surprised." She muses about something in her head. "Um, it was bound to happen. He kind of failed the mission he was on."

"Explain," I ask her when she stops talking and doesn't appear as though she'll continue.

"Well, he wanted Darius dead. He had wanted to use rescuing you as a guise to go after Darius and kill him. But, we derailed his plan; you derailed it."

"How did I do that?" It comes out a little more defensive and offended than I'd planned.

"You escaped. You went to the forest and we found out too quickly. We decided to go after you, rather than Darius.

James lost his chance to storm the castle and find Darius. He wanted to kill him to take out the leader of the region. James figured that he could drum up some support that way.

Darius is aware we are here, and after last night James probably thought that Darius wasn't going to stick around to be killed. He was going to grab Alexa and run off somewhere.

Or at least, be better guarded at the hotel.

Or, they have the numbers to come and kill us at any time.

I think James lost his faith in our group and thinks he should try for better elsewhere." I can see where she's coming from in her thoughts. She reiterates my thoughts earlier.

She has a lot, I feel, that she isn't telling me.

"I don't—I think he wanted our group to become the great rebellion legion type people." I look at her confused. She explains it a bit more once she looks at me. "Like, he wanted us to be the heroes of the story."

I get where she's coming from, but I think she's wrong in her tone. "We could be."

"No, not the group we have now. We're too conflicted with each other and some peoples' ideals don't line up."

"Like who?" I have a couple names that come to mind, but one already left this morning. The other is Kelly. She is very hostile toward humans, but she might just be hostile toward everyone.

"Brad." Her reveal surprises me. "I think he's a huge issue."

"I mean, he has his doubts about demons but he'll come around." I try to defend my friend.

He had his issues at the mall but I don't think he's the biggest problem person that we need to worry about. He was just in shock and needed time to adjust. Then, there's always whoever the spy is.

"I don't think so. I know he's your friend," she hesitates, "but he's extremely racist. He's a bully. And, he was planning on breaking off into an all-human group. He was saying some things that, well, his prejudice and hate is very deep seeded. Talking with a passion about how superior humans are. But he was willing to make an exception if you picked humans because you don't eat people."

A small part of me isn't surprised, which shocks me more. But, I guess the first blow at the mall wore away at the edges.

If that's true, and I'm certain Jaiden wouldn't lie to me, then he might be a big problem. We can't think like that and we can't divide people.

"I'll talk to him." I maintain a love of hope that he can see things differently. He's been my friend for so long, that it's hard to believe he'd be that way. But, we've never been in this situation before. This might be who he really is.

I'll have to watch him closer.

"You can try, but I don't think it'll help."

Somewhere near the top of the third switchback, I see where we need to break off by a little stone marking.

Through the trees is a large clearing.

I leave the path with Jaiden following. At the edge of the trees, I stop and take a look. This area is cleared from the near top to the near bottom of the mountain. There are quite a few steep drops that are mostly invisible because of the blanket of snow.

The area is dangerous enough when you can see your footing, but we now have to go across with snow and no visibility.

"Watch your step," I tell Jaiden.

One step out into the clearing, and I start my way across.

I try to erase the memory of what is below me. It's a long way down the mountain, with jagged rocks to break your fall and it's not how I'd like to go down.

Each step is carefully put down. I test the ground for its sturdiness and level before putting pressure down. Jaiden follows my steps behind me perfectly.

A loosened rock kicks out from beneath my foot; taking me with it. My whole body is thrown against the ground and starts a quick slide toward the very bottom of the mountain.

I slide to a stop not far from where I went down. A few small rocks roll into me and on top of me. I throw my arms up to cover my head until I stop feeling them collide into me.

I open closed eyes.

My lower half is bent at an odd angle from a bit of a drop off that goes down a couple of feet or so. My heels touch the angled bottom.

Suddenly, very aware of a tension in my jacket around my neck area I carefully reach up and grasp what holds me; a bare hand.

I look up at the person attached to that hand. Jaiden lays her head down at an angle. She must've grabbed me and been pulled a ways before we stopped.

By the looks of her other hand, she was able to stop us by grabbing onto a jagged rock sticking out of the ground.

Rolling over, I steady myself on all fours. Jaiden lets go and does the same.

She's in a better position to start climbing over again. I have a steeper climb. Her hand helps me crawl my way up to her. We hold hands until we safely latch onto a tree on the other side.

I let out a breath I'd been holding.

"See this is why I need you with me. I'd die if you weren't here." I confess. I'm amazed by her. She was able to grab my jacket, and grab onto a rock to stop us all before I could even react to my own falling. I take a deep breath in and let it out loudly. "God, you have amazing reflexes."

"I just reacted." Jaiden humbly declines.

"That, or it's like you knew it was going to happen." I nudge her.

"If I knew it was going to happen don't you think I would have prevented it; prevented this." She holds up her hand. I leap forward to grab the red bleeding appendage.

Jaiden's hand has one large cut and a few minor cuts among dirt and rocks. A few small bits of rock are still wedged in her hand. "Oh my god! How did that happen?"

"Grabbing sharps rocks might've had something to do with it." Her smart-aleck tone earns her a mental jab. I'm too worried about her injury to reprimand her about it.

I look up at her and blank on what I was going to say with the sight of red trailing down her temple. "Your head is bleeding."

"Probably, a few rocks hit me." She reaches up with her uninjured hand to feel around her head. She wobbles. I don't know if she's going to faint or not.

Grabbing her arms, I swing her around to lean her against a tree.

"Are you okay? How are you feeling?" I ask.

"I'm fine. I think." She reaches up with her hand again to

probe.

"Stop that! I'm trying to look at it." I stop her and put her hand to her side. With my natural height over her, I can see a deep red pool of blood coming from one area just behind her hairline over her right eye. Her hand comes up again, but I grab cloth when I try to put it down again.

"Can't use the glove anyway. Dab the blood away, and then you can see how bad it is." Jaiden calmly instructs me.

I dab away some of the blood to find a severely bleeding paper cut. The cut is about half an inch long and very thin. It doesn't appear to be deep.

Probing the wound with my finger I feel only smooth skin. "I don't think there is anything in it, and it's shallow."

"Head cuts tend to bleed worse." She explains.

"Good, because this is like a paper cut but from how much you're bleeding I'd say you got shot." I joke.

"Hn."

I know enough first aid to know that I should put pressure on the wound, and cold; to help it stop bleeding. Picking up some snow I form a ball and place it in the glove. I press the cloth against her head. Taking her hand I guide it to the glove. "Hold this. I want to look at your hand."

We switch over the glove and she takes over pushing it against her cut. I take her wounded hand.

"There are tweezers in the bag." She explains.

I look at her and say the first thought that comes to mind. "Were you planning on tweezing your eyebrows?"

Jaiden smiles at my joke. "They're in the first aid kit."

"Where'd you get a first aid kit?" I ask.

"Under your aunt and uncle's bathroom sink." She starts shrugging off the bag, so I help her. Jaiden freezes. She's looking beyond me; a bit up the mountain.

I follow her gaze to find three people standing at guard. Two of them have shotguns aimed at us. My first reaction is to hold my hand up in the air in surrender. Jaiden slowly lets the bag drop to the ground.

"Nikki?" He disarms himself, and pulls down his neck warmer from around his mouth. "Put your gun down. That's my niece." Uncle Bruce hands his gun to the other man and treks down to us.

The large man hugs me briefly and looks me over. "I'm fine. Jaiden got the worst of the fall; trying to save me."

"Jaiden, do you mind if I take a look?" Uncle Bruce doesn't quite wait for an answer. He's already reaching up by the time Jaiden agrees. "Henry, I'm going to need a bag."

The one with the guns hands both of them to the other man before making his way down. He pulls out a Ziploc back and opens it. Uncle Bruce puts the bloody glove in the bag.

Henry pulls out a small compact first aid kit. Together the men work on cleaning and bandaging Jaiden's wounds.

"How did you find us?" Uncle Bruce asks in wonder.

"Auntie left a note," I explain.

"Of course she did." He says mostly under his breath. "What are you doing here? Where are your parents? Why aren't they with you?"

"I don't know." I swallow the lump in my throat. "We weren't together when things happened. When I had a chance to go back to the house they weren't there. And, there was no note. I left a note of my own, but they never came. I got kidnapped, and they had brought me to the Banff Springs Hotel."

Jaiden's face twitches and scrunches slightly as a dampened towelette is placed against her head.

"Who are you?" Uncle Bruce directs his question to Jaiden.

"Jaiden Kensington." She announces; as if she expects that to explain everything.

"Who's your friend?" Uncle asks still at work. He finishes up with her head and moves onto her hand.

"She's my sister." The words slip out before I remember that we aren't supposed to talk about that. But, he's my uncle. Jaiden hisses as my uncle pours a bit of clear liquid on her hand, but I can't help but think she might have hissed at me for revealing that information. "This is dad's maybe-daughter."

That information had made its way through the family quickly; she was referred to as dad's maybe-daughter. Many were delighted at the prospect of a new family member, but mad at him for his life choices.

I suppose now that I know things, they might've been more mad that he could have let this happen. Risked having a prophet out there that no one knew about. For having a prophet out there not raised in the prophet family, learning and training her abilities.

She didn't have any of that support.

"Of course she is." He takes a good look at her face now that it's cleaned up. "Doesn't she look like your aunt? She looks exactly like Dannie did when she was her age." His wonder turns to reprimanding mock anger. "What is this maybe daughter thing? You can't look like that and not be part Marshall."

"It's a long story," I say hoping he won't ask to elaborate.

Jaiden picks up the explanation. "My mom slept around with a lot of men around the same time, and a few that had similar physical attributes. We never had a chance to do a blood test for any of them."

"Gotcha." He looks at me briefly. "As far as you're concerned she's your sister?"

"Yes," I say honestly.

"Then, she's family." Uncle Bruce finishes wrapping Jaiden's hand in bandages. "Did you injure anything else?"

"I don't think so. Thank you for helping me." Jaiden lowers her eyes and bows her head politely, then returns her eyes to his.

"Nothing to it. Let's get you girls to the shack and we'll get you warmed up." Uncle Bruce claps his hands together and rubs them for a moment.

The three men lead the way to a secluded area. Trees pepper the area, but mostly there is a lot of rock cover.

Built on the side of a rock is a shack only about a meter by a meter and a half. I remember it being bigger, but I was also smaller then.

Henry and the other man go to their own camouflage hidden tents.

There is one person sadly missing. A lump forms in my throat at the possibilities. "Where's Auntie?"

He looks deeply saddened at that moment. "She didn't make it." His hand and eyes guide me to a wooden grave marker a little ways away. Her name is carved into the wood right next to Brandon; I don't dare ask about my cousin too.

Immediately, tears fall down my cheeks. A sob breaks free from the hole in my chest. Uncle Bruce takes me up in a hug. Quickly aware of the noises I'm making, I smother them into his jacket.

I feel a separate patting on my back that's not coming from my uncle.

It takes a few minutes to gather myself together.

The tears still gather and fall, but I no longer feel uncontrollable pressure in my chest to let out; just an aching heart.

My uncle's tears break my heart more. "What happened?"

"We came back from hunting and her neck was ripped open.

There were other casualties, others missing and never found. Brandon- No one who stayed here had made it." He reveals solemnly.

"I'm sorry." I choke out.

"Me too." Uncle Bruce replies.

"Here." Henry hands me a tin cup full of clear liquid; I assume water. I can feel the heat coming off it and wrap my hands around it to absorb what I can. He gives Jaiden one too.

"Water?" Jaiden asks.

"Yes. Boiled." Henry answers.

"Thank you." She smiles at him.

I try to change the conversation and say the first trivial thing I can think of. "Jaiden showed me that you can put spruce needles in as tea so you won't get scurvy."

"Clever. I'll make sure I add some in next time." Uncle answers.

Henry goes back to his tent.

I go to the nearest spruce tree and gather a few needles for her tea and mine. I'm not one to drink just boiled water; it always has a weird taste.

Without asking I drop a few needles into Jaiden's tea, and place the rest in mine.

"So you said that the monsters had you kidnapped?" Uncle Bruce probes.

"Yeah, they thought I could see the future, so the leader kidnapped me. I was able to stall for time before Jaiden and a few other people rescued me."

"There are others, or did they-?" He trails off at the end.

"No, they're alive. They're actually at the house waiting for us to come back; with you. Then, we were going to leave."

"I'm not leaving." His voice cuts through the air. "I'll come down the mountain with you, but I'm not leaving Banff."

"Why?" I ask.

"Banff is my home. It has been my whole life. It's in my blood. I don't want to be anywhere else. Even if it means dying here." The smile disappears from my face. I can't say that I understand, but I can tell he means what he says. It's clear in his voice and in his eyes.

This is home to him. The mountains are home for him. His family is buried here, and he's not going to leave them.

I can't just leave him here alone. "What if we stayed? Do you think we'd survive the winter?"

"Of course, if the monsters don't kill us. Or, the bears and cougars. Or, the cold." Uncle Bruce's list is realistic, and reveals a bunch of dangers to us; few that we can do anything about.

Uncle is experienced in camping and survival, we'd certainly have a better chance of surviving this with him.

There is one danger we can do something about. "What if the demons were gone? There's only about fifty of them."

"If we could kill them or drive them off it would make it safer." He suggests.

"It would. Then we'd only have to survive the wild animals and the cold." The other man from earlier joins in with optimism.

"There are plenty of people hiding up the mountains. I think we could convince them to help; easy." Uncle Bruce says stroking his beard.

Henry comes over from his tent. He has a duffle bag at his waist and his gun in hand. "You've got me convinced. Mind taking the bag to your place, and I'll go find the Mackenzie's camp."

"I'll make sure it makes it, but you need to do the same."

Uncle Bruce warns Henry lightly to make it back safely.

"Will do. Ladies, I will see you soon." Henry smiles charmingly at Jaiden and me, then leaves.

Mackenzie is a name I remember from when I visited. James was just one year older. As his parents were friends of my aunt and uncle, he got the lucky job of keeping me company; and making out. "Like James Mackenzie?"

"Yes, his family and some others hid on the other side of the mountain. They thought it would be safer, turns out it was." He gives a small smile at his grim joke.

A small burning sensation at the bridge of my nose signals another onslaught of tears at the little jab.

I can't control the tears that fall down my cheeks. "I'm sorry. I can't-" I choke out.

"It's okay. It's new for you." Uncle Bruce consoles me. I feel like I should be the one consoling him, but he's not the one crying. "Let me pack a few things and we can go." I nod, and he pats my shoulder as he passes by. The other man leaves for his tent.

"So how are you planning on orchestrating an attack with a spy in the group?" Jaiden brings up a forgotten problem in a hushed tone. I dry up my freezing tears to concentrate on that issue.

"I don't know." I take a deep breath in. "Make information on a need-to-know basis."

Jaiden shakes her head. "That won't work. People are going to demand to know and be part of the planning, and as soon as we start they're going to know something's up."

"Well, it's not like we know who it is," I say loudly in my irritation.

"Who who is?" Uncle Bruce asks. My heart jumps at his sudden intrusion. I wasn't expecting him back so soon, but with the bag on his shoulder, it looks like he was already packed.

"There's a spy in the group," I tell him after just a moment of hesitation.

"They don't know they're a spy. It's a spell that allows a magic user to see and hear what is going on." Jaiden explains to him.

"Then we figure out who it is." Uncle Bruce's statement suggests this to be a simple task.

"Right, how?" I ask him.

"Did they think you were psychic when they took you?" Jaiden asks.

"Yes." They had taken me to that house in the middle of nowhere and told me I was going to be their prophet. When I fought back they put me in that bedroom and told me to cool down and get comfortable. That's when I put the notebook on the dresser and made the chair into a weapon.

"So something happened before that that made them think you were psychic." She deduces.

Nothing comes to my mind; I don't even know what I'd be trying to narrow it down to. "But what?"

"I don't know. You were there. Does anything stand out?" Jaiden asks.

"No. Nothing." I insist.

"Well, did you know anyone that kidnapped you beforehand?" Uncle Bruce tries to help.

"No," I state. I didn't recognize anyone. They seemed to be more of Jaiden's acquaintances.

"So, the connection there is James and a couple in his group. It had to have happened after they arrived to before they kidnapped you. It's a girl, so what about Stephanie?"

"She was with me before. I've known her forever. She's one

of my best friends. It's Leah, Taylor, Alexa, or Kelly." I list off the remaining girls.

"Assuming Alexa is crossed off, that leaves three; Leah, Taylor, or Kelly. Who did you talk with?" Jaiden remembers our previous conversation about this. I had forgotten we sort of crossed Alexa off the list.

"I don't know." That seems like a whole lifetime ago now. I think I talked with or around them all at one point or another. I go through the different girls' names. "I didn't interact much with Leah. And Taylor." Her name brings up a memory. "Taylor, she had my poetry book. That could be why they knew my last name and thought it was a prophecy book."

"So we think it's Taylor?" Jaiden concludes.

"It's as good of a guess as any." Uncle Bruce suggests.

"So, what do we do now?" I ask.

"We contain her." Uncle Bruce suggests. I'm pretty sure that means imprisoning her, but I don't want to jump to conclusions.

"We talk to her. She might not know, and we figure out if it's actually her. That type of magic is temporary and usually lasts a month. Once we figure things out we talk to the group and let them know, and ask them not to tell her anything important. We keep her in the dark, figuratively speaking until we can be sure the spell has worn off." Jaiden lays out a reasonable plan.

"That's not gonna work. A spy is a spy. You have to lock her up; for her protection and ours." Uncle Bruce brings up a point. How would people react to that information? If the three of us can't agree on this, we can't expect a group like ours to agree; not to mention when the Banff locals hear about it.

"We wouldn't want Taylor to know what's going on, but we aren't monsters. I don't want to imprison her. What if we don't tell anyone else? We keep it between us and Taylor. She avoids everyone while we plan the fight, and we attack immediately." I say. If we have it my way we'll attack in just a couple of days or so. Whether everyone is really ready or not. The demons in the hotel are a ticking time bomb. We don't want to give them too much time to have a chance to attack us first.

"She stays locked up in a room until we fight. It won't matter much after that. We can tell people she's not well." Uncle Bruce

"Fair enough," I say.

The other man comes back with a pack and about fifteen other people. "We're ready to go now."

Chapter 15

The people of Banff showed up in hoards.

People of all sorts rushed down from the mountain and out of their homes. They carried bags and dragged sleds behind them.

Some skied, and some snowshoed. One man even brought a buck he had shot on the way down.

I can't believe so many people were hidden away.

Darius is bound to notice. It's a matter of time before he does something to us. Hopefully, we make the first move.

It felt like a learning moment, as I stood by watching Bruce help Brad and the man hang the deer in the garage. As he backs away and stands to look at their handy work,

I question him about the whole process. "So what's the process from shooting the buck to eating it? Like I know you have to gut it."

He humours my inquiry. "Normally, I'd gut it right there. Slit the stomach open and pull out the insides. It's easier if you can get the buck up on the back of a truck, then you have it more at eye level, and you can work better.

If you come around this way." He trails off and uses his hand to instruct me to move.

He walks me around to the stomach cavity of the deer. "You

can see I've already gut this one.

We call it field dressing the deer. It makes the carcass lighter, and you want to get the guts out right away; max a couple of hours. Cut off the testicles, and cut shallow all the way down to its head.

Make sure you cut just the skin or you might run into the stomach and I'm sure you could imagine what that would mean. Pull the guts out, cut any membranes you need to, and cut out the asshole to let it all loose.

From there it depends on what you plan on doing with the carcass. You'd mainly want meat, so if you have the time, you want to leave it for two days minimum to get rid of rigour mortis."

"You should explain to her what rigour mortis is." His voice grates against my patience. It occurs to me that Brad's presence has taken on a negativity that shortens my tolerance for him and his words the more the days pass.

"I know what it is." I deadpan with a hint of a dare to question me further.

"Then what is it?" His head tilts side to side in a little shake.

"It's a stiffness of a dead body caused by chemical changes in the muscles of said dead body," I explain.

"Lucky guess." His poke bursts my patience. Why is he like this? Especially after finding out I'm Dominique's sister.

Because, he probably figured out that makes me not human. His leniency only extended to Dominique because of their history.

"When I found my mom dead she had fallen scrunched up between a wall and the computer desk. After the paramedics and the police left, my father made me go look at her dead body again; which they had laid in the bed to look more natural.

But, parts of her were still contorted because of the rigour mortis that had set in. It gave her a statuesque posed position threatening to jump back to life, rather than a peaceful sleeping one." I ignore Brad's slack jaw and change my attention back to the man.

His look of horror is one I expect from everyone when I mention things to do with my mother's death. It has to do with both the death and my nonchalance. After the years, I'm fine talking about it sometimes but people expect you to never get over it.

They expect tears and devastation forever.

I change the conversation to get back on track. "Assuming there isn't time to wait; I could just cut it up for meat and cook it?"

"Yes." He clears his throat after a meagre attempt at an answer. "Yes. You can. Your meat also tenderizes as it hangs, so it'll be tighter. You'll want to bang it up a bit before you cook it.

I assume you know how to cook it in an oven. If you want to cook over a fire, make it thin so it'll cook faster and turn it often to cook it evenly. You'll want to weave it on a stick, and stake the stick in the ground leaning over the fire. You want a hot coal fire, more than a flame fire."

"Hi, there you are. I need to borrow Jaiden and my uncle please." Dominique's head sticks in the doorway.

I'm done here, so I immediately thank the man and excuse myself to her beck and call. When I reach the door, I spot Taylor fidgeting anxiously behind Dominique. Her attendance explains why Bruce and I are beckoned.

Dominique leads us away from the house and away from any ears that could overhear the conversation about to happen.

I nearly think she's about to lead us back to her uncle's shack when she finally stops at the path's edge.

She uses a wooden fence as a leaning post.

I carefully examine the area for any eavesdroppers but catch none. I give Dominique and Bruce my attention. They are welcome to lead this conversation as long as there are no extreme outcomes.

"Are you a spy for Sandra?" Dominique surprises me with her direct question, though I should have expected it.

Taylor's upper body swings back an inch as she comprehends the question. Her brows furrow in confusion then her eyes widen. "No! No, I'm not. I swear!" Her chest rises and lowers in quick succession. Paling skin alerts me to an impending panic attack or equivalent bodily reaction.

Bruce and Dominique look tense and ready to pounce if she tries to run. I told them she wouldn't know.

Keeping my voice steady, calm, and light I resume the questioning in a way I hope to ease them. "Did you have any direct interaction with Sandra where she might have connected magically with you? Specifically, she might have done something to or near your eyes and ears."

"What?" She says breathlessly. I don't know if she didn't understand, or didn't hear.

I start to repeat my question when I see her mouth move to speak again. "Yeah." She takes a couple of deep breaths are we wait with bated breath for her to continue. "Umm, in an attack at James' house. Sandra had pressed her fingers into my ears and eye. I was hurt; an abrasion to my eye and I assumed a cut in my ear. They healed fast. What did she do to me?"

"Which ear and eye?" I ask. She points to her right eye and her left ear.

"Can you close your right eye please?" Taylor shuts both her eyes and squeezes tight. She slowly opens her left eye. "Maybe, also somehow plug your left ear." She sticks her finger in her ear to muffle noises. "Sandra placed a spell on you that makes it so she can see what you see and hear what you hear for up to one hundred twenty days from the point the spell was placed.

But it usually just lasts one month."

"Oh God! I had no idea! I swear!" She backs away. "Please don't make me leave. I'll die." Taylor begs.

"It's okay. We weren't going to make you go." Bruce tries to calm her.

"What are you going to do with me?" She panics.

"Put you in a room and keep you away from everyone and everything." He tells her.

"You're going to lock me up?" Some of the panic recedes from her voice, but she still looks like she's going to fly out of here.

I put up my hand and quickly respond to stop anything else from escalating hysterics further. "It's more like keep you away from any important information that Sandra could oversee and overhear until it's not a problem anymore.

We tell people you're sick and we're quarantining you, and you get a vacation in one of the bedrooms at Bruce's until we figure it out."

"For how long?" Taylor is a bit calmer than before, but she's still a little frantic from the information.

"We don't know. Hopefully not long. Just until there's no more important information Sandra could glean." I state.

"You can't lock me up for two months." Taylor defends herself.

"That's the maximum, and it's not like you'll never be allowed down. You just need to cover your eye and make sure you don't hear anything important. So you should spend a lot of time away from people." I try to cover myself and help calm her.

"We need you locked up for the next while," Dominique says. "It's safer for all of us. It's safer for you. You could get us attacked. Or, if someone else learns of this they might make you leave."

"You wouldn't tell anyone else would you?" Taylor asks.

"Not if you agree and you stay away from people," Dominique warns.

She looks at each of us for a moment. "Okay." Taylor nods.

"Okay. We'll go back now. You need to keep your eye closed and your ear covered. She could be trying to link with you any time." Dominique suggestively warns.

"Okay." Taylor agrees.

The whole walk back is quiet.

I quickly glance over to make sure Taylor is trying to cover her ear and eye. I try to be subtle about it each time, but Dominique and Bruce don't try to hide their actions. Taylor's tense posture informs me each time she notices their staring.

We lose Bruce in the yard to a few questioning people. Dominique and I lead her the rest of the way.

There is no talk as we put her in a room and go to leave her there. Dominique goes first and I follow after her.

Taylor holds my arm to keep me back in the room with her. "The mall was attacked after I got there. The attack came out of nowhere. Were they attacked because of me?"

"Probably," I tell her the truth. There is no reason to lie.

"A lot of people died, have died, and will die because of me." Her voice cracks and I can see her upset shining in her eyes.

"You didn't know and there is nothing that you could have done to this point. You just need to make sure that you're conscious of what you're seeing and hearing. Nothing bad is going to happen again. You just have to make sure of it. Maybe do an eye patch? Noise cancelling headphones."

"Thank you." Taylor hugs me.

I smile brightly at her to comfort her. "I'll see you later."

"Bye." She says.

I leave the room and escape to the garage. If I'm going to find an earplug it'll probably be in here.

There are numerous drawers to go through, and shelves to look on. Bruce has quite a collection of tools. While some seem to have a purpose and place, others are scattered more at random.

I search with meaning through one toolbox but adopt a more widespread approach as time passes.

The best I find is a set of headphone-type noise blockers hanging up near the saw. It's probably the best I'm going to find. I don't see why he would have the little earplugs if he has these.

I take them into the house and up to Taylor. Knocking on the door, she asks. "Who is it?"

"Jaiden," I respond. "Can I come in?"

"Yes." Taylor permits me to enter the room. I turn the door knob and let myself in; closing the door behind me.

"I brought these. They aren't pretty but they'll do the job. Just put those on an angle and you'll be able to hear with your other ear." I demonstrate in front of my face.

When I bring the headphones down, I notice she has a piece of fabric over her eye and her finger in her ear. She's working on remembering to cover them so Sandra doesn't hear or see anything.

We're so worried about what Sandra might see and hear that we aren't worried about what she might not see and hear. If Sandra is trying to link with Taylor and gets nothing but muffled noises she's going to realize we know.

We might be able to use the link.

"When you're up here by yourself, you don't need to wear the eyepatch or these things. Or, if you're not talking about anything important with others. If no one's saying anything important around you. It'll be more comfortable and they won't get anything from it." She smiles for just a moment and unplugs her ear. The smile drops, and she looks at her lap. "Do you want lunch? I can go grab you something."

"No, I'm good. I'm not hungry. Thank you. I'd just like to be left alone for a while." Taylor sounds like she's about to break down in tears.

I don't know what to do about it but leave her alone as she asked.

"I'll see you later," I tell her.

I leave and close the door. I pause and stare at the door. Taylor should be okay; she just needs some time to get through this and come to terms with it.

I take my own suggestion and make my way down to the yard for some food.

People from our group keep to themselves in the kitchen. They have bottles of hard liquor out and are shooting the liquid.

"Excuse me," I say to get by Daniel.

"You're excused." Daniel booms in laughter and the rest follow him in a drunken laughing fit.

I push past them, shaking my head.

"There you are." Dominique's voice bombards me as soon as I get outside. "Where were you?"

"I got earplugs for Taylor." My quiet voice seems to be unnoticed as she drags me off to somewhere with her presence alone and a quick tug on my shoulder.

She takes the lead. She walks beyond the garage to a few parked trucks. The tailgate is down on one of them.

Unknown faces welcome her with a hug. "Guys, this is Jaiden."

"Hi," I say meekly.

They each say their greetings. I feel uncomfortable. They're gazing between themselves and me. Their conversation goes back to jolly banter; likely continued from before our arrival.

Dominique grabs a beer and expertly opens it using the edge of the tailgate. She hands it to me and does the same with another.

Dominique whisks me off to another place. Each person we pass seems to know her.

Either she knows them from before all this, or she's met them in this short time. With her charisma, I wouldn't doubt the latter. She seems to make friends with anyone instantly.

I envy how easy conversation and relationships come for her, and how at ease she is in social situations. I would never be able to go up to people to grab a beer for a friend and myself and then walk away.

It was awkward enough in my position.

But, there is just something about her.

I remember it once said, I don't remember who or where that certain people have a gravity. People who have gravity have a special kind of presence that makes others around them gravitate toward the individual. People can't help but be naturally attracted to her.

We go off into the house and in through the sunroom.

Boisterous laughter bounces off the walls. Someone talks but it's almost completely inaudible with the laughter.

I look down at my boots and notice an inordinate amount of snow that has collected on them. Stomping my feet to get off the extra snow helps.

My ear twinges with what I think is the sound of my name, but with Dominique barely just out of the room, I assume she's asking me to hurry up.

"Are you fucking kidding me? Don't talk about her like that. What the Hell's your problem?" Dominique yells loudly to the people inhabiting the room.

It occurs to me immediately that they were talking about me again. And, that Dominique just caught them doing so.

My heart pounds in my ears. I know a male talks but his words don't register. I just rush into the room in time to see Dominique pushing Brad against the wall.

Oh no. She's gone ballistic; over defending me.

I don't know what to do. What do I do? I don't know what to do.

I rush over to them.

"It's okay. Just stop." I try telling them, but their screaming overpowers my words. She shouldn't be defending me. I'm not worth the fight.

"Do it. Punch me." Brad eggs Dominique on enough that her fist comes up lightning fast threatening to punch him, yet it never does.

As fast as the quarrel began it ends.

Dominique lets him loose and backs up a foot. He stays pinned against the wall on his own might. They glare intensely at each other.

Everyone watches, held still by the tension.

I don't know what to do. I know Dominique is trying to defend me, but I don't want all this fuss over me. I'm not worth it.

Is this because of what I said about him earlier?

I shouldn't have said anything.

She's friends with him, and we've got to be around him in the future.

We shouldn't anger all these people, because they like to pass their time by saying bad things about me.

I don't care that they're saying things about me; not that the words don't hurt. They can say whatever they want. I'd rather a person speak honestly about what they think about me than to bury it down in fake smiles and obligatory conversations.

I'd rather know exactly how they feel about me.

Can we just go back, and not have this happen?

He's probably talking about me because of our interaction earlier. He's probably telling them that I'm psychotic because of how I reacted while explaining rigour mortis

"If I ever hear any of you are bullying and gossiping about Jaiden again, I won't hesitate to throw you out in the snow. I don't care who you are, or how long we've known each other." She growls out her warning and walks into the dining room.

I know my cheeks are red. My face feels hot.

I wish I could disappear.

I just want this all to stop, and to have never happened.

I stop myself from apologizing; it wouldn't help anything.

Their eyes watch me as I follow after Dominique.

I expect to find her reeling from the events just past, but she calmly hugs me in the living room. "I'm sorry. I can't believe they'd say things like that. Have they done that before?"

I don't have the heart to tell her the truth and I don't want to make things worse. "No, I think I was a bit rude to them earlier. I ran into Daniel. They're drunk and it's probably just the drunken topic of the moment."

I try to take the heat off of Brad.

I've been bullied by classmates ever since I started public school. I've been bullied by people old and young for as long as I can remember. I've been bullied by basically everyone I've ever known and trusted. I was bullied by my parents. I've been bullied by complete strangers; and everyone in between. I'm used to people talking about me behind my back and to my face.

It's a fact of life. It's going to happen. There's no use in fighting it. Just endure it.

"That doesn't excuse them talking about you like that." She fumes.

"No, but it could the catalyst." Her brows scrunch up the slightest bit at the last word. "It could be the thing that started them talking about me; the reason for the conversation. They're drunk. They're bored. They're drunk. It doesn't take much when there's alcohol involved. But, thank you."

"You're welcome." Dominique smiles and takes a swig of her beer. "Let's go out the front."

"Where are we going?" I ask.

"I don't know yet." She admits.

"Why'd we come in here?"

"We were going to hang out and talk with those people but I don't like them right now," Dominique growls out.

"Okay?" I part ask, and part state.

She leads me out the front and to the neighbour's house. Dominique knocks on the door.

It takes a minute, freezing in the cold air, before Dominique tries the door knob. It opens.

We let ourselves into the dark house.

"Hello?" She calls through the house. "Hello?" She shouts a little louder.

Dominique sets about opening the curtains for the dining room. Light floods into the house. It looks untouched like a prop house.

Not a thing is out of place, and everything has its place.

We check the house for occupants in the upstairs. I don't dare venture to the basement without a flashlight, but we call down there, and no one responded. When the whole house is checked we raid their pantry.

I grab a box of crackers and a vacuum-sealed stick of jerky meat. It's cooked and preserved right so it'll be edible. Dominique helps me find a plate. I grab a knife from a knife block and quickly find a cutting board.

We cut up the meat and stack them on the plate. The meat and the crackers are separated for her food preferences.

We set out the plate of crackers and meat. Dominique pulls out some canned corn from the pantry. While she gets that ready I bring the plate into the lit dining room.

She brings out the can of corn and a spoon.

I'm ready to share my crackers if she wants one. I put the plate in the middle of where we both sit down. I take a cracker and slice of meat and take a crumb-spilling bite. The jerky is good and flavourful. There are lots of spices in the meat.

Dominique sticks to eating her bowl of corn. I won't push the matter. If she wants to eat vegetarian in a world that won't support it, then I'll support her until it becomes life-threatening.

I eat the whole plate of crackers and meat to myself. She declines crackers when offered.

Dominique finishes her bowl of corn and gets up to wander around. I watch her until I can't see her anymore. Clinks and taps come from wherever she goes.

I sit and watch out the window. I look back for her every once in a while but think it better to stay put and watch the picture-like view.

From my position, I can see snow-peppered trees and behind that is the frozen river.

"Here let me shape your eyebrows." Dominique has returned.

In her hands is a makeup kit. Her lips are bright red now.

"Sure." What's wrong with my eyebrows? I've never plucked them before. It's not like they're unruly but they aren't perfectly lined like some people have them.

"Put your head in my lap. It's easier to shape them that way. I used to do this with all my friends but we did it a little too much. I'm still waiting for my eyebrows to grow back properly." That doesn't bode well for my confidence, but I've never noticed anything unusual about her eyebrows. "I won't pluck too much. Just some of the hairs growing outside your natural eyebrow shape."

I look at her eyebrows and notice they are thinner than mine. I don't want my eyebrows to look like that, but if she realizes they were over plucked she would know not to do the same to mine. I decide to trust her and lay my head on her lap.

It's not exactly that comfortable. It's awkward so I close my eyes.

I can feel her hot breath on my face as the hairs pull out with a pinch. She starts in the middle and then works around each eyebrow. We don't talk as she concentrates on shaping my eyebrows.

The burning in that area makes me imagine that I have a ring of red around my eyebrows.

Sooner than I thought, she stops. "All done," Dominique announces. "Would you like me to do your makeup next?"

"No, thank you." I burst.

"Are you sure? She has plenty here." She insists.

I decline once more. "No, it's fine. I don't really like makeup."

"You don't like makeup?" She's incredulous at my statement. Everyone always is, for some reason.

"No. It always feels like my face is dirty, and it feels itchy to have something constantly touching my face. I always end up eating some of the lipstick and get a bad taste in my mouth. No one can get near my eyes to put on eyeliner or mascara."

"What happens?" Dominique interrupts.

"I twitch. My eyes panic and I feel like they're going to poke my eyes out. It's not a good time."

She smiles at me, but finally accepts it. "That's fine. You have a face that you don't need makeup to look beautiful."

I don't think that way; I'm not beautiful. There are sometimes that I look okay in the mirror. But, certainly far from being beautiful. She's a thousand times more beautiful than I am; with or without makeup.

"So do you." The response is awkward and I mentally shake myself for sounding weird.

"Thank you, but I need makeup. It hides things, and I like the statement." I look at the red lips and remember her past looks. She does tend to go big and bold with her makeup.

It always bothers me when beautiful people think lowly about their looks and hide it in makeup. It speaks to the power and control of a multibillion-dollar industry.

Though I suppose someone could point out the hypocrisy in this.

I take a long drink from my beer to kill the current conversation. It never takes long for her to talk about something else. I mainly listen to her ramble on about everything and give a few words of input here and there.

She talks about the house and what she's found. She talks about the people she's met today. She talks about her trip up the mountain, and her trouble finding the stone sculptures in the snow. My small input is given in a name to the sculptures; an inuksuk.

She talks about how good my eyebrows look and that my face

isn't red anymore. She talks about the people who owned this house. She talks about her family and I hear her fears about where they are now.

I panic. I lie once more to appease her. I don't want to ruin the moment. I'll tell her another time when timing works out better.

We talk for hours.

After a natural break, when we could no longer hold our bladders, we decide to go back to her uncle's house.

I leave Dominique to a group of people and trek with a can of fruit cocktail up to Taylor's room. No one answers. I let myself in to find a sleeping lump. Leaving the can on the dresser, I vacate the room.

There goes that idea.

Not quite ready for bed yet, so I decide to find Dominique again.

At the bottom of the stairs, I peek through the open door to the filled benches of a party still going.

They have their attention on someone not in my view. I quietly bound out into the living room, and leave through the front door.

I'd much rather go around the whole house than possibly have to have another encounter with that group so soon.

Flashlights and campfires light up the faces of people, and rooms. Joyful banter fills my ears along with the quiet pops of the lumber.

I have no idea where Dominique could have gotten. I don't suspect it will be too hard to find her, and if it is I'll just return to my room.

Peeking into the garage I see another animal carcass has joined the first.

I walk down the alley and I can see everything. I can see lights from people's houses and backyards and garages. I can see the moving lights of people on the move.

With all this light we are likely teasing the group at the mountain. We'd be idiots not to think that they don't know where we are.

This light is a tease. It could also betray our numbers.

I don't think I'll sleep restfully tonight with the threat of attack.

A few people pass me by. I don't notice them so much as what they are carrying. They each carry a bundle of long guns; by my completely nonexistent expertise, I would say they're rifles.

They must be collecting all their guns for the fight.

A supernatural being probably isn't much good against a gun, no matter what type they are.

"Boo-yah!" The sung word tells me so many things; Dominique's gotten a few more drinks in and is in a happy mood.

I ascertain the direction I need to head in; somehow I had passed by her. The word is sung once more. She's in one neighbour's yard around a fire.

She sees me immediately. "There she is." Dominique gets up from her spot to come over to hug me. "Jaiden. James, I want you to meet Jaiden."

She pulls me over to a tank of a young ginger-haired man named James. "Most people call me Jamie."

"Nice to meet you." I shake his hand. Dominique sits me down next to her on a seat meant for one. I almost spill off the seat. "So Dominique says you're her sort of sister?"

Annoyance set aside I explain. "My mom slept around and there's a question as to who my dad is out of multiple possibilities," I swear the story gets shorter each time I tell it.

"Sounds like you need to go on one of those TV shows that do the DNA tests for paternity testing," Jamie suggests.

"Yeah, we should have gone on one." Dominique gets really

excited and nearly knocks me off the seat.

"I don't know what that is," I admit.

"What?" Her voice screeches in high pitch.

"Basically the only TV I was allowed to watch was educational. So that's all I know about." I confess. There were a few shows I caught in secret, but my knowledge isn't extensive.

"So what did you watch?" Jamie asks.

"The History Channel and Discovery Channel." I surmise.

Dominique spends fifteen minutes asking about various shows, actors, bands, and references. Most, I answer having never heard about them before. If I do know of them, it's only in name or having had someone reference it before.

"I think I need to contaminate you." She finally ends with.

I don't think she means that word, but it could work; I guess. I offer a correction. "Do you mean corrupt?"

"Yes. You're so smart." She scrunches her nose. "I love you."

"I love you too," I respond in obligation; I don't know if I love her. I think she might be a lovey drunk.

And one who can't keep secrets.

"I'm really glad you're here." Dominique hugs me and kisses my cheek. Her hug doesn't fully release. "I love you. I really hope you know that. You're my sister."

"I know. I'm glad you're here too. I consider you my sister too." I don't know about love, but this much is true. I do consider her my sister. The hug is released and Dominique returns to her previous position.

I added the word consider to hopefully pull away suspicions. I think we need to have a talk about how that's supposed to be a secret again.

There's only so much doubt I can sew before people come to the right conclusions.

At this point, I'm half sure everyone knows the truth.

She smiles a drunken sloppy smile then frowns. "I don't feel good."

"Oh no. Up." I spring up from my seat.

Her statement sounds like the famous last words of every drunk before they throw up. I need to get her off to a corner.

She has other plans when she turns over the arm of the chair and starts throwing up on the ground there.

I grab up her hair to keep it out of the way while resisting the urge to gag. Breathing through my mouth and looking away get me through without throwing up.

I'm not cleaning that up.

I'm stuck in this position. The people around me do nothing, so I decide to put them to work.

"Can you get water and something to eat please?" Jamie gets up to go. I quickly add. "Vegetarian." I don't know if he knows her food preferences or not.

Jamie is back before Dominique finishes hurling. She starts gagging and throwing up practically nothing. Her body finally draws back to a proper seated position.

"Here. Drink," I order. I take the water from Jamie, unscrew the lid, and give it to her. She takes it and takes a sip. I shove a piece of dried bread at her next. "Eat."

I watch over her telling her to drink water and eat the bread until I'm satisfied and they are all gone.

"Better?" She asks.

"Yes." At this point, she has alcohol poisoning. She needs to quit drinking alcohol, drink some water, eat some food, and sleep it off. She's done three of those.

The last action she needs to complete is to sleep it off, or at the least pass some time.

"We should get you to bed. You'll need to sleep that off." I tell her.

She nods and stands up. A groan releases from her as she grasps her mouth. "I'm not going to make it."

"You girls can take my bed. It's closer and no stairs." Jamie offers.

"Yes," Dominique answers for us.

She starts to stumble that way. I grab her arm and put myself under it to support her. Jamie takes her other side. With his help, I almost don't need to do anything. My height makes me useless.

His house is noticeably colder than Bruce's. They probably don't have a wood stove here; could be the lack of people.

Jamie guides us to his room.

I help lay Dominique on the bed. She goes to lie on her back. "You should be on your side. I don't want you to aspirate vomit."

"Okay mom." She tells me. A deep pain strikes through me.

Jamie comes back from a trip to the kitchen I didn't know he took. "I got this if she can't make it outside." He hands me a mixing bowl.

"Thank you."

"If you need anything else let me know. I'll be outside, and then my parents' room is just down the hall second door on the left." He points, but it is redundant as there is only one direction to go that doesn't lead to the backyard.

"Thank you. I'll let you know. Have a good night."

"Good night." He leaves the room.

I crawl into bed on the other side. Dominique is already snoring away. I fear she'll go to her back again. Removing the pillow from under my head, I press it against her back. It should stop her from fully rolling onto her back.

I close my eyes and breathe in spicy cologne emanating from the sheets. It's funny. Before this, I'd prefer sleeping on the floor rather than sleeping in someone else's bed. But, it's entirely too cold for that.

He forgot his phone; of course he did. He needs his phone.

How could he forget something so important? I turn the car around and drive back to where I came from. Luckily, I didn't get too far away when I noticed.

I should be able to catch up with him.

A phone buzzes. I pick up my phone in the cup holder, but there isn't anything on there. I pick the other up to see that he has received a message.

When my eyes return to the road I see a very unwelcome sight. An officer straight ahead is telling me to stop with his hand straight out.

The consequences would be higher if I don't stop. I slow down to a crawl and pep talk myself silently.

I can do this.

I roll down the window.

"Hi, how are you?" I ask sweetly.

He looks at his tablet. "I'm well. I'm going to have to see your ID." His voice thick in accent.

"I don't have an ID." I feel like someone getting ID'd that's underage; embarrassed at being called out. Scared for the possibilities of being caught without one.

"Are you a human?"

"I-uh." I stumble for words. What answer is going to get me in the least amount of trouble this time?

He's the police. But, is he human police or supernatural? Is this an official stop or unofficial? Is he a fake?

I hesitate too long. "Step out of the vehicle please." The officer orders.

He could be Council police; I should've looked up what their uniforms look like here. Whether this was an official stop or not, he's now taking steps to ensure I'm not a danger. Or, he's trying to put me in danger.

"Why?" I ask.

"You are being detained for the theft of supernatural property." I know I'm in trouble. My heart pounds and I can't help but think this is where I will die.

He reaches into the car and opens the door. I have no choice as I unbuckle my seatbelt and step out of the car. "What? Why?"

"The phones."

"One's mine. The other is a friend's. I just dropped him off and he forgot it in the car. I was driving back to give it to him." He pauses and pulls out a tablet from his bag.

"What's your name?"

"Why?"

"DataBase." No. "What's your name?"

"Jaiden," I tell him reluctantly. I should have registered. The hairs stand up on the back of my neck.

"Spell it."

"J-A-I-D-E-N." He types each letter into his tablet.

"Last name?"

"Kensington. K-E-N-S-I-N-G-T-O-N."

"There is no one by that name in DataBase. You are a human, correct?"

"I-"

The world goes black.

I shine a light near her to illuminate her face. "YOU DON'T GET IT!" Dominique screams at me from the other side of the train room. "I can't do this anymore."

"Then explain it to me. Tell me what you can't do anymore and I can help you." I say calmly. I inch closer to her.

"I killed people.

I killed innocent people.

I killed Jamie's mom.

I killed Henry's nephew.

I killed loved ones of the people here; people who miss them.

And, they know. They know their loved ones are dead because I killed them." She stops to deeply sob.

I have no idea what to say. Even if I did, any words I could possibly try to form right now would get stuck on my tongue.

"Why did they do that Jaiden?" She asks in a hoarse whisper "Why did they just let them go? It was dark. They were running at me. I thought they were demons. I thought they were going to attack me. I just shot them all."

"You couldn't have known. It was too dark in there. No one can blame you."

"They all blame me. I blame me. I can't. We need to go. We need to leave. I can't stay here. I can't do this." She gets up from her spot on the floor.

"What do we need to do next? Tell me what I need to do?" Her eyes are bloodshot from her crying. I don't know what to tell her as I look at someone who has had their soul broken by actions they can't take back.

Somehow, telling her that time will heal it, doesn't begin to cover it. Nor do I really believe it. Time can't heal something like this. This is a tragic event that haunts a person for the rest of their life.

Such a strong woman has been broken beyond repair in an action that took less than a minute to commit.

Chapter 16

A knock on the door scares me. We've been shut away in this room too long. Food never arrived, unless that's Ram now with it. My stomach growls with the reminder.

A bubble of hope fills the empty spot in my stomach. Either food has arrived or Darius has returned. Either would be welcome right now.

I walk over to the door and unlock the latch. I twist the doorknob and reveal Ram.

"Come in." I sing-song.

Ram enters the room; without food. "Darius is back. He's requested you meet him in the lounge." He dashes out my earlier negative thoughts; that Sandra would lock us up here to die and not tell Darius.

"Okay." I gather up Rayleen and usher her out after Ram. Two demons follow behind us. It unnerves me to have the guards, but I guess they are trying to make sure we are protected here.

The long trip down to the main floor is cold and dark. Between the twists and turns, I don't know where I am.

We walk into an open bar area. I spot Sandra and Darius immediately. They are wrapped around each other. Lips clash against lips. Eye closed as they focus their other senses in on each other. Hands move to cradle her and hold her to his body.

She said they had broken up. He said they were broken up. He won't turn me into a vampire.

My chest hurts, and my breath quickens. Tears flood my eyes. I clench my fists in a fit of flowing anger. The blood pumps through my veins fast.

Neither looks up from their entanglement. No one says anything so as not to disturb the couple. I clear my throat to catch their attention.

Darius' eyes flash open. He breaks away from Sandra and deposits her on the couch. She is confused for a moment then a scowl carves her face when she spots me.

Darius walks over to me. A cocky grin plastered on his mouth.

I meet him with a glare.

"Lexy." He words breathlessly. I've never hated a nickname more than this moment and that name. He leans in for a kiss.

I back away. "You were just kissing Sandra. I'm not gonna kiss you. You can't possibly think I'd be okay with that."

"Yes." I lift one eyebrow. "You came back to be with me. Nothing else should matter."

"It does matter. I came back to be with you. But you're still involved with Sandra."

There is no change in his expression. I can't read him, but he looks smug. "Yes. That's how it's going to be."

My eyes widen for a moment. I've been tricked again; betrayed again. I shake my head. "No. I'm not agreeing to that. She needs to go. That's not what we had agreed to."

"There's nothing wrong with being in a relationship with both of you. You should be happy that you get to be with me again." His words make me do a double take; could he be right? Should I be happy being with him even if it means that I'm not the only one? The arrangement would still get us protection. I'd still become a vampire.

Sandra sends a dirty look to me. The look promises that she won't make this easy on me. She doesn't like this arrangement either.

My memory flashes back to the hobgoblins. I doubt it would take much for Sandra to convince him to kill me. If she doesn't just try to get rid of me herself.

His look solidifies my decision immediately in a bubble of endangered panic.

"No, not like this. It's her or me." I give him an ultimatum.

"I'm not choosing." He says. "I'll have both of you."

"I want to go." I barely move an inch before he grabs both of my arms. "I'm leaving."

"You're not leaving." He growls. The pressure on my arms pinches.

"The Hell I'm not!" I shout as I let loose all my anger.

A whistle raises the hairs on the back of my neck. I feel trepidation about what it could mean. His lips are pursed and I know he's saying something to the other vampires.

Sandra grins smugly. Her stare now tells me that she's won once again. She played me. She played Darius.

He lets me go. It is only so that a woman can grab me and drag me off. I try to create resistance and grab things, but nothing slows her down. Rayleen screams and cries. I look back at her to see a man has her up on his shoulder and he's holding her there. He's following behind us at least.

I resist the pull, but it's too much. I'm helpless against her strength. I change my mind. I'll do it, but it's too late.

When we reach the stairs I stop resisting to make it over them safely. I check on Rayleen. She still looks the same, struggling on the man's shoulder. Her cries echo through the halls. They drop my stomach. I'm so sorry.

She leads us into the lobby, then up some stairs. We come to a hall with guards at the entry. We are dragged down a long hallway.

They stop in front of one of the doors and open it. I'm flung inside with a tug on my wrist.

Catching my footing, I look up to see the room is filled with frightened-looking people. Turning around, I barely react fast enough to catch Rayleen before she trips to the ground.

My actions bring me to the ground on one knee. It stings from the impact. But, I am thankful that Rayleen doesn't seem injured.

"You made it through the forest once, think you could do it again?" I pull Rayleen closer at his words. He laughs and shuts the door.

People spring forth in an effort to help Rayleen and me up. "Thank you," I tell them.

The stench hits me like a brick wall. The filth of people caged in a hotel room for a long time toxifies the air. I cough.

The light from the window filters in around all the people's bodies. Those closest to me smell of body odour a few weeks old. A few people in here are outfitted in hotel attire. They must've been working here when they were attacked and captured. That also means that they have been here since this all started.

Very few people have any winter gear on. The room is cold, much colder than the rest of the hotel areas I've been in, and these people's clothes are not suited for the outside. The only thing keeping the temperature up must be the number of people in here and the insulation.

To get rid of the smell wouldn't be worth trying to open the window and letting cold air in.

Maniacal laughter cuts through the room like a hot spoon through ice cream. "I knew they wouldn't let us go free." She cries.

"You don't know that." A man exclaims.

"I do. You heard him. They made it through the forest. Now they're back here again." She explains. The woman is wearing a hotel uniform. Her hair is wrapped up in a falling-out bun.

"We don't know what happened." He looks to me in hope and desperation. "Please tell us why you're back here. Did they keep their word?"

"I wasn't. I." I take a deep breath in and out. "Rayleen was here. I rescued her and we made it through the forest with a big group of people. We made it back to town. We didn't leave town." I trail off. They can get the idea without knowing that I came here on purpose.

"So, you're stupid." The lady laughs again.

I don't need the reminder. My heart acted, my brain had a dumb plan, and it put Rayleen in danger again.

How could I be so stupid?

How could I think that this would work? How could I think that we could just walk in and everything would be alright? I should've asked Kelly to change me instead.

Jaiden ruined my chance to be with Darius; gave Sandra a chance to corrupt him. Jaiden screwed everything up. If she hadn't interrupted us then Darius would have taken us to be with him that night. Everything would be alright. Sandra wouldn't have gotten her claws in him again. Jaiden gave Sandra time to convince him that he could be shared.

She's the reason why we're here now, and not with Darius.

"Jane." A man says sternly. He turns to me. "If you made it through once, you know where to go. You know what's waiting for us. You can tell us so we can all get through it together."

A little hope fills my chest. "Okay."

"Well?" Jane asks expectantly.

I guess I'm supposed to tell them what I've seen now. "It's the forest. The demons hunt you down while you have to watch out for traps."

"What kind of traps?" She asks abruptly.

"Everything, like death pits and bear traps. They had a giant demon in there that had Rayleen hanging from a post."

The man writes something down on a notepad.

He walks with purpose to the wall and knocks on it three times. Without hesitation three thumps sound against the wall on the other side.

He moves the picture to reveal a hole and a shaded hand. He hands the note through then puts the picture back on the wall.

Each room is meant to section off prisoners but they've found a way to get around that.

The room goes quiet and people move off to huddle in groups.

It's clear that there isn't much to do but wait for the moment the demons come to grab us.

So, we wait.

Chapter 17

"Are you okay? You've been really quiet all morning." Jaiden's been too quiet for the whole morning; more than usual. She's been in her head; anxious about something. I pull her aside to talk with her. We stop in the living room.

She bites her bottom lip at the corner and inhales deeply. Air rushes out in a quick exhale. "I don't want to do this."

"Do what?" I ask quickly.

Jaiden looks up at the ceiling, and then focuses back on me. "I'm not a fighter."

I scrunch my eyebrows in confusion. How can she say that? "You already did when you rescued me. And, what about the farm?"

She points to make her point. "I didn't have to physically fight anyone and that was about rescuing people."

"And, this time we're rescuing Alexa and Rayleen." I remind her.

"And, if Alexa doesn't want to be rescued?"

"Then we rescue Rayleen." The regret strikes me. I should have gone after Alexa. She's an adult and can make her own decisions, but it doesn't mean she should be imposing them on the little girl.

Rayleen looked so frightened as they were leaving. I know the nightmare we faced while captive, so I know that there is no way she would want to willingly return to that. She was terrified, but I let her go because Alexa is her guardian.

It was a terrible mistake.

I know if I go get her, Rayleen will come back with me; probably. The only wild card is her love for Alexa.

"And, if Rayleen doesn't want to leave Alexa no matter how frightened she is?" Jaiden picks up on this problem too.

"Then, we figure it out then." I shrug.

"It's not a rescue mission. You know very well that Alexa chose to go. We'd be pulling her out kicking and screaming. This is revenge. You and everyone from Banff, are going so you can kill everyone there for the wrongs done to you." Jaiden surmises. "Secondary to that, getting rid of them lets us stay here. But, we could very well just go somewhere else. It would be easier, safer."

"You've already killed people so what's the problem?" I point out.

Jaiden is taken aback. She shakes her head. "That's not the point and that was a rescue mission that turned into self-defence. And, those people senselessly killed innocent people, not used them for food. They shot at us first. I also shot them from a gun from a high vantage point. I didn't have to do any fighting. I didn't even know I had killed anyone until I was told later that night because I wasn't meaning to kill people; just distract so they wouldn't kill anyone." She takes a deep breath, I assume, to calm herself. With her tone, I wouldn't even know she was upset, but the deep breath gives her away. "I didn't want this to turn into an argument. I just don't understand why we have to do it this way. There has to be another way of doing this."

"Everything's going to turn into a fight Jaiden. You're smart, so I know you can't be this naïve." I reply sharply.

Her mouth pulls straight. "I'm not naïve. I'm just looking at this from a different angle. You all are like 'all the evil demons must die, so we can take back our lives and homes.' You are all so blinded by that one way of thinking that none of you are taking a moment to look at this from their point of view or thinking about whether or not we should attack."

"I know their point of view. They want to take over the world, and they're succeeding." They're the revolution.

"Some of them, yeah. Some of them want to take over the world and use humans for food. But, this was also a revolution led by people who declared that if a supernatural being didn't join them then they'd be killed too. There are bound to be lots of supernaturals in that building who are there because of that. People will abandon the cause in a heartbeat if we convince them that we stand for something better and can win. People could get caught in the crossfire. I just don't see why we can't talk to these people first, and ask them to turn sides. Instead of killing first, ask questions later. Not everyone is evil."

She doesn't get it. Jaiden's living in a whole other happy sunshine world. She hasn't seen the evil these people can do. That those people who go with the status quo are just as culpable. "Because they'd kill us first. They made their choice and they don't get to take it back."

"They did what they had to do to survive-"

I cut her off. "And so are we. We have to fight to survive. Why don't you just stay here if you are so against it?"

She tilts her head. "That's not really an option, is it?"

"No. Jaiden. You're going to have to fight at some point." I burst the bubble on her perfect little world.

"I know, and I'm perfectly fine killing people that deserve it; if I need to. I'm prepared for that. I've done that, and I felt nothing for it. But, I hate senseless fighting. I won't kill senselessly." She puts both her hands in front of her. "Storming a place with, who knows how many people are in there, with fifty people isn't the way to go. We're going to die if we just go in with nothing but a plan to fight to the death."

"Then we'll take some of them out with us. Jaiden these are bad people." I raise my voice to make my point dig in.

She takes a deep breath in and lets it out. It's the only sign I can see of her losing her cool once again. I almost wish she'd yell at me. Each time I raise my voice, she brings it right back down with her calm voice. "We don't have to fight. Not all of them are bad. Some would change sides if we gave them the chance."

A name comes to mind; Shale. "One person helped you out. You can't guarantee anything else. You can't just not fight because one person helped you; probably because he was scared you were going to kill him."

"He wasn't scared of me." Jaiden motions to herself. "Look at me and tell me seriously who would be scared of me? It's a revolution. Not all people who do bad things in a revolution are bad people. They had no choice or felt they had no other options. Just like you think we have no choice now, but we do. Violence isn't always the only answer."

"I don't want violence to be the answer. But there isn't a way around it." Her words make her sound deluded. "So, what do you want to offer Darius a chance at changing sides?"

"No, Darius, I'll kill him myself. Sandra, I'll kill Sandra too. They're both evil and need to die. They aren't redeemable. But, not everyone is like that. They made their choice under duress."

"So what are you saying?" I shout at her. Her speech is confusing to me, and I don't understand what exactly her point is. We're going in circles.

She hates fighting, but is willing to kill people; she already has killed people and feels nothing. She's willing to fight, but she doesn't want to fight. She won't stay behind because that's not a real option. She wants to find another way, when there isn't another way.

It occurs to me that she might not know where she's going with this. I asked her to talk, and maybe she hadn't worked it out herself.

"I don't know anymore. I just." A deep breath in and out. "I think you going in and killing everyone indiscriminately is wrong. I think you going in to kill for revenge is wrong and not something that you'll come back from."

How did this become about me? "I'm tougher than I look. I know how to fight."

"Have you killed anyone? Demon or human?"

I answer immediately, "No."

"What would you do if you accidentally killed an innocent person?" Her question throws me off.

"I won't." I insist.

"There are a lot of innocent prisoners in the hotel. What if you did? What if you accidentally killed some of them? It would ruin you."

"There's no way I'd kill them."

"Dominique." My name is screamed from her lips, in a way only Jaiden could achieve by very slightly raising her voice and hardening her tone. "You won't come back from this the same person. Your actions are going to kill you inside. It'll ruin you."

"You keep saying that! I'll be fine! I'm not going to kill any humans. We have to do this!" I yell.

"Is everything okay in here?" Miles comes rushing in.

"Yes, it's fine. We're just disagreeing on how to attack." I tell him.

"It sounded more like Jaiden was suggesting we try to get some people to switch sides." He must've been listening in on our conversation. More people follow in after him. We should've had this conversation in a more secluded place than an empty living room. "We could talk to some who are already questioning leadership, and the methods of the revolution. And some, like she was saying, may just be there because they are scared. We could get some to turn sides before we kill them all."

Every second our audience gets bigger and bigger. More people to put their input in; Derek goes next. "But, it's not something you could guarantee. We need to go in guns blazing. That was the plan and it's staying the plan."

Different people start talking at once.

"We do that and we are as bad as they are." Uncle Bruce steps up. His loud voice drowns out all others. "Jaiden is right. We need to think more diplomatically. We offer them a peaceful surrender. Whoever wants to switch sides, can do so without repercussion. If they don't and they attack then we shoot back."

Maybe they do have a bit of a point. It doesn't take much to make a quick offer if they don't attack us.

"Why should we do that?" A man asks.

"Because not everyone is evil." I echo part of Jaiden's speech. I look over at her but she's looking off at the floor. I thought she might be happy about that, but I guess not.

"It's what makes us human. We need to remember that. To be human is to show mercy; to forgive. We will fight for our home and we will succeed. We will kill out of necessity not for the sake of killing; not for sport. We are more civilized than that.

We will go up to the hotel. We will request their surrender. We will fight if need be, and they will know that they should have never come here.

If you don't agree you are welcome to leave. You all have work to do, you should get to it. Be ready to leave in two hours." Uncle Bruce's word becomes law immediately.

People clear the room quickly. Jaiden has disappeared with them.

"Nikki?" Uncle Bruce's voice calls me back to him. "Don't be too upset at Jaiden. It sounded like half her point was that she's worried for you."

How many people heard our conversation?

"Then why didn't she just say that?" I ask not looking for an answer. I don't think he gets it. He wasn't there.

"She did. Just in a few more words. She was telling you that she is worried about you and what could happen to you; she may not have said the words, but it's what she meant." He comes in closer and lowers his voice to almost a whisper. "She's exactly like your aunt. Sometimes they can't say exactly what they mean. It's either your job to figure it out before something bad happens, or you need to let her do whatever it is that she needs to do."

He walks away after dousing me in imaginary ice water.

Realization hits me. Jaiden must've had a vision. Uncle Bruce knows Jaiden can see the future, and Auntie was a prophet too. And, Uncle Bruce knew. It's the only explanation that fits.

I have to find Jaiden.

I charge out to the back to find her. It's easier and faster than I thought it would be. I find her in no time at all in the kitchen with a bowl of stew.

It's like she didn't even try to hide.

"I get it now," I tell her. "Just do what you need to do, and let me know what I need to do."

After her initial confusion, she smiles a bit more, then returns to her regular smile. "Breakfast is ready; backyard. Get in line before it's gone."

"I'm sorry that I-."

She waves me off. "Don't worry about it."

"Thank you."

I grab lunch and return to eat it beside her. She's been joined by quite a few people since I left.

"Alcohol thins your blood. It makes it so that you clot less. So, not only will you bleed more if cut, but you also get cold faster. Which I'd like to avoid when planning to go out to battle in a cold winter." She explains to Brad. His arrogant grin is wiped from his face as he lowers his beer.

"What was that?" I ask Jaiden. Brad better not be starting anything with her again.

"I was explaining to Brad my decision to abstain from drinking alcohol so I won't bleed out or get hypothermia as easily." I start watching Brad halfway through her talking. He doesn't look too happy. He has a dulled look in his eyes that makes me question how many drinks he's already had this morning. What the Hell is going on with him?

If Jaiden is right, and she always is, I don't feel like finding out how fast I'd bleed out or get hypothermia.

Chapter 18

The memory of my vision haunts my waking thoughts as we walk to a certain doom. We win, I can assume that much, but Dominique loses herself.

She killed people; human innocent people. The supernatural beings let the humans out of their rooms and Dominique killed them; accidentally.

I tried talking with her, to get her to abandon the fight, but she's stubborn and determined. That means the fight should happen more or less as planned.

Dominique is still going to kill those innocent people because they will still let the humans loose. She has a high-powered gun, with a jimmy-rigged bullet slot to allow for more bullets than normal. The gun will shoot them in quick succession. She will kill the maximum amount of people.

I trail behind Dominique; vowing to stick with her the whole battle to prevent her from making any life-changing mistakes. I'll protect her from one possible outcome.

I think she'll let me too. She had a weird thing after the meeting, where she told me to do whatever I had to do.

I don't know what I was supposed to do originally as I have no vision, that I know of, about what is going to happen. My only clue to the battle is a vision of Dominique breaking down in the train room.

But no matter what, this time, I will follow her to make sure she doesn't kill people. Or, at least, not anyone innocent. Though, I don't think she'll be able to handle killing anyone at all. Self-defence might be easier for her to handle and reason away.

I doubt I would've had any huge impact originally. I likely would have stayed with Dominique anyway. I don't imagine I would do anything that would decide the course of battle.

A chill runs through me. I opted for sweaters and jeans rather than my winter jacket and snow pants. I need stealth and mobility that the thick crinkly material won't allow for.

My face is chilling, and my nose is running. I wipe the drips on my sleeve cuff. Uncovered ears are the coldest part of me, and I know I'll have an earache later if I don't get out of this cold.

A lone figure walks down the hill. He sees us after we see him; after some people already have their guns trained on him. He stops in his imprint in the snow. Staring at us for a couple moments until he ascertains our purpose, then takes off towards the trees. He runs towards town.

He's running to save his own hide.

The people in the hotel will not get any warning from him.

Our guns are brought down, and our pace is picked up. I'm glad about the win. Our people didn't shoot needlessly.

With the entrance in view, I spot people gathering in the drop-off zone. They come from everywhere; the hotel, the forest, and further up the road.

People start moving about, commanded by a tall male with his back facing us. They go back into the hotel, and out to the forest.

Darius turns around to look at the army approaching. He walks to the entrance.

I get the idea that they knew we were on our way.

I'm thrust sideways out of pure instinctual reaction to a series of loud pops deafening my right ear. It's the unmistakable bang of a gun. It's louder than I thought it would be.

I crouch as more people join in shooting at the people escaping. Some are hit and go down; presumably dead.

Bruce yells at them. "Stop! You fucking idiots!" I make out between the bangs and fill in the blanks. "If you're going to be trigger-happy you can leave!"

I stand up when Dominique walks forward. We approach the vacated area. A few people lay dead where they were shot.

People shout at the back of our pack. I turn to the troll swinging a large branch and striking three people simultaneously. Their bodies are knocked back a few feet.

Bullets riddle his body and face when people gather their wits after the surprise attack.

I look to my left where Dominique should be, but I find someone else. I jerk my head around searching for her, to see the tail end of her going inside the hotel.

Sprinting after her, I open the door and greet the darkness. There's no time to adjust to the dark properly. They've made it darker in here; on purpose I suspect.

I grasp the flashlight in my pocket. The new light gives me something to see. I scan with the light. A person is only a couple of feet away from me.

I yelp and jump in surprise. Then, quickly realize it's Dominique.

"What?" Dominique tenses with worry. She spins to look around for potential danger.

"I didn't realize you were right there," I say holding my thumping heart.

"I forgot a flashlight. I couldn't see much to go anywhere until my eyes adjusted. Come on. Let's go this way." She points and starts walking. I light the way.

"Where are we going?" I ask her. There is a distinct lack of people inside.

There is a distinctive difference in our actions that I notice. Dominique is on edge. Her gun is raised and she is prepared for an attack. My gun is lowered in one hand and safety is on, and my flashlight is prone in my other.

If someone attacked, I would be useless immediately.

"The conference room Darius and Sandra used as their base of operations." I make a noncommittal noise. "What's wrong?" She asks me.

"Nothing," I tell her.

"Are you sure?"

"They knew we were coming." I leave it at that, and so does she. There are many implications from that sentence alone. The main point is that Sandra and Darius likely aren't here. Taylor might not be the spy.

We walk around empty corridors until we make it to a set of large wooden doors.

Dominque opens the one and slips inside. I catch the door with my foot and open it so that I can get through. I watch as she searches the room. There is plenty of light inside due to a wall full of windows. It's cold in here; almost as cold as outside. The reason being, a busted window letting the cold air into the room.

It looks like a battle occurred in this room. The furniture is destroyed and thrown around.

"No one's here." She says.

My search concludes the same. I can see why they wouldn't be in here with the temperature.

"They're probably outside," I suggest.

"I saw Darius come inside the hotel. He has to be here." She determines.

"It's a big place. We went one way. He could have gone another and went right out to a dragon." I reason.

"Then we go back and look for him." Dominique snips back.

"It's a huge hotel with many exits. And, he's a vampire. He could make his own exit out a second-floor window for all we know. I'm just saying maybe we should focus on freeing people, and search for Darius and Sandra along the way."

She hesitates to agree with me. Her own objective is getting in the way. "Okay. I'll show you where I saw the prisoners come from."

"Perfect."

She takes me back right near the entrance to a set of stairs. I give her an unnoticed eyebrow raise, and a sassy thought out 'really?' Her lead took us completely out of our way.

Though, it may have uncovered a different problem. "Was this place always so empty?" I ask because no one is here. Absolutely no one. She had said there were lots of people. Maybe, they stuck to other areas of the hotel.

"No. There were a lot of people here. Or, I thought there was. People were always at the entrance. Filled it up okay. And, guards were covering some rooms. I thought the whole hotel might be the same."

Her assumption would mean there had to be at least a couple hundred people here. "Okay, so assuming there are supposed to be a lot of people here, where are they? Because a hundred people weren't outside when we got here."

"Good question." Meaning she doesn't know either. "Hiding in rooms?" Or, were there not many people here?

I look out a stairwell window to see supernaturals fighting against gun-armed people. Many bodies litter the ground.

Listening carefully I can hear the guns popping.

That might account for some of the people. There is a large crowd out there, but half look like they belong to us.

Maybe those that escaped to the trees came back. Maybe the rest abandoned the cause as soon as they found out. Maybe some are hiding in rooms until we leave.

Dominique moves into a stance that braces herself. Her gun sits in position against her shoulder. I breach the stairwell and see a group of shadowed people running toward us.

"Surrender or I'll shoot!" She yells at the crowd approaching.

I recognize the situation for what it is before she does; if only because I know something is supposed to happen.

Up goes the flashlight. I am looking for frightened looks. For the people looking behind them to make sure a captor is not about to detain them once more. I am looking for human features or rather inhuman features. I can't distinguish anything in the brief look.

I don't have time.

"Don't shoot!" I plead to her to hear me before the unthinkable happens.

In case she doesn't, I stretch my hand up and barely push her hand so the gun points off to the wall.

The recoil jolts to my hand multiple times before everything else registers. The bangs echo in the hall and contains the noise to the smaller area making it sound all the louder.

I pick up a forgotten flashlight and gun, dropped on either side of where I was.

In a swift move, I shine it down the hall. Dust fills the beams from the broken drywall. The left wall has holes in a distinct line. I can see where each bullet hit.

The people get up from the floor. Little cries muffle as they hug into adults. No one has visible supernatural features. These have to be the prisoners.

"Jaiden!" I saved her from killing the people, but I wasn't fast enough to save her from the possibility.

Hopefully, this is enough to save her from being permanently broken.

"They were the prisoners!" I shout.

Her voice drops. "I was going to kill them. They weren't stopping. I thought-"

I open my mouth but nothing comes out. It takes a moment to find any words to comfort her. "But you didn't. They're alive."

I look over to the hall. People are crouched down and quivering from their fright of a near-death experience.

"We're here to rescue you. The exit is this way." I extend my voice so they all can hear.

Dominique doesn't look like she's about to move anywhere. Her hands shake the gun. She's in shock. I pull the gun from her grasp. A few people have made their way over to us.

The ones who haven't sprinted by in their excitement for the exit, stop for further instruction. "Please help her outside. All prisoners need to make their way out of the hotel and back to town. Go to Buffalo Street."

I juggle the guns in each hand. Both are useless to me right now. I can't hold the safety on either with both hands full.

I hand Dominique's gun to the closest person with no idea if they know how to use it. No idea if they'll use it wisely, but it might be better than leaving it here.

We go down the stairs and the short lobby space to the entrance. There is not one soul in the grand room.

The bright light and the cold air hit at the same time.

I almost go with the group. I almost decide to abandon everyone here to help them escape. To get Dominique safely away from what could have been, and maybe that was what I was originally supposed to do, but I can't.

Other people here need me more. There must be more prisoners. I'm drawn to choosing to stay.

I stand guard as the rescued prisoners make their escape.

Gunshots echo all around me. I can't help but feel like this is wrong.

There have to be more prisoners inside, there has to be some supernaturals hiding from the fight inside; someone who let the prisoners free.

I go back inside the hotel, back up to the second floor where we were going. I run into more people and direct them to town.

Some doors are already open along my way around the halls and up more stairs.

An unthinkable stench fills the air and practically suffocates me. My overworking lungs need the air so holding my breath isn't an option. Through the nose, I can smell it, but worse is through the mouth where I can taste the rot. Clamping my jaw tightly, I opt for the unpleasant smell.

The people stop passing me by. I don't dare holler and alert the wrong person to my whereabouts.

Then I spot him; the one I assume was opening the doors.

"Shale." I greet him when I recognize him.

He is startled by my arrival. "You should go before I have to kill you."

"Right." I breathe deeply trying to catch my breath. "You'd of done it by now if you were going to." I gasp for air again.

"Why are you here?"

"Directing people you're setting free," I explain.

"I'm not-"

I interrupt him. "You have been."

"The doors are unlocked. The prisoners can leave whenever they want." His words make me realize the people were only locked in the rooms by their fear of what was lurking in the halls. I should have been yelling all along.

People could have been in rooms I passed.

Shale's actions speak to his loyalties, and his compassion. Everything I've seen has led me to a couple of assumptions. I believe Shale is James' spy. I believe Shale was the person who helped Dominique realize she had to act like a prophet.

I hope I'm not wrong or I might be dead.

I could use a spy, especially with the track record of Darius' involvement with our group, and Alexa. But, to reveal him in this place might be leading him to death. To let him know I know in such a way that doesn't reveal what he's been up to will be difficult.

If I'm even correct at all.

Though my breath is a bit more even I still take a deep breath in necessity. "James left because he has work to do with the council. Thought you should know. I understand you still have work to do, but I'll offer anyway. Do you want to come back with us? Miles and Kelly would appreciate it I'm sure."

I leave out my thoughts about our group gathering as a mere convenience for James and his needs. We lost our usefulness and no longer served a purpose, so he left. We are likely not going to see him again, and are no longer associated with him. But, the name-dropping I can use for my own purpose. Especially, with my suspected spy, or possible ally.

His bewilderment is either because he has no idea what is going on, or he is confused as to how I know. "You're right; I still have work to do."

"You should go then before I shoot you." I joke.

He calls me on it like I did to him a few short seconds ago. "You wouldn't shoot me."

"I don't know; I might," I smirk.

He stops for a moment, then lets me go.

He runs quickly into an open room, and back out only a couple of seconds later. He writes something on the piece of paper against the wall. "You're running out of time. You should go before I decide to kill you." When he finishes, he hands me the note.

The note is hastily written. Scrawled in flowing messy letters spells a daunting message barely legible.

Evacuate

Sandra blowing building up

He's gone when I look up. I start to panic. At any moment this building will come down on top of me; on top of everyone still inside.

I don't know how much time I have. I can't dawdle.

But, there are still people to rescue.

I elect to escape while also rescuing as many people as I can.

"EVACUATE! EVERYONE OUT! THE DOORS ARE OPEN!" I yell out louder than I've ever done before.

In the immediate area, I pull open doors. Only two reveal people. I repeat the message. "Evacuate now! Everyone needs to leave now!" A hoard of people lurches by. "HELP AS MANY AS YOU CAN TO ESCAPE! DOORS ARE UNLOCKED!" I shout to them. "THE BUILDING IS GOING TO EXPLODE!"

I'm in full panic mode. Nothing is ever so clearer and so muddied. It's clear what needs to be done, but at what risk to my life do I stay here longer than a moment; when each moment is an invisible ticking time bomb ready to blow?

The lack of people inside now makes complete sense. Why stay in a building when you know it's coming down?

Flight kicks in at that moment and I am gone in the opposite direction from the rest. I know there is an exit this way, and I know there could be more people this way.

Each door I come to I open and yell, "RUN!" It doesn't take much for people to leave their rooms once the doors open.

At the commotion, others start leaving their rooms on their own. Some are supernaturals and many appear human.

Why would the supernaturals stay if they knew the building was going to explode?

They wouldn't.

Sandra didn't tell everyone. That's why Shale wrote it. He couldn't be heard warning me.

The ground shakes.

It unsteadies my feet enough for me to notice something is wrong. The crashing tear of a building coming down on top of us deafens me to everything else but my heartbeat in my ears.

My words catch in my throat. I'm mute as the realization sets in that the building is coming down right now. There is no more time. No stairs in sight, and I'm running at breakneck speed to who knows where.

The thought of an exit brings to mind a desperate thought; to get to the nearest window.

I duck inside a room to find it empty.

The window's bright light is my beacon. Grabbing onto it, I open it as much as it goes which is only a quarter of the way and look down. I am higher than I'd like to risk jumping; for surely I'd die.

The second-floor window is something much higher than a

normal second-floor; as such I think I might not be on the equivalent of a second-floor height.

In my peripheral I see stone. There is a walkway between the two buildings that is only a couple of rooms over and one floor down, but the top is perfectly lined for this floor.

I backtrack a couple of rooms and enter. With no room for error, I pick the right room on the first try with a bit of luck and reasoning.

This window doesn't open, but the coffee table fixes that as I smash it through the delicate material.

My hand steadies my jump through the jagged opening. I land briefly on my right leg, but it gives out, and I stumble to all fours. Moving all appendages I push my hands up and sprint over to the roof adjoining.

As I reach the wall of the tower a force pushes me forward. Grey-brown dust clouds my vision. I close my burning eyes. I stop breathing so I don't breathe it in; only a temporary fix until I will be forced to breathe.

I make myself as small as I can by drawing myself into a lopsided ball. My arms wrap up around my head to protect it from a crumbling building.

The only good sign I have is that I don't seem to be falling. The ground beneath me quakes, and I'm certain that my stomach will float to my throat at any moment.

Being squashed to death would be a quick death at least.

Spasms emit from my chest when my lungs need air. I tuck my mouth into the sweater. Heaving a large breath in feels good. The air filters well enough through the cloth that I don't breathe in anything large, but the earthy dust still makes its way to my taste buds.

I have enough time to worry about the long-term effects this will have on my lungs.

I'll probably get sick and cough up dust gunk. Cancer or something equally as deadly could be an issue. I don't know the building's construction materials, but I don't imagine any of it is particularly healthy to breathe.

I have enough time to complain.

Come on, my visions couldn't have warned me about this? Out of everything that I see, this had to be something I didn't see. I can have a vision of nails being painted in the spring or a meaningless conversation over tea, but I don't see a huge building coming down on top of me.

Though, I suppose that one could be my fault. I changed things. I might've been down the mountain when this building came down.

I only have myself to blame when I don't follow the set-out timeline.

The noise settles from the building. It's too quiet. I don't know if my ears gave out or if everyone and everything is dead quiet.

I know that dust can take a little bit to settle, so I wait as long as I figure it will be to make it safe.

Peeking through my eyelids hurts. I know I have dust in them. They water to clear themselves. I don't dare rub them and possibly cause any further damage.

I'm happy for my glasses as I'm sure they blocked a lot of the dust. I remove the glasses for a good cleaning.

Slowly the world clears, and I can see that the air is relatively clear. I put my glasses back on when clean. They reveal a dust-laden sky, which makes me still weary of breathing without a filter.

My clothes are grey with dust. I'm certain all of me is just one large grey dust ball.

Three-quarters of the bridge I just passed over a minute ago is now rubble on the pavement below. I hug myself closer to the wall as if I'd fall over the edge if I didn't.

Beyond that, is nothing but a large pile of furniture, and stone. The hotel is completely levelled. Nothing could've survived inside the building.

All the people I worked to free are likely dead. I was almost taken out with them.

This is what I get for changing the future. Now I'm stuck up here, and no one is going to come for me. They'll assume that everyone inside is dead; that I'm dead.

In my rush, I didn't figure into my escape how I'd get down from here. The bridge was still a couple of stories up and I'm on the roof of another building. The tower I cling to has windows, but they'd drop into the tunnel, and that's a large drop; not as big as dropping to the ground.

I can't stay here.

I pull myself up onto the ledge of the tower roof. It is large enough that I shimmy myself over to the opposite corner where a ceiling greets me within dropping distance. A path clearly defines itself.

One drop-down at a time, I can make my way down to the ground. I sit myself down on the ledge and jump down one level. It's about as tall as I am. The next step down is taller. I go down on my stomach lowering myself on the ledge with my arms before I fall the rest of the way to the ground.

Above all else, there is a persistent sting in my right leg. I still have a ways to go. I look at the area that hurts and don't see anything major. A rip in my pants and there is a fair amount of blood. Nothing I'll need to worry about right now. It's not broken.

The path leads to stairs that take me to the ground. I limp down using the railing for help as my leg hurts with the aggravation.

I can clearly hear each noise I make down to the steps in the snow. There is truly no other noise to be heard. Walking around the front of the building reveals many people gawking at the demolished building. Everyone is too shocked to move. I painfully stumble over to the nearest person; my leg throbs and screams.

I know they are a supernatural being by the purple skin spots beneath the dust and yellow eyes. His hands only have three fingers each.

"We're asking for a truce. Supernaturals can either live in Banff in peace alongside the humans, or they can leave. There's been enough death on both sides for a lifetime." I wait a moment before they blink and turn to acknowledge me.

"You really think we could live with each other." He says in a gruff voice.

I nod. "I've been sharing a house with a vampire, two elves, a succubus, and James the Representative of the Magic Folk in the Council; many other supernaturals too. I'm friends with many more supernaturals. You don't have to hide. We can live side by side if everyone is willing to work at it. I'm human and I don't care what anyone is as long as you're generally a good person. A lot of people feel this way. Some don't but they'll get there. It's not too late."

He stares at me for a moment. I drop my smile when he turns away from me. "Sota! Get over here." A humanoid-appearing supernatural being jogs over to us. "Fight's over. Tell everyone to help the humans back to town and find anyone alive in the wreckage."

"No one could've survived that," Sota says realistically.

"There's always a chance."

Sota nods and walks over to the next person. It creates a chain reaction and soon everyone is moving. No one has the mind to fight after such a cataclysmic event.

Those with their minds somewhat intact help to lead those

without away from the rubble hill.

With my mind set on the hill, I walk towards it. As if part of my imagination, I hear a faint screaming in the back of my mind.

I stop and turn. Hearing the screaming toward the rubble. I step closer.

"Hey, where are you going?" He asks after me.

"Do you hear that?" I nearly whisper.

"Hear what?" He goes silent for a moment. "I don't hear anything."

"I think I heard someone." The screaming doesn't get any louder until I reach the mountain and start climbing.

"Would you get back here? Don't climb that." He stops protesting. "Is that someone screaming?" Pieces of rock fall behind me in places I've finished climbing as a sign of his following after me.

The noise is hard to pinpoint. As I start leaning more towards the right the screaming increases slightly from that direction. I crawl my way back to the bottom and stand up.

It's clear enough that I assume the screaming is coming from a girl.

Slow and steady scanning brings me over to where the walkway had collapsed. Her screams gradually get louder and louder. She begs for help.

"Hello? Where are you? We're here to help." I yell loudly. It is enough that the screams subside for a moment. "Hello?"

"Oh God. I'm here! I'm here! Please help me. I'm trapped." There is desperation in her voice that riles my heartbeat.

The voice seems to be coming from nowhere and everywhere. "I can't see you. Can you see anything? Do you know where you are?"

"I can see a little crack of light. I'm in the bridge. I was in the bridge."

Both me and the other guy speed up as she gives us a bit of an idea. "Keep talking. Are you okay? Are you injured?"

"I don't know. I can't see. I can't move much."

She talks long enough for me to make it down to the ground where her voice seems to be coming from. I stand near where the walkway was held.

The walls gave away, but there is a portion of the roof that stayed intact lying against the pile. Her voice sounds like it's coming from right behind.

"Adelmira?" The purple male's voice asks in recognition.

"Ethan? Is that you?" She responds.

"Of course, you'd have a building fall on you and survive." He jokes about the dire situation to lighten the mood.

"Shut up and get me out of here." Her voice comes out from a crack between the roof and the debris. I move a small piece of wood that doesn't look like it stabilizes anything. "The light; it got bigger!" She cries excitedly.

I back away to talk with Ethan. "Are you able to move that ceiling piece?"

"No. It looks too heavy. I'm going to get strong help." He sprints out toward the front of the hotel.

After a moment of silence, her voice comes through the hole. "Are you there?"

"Adelmira was it?" I ask.

"Yes." She confirms.

"Ethan just went to get help. We can't move the large piece on top of you." I explain.

"Oh okay." She dismays. "Who are you?"

It occurs that she wants a conversation to help keep her mind at ease. "I'm Jaiden. Hi."

"Hi." Her voice wavers slightly.

The gap in conversation worries me as much as her wavering voice. I need her to talk again so I know she's alright. "So, what brings you here?" The words sound lame as they come out of my mouth. I wish to take them back and ask something else, but it was the first thing to come to mind. I suck at conversation.

Hard laughter comes out of the crack. Well, I'm glad she found that so amusing. At least it's an indication that she's alive.

"You know; the usual. I wanted to hike the mountains, do some shopping, see the sights; the usual."

"See any deer around?" I ask.

"A few, but I've seen a lot of cougars."

The chit-chat ends when I see Ethan and four others coming. "Ethan's back. He's brought help." I advise.

He approaches quickly. "Move back." He guides me away from the others and the building slab.

Before I'm turned back around the five of them have the slab up straight. They let it fall the other way. The resounding thud makes me cringe.

Revealed in the tiny space is a huddled person laying on the ground of what was the walkway. I go over to help her up. Holding my hand out for her to grasp I help her onto her feet. Tensing in preparation for her to fall over if she's been wounded, but she doesn't. From head to toe, she's covered in a cloud of grey dust.

Instead, she steps forward and wraps her arms around me in a hug. I reciprocate as I'm sure she's grateful for being alive after her ordeal.

She lets go quickly. Adelmira rushes to Ethan and hugs him. "Thank you." She tells Ethan when she lets go of him.

I climb my way out of a little pit I had stepped into.

Humbly he shakes his head and points her to me. "She did it. I thought everyone in the hotel had to be dead. She went to look and heard your screaming."

With as much enthusiasm as she launched herself at Ethan Adelmira comes at me for another hug. "Thank you, Jaiden."

"You're welcome," I say.

"Is she okay? I smell a lot of blood." A male voice comments.

Adelmira and I break apart. I look her up and down. She quickly looks herself over while I look her over. "I don't see anything." Her hands go up to her head to search for blood she can't see.

"No, her." He points at me. Me? The pain in my leg.

"What? Are you hurt?" Adelmira uses as much scrutiny in searching for a wound on me as she did herself.

"My leg, probably. I think I cut it on glass from the window I jumped out of." I look down at my right leg. Right above the right side of my knee, where the cut in my pants is, and down there is a growing length of brown-red blood darkening my pants. "I'll need to bandage it when we get back to town."

"Back to town?" Adelmira asks confused.

"She's human. We've called a truce." Ethan tells her.

Her voice deadens in seriousness. "Where's Darius?"

"Gone, him and Sandra, as she was pulling down the building on top of you." One of the men exclaims. He's tall and muscly. His darker complexion peeks through spots without grey dust.

"Are they going to kill us?" I notice her rough gesture toward me.

"I don't think so." Ethan looks over to me for help.

An urge to defend myself rises as does the need to say something. "We're not taking prisoners. We're a mixed group of all sorts. We just, Darius and Sandra had kidnapped some of our own. We just wanted them back." I trail off because I feel like I'm going to start rambling.

"So, we should get the wounded back to town." Adelmira finally says as she breaks out with a smile. "Who wants to run Jaiden to where ever she needs to go?"

"I'm okay. Some other people need the help more than I do." I decline.

"Sweetie, I think you might be hurt more than you think." She points down. I can't help but look down at the growing dark spot she is referencing.

"I'll be fine." A deathly glare changes my answer. "Okay. I'll go."

The one who talked with Ethan earlier walks over to me. "Hi, I'm DeAngelo. May I?"

I nod to his question, though I'm not exactly sure what he's asking until his arms knock me over and he lifts me. My arms loop around his neck and clench his shoulder.

The position is a cross between uncomfortable and frightening. I stop myself from apologizing about how heavy I must be.

My wound knocks against his arm. I hold my breath in pain. There feels like something is grating inside the wound, but it could be the pressure held against it.

"Are you okay?" DeAngelo asks concerned.

"Her leg, you idiot." Adelmira scolds him. If she could reach I'm sure she would wave knock him upside his head.

DeAngelo quickly places me down to pick me up from the other side. "I'm sorry."

"It's okay," I say when I finally breathe again.

I reposition to latch on this side. When I finish shifting he asks, "are you ready?"

"Yes."

He sprints off down the mountain through the trees. The air bites against my wound and face. There is only so much I can do to rectify this. I turn my head towards his chest more to shield it.

The trip makes me queasy. My stomach doesn't approve of the quick jolty ride. But he runs a lot faster than I could limp.

A bunch of people are congregated over the bridge, dashing to make it to the hotel.

"We should talk to them," I mention to DeAngelo.

He sets his strides to meet up with them. DeAngelo places us right in front of the surging group. They stop.

"Jaiden!" Dominique races to me. "What happened? Are you okay?"

"Sandra pulled down the hotel. We called a truce. Everyone left are coming down or trying to help find people who might still be alive. This is DeAngelo. He was nice enough to bring me down. I had to jump through a broken window, and I cut my leg."

"Oh God, Jaiden! I need a doctor!" She screams to the crowd. "I shouldn't have left you. I'm so sorry. I-."

"It's fine. I told you to go and sent you with people. I'm okay. Really. It's just a cut. DeAngelo, you could put me down now. Thank you for helping me." I hope my standing upright will help ease her mind.

"You're welcome." He settles me on the ground.

"Jaiden, right? I'm Harold. You need first aid? Where are you injured?" My doubts soar with his introduction to his credibility of doctor qualifications; however, anyone could put a band-aid on.

"It's my leg. I cut it." I set my right leg in front of me at a vantage point visible to the doctor.

I lift away the edges of my ripped pant to reveal a two-inch-long gash. The form is perfectly straight with the edges pulled apart. Embedded in the red tissue is a clear shard of glass.

That doesn't look good. The edges of my sight close in.

Chapter 19

The room freezes the moment the ruckus starts.

Normally, muddied conversations leak into the room; one or two people talking at a time.

Sometimes, it's clearer. As though the person would be up against the door while they talked. Before, this was usually intentional conversations about what they would do to us. Or, what they had done to others. How they killed the other people.

Maybe screams could be heard while someone was being taken from another room.

This is different.

Large numbers of people pound the floors outside in small bursts. Like small stampedes in a horse race.

Everyone freezes when the door knob turns. Anxiously waiting for someone to come inside to take people to the forest.

And, we wait.

The door bursts open. It's a man in dirty clothes. "We're free. Run!"

Like a dam bursting, people surge to leave the room. With Rayleen in arms reach I pull her up to carry her. She latches to the front of me.

I follow the others, guided by their force down the hall. We are dragged with the ebb and flow of the escaping crowd. It feels dangerous. I don't have control of where I go. The only inkling of control being in running with the crowd.

BANG! BANG! BANG! BANG! BANG! BANG!

In quick succession, a gun shoots its bullets. The sound blowing all around me.

I duck with the people around me and scurry to a wall. Pressing Rayleen against the wall to shield her as I curl us down.

Someone wraps around us both; pressing the breath out of me.

The drywall dust tickles my nose and throat.

"We're here to rescue you! The exit is this way!" A strangely familiar female voice yells down the hall. She's not supposed to be here.

The gun shots. They were supposed to be the guards; the supernaturals keeping us here. Why would Jaiden's voice be coming from there.

The body against my back leaves.

It's time to go. I can't question this any longer. Not when it could risk our rescue.

With my ears still ringing I lurch backwards and bring us up. We start running with the rest of them.

Everyone bursts to escape at their own pace; mine faster than most.

I pass the two people with no care as to who they might be. Golden hair links with the voice to tell me Jaiden is that one. Is she the one who shot at us? Or, was it the other one?

Did Jaiden save us from a guard shooting at us?

I take Rayleen down the stairs and to the lobby door. As we break free, we fall into another mess.

In blinding light, I can still make out people with guns are shooting at all sorts of demons. Blood dyes the snow around all the dead and wounded.

"Close your eyes," I tell Rayleen. I don't know if she does as I say but she squeezes me tighter. I hope her eyes were already closed from the blinding sun.

Just now, I notice her cries.

I run with a group to the road down the mountain. We run until we can't run anymore. My lungs hurt from the effort and the cold.

A chill freezes me. I am not dressed for this sort of cold.

I set Rayleen down when I get too exhausted to continue to carry her; she complains but follows. People pass us in their rush to put as much distance between them and the hotel.

At the bottom of the mountain, we reach the bridge. People are ahead on the main street reuniting with loved ones, and receiving the help they need. Generally, celebrating their safety.

A crumbling rumble echoes in the air. People ahead gaze with mouths open at the mountain.

I look back to see the hotel shrinking into the mountain and trees. A cloud of dust replaces it.

Did the hotel just come down?

Did they blow up the hotel?

I stare in awe and confusion at the empty air where the hotel just was. A cloud of dust spread up and out until it disappears.

We would have been crushed if we hadn't been set free.

Some people rush by me. They run up the road and toward the hotel. After getting away, I have no desire to return. Whatever happened and happens up there, I have no business in.

Rayleen and I are safe down here and that is what matters.

I walk Rayleen and me to a smaller grouping on the other side of the bridge. Walking passed people frozen like statues.

We are overlooked by the couple going around to medically look over the injured. We don't look near as bad as any of them.

We hover in limbo unsure where to go. In one thought, I think of going to the house. In another, I think I should stay here.

We are handed a couple of items here and there; water, food, and a blanket.

"Jaiden!" A scream rips through the air.

I look in the direction of the scream. Nikki runs like a bullet towards Jaiden in the arms of someone. She must be seriously injured.

It's then that I decide to return to the house. Rayleen doesn't need to see the injured coming down the mountain.

A few people are returning that way so I tag along with them.

We return to the house where warmth greats us. Heat after what feels like so long without is everything. Despite the burns I'd receive, I could just go up to the wood stove and hug it. It might be worth it.

I settle for depositing Rayleen and myself in front of it until our bones thaw.

People stomp in their rush through the door.

The doctor, Nikki, a black man, and a knocked-out Jaiden rush in.

"Put her on the table. I need blankets. She needs to be warmed. I need someone to hold her leg while I get the glass out." He gives his instructions.

To protect Rayleen, I pull her out. I take her upstairs to, at least, muffle the noises.

I hope they won't use this house as a hospital for the whole lot of them.

A stomping follows us up the stair. "Alexa. I could use you. Rayleen, go talk to Taylor. She could use some company."

Nikki points to a room. She goes into the linen closet and pulls out a few blankets. She hands them to me.

"Rayleen go talk to Taylor. I'll be downstairs." I tell Rayleen. Nikki quickly hurries me downstairs.

We go back into the kitchen. Jaiden is lying down on the table with her eyes closed.

Her body tenses as the doctor digs into her wound and pulls a good-sized chuck of glass out. It shines with her blood on it.

"Just a bit more and we'll be done. Hang in there." He says.

"Yep." Jaiden squeaks.

"God, you're awake?" Nikki drops her set of blankets on the bench and leans over Jaiden's body.

Jaiden tenses as the doctor digs into her wound. Jaiden's clenched hand tenses and moves in on itself. Not one sound comes out of her.

"Did you freeze it?" Nikki asks the doctor when she sees Jaiden's reaction.

"Don't have anything to freeze it with." He says.

"Let the doctor do what he needs to," Jaiden tells her.

"Do you want pain medication? Vodka?" Nikki offers.

"No, thank you." She quickly pushes out.

Nikki latches her hand with Jaiden's. "Squeeze my hand as hard as you need to."

I don't know what I'm supposed to do. Nikki said she needed me for something, but she didn't say what. I don't see anything that I could do, if anything I could just be in the way.

"All out. Do you want stitches or just a bandage?" The doctor asks.

"Bandage please," Jaiden says.

"But stitches will minimize scarring." Nikki counters.

"I don't care about a scar. I do care about getting sewn up with no anesthesia or drugs." Jaiden reasons.

"Well, what about that thing that Shawn did to me? Couldn't he heal you too?" Nikki suggests.

"No. It's fine. I don't care about the scar."

The doctor clears his throat to get their attention. "So bandage?"

"Yes please," Jaiden says.

He sticks some weird stickers across her wound. It binds the edges closer together. Then, he puts a gaze pad on it and tapes it on.

"Do you normally faint at the sight of blood?" The doctor asks professionally inquisitive.

"No." She is bashful.

"Do you have a history of fainting spells?" He probes.

"Only this time, and the last about a week ago, but I have almost fainted a few other times over the last few months," Jaiden reveals.

"Do you have a family history?"

"I don't know. I don't know anything about my family history." Jaiden reveals.

"Have you seen a doctor about it?" He asks.

"No, but I have an idea." He looks at her expectantly. She looks like she wishes she could take it back. She looks down sheepishly. "I've been anorexic for months. I had been at a fifty-pound weight loss before the revolution, probably another ten pounds since."

"Eating disorders are complicated with physical and psychological-" The doctor starts explaining by Jaiden cuts him off.

"I know. I don't need the spiel about it. I'm very self-aware. I know exactly why I did it and my triggers. The past month has been more situational to survival.

I know all the facts about eating disorders; I've done all my research. I know. And, I'm assuming that my passing out has to do with the physical side effects of not eating enough and not getting enough nutritionally.

Right now there is only so much I can do when I have to scavenge and ration food, but I can tell you I'm mentally in a regression of my eating disorder. My body just needs to catch up." Jaiden's voice is strong and sure. She has me convinced, but not Nikki; by the looks of it.

The doctor mulls this over. "Okay, but I'd like two things from you. One, you find someone who you trust to help you if you relapse. Someone who will work with you, and if need be, make sure that you are eating regularly.

Two, I will bring you vitamins and you will take them. They are not to replace food, but they will help you regain lost nutrition. I would like to see you once a week for observation."

"Me," Nikki tells the doctor. "Why didn't you tell me you were anorexic?" Her anger shines in her voice as she reprimands Jaiden.

"It's not really something people normally share while they're in the midst of it. I'm over it, so it's easier to talk about." Jaiden explains simply, but it doesn't seem like that is all of it.

"Why would you starve yourself?" Nikki fumes.

"It's mostly a control thing. I had no control over anything in my life, but I could control my food intake. It was also a bonus to lose weight. Dad hated me being fat. Great timing, eh? Right before the apocalypse." I try not to smile at her joke but I can't help it.

"Jaiden!" Nikki doesn't appreciate the joke as much as I do.

The doctor catches my attention. "I'm going to go. Make sure they get her warmed up. She could still have shock. And, she should stay down until she can get some food in her. Something with sugar. She shouldn't move her leg too much or she will reopen everything."

"Okay, I'll tell her," I say. The doctor leaves while the rest are unaware. I decide to save Jaiden from Nikki's wrath; at least for now. "Doc's gone. We need to get you wherever you feel like staying for a long time. Probably the couch? Or a bed? He said you could be in shock. Umm, so we're supposed to wrap you in blankets and get you food. All of this without moving that leg or it'll reopen."

Jaiden sits up and tries to scoot herself off the table. "What are you doing?" Nikki's shrill voice stops Jaiden.

"Nothing," Jaiden says clearly guilty.

"That's what I thought. Would you please carry her to the couch?" She asks the man.

He doesn't say anything but does nod.

He picks Jaiden up, careful of her leg, and Nikki leads him to the living room.

He sets Jaiden down carefully on the couch. I follow up quickly with the blankets in my arms.

Nikki disappears, coming back almost immediately with her nearly forgotten blankets. Jaiden should be nice and warm with all the blankets on her.

She's propped on the couch in such a way that she'd just lie back if she were to pass out again.

I feel like I'm no longer needed here if I was ever actually needed in the first place, so I duck out to check on Rayleen.

I walk upstairs and into the open door; following Rayleen's happy squealing. Taylor and Rayleen are roughhousing in what appears to be a tickle war.

I watch them for a moment before I notice Taylor has something tied around her head. "What's with the headband?"

"What headband?" I point to the cloth. "Oh, my eye has been acting up. I thought it was healed but I guess not."

I pretend to know what she's talking about and nod. A flash of memory reminds me of her eye injury at James' house. That must be it.

"So, what have you been up to?" I ask.

"Pretty much just this," Taylor informs me.

"Is she going to be okay?" Rayleen asks.

"Oh yeah. Of course. She just fell asleep because she was tired, and she has a cut on her leg so she needed a bandage. But, she's going to be okay." I soothe her worries.

"Can I go see her?" Rayleen asks.

"Sure." Rayleen immediately gets up and rushes downstairs. I give Taylor a questioning look, but she returns it with her own confusion.

Rayleen beats me to the living room. "Are you okay?"

"Yes, of course. Thank you." Jaiden says politely.

"What happened?" Rayleen asks her.

Her mouth gapes open for a moment while she searches for the right thing to say. "I'm clumsy. I had an accident and got a large cut on my leg. It needs time to heal, so I have to lie down for a while to let the cut scab over."

"Okay." Rayleen's voice wavers. She sounds near to crying.

"Would you like to help Jaiden?" Nikki kneels down to Rayleen.

"Mmhm."

Nikki smiles big for her. "Well, what would be a big help is if you could come with me to help make her some tea. Would you like that?"

"I'll go make you tea and be right back." Rayleen tells Jaiden.

Her voice now perked up. She grabs Nikki's hand and pulls her. "Come on Nikki. We have to go make her a tea."

"Okay. I'm coming." Nikki tells Rayleen. To the rest of the room, she says, "We'll be right back."

Jaiden's smile falls a bit as Nikki and Rayleen leave. By no means does she frown, but there is only the barest smile twisting her lips.

"If you're okay now. I'm going to head back. They're going to need my help up there." The man explains.

Her bigger smile returns.

"Thank you, for everything." Jaiden thanks him.

"You're welcome. If you need a lift anywhere, let me know." He smirks.

"Yes, I will. Thank you." Jaiden responds.

"See you later." He waves with his goodbye.

"Bye," Jaiden says.

"Bye," I echo.

Jaiden drops to the barest smile again. I figure it out. She was using a customer service face with them. I'm guessing she doesn't really mean to contact him for a lift. She was putting on a show for Rayleen not to feel bad. She doesn't want Nikki to worry over her.

I sit down at the end of the couch and whisper the question I've been wondering. "So, what happened up there? What really happened to your leg?"

"Sandra used her magic to collapse the building. I was inside and had to jump out a window onto the walkthrough roof. So I could get to the other side. Once it was all done, I climbed down." She's completely nonchalant about the coolest thing I've heard anyone do.

"Wow." I imagine it played like something out of an action

movie. She tackles a window and breaks through to fall down one story to the roof below.

"Yeah. Sandra took Darius and abandoned everyone inside. Whoever's left has called a truce. No more fighting."

At the least, I know Darius made it out and escaped unharmed. However, there are a lot of others people that went up to the hotel, and any number of them might be dead. "Who was all inside?"

"I don't know yet. I can only assume that everyone I had seen in the last minute or so didn't make it out. But, I don't know who else might have been inside."

"Oh." I'm a little disappointed that she can't tell me much more.

"We'll know soon enough." She tries to reassure me.

"Yeah." I let the conversation fall into an uncomfortable silence. I stare out the window until I hear soft snoring.

Apparently, the silence wasn't that uncomfortable for her.

I stand up and glance out the window. Some more people are making their way into the backyard. Nikki and Rayleen are out front picking needles off the tree.

I'd go out to tell them they don't have to make the tea anymore but whatever they do make, there will be no shortage of people to drink it.

The back door opens with a bit of a slam.

I look at Jaiden but she doesn't seem disturbed by it.

Someone goes up the stairs. I look over there to see winter boots before they step up out of view.

I wonder who that was.

I go back to the living room to check on Jaiden again. She's still sound asleep. She looks like she's situated well on the couch. I wouldn't want her to fall off and hurt herself more.

The footsteps come thundering down the stairs. I look at Jaiden and see that she's shot up and awake; confused about the loud bangs.

I swiftly go to the bottom of the stairs and shush the people coming down. They both stop; Taylor and a man I don't recognize. "Injured people are resting. Could you please keep it down?"

"Sorry." Taylor apologizes. The man grunts.

I go back into the living room once more to check on Jaiden. Her position has relaxed slightly. I shrug at her unasked question.

"Wait! Let me go! Alexa! Help!" Taylor's desperate cries reach my ears.

"What was that?" Jaiden's eyes are wide and she's pushing the blankets off her.

"Stay there," I tell her. I run to the back, where Taylor's voice came from. The back door swings shut as I reach the boot room.

I push the door open and go outside. A mob has gathered in the yard. Taylor is pulled to the center of them.

"You can't do this!" A woman protests.

"You heard them. She's a spy. She told them we were coming!" A man cries out.

"I'm not a spy. I didn't say anything. They put a spell on me. I didn't know. After I found out I hid myself away so they couldn't get any information. I didn't know you were going to the hotel, so they wouldn't have gotten that information from me. Please! I didn't do anything." No one listens to Taylor as she screams out in her defence. Other people have their say as she pleads with them. It all jumbles together. Was she a spy for Darius?

"My son is dead because of you!" The anguished accusation stands out. My eyes ping to him immediately.

The gun in his hand raises and aims at Taylor's head. It happens too fast, as the gun bangs, and Taylor crumples to the ground as round pellets destroy her face.

There is no way for her to live through that.

A hand tugs on mine. I look behind me to see Jaiden. She pulls me inside the house. She locks the door behind us.

"What are you doing?" I ask her.

"What do you think they'd do to you if they find out who you are? Right now?" She asks rhetorically, quietly rushed. We both can imagine that.

"Nikki and Rayleen are outside. They were picking needles for your tea." I tell her.

"I'll find them. You need to hide. Right beside the stairs is a door to the downstairs. At the bottom, go left. Hide under a table. Don't let anyone see you." She pushes me towards the kitchen. Then, she dashes through the house. I hear the front door open.

Before I follow her instructions I run to the front room window. Nikki and Rayleen are gone. The pot they were filling is on the ground.

Anxiety builds in me. Where are they? Where is Jaiden?

The back door opens again. I sprint to the door, and quietly open it. Just as quickly close it behind me.

It's pitch black in here. I know I have to go downstairs so I reach for a handle on each side.

Flashbacks from the last time I had to do this makes my heart beat fast and my breath catch in my chest.

Jaiden wouldn't send me down here if there were hobgoblins, right?

Feet stomp by the door.

I hold my breath and freeze. A hiding place is no good when

you make noise.

Slowly, I creep down the stairs. Jaiden said to go to the left.

It takes only a moment to find the door impression and door knob. I tip-toe through the room, until I run into a table. The floor is cold so I stand leaning against the table.

I hope Rayleen will be alright. Please, protect her Nikki.

I hope no one is looking for me.

Chapter 20

A shot spooks me, as it reverberates through the air. Rayleen screams as she covers her ears.

I try to reassure her. "It's probably just some idiot, shooting off a gun by accident. There shouldn't be anything to worry about. Let's just go back to picking the needles."

I lead by action and she quickly resumes.

A muffled voice so quiet, I initially think it's solely in my imagination calls out, "you killed her!"

The dots connect. A gunshot. You killed her!

Someone shot someone.

I drop the bucket to the ground and grab Rayleen's hand. The sound had come from around the back of the house. "Come on," I tell her.

We jog towards the gate, open it and go along the path toward the yard. I stop suddenly at another soft shout. "Dominique!"

The shout breaks my adrenaline fog. I shouldn't be taking a small child to investigate someone being shot and killed.

"Back up. Let's go back." I tell Rayleen.

We speed back towards the front of the house and through the gate. Jaiden calls out my name again. She stands near the bucket with her hands cupped around her mouth.

"Here! What happened?" I ask.

"They just killed Taylor. Someone told them that she was a spy, and someone blamed her for his son dying." She says.

"Fuck!" I turn to Rayleen and let go of her hand. Tears well in her eyes, and her face is scrunched. She and Taylor might've been close. I realize, I don't have time to deal with her upset. Did Bruce tell the group? What else would he tell them? "Get her inside the house, and hide; both of you," I instruct Jaiden.

"But-" she cuts herself off as I sprint away.

The gate and sidewalk blur by. I stop and freeze at an angered crowd. A man is held into the snowy ground, blood looks almost black near the body it pools around. Splatters of red, dot a wide area.

Uncle Bruce stares down at the remains. He's frozen from the moment. Blood spots speckle him. He must've been close to Taylor when it happened. His mouth hangs open as his chest heaves.

I walk up to him. "Uncle." He snaps out of his shock to look at me. "This can't happen again." His blank stare infuriates me. Bruce is looked up to by these people. Or, at least by the people who have lived here for years. And, as far as I'm concerned he had a hand in this. There was no need to tell anyone else about Taylor's unfortunate situation. "Do something!"

"I don't-," He shakes his head as he stumbles through getting words out.

"End this now! We called a truce!" I shout at the top of my lungs.

It affects some but not all. A few back up to draw out of the main fight.

I barge my way between two of the main people shouting. Putting my hands on each of the men's chests, I push them away from each other. They both stay at the end of my hands as if that's the only thing keeping them apart.

"Enough!" I yell.

I switch between looking at both of them. The one on my left backs away from my hand, but the other keeps firm against it.

I drop my left hand. Pushing again with my right, the man bounces against my hand. He's not letting up.

"I didn't kill anyone. Not all of us killed your people." The one on my left defends. I think he might've been from the hotel from his words. He doesn't look supernatural in appearance.

"You didn't do anything to stop it! That means you're just as culpable and capable of it." With his fury, the man spits out his words.

In deep contrast, the hotel man stays calm but firm with his voice. "You're right, we didn't stop it, or else we wouldn't be here right now. We'd be dead too. They killed anyone who tried to stop anything."

Angry man's finger comes up to physically point blame. "You're responsible for their deaths. You should pay for it."

"I'm not putting a stranger's life over my own, and neither would any of you. Yes, we made a choice not to intervene, but it was gun to my head. Save the humans and die, or quietly go along with whatever they decided.

Most people would pick the same thing. Most of you would pick living with regret, over dying in horrible ways." It goes quiet.

The angry man's steam seeps out of him and his accusing finger falls to his side. His body pushes less against my hand. I don't dare to take it down yet, just in case he decides to try something.

The deep pause allows the hotel man to continue. "It was never a simple decision. We never thought they would start a war over this. Many thought we were just one viral video away from humans knowing we exist.

That someone would have the guts to make a video and post it, and before the Council could bury it and the poster, that it would go viral, and humans would know we exist. That we could stop hiding that part of us."

He pauses to shake his head. "The wrong people got together. Got in charge. It spread like a plague. They used fear and threats against their own people to get compliance."

"I am so sorry about your loved ones. If it feels better to hate me, then go ahead. But just know, I had people to protect too. People I have to live for. People I loved who also died." No one tries to speak after his impassioned speech.

In the quiet, the sobs of the man on the ground pierces the air. He must be the one who killed Taylor. He killed her in a desperate grasp of utter despair. His son was killed, and this felt like a way to even things out.

Doesn't mean it was right, but I can understand.

So much of this is about understanding each person's side. We like to paint everyone with titles; good and evil. But history has always been about winners skewing the story.

Ensuring the winners were labelled good, and did no wrong, while the losers were evil and did all these horrible things. Many times over, the winners did horrendous things too; they just got buried.

I take the moment to end this once and for all; hopefully. "This ends here. We called a truce. No one else dies. No one else pays for past indiscretions. We work together going forward. We all need to survive. And, we have a lot better things to be doing right now, than turning on each other."

A few heads nod in agreeance. Nothing much more is said. The crowd dissipates in opposing feelings quietly in varied directions.

The man is let up by the restraining bodies and handed off to other people. His body is supported as he's led away.

"No." Uncle Bruce says quietly. "You can't just give them a free pass. This was wrong, but so is letting everyone go free."

"We-"

He cuts me off. "They killed her. Dannie was ripped apart by those monsters. I could barely find half of her to bury. Brandon's disappeared; just gone. They're all responsible for something." Uncle Bruce's pure shaking rage shocks me into silence.

My heart pounds; I didn't know about auntie. He continues. "I will give it to you that not all of them deserve to die, but they should be locked up. They need to answer for all the murder and destruction. They ruined lives! I need you, of all people, to be on my side."

It takes a moment to gather myself together for a response. "No, sorry. We need peace. We need this truce. You heard him. They didn't have a choice."

"They had a choice. They made their choice. They could have chosen to die, but they didn't. They could have fought against the war, but they didn't. You won't have long to change your mind. Make sure you can live with your choice." Bruce turns his back and walks towards the garage. He goes out through the back gate and out of sight.

I replay Uncle's words again and again until my brain focuses on the last bits.

Make sure you can live with your choice.

Is it wrong not to lock them up?

Some of them could be dangerous; potentially. I can understand that. But, I have to believe that they are generally good; that they had no choice. Or else, we'd be condemning a whole group of people for what could be the actions of a few of them.

I'm left alone with Taylor's body. I don't know what to do with it. Looking at it makes me woozy, so I look away and try not to think about the gaping hole in her face.

The back of my hand seals my mouth as if that would help me not throw up.

Jaiden, no. Her leg is hurt and she'd help me anyway. I can't ask her, or anyone around her.

I need strength. Someone strong enough to bury her in the freezing ground. Most of the supernaturals are gathered up the road. Some in the next-door house. I'll try there first.

We can't leave her here for long. We might attract wildlife.

I walk to the front door of the next house over. The door is open and people are wandering in and out.

I look for familiar faces first, but then realize that it really wouldn't matter. I need strength, not familiarity.

"There's a dead body next door; in the backyard. I need help cleaning it up and help to dig a grave for her. Is anyone willing to help me?" I ask loud enough for anyone on the main floor of the house to hear.

At least a dozen people are milling about. Someone has to be willing to help me. I need at least one person.

"How dead?" One asks. I recognize her. She was new from Jaiden's group. I don't remember her name though.

"She was shot in the head," I answer.

She shakes her head at me like I misunderstood the question. "How long ago?"

What would that matter? I briefly frown my eyebrows. "A few minutes. Maybe ten minutes, or longer."

I have no idea how long has actually passed. It feels like forever, but I know it hasn't been too long.

"Hmm. Probably too late for me, pass." She turns to go back the way she came.

"You could try anyways. Just in case." Someone suggests.

She stops to mull it over, then turns around. "Hm, I guess so."

"Try what?" I ask. Curiosity getting the best of me. I don't think I'm going to like the answer.

"Eat her soul." She says simply.

"What?" I say without meaning to.

"Well, she's dead anyways. Not too many chances to eat souls around here." She walks by me and leaves through the front door.

I want to stop her or follow her. But maybe I should leave her alone. I don't know what eating a soul entails.

Is there going to be a body left over?

"You have shovels?" A tall guy asks. He brings my attention back to the crowd. He looks like he would be strong. Hopefully, this is the beginning of his offer to help out.

"Um, no. We could find some around, I'm sure." I think Uncle has one in his garage that we could use. It's not an unusual item for people to keep around.

A woman comes out from behind the tall man. She gets close to me. "There should be some in the garages around here. How about you let us deal with this? We'll get the body moved and buried. Somewhere near the lake, maybe? So we aren't attracting wild animals near the houses."

Putting both her hands up, she means to usher me out of the house. One hand points with an open palm toward the exit, while the other makes a sweeping motion.

"I could help." I hadn't meant for them to take on everything themselves. Maybe they misunderstood me asking for help.

"No offence, but it'll take way less time if you don't. It's kind of like, trying to get something done while babysitting a toddler. You get half as much done in twice the time." She sneers.

The tall man interjects. "What she means, is that we're stronger and faster, so it makes sense to let us do all the heavy lifting. We'll let you know where we bury her, so you can hold a funeral and go back to pay your respects; if you want."

"Okay, yeah, sure." They seem determined so I'll let them take this. I make an excuse so I feel less awkward. "I have some people I could check on instead. Thank you."

"No problem." The woman walks me out the door and closes it behind me.

I stand stunned for a minute.

Should I go see the soul eating girl?

Should I go back to supervise and offer my help again?

Should I go check on Rayleen and Jaiden?

She was walking around with her leg wound. I bet she reopened it.

I need to go find them. Check on Rayleen and how she's doing. I hope Jaiden was able to comfort her. I hope Jaiden didn't pass out again.

I think they went into Uncle Bruce's house, so I go next door and inside the house.

Straight away, the house feels colder. Not physically, but psychologically. Bruce's rage sends shivers through me and taints the feel of the house. Auntie's tragic death mention brings her death into focus.

Did she die in here? Or did she die escaping to the mountain? Or did she die at the campsite?

I try not to imagine what happened. How she could have been torn into pieces. Maybe the ogre has the strength to do that.

Or, something else.

It doesn't make sense to just tear her apart. Someone who did that did it for the sheer terror of it. They didn't do it for food. And Brandon-

Something clatters in the kitchen. "Shit, sorry." The female voice apologizes.

I walk through the door to the kitchen. Jaiden is on the bench with her leg stretched out. Blood drips down the side of her leg and onto a paper towel she holds below the wound.

Shawn, Stephanie, Alexa, Rayleen, and a few others crowd the kitchen.

"Could you stop bleeding everywhere?" I joke seriously.

"Trying. I reopened things earlier." Jaiden responds. She points briefly towards the backyard. "What happened?"

I sit down on the bench with a sigh. "One of the dads was upset and blamed Taylor for his son dying. I guess Bruce told them that Taylor was spying on us."

"She was spying on us?" Steph asks.

"No, not on purpose. Sandra had done a blood spell on her that made it so she could see and hear what Taylor did only when Sandra concentrated. It had a time limit on it. Once we found out, once Taylor found out, she hid away from everyone and made sure she wouldn't see or hear anything important." Jaiden explains. "So, she wouldn't have been the one to warn them we were coming."

"Why didn't you say anything?" Shawn's question is aimed at me.

I sweep a hand towards the back door. "That's why. People found out, and killed her for it."

"Fair enough." He says, holding his hands up in defence.

"Are we healing Jaiden? Are you going to do that thing?" I ask him. There is no sense of urgency in the room to get her wound under control; that would make sense why.

"No." Shawn answers.

"Why not?" My question spikes with an unintended edge.

"She said no." Shawn pushes the focus to Jaiden.

"Jaiden!?" I exclaim a whole sentence's worth of question in the form of her name.

"It's fine." She brushes it off. A woman comes over to dab at the extra blood. She works to close it with butterfly stickers and redress it in gauze.

I turn to Shawn. "Well just do it anyways."

"No, she said no," Shawn says succinctly.

"You did it to me without telling me everything, but her saying no is where you're drawing the line?" I push further.

"She said no. No means no. I stopped once you said no." I glare at him and then turn to Jaiden.

If I can't change his mind, then I'll have to change hers. "Why are you saying no?"

"I'm fine." Jaiden shrugs. "It's just a cut."

"You had a whole chunk of glass in your leg. It's not just a cut, you were stabbed. You're dripping blood everywhere. It's going to scar." I list off.

"I'm not afraid of scars. It'll heal just fine on its own." Jaiden responds.

I huff a small breath of air out then switch tactics a little. "What if we need to run away from something? Are you going to be able to run?"

"Sure. I'll just bleed everywhere in my getaway. I'll be fine. Nothing's going to happen." She tries to reassure me, but it has the opposite effect.

"Something already happened," I shout a bit louder than intended. She jumps back a little. I lower my volume a little. "You got fixed up and lasted five minutes before reopening everything; having to run away from a mob."

"Are you okay?" Jaiden changes the focus. The woman gets done with her leg. Jaiden quickly switches to thanking her before looking back at me for our conversation.

"I'm fine!" I bite back.

"You don't seem fine." She states.

"Do you need a hug?" Shawn asks.

"Yes, but don't do anything weird." I snap at him.

"Dude!" He throws both his hands up near his head. "Don't say it like that. You make me sound like a creep."

Looking back at my wording, I realize what I did and burst out laughing. "I'm sorry."

The laugh turns into a deeply pained cry. I take a deep breath. Shawn gets up from the bench and wraps his arms around me as tears flood down my cheeks.

"What happened?" He asks softly.

I pull away and snap at Jaiden. "You need to take better care of yourself." I don't want to lose you too.

"Okay," Jaiden answers quietly.

"Uncle Bruce wants me to pick his side. I'm not entirely sure what it means, but at the least, he wants supernaturals to pay for their parts in what happened to Banff. And, he said someone tore Aunt Dannie apart. That's how she died. And, my cousin disappeared. And, Taylor-" I trail off.

And, my kidnapping.

And, my family is probably dead. I might never see them again, even if they are alive.

And, Jaiden's anorexic and hurt and fainting frequently. And, she's not letting us heal her. She needs to take better care of herself. I need her to be okay.

I take a deep breath, and let it out slowly. Tingling pressure appears in my eye's tear ducts.

Outside of Shawn, I can feel people staring at me. The heated pressure of it chips away at me.

"I'm going to go to my room. Alone." I announce while spinning to go back out the door.

Chapter 21

Arching my back, I let out an exasperated sigh as my head hits the top of the pillow.

I'm so bored.

I sweep my tongue along the back of my front top teeth. I'm glad my tooth never fell out fully. It seems fine after being bent backwards. It doesn't hurt and it's not wiggly, so hopefully, it's all good in there.

The phone told me I did exactly what I should have. It didn't fall out or turn gray. So, maybe it's fine.

The rib pain I acquired is already nothing.

That brings me back to my other wound. The giant cut on my leg is sore, but a dull manageable ache. It's got a huge white bandage patch taped onto it now, but earlier, while changing the bandage, it looked like it was healing well. A scab had formed and there was no sign of infection.

As long as I don't keep reopening the wound, it should keep healing just fine.

I, maybe, should have agreed to the stitches. But, I think it's too late now. All I kept thinking in the moment was about how I can run or fight if I have stitches. But, I don't know how well I can do that now either.

It's going to take time to heal.

In the meantime, I've been honour bound to the couch. I promised Dominique that I would take it easy for a few days. So far, that's meant not being allowed to leave the couch. I wasn't even allowed to go a few houses down to sit in on the town hall meeting Bruce called.

Though, I guess it's more of a meeting of Banff residents since he conveniently and suspiciously waited to call the meeting until after most of the hotel people had left to start scavenging.

Bruce didn't return here last night. I guess he's still mad.

Or, if he's drawing lines, maybe he doesn't want to stay with supernaturals.

Or, maybe it's the full house of people he can't stand.

His wife was a supernatural, it doesn't make sense that it would be supernaturals specifically that he'd have a problem with. It could be because of his wife that he can't stay; too many memories haunt the house.

Jacob got rid of every reminder of mom in the days after her death. We hadn't even had her funeral yet, and he was tossing out photo albums, her clothing, her car, and anything she bought. He even had her favourite accent wall painted over in the living room.

I got banished to the basement then, and he started being cold to me after that. In hindsight, maybe that's when he figured out I wasn't his. Or, maybe I was a reminder of his dead wife that he didn't want around.

Maybe, he just wanted to move on quickly.

It makes sense that Bruce doesn't want to come back to the home where reminders of his wife are everywhere. Where he has to relive her being torn apart again and again.

It's only been a few hours since I woke, and I'm bored out of my mind. There's nothing to do except wait for nuggets of excitement when people return briefly.

Even the organizational busywork I offered to take up isn't enough to keep me going.

I ignore the heavy footsteps that come into the room. "Are you sleeping?" His deep voice asks quietly.

I pop my head up to see DeAngelo sneaking in. "Nope. Did you find anything fun this time?"

"Load of wood. Half-ton truck." He responds.

At least we should have lots to burn all winter. We're lucky the second most common item used at the hotel was wood.

I realize we have trees all around us, but this way we don't have to go chopping anything down and it's already dried out.

I mark down the one line item on our scavenged supplies list. "Alright, put it where the last one went."

"You hear back from the meeting?" He asks.

I look up at him from where I'm writing. "Not yet."

DeAngelo hadn't been surprised when I told him about the meeting Bruce called. Said it made sense that he might want to discuss things amongst his own group first.

He was very understanding about it. More than I might've been. They'll be seen as outsiders for a little while, and they are prepared for that. He said they're ready to make amends.

Word quickly spread within their own group. Each person who comes by either gives a lingering look around, I assume to look for other people, or they directly ask if I've heard anything.

"Bored out of your mind?" DeAngelo switches topics.

"Yes!" I exclaim dramatically.

He smiles wide. "Maybe think of that next time you decide to leap out of a falling building."

"Yeah, because at least if I was dead, I wouldn't be bored." I prepare to tell him that I'm joking just in case he doesn't get it.

DeAngelo breathes out through his teeth, but his smile lets me know he got the joke. "Have fun. I'm going to get back to it." He laughs as he leaves.

The excitement leaves with him. I eye the papers I've organized, the lists I've made, and all the information I've sorted through.

I thought it would take longer. I thought they'd be able to scavenge things from the hotel faster.

The stone is giving them trouble. There's so much of it and in huge heavy chunks. Some pieces are impossible to move, while others take ages.

On the opposite scale of things, the small rubble is slow to gather and move enough to make an impact.

There are enough people up there helping; less than expected though. On his first visit back, DeAngelo mentioned that a few people had disappeared in the middle of the night.

They were all staying at one house and decided to leave. A few that decided to stay, said that the others felt like they would be safer on their own.

I can respect that.

However, DeAngelo also mentioned that we would be better off without Chris. Specifically mentioning him by name, but not elaborating. There were too many people in the room to ask him to tell me that back story comfortably.

My imagination went from a personal life-long feud between Chris and DeAngelo to Chris being a Mengele-type character and the brain behind the torture forest game.

If I can get him alone at some point, I might ask.

They got the bodies sorted first. Counting the dead, and identifying them where they could. Squashed bodies from the building are barely recognizable, having to be identified by their clothes, scent, or hair.

It's not a perfect system. I'm sure some are misidentified. But, if the person hasn't been seen alive, people are assuming they were in the building when it collapsed.

"That was a waste of time!" Dominique barges into the house. Stephanie follows after her.

"What happened?" I ask.

"Nothing! He talked in circles for hours and hours." She falls in a heap on the couch.

"I almost fell asleep. The whole meeting could have been twenty minutes. But he just kept circling back and restating everything he already said before, but this time he said it slightly differently and maybe added an extra thought." Stephanie elaborates.

"So in the twenty minutes, what was actually accomplished?" I ask.

"Accomplished; no. Homework; yes." Dominique sits up straighter to look at me as she talks. "Mostly he wants to know things and we all need to collect the information and bring it back to him for another meeting later this afternoon."

"What does he want to know?" I ask.

"Supplies mostly. Taking stock of what we have, so that we can figure out what we need to be able to survive winter." Stephanie replies.

"That was the whole thing." Dominique lowers her voice in a mock Bruce voice. "Hey, we don't even need this meeting right now, but if you all could go out and figure out what we have so that we can discuss if we can survive winter, and what we might need. The rest of this meeting will be put off until the afternoon."

"Sounds horrible." Knowing that most of the supernatural beings were excluded from the meeting, I have to ask. "Did anyone bring up what extra food type dietary things the supernaturals need? Like human blood for the vampires?"

Dominique taps her finger toward me. "I will bring that up."

"Did they talk about how the truce will go? If Bruce isn't happy with letting it go, it's not hard to guess that'll be the same for others." I ask.

"Not one mention of it. I'll talk with him later. Alone. See if he's cooled down yet." Dominique says. "It might be a nonissue."

"Almost an entire house of supernaturals took off last night. Took some vehicles and some supplies. Sounds like they figured it would be safer to leave." I figure it would be best to tell her the rest. It might help out. She looks over at me and straightens up in her seat. "Rumours are that they might've been some of the ones who believed in the cause. Maybe you can spin that to help convince him that nothing else needs to be done to the ones who stayed."

"Maybe." Dominique gets up from the couch. "I'll go find Uncle now. That might be enough to put it to rest. Can you handle my counts?" She asks Stephanie.

"Sure." Dominique hands Stephanie a folded sheet of paper she pulls out of her pocket.

Dominique leaving disperses Stephanie in a silent signal to get going with whatever she had to do. I'm left alone once again in a roller-coaster of boredom and excitement.

I eat some lunch, in the form of jerky and canned mandarin oranges, from the selection of snacks placed on the side table. They didn't want me to have to go anywhere except for the bathroom.

Eyeing up the cane, they gave me for that circumstance, with a glare. I didn't use it when I last had to go.

The elderly man the cane belonged to had died, so he has no use for it. But, I can tell the cane meant much to him. The whole cane was intricately carved by the man himself, with a design of all the important things in his life and things he liked. Animals he liked, names of his loved ones inside of hearts, cars, boats, flowers, and leaves. The cane felt too much like an object that I shouldn't touch.

Jumping from the door opening abruptly, a woman comes in. "Jaiden?"

"Yes?" I ask.

"DeAngelo asked me to collect you. He said you're bored and it makes more sense for you to do this from the hotel." She has a point, but it wouldn't take much to convince me at this stage.

"Yeah, sure. Let me just collect my things." I get up with the use of my good leg and my arms.

I gather up papers and my pencil. I quickly write a note on the corner of a paper, then rip it off and leave it on the table.

"I'm Michelle, by the way." She introduces herself.

"Hi." I have to deliberately stop myself from saying my name. She already knows that. I don't need to say it again.

"He was right. I'm about your height." She quickly answers my unasked question. "DeAngelo told me about your leg and said you might need some help to get into the SUV."

"Oh, no, that's alright. I just have to favour one side so I don't reopen things. But, I can move around alright." I decline. Even if I needed the help, I wouldn't want to bother her. Besides, while walking around earlier, I found that I just had to walk stiffly with one leg, and all was good.

"Okay, just so long as you don't start bleeding everywhere. Some of us are a little sensitive to that." She abruptly jerks up her hands to face her palms towards me. Her eyes are wide. "Not that we'll attack you or anything if you do start to bleed."

"It's okay. I've travelled with vampires. It's- I'm good. It's fine. Um- yeah. I understand." I try to reassure her awkwardly.

She grabs the papers and pencil from me. I slowly follow her with intentional steps to the red SUV. Climbing in the passenger seat is tricky, but manageable by backing in.

Michelle starts up the SUV and we drive up the road.

"You know, if I was trying to kidnap you, you really made this easy for me." She laughs.

The thought hadn't crossed my mind, but now that it has, instant panic sets in. "You're not though, right?" I ask suspiciously, yet calmly.

"No. God. No. Sorry. I have a wicked sense of humour sometimes. I wasn't trying to make you feel uncomfortable." She turns towards the castle. "See we're going exactly where I said we would."

"It's fine. It's okay. We're good. I believe you." I lie. Now the thought won't leave. The trust is gone. Maybe she was one of the people who left. They could have gone to the other mountain hotel. She could be taking me there.

They might've figured out what I am. Dominique has certainly let enough people know that I can't rule it out. Bruce could have said something. Calli or Lucas could have spilled it. Brad, Shawn, Stephanie; anyone who overheard us at the other hotel. Apparently, there's a deep genetic resemblance that could clue people in. The information is out there; it's a matter of time.

Seeing the pile of hotel remnants sinks into the reality that I barely escaped being crushed yesterday. I look up to the spot I managed to escape to, and the rubble I escaped from. If I had been moments later, I'd be dead. Hopefully, it would have been a quick death.

Hopefully, anyone who had been inside when it came down, had a quick death. I'd hate to find out that people survived the collapse, just to suffocate or starve to death in a pocket space.

It's entirely possible though. Sandra, you better have done a good job at collapsing the building so that no one suffered.

"Jaiden!" I snap my attention to the other side of the SUV. Shawn is at the open driver's window. I hadn't realized he was there. "What are you doing here? You're supposed to be at the house."

"I was bored. It's more efficient to be here. Fresh air. Mental health is a big part of physical healing." I list off a couple of things to make my case. "I promise, I won't walk around much."

"Remember all those excuses when Nikki is yelling at you later," Shawn warns me.

"I'll take it easy. There shouldn't be a difference between me sitting here, or me sitting at the house." I try to reason, but there really shouldn't be a difference.

"Try telling her that," Shawn says.

A knock on my window alerts me. DeAngelo waves and points down. I press the button to roll down the window. "Hey. You bring your papers?"

"Yes." I hold up the papers to show them.

DeAngelo grabs the papers from me. "We'll fill these out. How about you go check on our furry friend? It'll be a whole lot more exciting than this." He taps on the door twice before leaving.

I've been swindled, but I'm not mad about it. "Who's the furry friend?" I ask Michelle.

She smiles. "Do you like dogs?"

"Hm. Not entirely. My mom used to have a dog that terrorized me. Bit me a few times. It would growl at me lots. She refused to get rid of it because it was her baby and I needed to get along with my sister; who was the dog." By the drop in her smile, I realize I should have just said yes.

"Well, I'm sorry for that. That was really shitty of her." Shawn says.

"Yeah, that. I'm sorry too. Are you scared of dogs?" Michelle asks. "Should we stay here?"

"No. No. I'm good. More cautious and aware that not every

dog is nice." I reassure.

At least they didn't say they now don't trust me. Some dog people base their whole assumptions of people based on whether dogs like them or if the person likes dogs.

"Okay, well, they are a sweetheart. So, let's go see them then." I hope she's right.

"I'll come with." Shawn gets into the back of the SUV. "Nikki'll kill me if something happens to you. Congratulations, you've now made me an accomplice."

"Oh, you'll be fine. I'll be fine." I reassure.

Shawn gets into the middle row. Michelle drives and swings the SUV around to go back the way we came. She turns to go further up the mountain. We stop on the further side of the torture forest.

Michelle rolls down the window and lets out a loud whistle. When nothing appears, she whistles again; repeating every minute.

A husky face bounds up to Michelle's window. Clicking claws scratch up the SUV as she hops up. I look further toward where Shawn sits. Three husky faces nose at the windows on the driver's side.

All three are fluffy black and white huskies, but their eyes vary. One has brown eyes. One has light blue eyes. And, one has a mix of both.

"Down." Michelle orders. They listen to her and back away from the SUV. There's something odd about their movement. How in sync they are with each other.

I understand why as Michelle opens the door. The three heads are attached to one body.

"Meet Artemis, Apollo and Athena. Artemis is on the left with brown eyes, Apollo is in the middle, and Athena is the blue-eyed one." Michelle goes up to the cerberus dog and gives them pets.

As they lick and she pets them, I get the courage to leave the SUV. They don't look mean.

"Artemis, Apollo, and Athena meet Jaiden and Shawn. They are friends and we don't eat friends." She looks at me with a hand outreached. "I have to properly introduce you."

I give her my hand. She guides me closer and puts my hand in reach for the dogs to sniff and lick.

All three take their turn. The last one is the middle one. The one with one of each colour eyes licks my hand, then nuzzles for pets.

I realize that the eye colours match the same sides as the other dog's head with that colour of eyes.

Michelle calls over Shawn to do the same, so I take a step back while she introduces him.

"They were supposed to guard the land and kill anyone who trespassed, but obviously they were taking a nap the other day while they were supposed to be working," Michelle says.

"Lucky us," Shawn says.

"Honestly, I think her owner oversold her vicious guard dog ability. Though they do seem to hate particular men, so that's fine." I wonder if she means that they hated Darius, or maybe Chris; maybe someone else she doesn't like.

The blue-eyed head wants attention now. Nuzzling at my relaxed hand to get pets. When I oblige, the next head over tries knocking into that hand, so I bring up my other to pet her. I feel like the last head is left out, but I only have two hands. "What are we going to do with her?"

Michelle takes pity on the last head and starts petting her. "Leave her here and come visit. She's a husky and built for the cold. She loves the exercise and freedom. She's killed a cougar, so she can hunt at least and eat what she kills. It's what makes the most sense."

The one Michelle is petting stops the attention to move toward me. The others move away to adjust so she is closer.

She pokes her head forward to gently nuzzle at my leg. She looks up at me. When I don't answer, she huffs, pokes near my wound again, and looks at me expectantly.

"Careful Athena," Michelle warns.

"I'm okay. Just a big cut." I tell her.

She accepts the answer with a huff and backs away. I guess she understood me. How smart are cerberus dogs?

All six ears perk up, three heads turn at the same time. They rise to all fours, then take off in a sprint. Kicking up snow as they speed away.

"I guess they're done with us. Let's go back." Michelle motions to the SUV. I wonder if someone else called her away.

Shawn holds up his arm to help me walk back to the vehicle. I take it to show that I'm working to not reinjure the cut. He could report back to Nikki negatively or positively and I'd rather the latter.

We all get back into the vehicle and start a comfortably silent ride back.

The back of the SUV kicks out from the alignment, turning us sideways. We slide for a couple of meters before we catch traction and take off down into the ditch.

The SUV stops suddenly before it hits some trees.

"Everyone okay?" Michelle quickly asks.

"Yes." Shawn and I say together.

"Oh my God, is your leg okay?" Michelle shouts.

I panic for a moment as I look for some oddity. My leg looks fine. It didn't require the yelling she just did. "Yes. I'm good."

"Are we stuck or can we get out of here?" Shawn asks.

"I don't know yet." Michelle backs up the SUV and works to slowly turn us around in the space provided.

We go up a bit of a hill and she puts us back up on the road with ease. For a moment, I was anxious that she might slide us down the other side, but the vehicle gripped where it was supposed to.

With bated breath, we all wait for the SUV to slide again, but it doesn't. Michelle drives at a small fraction of the speed she had been using.

You never know under all of this snow, where a frictionless patch of ice awaits. The snow isn't packed down enough to provide friction. Who knows if snow tires were put on or not?

Shawn breaks the silence. "Do me a favour. Please, don't tell anyone about this. Especially, not Nikki."

"Afraid she'll never let Jaiden out again?" Michelle jokes.

"Probably," I add. "Maybe after she's done killing the both of us."

"Would she kill me too?" Michelle asks.

Shawn answers jokingly. "No. She'll kill me because I let something happen to Jaiden. And she'll kill Jaiden for getting hurt after she told her not to leave the house. Then she'll kill me again to make sure the message got across. Don't worry. We'll leave your name out of it."

Shawn cuts the tense air I created with my initial jest. "We're joking about the killing part, of course. I've known Nikki since kindergarten. She used to cry if someone else killed a mosquito that was sucking her blood. But, she does fiercely protect those she cares about. Even from themselves."

"Sounds like a good friend. I'm sorry we locked her up." Michelle backtracks. "I'm sorry, I didn't help her while she was here."

"What were you supposed to do? Walk her out of the building full of people who might stop you? You probably would have ended up dead." Shawn calms her worries.

I have a feeling we'll encounter a lot of people regretting their actions. I wonder if there are any therapists around.

Chapter 22

Daniel pokes his head into the room. "I'm ready to talk to you now," he says softly.

My heart pounds from both his sudden appearance and because I haven't seen him since we returned. He fiercely yelled at me, then got dragged away while he was told to cool off and talk to me once calmed down.

I guess that's what's happening now.

Daniel invites himself inside and quietly shuts the door behind him. He comes over to sit down on the bed's edge.

I peer over to Rayleen's sleeping form, weary that we might wake her.

"We'll keep it quiet. I won't wake her." He says, but I don't see this conversation happening without yelling. "You owe me an explanation."

"Okay," I say. Everything that I thought to say to him, everything I figured out, clears out of my mind.

The silence is constricting. Each passing moment increases the difficulty to start. I don't know where to start. I don't know what exactly would make this all better; I want it to be better.

With the expectant look and pleading eyes, it all becomes suffocating. He twists and grips his hands to keep himself steady.

"Talk to me. Because if I talk first, this won't go well. Why? What the fuck were you thinking?" Daniel reveals the rage he's keeping the surface.

Being locked up, having time to think about why I did it, an answer that doesn't sound wild, it all comes down to Rayleen; needing to protect her.

It's the only answer I think people will accept with any understanding.

I sit down on the opposite bottom edge of the bed. It feels too threatening to be standing while having this particular conversation. "They were organized and stronger. They took down the world in hours.-"

"So you want to take over the world?" Daniel looks over to Rayleen. He realizes that his words got a bit loud in his interruption.

"No." Does he think I'd want to take over the world? I'm not some villain. "I want to protect Rayleen."

"We can protect Rayleen here." He suggests.

Not the same way. Not enough.

They have too many strengths and advantages to ignore.

"Darius promised to turn me into a vampire. I would be strong enough to protect Rayleen without having to rely on anyone. I could protect her from everything." He cuts me off at a breathing pause.

"If that was it, you would have asked someone here to turn you." Daniel has a point. I could have asked any vampire to change me. There were plenty of chances. Kelly or Leah, either could have changed me.

Although, who knows if they would have agreed? I don't think either had crossed my mind, because I didn't see any option in it. Neither would change me, if I asked.

But now, there would be plenty of other vampires who might

be willing to. I could still fulfill this wish.

But, that's not the whole thing. "Being with Darius comes with its own protection. No one would try anything."

"So you went to pimp yourself out for protection." His accusation instantly heats my chest.

I strike back with equal ferocity. "If that's what it takes to keep Rayleen safe, then yes."

"And, what about you? Would you be safe?" The subtext is woven into his harsh tone.

He knows about Darius' abuse. He knows I would be abused going back to Darius, and he doesn't understand why I would choose that.

"Not from him." I acknowledge. "But, Rayleen would be safe from everything. No one would dare attack her. She could actually live a childhood; be a kid. And, if something did happen, as a vampire, I could actually do something about it."

"I don't want you to be a vampire." Her little voice cuts through the air and guts me.

I push through the pain. Standing up, I walk over to her. She's laying down exactly how she had been sleeping. I thought she was sleeping, but she could have woken up at any point.

Staying here helped with privacy, but I might've just let Rayleen know a bit too much. I never wanted her to find out about my abuse.

"Did we wake you up? I'm so sorry." I kiss her forehead and rub my thumb across her cheek.

Rayleen turns over to her back to look up at me. "I don't want you to be a vampire."

"But I'd be so much stronger and faster. I could protect you so much better." I try to explain in a way she might understand.

"I like you the way you are. I don't want you to change." She says stronger.

"I'd still be me, just faster and stronger." I insist.

"You don't know that," Daniel interjects. "Becoming a vampire might change you. And, what if you can't control yourself? You could end up hurting Rayleen."

"I wouldn't," I say.

"You don't know that." He says.

"Neither do you." I counter.

"Promise you won't be a vampire." My heart aches with her plea. My voice gets caught in my throat.

"They're gone. We're safe now." Daniel is up from his spot and behind me now. "You don't have to put yourself in danger to protect her anymore. She doesn't want you to become a vampire, so listen to her."

"Promise you won't be a vampire." Her voice wavers. Rayleen's pout threatens to turn into crying with one wrong word.

I can't deny her plea. "Okay. I promise."

"Good," Daniel confirms. "We have some more to discuss, without little ears around, but it's going to hinge on this question. Will you move to a different house with me?"

I turn to face him. "You want to move houses?"

"I've already moved, but I want to know if you're willing to work at this, and that starts with moving out of this house." I look him over incredulously. A large part of me can't believe he's willing to try again.

What kind of a guy is willing to work things out after they've been left for another man? Is he really that nice and forgiving, or is it something else entirely?

He stands near with pleading eyes. A crease of worry furrows between his eyebrows.

Rayleen's eyes glisten with extra moisture. If I can't become a vampire then she'll need extra protection. More people who will aid her, people who will care for her.

"Yeah. Okay." I agree to the ultimatum. If he's willing to take me back after that, then I'm willing to try to work with him.

A wide grin draws up Daniel's face.

He swoops his hands into an abrupt clap. "Alright, let's pack up your things." Daniel looks around the room.

"I don't have any things," Rayleen says.

Daniel pffts. "That's okay. We'll get you lots of things for the new place."

"Oh! We can't forget our Christmas presents!" Rayleen dashes over to the dresser and pulls out drawings we made for each other.

"Do you have one for me?" Daniel asks.

"No." Rayleen replies sheepishly.

The moment is a stark reminder that we weren't together then. We had figured he would hate me forever and he'd sign off on Rayleen because of it.

Daniel takes it in stride. "That's okay. I forgot it was Christmas. Can you believe that? Who forgets about Christmas? How about, once we get back to my house, our house, we can make each other our gifts then?"

"Yes!" Rayleen perks up.

It takes two minutes to pack up everything we want to take with us. Most things would be considered stolen property rather than our own possessions. I've gotten used to it though; Rayleen too.

To my surprise and delight, no one stops us on the way out of the house. We go out the front door, then to the sidewalk.

Daniel leads us down two houses to the left. He lets us inside first by holding the door open for us.

"I'm back," Daniel announces.

"How'd it go?" As Bruce asks, we walk around the small entry partition. "Well, I see. Welcome."

"Thank you," I tell him.

I wave shortly at the others in the room, a bunch of men around the same age as Bruce. Everyone is settled deeply into an arm chair, rocking chair, or couch.

Do they live here, or are they visiting?

"Go get settled in, and we'll talk later." He dismisses us.

Daniel instructs us to take off our boots. To my surprise, my feet don't freeze once they hit the floor. Then, I notice, that this house isn't so cold. It's like the other one when the fire is going in the kitchen and the heat reaches out to the living room.

Daniel shows us to his room. There's an unmade bed and set out sleeping bags. Multiple people share this room; I realize in disappointment.

Rayleen jumps onto the bed. I don't know whether it would be okay or if I should tell her to stop.

"Bruce has the bed, but we get to sleep in sleeping bags. Isn't that fun? Like camping." Daniel tries to convince her.

I'm already regretting leaving the other house, if for nothing more than being able to sleep in a bed.

I wonder if Daniel knows Taylor died because of Bruce.

Or, if he cares.

Either way, this isn't the time to bring it up. I don't want to upset Rayleen again.

Daniel leaves the room without saying anything but comes back quickly with a large box of assorted crayons and markers, and some green and red construction paper.

"Who wants to make presents?" Daniel asks. He sets down the drawing utensils and paper on the ground in front of the bubbling little girl.

Rayleen jumps up with joy. "Do you want to hear my Christmas song I wrote?"

"You wrote a Christmas song?" Rayleen nods. Daniel jests. "What? No way! Did you really write a whole song?"

"I did. Do you want to hear it?" Rayleen asks.

"I sure do," Daniel responds excitedly.

Rayleen stands up straight and takes a few calming breaths. She had no problem singing it in front of me over and over again in the hotel room.

This is different. Like she's preparing to sing in front of an audience. This is a production.

"Wait!" She declares. Rayleen launches for our abandoned things, and ruffles through the papers until she finds the one she wrote her song on. "I don't want to forget anything."

She goes back exactly where she started, in the exact same spot, and breathes deeply again before starting to sing.

Snow, Snow a white blanket of snow.
Snow, Snow comes in the winter.
Snow, Snow comes on Christmas.

Oh, Oh, Oh, Oh.
All the decorations shimmer and shine.
Oh, Oh, Oh, Oh, Oh, Oh.

On Christmas night Santa brings all of us presents.
Santa goes all around the world giving us presents.

Oh, the tree ornaments shimmer and shine.

Santa makes our wish come true!
Santa makes our wish come true!

Sharp clapping shocks me from the doorway. "That was beautiful! I love having a kid in the house again. They're always so joyful." An older man gives a thumbs up to Rayleen and then walks away.

The interaction brings joy to my heart and tears well. Maybe this won't be so bad after all. It might be good for Rayleen to be around people who find her joyful and celebrate her being a kid.

We spend the rest of the morning drawing pictures for each other. It's almost enough normalcy to make me forget about everything going on; almost.

Chapter 23

"Merry Christmas!" A small woman says approaching us. She's not human, but I can't place what she is. Her face and arms are covered in a moving black tattoo. The lines sway and swirl in stark contrast with her light brown skin.

It's mesmerizing. Can anyone get a magic moving tattoo?

"It's Christmas?" I half ask and half state. Keeping track of the days hasn't occurred to me too much. I lost track of any sense of time while kidnapped.

"Yeah." She smiles. "We've been keeping track. There was even a Christmas party and feast planned at one point. I guess there was a turkey farm we were going to get the turkeys from, but there wasn't any turkeys there."

"I had no idea," I tell her. I had no idea what day it was.

It makes sense that a fresh blanket of snow tucked us in. That the cold air turns our breath visible as it attacks our bare skin.

My face and hands burned from the temperature yesterday. I turned right back inside the house. I have no business important enough to face air cold enough that it hurts my bare skin in just five seconds of being outside.

Today, it's not so bad. The fire pit gives off enough heat to keep us comfortable. The air is fresh and crisp, but not painful. I don't know how she's not wearing a jacket though; it's too cold for that. But, I guess some supernatural run different temperatures than humans do.

So, it's Christmas. Merry Christmas to me.

The woman approaches closer to Jaiden beside me. "Hi."

Jaiden peers up from the book she's reading. "Hey." She smiles and greets the woman with some level of recognition. I don't remember her from any of my introductions or wanderings.

She must be from the people rescued at the hotel. Maybe Jaiden met her while up she was up at the hotel ignoring her promise to stay on the couch.

"I have something for you; a Christmas present." The woman opens her jacket halfway to pull out a rolled-up lime green fabric.

"You do?" Jaiden is taken aback by the gesture. "You didn't have to give me anything. I don't have something for you."

"It doubles as a thank you." The woman unravels a bright green scarf and drapes it around Jaiden's neck. It's thin and finely woven. Small tassels line the very ends.

"It's beautiful." Her smile drops ever so slightly in concentration as she examines a section at the end right above the tassels.

I lean over more, so I can see her finger brush over her name in a coarse stitch. There is a delicate design beside her name in a light yellow thread.

"I hope I spelled it right. I asked around." She says anxiously.

"You did. I can't thank you enough. This is beautiful. Thank you." Jaiden smiles widely.

In a rare gesture, Jaiden gets up from her spot to hug the woman. She welcomes the hug and grasps my sister tightly.

Bringing the can up to my lips, I taste the last bit of pop in a one-half gulp. Wanting more to drink, I get up and go inside the house.

"Can you help me move a table?" A girl asks from the door to the kitchen. "

"Sure." She takes me to the dining room, and I help her put the table flat against the wall. We remove the top legs by spinning them off.

"Thank you. I wanted to give us a bit more room. No one's been using the table anyway. You all seem to like to freeze outside." She jokes.

"It's not bad today, and we stay by the fire. Yesterday though, I walked outside and my face and lungs started hurting. Went right back inside. No way, I was dealing with that." I inform her.

"Yeah, no one needs frostbite these days. Gets worse in January and February lately. So, we'll need to be prepared for that." She says thoughtfully.

"Yeah, maybe. Maybe the weather will be nice to us this year." I can hope that with all that's going on, our winter will be nice to us, but it might be a fool's hope.

"I heard it's supposed to be a snowy year with few days that are -30 degrees, but we'll see." She informs.

I scrunch my nose in disgust. "Yeah we'll see. Did you need anything else?"

"No, thank you." She declines.

"I'll see you later then. Bye." I send a short wave her way then head back to the kitchen.

"Bye. Thanks for the help."

"You're welcome." Without turning my back, I go back to the kitchen and grab a pop from the cooler, then back out to the yard. The cold air nips at my skin before I make it back to sit around the fire.

I drop back into the conversation to find it's twisted around to the boys talking about hockey. I've never cared for it, but my family are huge WWE and boxing fans.

"Awfully quiet Jaiden," Brad notes. My anger rises immediately. I hold back to see if he means anything by it. Lately, he seems to antagonize people more than not.

"I have nothing to contribute." She states.

"Why not?" He goads her.

"I don't watch hockey." Jaiden confesses. Me neither.

"What?" A collective sarcastic gasp comes from the group. We're Canadians, so obviously we're supposed to be obsessed with hockey. It's an annoying stereotype.

"Of course you watch hockey. You have to watch hockey. Everyone watches hockey." Shawn exaggerates.

She shakes her head slightly. "I think watching sports is a complete waste of time. I went to a game once, because our school got free tickets, and I sat there thinking it was the most boring thing in the world. I don't understand it."

"Keep talking like that and we will revoke your Canadian Citizenship." Shawn points at her and mocks an angry tone.

"You don't have that power, not that it matters much anymore." Jaiden pulls on his joke and then directs her attention to the group. "But, for me, it's true. I don't understand how watching other people play sports and paying hundreds to thousands of dollars to do so, is so popular.

The whole culture behind it bewilders me. And, I don't understand how people get so into it and make it their whole personality. And, the temper tantrums people throw when their team loses is ridiculous."

"You're just not doing it right." Brad accuses her.

"I'm fine not doing it right for the rest of my life." Jaiden is stubborn to the core.

"So, you don't watch sports and you don't know anything

about celebrities. What are you interested in?" Jamie asks Jaiden.

"Wait, you don't know anything about celebrities?" Steph looks at Jaiden with disbelief.

"I know some things, impossible to miss things that others have talked about around me, but I don't care about them. I don't care what they do and who they are. I don't know them, and I'm never going to, so why should I care about who they are and what they do? All I care about is whether I liked the movie or show or not. Did they do a good job? Again, the whole culture around that bewilders me."

"So, back to my question. What do you like?" Jamie pulls the conversation back on track.

"Umm. I don't know." She thinks hard for a moment. "I like knowledge."

"Obviously, not all knowledge. Knowing about celebrities and hockey is its own type of knowledge. What fascinates you the most?" Jamie probes a little further. The question interests me. Jaiden isn't one to share information about herself, and I couldn't list any of her favourites.

She hesitates. "Ancient history. History."

"Cool. So were you going to be a history teacher, museum director or archaeologist or something?" Jamie asks.

She shakes her head. "No."

"Why not?" Jamie probes.

"None of those were acceptable career options according to my father," Jaiden reveals. I should have known the answer would have been something like that. Not every parent is as accepting of every career choice as mine are.

"So what were acceptable career options?" Jamie asks.

"At one point, I was being groomed to take over the family business, and that was the only option. Then, when he found out he was going to have a son, I was supposed to be a doctor or a lawyer. Both, I would be horrible at because I don't like germs, and I can't debate anything to save my life. Or, I was supposed to be a trophy wife in a strategic marriage with someone of equal or greater status as my father. But, he also told me frequently that I'd make a horrible wife, so I think that plan was off." Her response is a tragedy.

"Well, you're just a disappointment aren't you?" Brad chuckles as he jokes.

"Yes." Her stark acceptance of it is sobering.

Brad frowns. "Believe it or not, I was joking."

Jaiden shrugs her shoulders. "My father was not."

I swallow a lump formed in my throat. "So if you had the choice, what would you have done?"

Jaiden shrugs and shakes her head a little. "I don't know. Doing what I wanted was never an option, so I never thought about it."

There is an awkward silence for a few minutes after.

People move on from Jaiden as the conversation piece. I, however, received a bit more insight into Jaiden's home life from that small conversation.

Small conversations and comments since I met her have been gathering in my mind.

Piece by piece I have put together an image of Jaiden's home life. What I see, is an abusively controlling father and a shattered shell of a girl who's an ounce of the person she was meant to be. Her mom died but didn't seem to be stellar either.

And, no one else seems to notice. She does put on a good front. A smile to wipe away everything.

But, it explains everything about who she is. Why she is so reserved. Why she hugs so awkwardly. Why she simultaneously doesn't seem to care about you but will do anything for those she loves.

"Nikki!" Uncle Bruce gets my attention with an inpatient voicing of my name. He beckons me to follow him.

A bit reluctantly, I get up and go. The lines were clearly drawn when I confirmed he betrayed Taylor and us.

Furthermore, when he conveniently put all the supernaturals in separate homes from the humans. He surrounded his living space with humans.

He did it subtly. But one mention from Jaiden about her theory and it immediately clicked in place. I'm no longer sure of where my uncle's intentions and views lay.

"Will everyone be staying for the winter?" He asks when we get to his garage.

I had been thinking of this when I noticed all the snow that had dropped on us. "I don't think we have much of a choice now."

I don't imagine unless something drastic happens, that anyone else would leave in this. It's hard enough to travel around without snow and cold adding to the dangers.

It was different before this last dump of snow. The roads we somewhat drivable.

People had to turn back on foot this morning. They got stuck trying to go up to the hotel. So far as I know, no one has tried to get the vehicle out yet.

"Good. It'll give me more time to convince you to stay longer." He smiles charmingly. I'm not sure if he's joking or serious; perhaps a bit of both.

"Still planning on leaving as soon as it gets warmer out and some of the snow melts. I need to try to find the rest of my family." I gently remind him.

We talked about this back on his meeting day. His boring, useless, meeting day.

When I went back to him to ask questions related to the supernatural people, he didn't have answers for me. But said he would figure something out. The afternoon meeting didn't have anything mentioned until I interrupted the end to mention it.

"You're still my family. If you can't find your mom and dad, then you come right back here. You'll always be welcome." He tries to be welcoming but I shove it off.

"Thank you," I say. But, I'm not quite sure that I'll return.

"On to business, a few people have requested justice for the false imprisonment and the deaths of their loved ones," Bruce announces. I thought this was put to rest, but I guess not.

I interrupt anything he's planning on saying next. "What about justice for Taylor? She didn't ask to be murdered by your lynch mob. We called a truce."

"Jaiden called the truce, not me." Seems Uncle believes his hierarchy is worth more than everyone else agreeing to get along.

"Jaiden called a truce as soon as the hotel blew up, and fixed the fuck up that was that day.

They were letting the prisoners go. The leaders fled because they knew their people wouldn't follow them. No one had to die.

Jaiden called the truce and brought everyone together. The hotel people agreed to a truce and are helping us.

You opened your mouth and fucked things up. You told them about Taylor, and they killed her." He tries to interrupt me. "You don't get any say in this. Because we'd be putting part of Taylor's justice on you.

People died on both sides. If everyone wants justice then no one will be alive at the end of it. We called a truce. That means everything previous is forgiven, and we move on."

"Nikki!" He shouts in anger and parental reprimand.

"No! That's the end of this. Go tell your people that retaliation will not be tolerated. We have a truce. No more fighting." I storm out with my blood boiling.

I sit in my previous spot beside Jaiden. I've never craved a smoke more. Anger does that to me, but so does not having any on me. I know that it's horrible for my health, and better that I quit, but it's still engraved as a coping mechanism.

I fidget with my fingers instead.

Jaiden's immersed in listening to the conversation, but I can't pay attention.

Her hair is so long. I reach out and start playing with her hair almost subconsciously. I feel her tense up as she feels the slight tugs against her scalp.

"Sorry. I need a distraction." I let out the confession.

Her eyebrows twitch. "No, it's okay. I don't mind. You can go back to playing with my hair if you want."

I take that as full permission to do what I want with her hair. The fidgeting is a good distraction from both the craving and the anger.

The first thing I notice as I manipulate her hair is how clean it is. I'd expect it to be ultra-greasy like so many here. My hair is permanently in a bun so I don't have to deal with it.

The movements awaken a flowery scent. Leaning in and pulling the hair up at the same time I smell it. "Why does your hair smell like flowers?" I ask under my breath.

"Did you smell my hair?" She doesn't wait for me to answer. "I had a shower this morning."

"There's a working shower and you didn't tell me." Leftover irritation spills over to Jaiden.

"Because, it's more like melting some ice and sponge bathing yourself." She explains. I immediately back off. It's not exactly what I would call a shower.

"Why didn't I think of that?" Calli mutters to herself. "Of course, you'd think of doing something like that; Miss it's the apocalypse and I somehow remember to brush my teeth every day. You're making the rest of us look bad."

Her eyes widen slightly and she looks flustered. "I just—I'm not doing it to make you look bad. I do it because I can't stand fuzzy teeth, and oily hair, and being dirty."

Calli chuckles. "You're so fun to tease. Relax."

"I think the most important question here is whose toothbrush are you using?" Lucas asks.

"Probably one a guest can buy or use. It was still packaged up. I'm not desperate enough to use another person's used toothbrush." She scrunches her nose in disgust.

I laugh.

Chapter 24

A knock at the door interrupts my bedtime routine.

"One minute." I finish dressing in pyjamas, then open the door.

Shawn waves his hand once. "Hey, sorry, I was hoping you'd come next door to talk. Were you getting ready for bed?"

It's just after supper, maybe five thirty, I understand his confusion. "Yeah, I didn't sleep well the last few nights. I thought I might catch up on sleep. But, I can change and go talk; if you need me to."

"I would appreciate it." He says.

Through my disappointment, I nod and put my finger up to signal that I need a minute.

I close the door and change back into the clothes I had worn throughout the day.

Slight disappointment is sharpened by the stiff clothes. We need to figure out a better solution for laundry sooner rather than later.

I open the door.

Shawn leads me downstairs and we go to the front door. He opens it once we're in outside gear.

"Should we get Dominique, or…?" I trail off my question.

Is she already there?

"No." We get out the door and I shut it behind me. He continues quieter as we walk away. "They don't trust her. They think she's too close to Bruce and will ultimately side with him over people who kept her captive."

I can see the objective point, she's his family, but I don't think she would from her personality.

Then again, I don't know her as well as Shawn would, maybe she would. "I don't think she would."

"Neither do I," he looks behind to smile at me, "but this doesn't work if they don't think they have a voice that will advocate for them. Someone that the other side doesn't immediately shut down because of what they are."

"Wait, why, am I the advocate?" My heart panics and an instant pit lodges in my throat.

I can't do that.

I don't advocate.

I can't even advocate for myself.

How am I supposed to advocate for other people?

Suddenly, the necessity of us talking next door, right now, is making a little more sense.

"Yes," Shawn confirms.

"How'd that happen?" Was there a vote? Do I get a say?

"You've been doing it. They trust you enough. Now it's official." He reasons.

I don't see how I've already been doing it.

Unless, they took my saying there would be a truce back at the hotel, as me being trustworthy and in charge. I've just been friendly otherwise.

"I'm a horrible advocate," I admit.

Maybe I can still get out of this.

They should have someone better. They should know I'm not going to be good for them.

"Should have thought about that before you made them trust you." He responds.

I can't tell if he's joking or serious.

We go inside the neighbouring house. It's cooler here than in our place, but warmer than outside.

Our wood stove helps warm much of the main floor to a comfortable sweater temperature. The rest of the house is a bit cooler, but not this cold.

I opt to keep my jacket on in here, and so do many others.

The living room and dining room are full of people sitting on anything they can.

Some people moving around, hop in small spots between people; typically needing people to lean so they aren't knocked into.

The stiff material of winter gear crunches continuously between all.

"Hey, thanks for coming." DeAngelo welcomes.

"Thanks for having me," I respond politely.

I'm not entirely sure what I'm doing here, but Shawn mentioned that they want me to advocate for them, so something to do with grievances; I'm sure.

Bruce had his meeting; a very human only residents and vacationers in Banff meeting.

Now, the supernaturals are having their own meeting.

"So, we don't want to take too much of your time, but there have been concerns tossed around, and we'd like to make sure everyone is on the same page." DeAngelo talks between myself and the group.

I'm not certain who the message is intended for. I settle on it being for everyone.

He continues as everyone quietens, "we made a list to help organize this. But, if you have additional concerns, please, wait until the very end."

People nod in agreeance and understanding.

Shawn and I are left standing near the house entrance. It feels oddly like being up on a stage since everyone else is sitting, watching us along with DeAngelo.

But, I won't be the first to sit out of the two of us. I don't know what would be more awkward; sitting down when Shawn doesn't or standing the whole meeting.

On second thought, it would definitely be sitting down when Shawn doesn't.

Maybe he's waiting for me to sit down first, in an ironic battle of anxiety.

"First issue is food. We all subsist on a variety of plants and animals, but for those of us who also intake a different diet in ways that can't be met by animals, we need options. We also need to make sure we are meeting nutrition needs by other food, enough, to ensure we aren't suffering negative effects."

"We need human blood." A man shouts from the crowd. "You need to organize a blood drive."

With the air of supernatural distrust, I don't think that will go over well. "Sorry if this is a dumb question, but what about supernatural blood, could that also be used? Or animal blood?"

"Animal blood doesn't have the right stuff." A woman answers.

"We've already gone through all the supernaturals that can donate." A different man says.

"Most don't count," Shawn says. I look over at him. "Like vampires don't drink from other vampires because of different strains of vampirism, can do funky things to the drinking vampire.

Could make them stronger, or weaker, kill them, or do nothing. You don't want to take that chance.

Some supernaturals are too different blood-wise. It would be like you eating food that's gone bad or stuff that has no nutritional value at all. Which defeats the purpose of drinking the blood.

And then, as with all blood, you have to make sure you're in taking compatible blood. Much like blood typing for blood transfusions. Some blood works for some, but not others. It's not compatible for nutrition or absorption."

"You could be the first to donate." The same man from earlier shouts.

"Stop interrupting, and stop being an ass. She's here to help." DeAngelo scolds.

"She's O-. Sorry, I got a whiff of it earlier with you bleeding everywhere." DeAngelo throws his hands up to make the question W form at the woman's statement. She mouths the word sorry again.

"It's fine. I can donate if needed." I think. I hope. Does that soul protection thing translate over to blood too? They said some supernatural blood works, and some doesn't. Let's hope mine does or at least doesn't harm anyone. "But, obviously you need more than just me.

I can ask people to donate, but how much would we need realistically?"

"Ideally, eight ounces per vampire, per day," DeAngelo informs me.

"There's wiggle room in that." A woman interjects as she raises her hand to talk. "It's like the doctor's answer equivalent to how much water a person needs in a day.

They tell you to have a cup of blood a day, but some people need more and some less. Some days you need more, like after an injury, and some days you can do with less. You can also skim a bit off the top and be more or less fine for a little bit.

What you need to know, is that a regular blood donation, that you would do at a hospital blood drive, is typically just over fifteen ounces and is usually fine to cover two full portions.

Unfortunately, this means we need about six people to donate every day.

And, once you donate, doctors want you to wait two to three months before donating again. Which obviously puts us in a supply problem, even if you can convince every single capable person to donate and blood typing works out."

"There had to of been some vampires who lived in Banff. Maybe we can find a hidden store, or somewhere that has supplements." My ears perk at his mention of supplements.

"That's worse than a needle in a haystack."

"We had supplements at the hotel, but good luck finding those, even if they survived."

Shawn turns to me and says in a hushed voice. "Supplements are like human blood vitamins, many preferred to take those instead of the blood substitute, or human blood."

A thought hits me. I instantly draw my gaze to the vampires we had travelled with. Each of them has been quiet through this. Throughout our journey, not one of them had to drink our blood. They must have their own stashes of blood supplements.

It's the only thing that makes sense because I doubt this would be as much of an issue if vampires could go weeks at a time without blood.

I won't tell on them, but I might ask privately how much they have and if they'd be willing to share some.

The conversation seems to be spiralling, so I make a

summarizing comment. "Obviously, blood donation is the tangible answer. I'll ask around.

But, we also should try to find other options, since we already know that it's not going to be enough. So we'll need to search for hidden shops or personal stashes around Banff.

Were there any supernaturals that lived in Banff, that are still around and could tell us the locations of the hidden stores?"

"None that lived." Someone calls out.

"There was Cory. He owned a shop, but he donated everything to the hotel. Maybe he kept a back stock somewhere he didn't tell Darius about." DeAngelo tells me.

"That's a big maybe." Some people snicker. I assume Cory was all in on the cause.

I'll have to check my phone later. There has to be some sort of directory for shops.

"What about supernatural residents that are still pretending to be human?" I ask.

"No idiot would continue to pretend to be human after what they were going to be put through." A man scoffs.

They might.

DeAngelo cuts off the group discussion. "Okay, we're done with this topic. We have a plan. So it's done.

Moving on, but on the same note, Calli needs souls. It's not as dire, but at some point, we will need to start looking at human donations."

"They won't do it. Humans are weird about their souls."

"Unless you want to offer?" The same man asking me to donate blood, asks about me donating souls.

He has a grudge to burn, I feel.

I open my mouth to talk but, I'm still thinking about how I can excuse this one. Should I just agree? Calli knows why I can't.

"She already did." Calli saves me. "I won't take more unless necessary. Just ask if people are willing to donate a year or two off their soul life, tell them it won't affect their human life at all, and we can move on."

"Okay." DeAngelo moves it along. "The last note on food is that we need you to make sure we're getting our equal portions. There's thought that Bruce might give humans more food than us."

I nod, so he continues. "Next item on the agenda is Sunshield. This will go along with finding hidden stores. However, unless we find those shops, we have limited quantities of Sunshield left.

We're asking as many vampires as possible to only go out at night. Conserve the Sunshield for emergencies and necessities, please.

Next, we are officially calling off efforts on the hotel. We haven't found anyone alive, and we haven't found anything useful beyond stuff to burn. There's too much snow, and our efforts would be better off elsewhere.

Can we, please, all agree?"

There is a general agreeance, but some stay quiet.

"What about the cerberus?" A girl asks.

"They caught a wolf to eat the other day, so we believe they won't need us feeding them. They have a good shelter. But, it would be a good idea to have people visit them, to make sure they keep socialized." Michelle answers cheerfully.

"Last item. We found out some humans have generators. And, they aren't sharing." DeAngelo says.

"How do you know?" I realize how guilty that sounds as soon as it leaves my mouth. "We don't have a generator next door. But, I haven't seen anything from the other houses. No ones' mentioned having one."

"See, the silly humans forgot that vampires are naturally nocturnal. And, they were using it to light up three houses in the middle of the night." A woman sneers.

"We can do this without insulting the humans," DeAngelo says.

Proof enough, for now. "I'll go talk to Bruce and see what he says. Obviously, it's not fair if there are generators, and they are being used only at specific houses." At human houses. "And, they aren't being shared amongst everyone."

"They might argue ownership rules over sharing it at a house where the owners aren't staying." A woman tries to reason.

"Why hide it then?" A guy counters.

Before this continues, I put out other thoughts on this subject. "But, if there are generators, there could be more out there. We could check around. But, we'll also run out of gas sooner or later. We could attempt to make or find a different solution: batteries, solar energy, or wind energy. I once made a cardboard science experiment generator. We could attempt to large-scale that."

"You made a generator?" Shawn asks.

"Yeah. It's actually pretty simple." I make hand motions to help explain the directions. "Make a cardboard box, stick a bent nail through it, wrap it in lots of copper wire, and glue magnets to the nail inside the box. Then as you crank the shaft, the magnets inside spin, and the magnetic field creates an electric charge in the wire.

Obviously, the science experiment only lights up a small lightbulb and only for as long as you crank the nail, but generators work off of this same principle. And, if you can hook it up to a rechargeable battery, you could save the power."

"Sounds like too much work, for not enough electricity." His comment pulls me out of my explanation to Shawn.

I shrug. "Might be better than absolutely nothing at all.

We could get a bike to crank a couple of larger-scale models and maybe it would be enough to power an electric heater. If that's what saves us from becoming popsicles this winter, then that's what we'll do.

We might want to look into hardware stores around, and see what we can do to help insulate the houses better. See if they have generators. If nothing else comes about we have a wood stove next door, we can move everyone in if it gets too cold."

"We'll be stepping over each other like cockroaches." He sneers.

"If it's that or death. I think you'll choose to move in." Shawn defends.

"I think this is where we will end things," DeAngelo interjects. "Jaiden, if you can action what you need to do, we'd appreciate it.

For the rest of us, we can start on our share of the work. Tonight, vampires will go out to Cory's shop and see if there's anything left over, or any information that points to his home or another shop, storage, or anything.

Tomorrow, the rest of us will work on weatherproofing and generators."

People get up in a rush. Shawn tugs at my jacket to jumpstart me. We go out the door before some of the crowd get to us.

"Do you want to talk to Bruce now? Get it over with." Shawn asks as we approach our house.

I want to answer no, but since I'm already having to be outside of my comfort zone, I might as well keep going. "Might as well get it over with; I guess."

Shawn escorts me over to the house Bruce is staying at. I look at the houses suspiciously, but I don't see any lights on.

"Good luck." He says.

"Thanks," I respond instinctively.

He turns back the way we came. Of course, he's not coming with me. Why did I think he would?

I knock on the door three separate times before an elder man answers. "Hi, is Bruce here?"

"Yes, come in." He opens the door wider and steps aside.

A dozen boots on the boot mats cue me to remove my own. I line them up with the end neatly.

It's distinctly warm inside. A sharp contrast to the previous house. No one is wearing a jacket or snow pants. It's already warm enough that I want to take my jacket off.

I doubt the candles are contributing to all this heat.

"Jaiden, welcome! To what do I owe the pleasure?" Bruce snatches my attention.

He sits on one side of a green velvet loveseat.

A matching couch holds three men at the window while the man who greeted me takes his seat in a matching lounging chair.

"Thank you." I walk into the center of the room. "Umm. Some concerns were brought to me and I was hoping we could talk."

"Of course. Sit down. Let's talk." I sit down in the spot available next to him. "What concerns do people have?"

"Vampires need a nutrient that's in human blood to survive, but it's not in animal blood. So they either need human blood or a special supplement vitamin.

They've started a search to find hidden shops that sold supernatural stuff like those special supplements, and I was hoping maybe some of the Banff residents might have a better idea of where to look. If you could pass the word around?"

"Of course. I will see if anyone knows." Bruce replies pleasantly.

"Otherwise, they will need volunteers for a blood drive. If anyone is willing to donate?" I wait nervously for his response when his smile falls slightly.

"Anything else?" He brushes off this one.

I instantly change tactics knowing Bruce won't be as responsive to supernatural requests that require human sacrifice.

"There's a general food concern. I don't know if Dominique told you. I fainted the other day because I haven't been eating enough. Happened a couple of weeks ago too.

So this has sparked concerns about long-term food, and having enough to survive the winter."

"We'll make sure we have enough. You don't have to worry about having enough food to last the winter. Plenty of survivalists and hunters in Banff." He places his hand on my arm and squeezes briefly.

I smile sweetly, and it helps put the smile back on his face.

I try not to word the last one as though I'm accusing him of something. "Wonderful. The last thing, it's just a rumour I heard. Do you have a generator?"

"Yes," Bruce answers simply. I wait a moment for an elaboration, but he doesn't continue.

"Oh. Is that how it's so warm in here?" I ask while knowing the answer.

"Yes, we've got some electrical heaters throughout the house." I nod at his response.

"That makes sense. The wood stove does alright, but this is the warmest I've been in a long while.

Are there any more? Do you think there would be enough to warm all the houses?"

The men look between each other. I might be pushing for too much information. "We could see if we could find you one. We only have this one because it was for John's camper." Bruce answers.

I don't know anything about generators, but I doubt one camper generator would be good to keep multiple houses going and I don't think they'll be willing to pass it around.

The passing looks between the old men suggest he's not telling me the full truth.

I smile charmingly. "That would be great. The more generators the better, right?"

"Excuse me." A tear falls down his cheek. This feels exactly like a change of conversation tactic I would use on my father. "I'm a sentimental old man. You look so much like my Dannie when she was your age. You have the same expressions. Doesn't she?" He opens up the question to the other older men in the room.

They all agree. They all must've been friends before all this, maybe going back decades.

"You knew Dannie when she was fifteen?" I inquire.

He raises his eyebrows in surprise for a moment. "We didn't meet until she was twenty. That's a story; would you like to hear it?"

"Yes, please."

Bruce moistens his lips. "She had come to Banff with her sister and brother; Dominique's grandfather. They were young and on a road trip. They had told their parents they were going on a hiking vacation and sibling bonding trip.

I was a cool young motorcycle guy and had lived in Banff my whole life. I was a bit of a troublemaker." He smiles at the memories that likely pop up in his mind.

"But back in those days, the police never did anything about it. I would speed up and down the highway as fast as I could go. They used to radio between police cars to warn that I'd be coming through.

That all changed just five years ago. The police chief changed and personally warned me they would now be charging me if I speed. He personally came to give me my two tickets too." Bruce smirks.

"Dannie made me stop after that. Threatened to sell my bike, if I went to jail." I smile largely at the image of Dannie making her threat, then storming out.

The knowing smiles around the room suggest the others are reminiscing through this, likely, often-told tale. Maybe they were even there, or around during the time, this was occurring.

Years of history between these friends won't be rivalled.

"She was always the spitfire. Had to be; being the youngest in that family. That's what caught my attention first, that and her golden hair. She was arguing with her siblings about the trip and refusing everything she suggested.

I caught up to her when she ran off, and offered to show her around; being a resident I would obviously know all the best spots. She agreed and we did all the things she wanted. I showed her around to some local spots tourists rarely venture to.

She rode on my motorcycle, and I showed her how fast it could go."

He continues after a thoughtful pause. "By the end of the week, we exchanged numbers and kept in contact. After just one month of her being home, she decided to come back to Banff permanently.

You're probably bored of an old man's stories."

"No, not at all. I really appreciate it. I haven't heard many stories about the family."

About my family. About someone who also has visions. An Aunt, I likely would have loved to have grown up with.

"Would you like to hear more?" Bruce asks.

"Yes, please."

Chapter 25

The spectacle at the window instantly surges chills down my spine. Grabbing Rayleen a little tighter, I get ready to bolt in the other direction.

"He's a fat one."

"He's obviously still finding food, or else he'd be hibernating already."

"Who left the food out last night?"

"I don't know."

"Probably the tourists."

They talk between themselves as they watch the bear through the window.

"Well, this is your reminder, to everyone, that we need to make sure we're not leaving food out. Food attracts animals. Clean up after yourself, and clean up after others, because it's everyone's problem when we get bears." An older man boosts his voice so everyone can hear.

"I thought bears hibernated in the winter," Rayleen says.

The older man turns around from the window to face us. He smiles big and leans down to talk to Rayleen at her level. "They do, but there's no set timeline on that, and it can be disrupted. It's not completely abnormal for male bears to be out until the end of December if there's been enough food around to keep him going. Judging by how fat he is, that's likely what's happened."

"So, what do we do? Are we safe in here?" I ask him.

He stands up to talk with me. "He probably won't try to break in, and unless he does, then we do nothing."

He turns his attention back to the bear.

I bring Rayleen away from the back. I don't want to chance being nearby if he does decide to break in.

I decide to go search the house for Daniel. I haven't seen him in a while.

A teen boy listens closely to a closed door. As soon as he sees us, he puts his head down and runs off.

I get curious, so I put my finger up to my lips to shush Rayleen. I lean into the door and concentrate to listen quietly.

"Everyone's distracted by the bear. We should go now."

"What if someone sees us? We'll immediately give the location away. We find a reason to go to the shop that no one would question, take the blood vitamins, and hide them in other cargo until we can unpack them here and come up with another reason for why we have them. We control the vitamins, we control the vampires."

"Right, we have to be smart about this. Where did you say it was?"

"I'm not telling. I know where it is, and that's good enough."

"Why won't you tell us?"

"Because, he's afraid I'll burn it down."

"We already nixed that plan."

"You did. And, I get it. I won't burn the whole house down. But, it doesn't mean we should give them anything."

"The supplements mean the vampires don't have to drink our blood." I recognize Daniel's voice.

"Fine, then we leverage the vitamins so we can control the vampires. Destroy their sunscreen so we're safe during the day, and destroy anything else. We control the demons, so we can survive."

The teen boy walks swiftly by us, this time he catches us eavesdropping. He ignores it to go out the front door. I notice the bags he now carries, and knowing the conversation topic, I wonder what he's going to do about the shop. He doesn't seem like he's with the men in the room.

I pull Rayleen's arm away from the door.

Multiple male voices continue their argument as we follow the teen out the door. Putting on our winter boots and grabbing our jackets before we leave, then putting on our jackets as we follow him.

He speeds around the block, down a few rows, and disappears into the yard of another house. The gate snaps loudly. We won't be able to follow him if we make that much noise.

The side door of the house opens and, after a few moments, shuts.

I look around in part to make sure the bear is nowhere around and to make sure we weren't followed.

Hopefully, the bear sticks to that house for a while and we don't run into him on the way back.

The teen is in the house, where the shop likely is, and is doing who knows what.

"I'm going after him. I need you to stay in the doorway, and run if I scream." I order Rayleen.

"No, what if he's dangerous?" She asks.

"I can handle it. I need to make sure he's not destroying the stuff." Rayleen tugs on my jacket as soon as I move one foot forward.

Rayleen reasons. "He had bags. He's not destroying, he's gathering."

"Then we need to know why he's gathering it. The other guys want to destroy it or control the vampires with it. We can't let that happen."

"I think he's trying to save it." She responds optimistically.

"Chances are, he's not." We can't trust people have the best of intentions.

Our talking wasted too much time. He's out of the house and struggles to come out of the gate with four large bags filled.

"What are you doing with those?" I strengthen my voice.

"Shit!" He jumps. "Nothing. I was just getting some personal objects."

"You were getting the blood supplements before they could. Why?" I question; straight to the point.

"To give to the vampires." He says.

"Give me half, we can split up. If one of us is caught by the men behind the door, then they don't get them all." With this, at least they'll get half.

"Why should I trust you?" He questions.

"Why should I trust you?" I echo.

"I'm a witch, you can trust me." Rayleen's little voice announces proudly.

I scold her in a higher voice. "We talked about this. You can't tell people that."

"Show me something magical." The boy demands.

"I'm not very good," Rayleen admits. "James was trying to get me to roast a marshmallow but I couldn't. I didn't grow up with magic so James said I don't have any instincts."

"You were with James' group?" He asks me. I nod. He smiles warmly and turns his eyes back to Rayleen. "I'm still learning too. I could show you some things if you want. But, you need to promise me that you won't tell anyone you and I know magic, could be dangerous for us."

"Okay." She beams.

The lanky teen walks over and hands me two of the four bags. "Do you know your way to the supernatural houses?"

"Only back the way we came," I admit.

"Best we go together then. We don't want to pass by the house. I'm Cam, by the way." He starts walking away at a brisk speed.

Ushering Rayleen forward, we quickly keep pace with him. "I'm Alexa and this is Rayleen."

"Nice to meet you."

"So how did you know about this place, did you live here?" I ask.

"My parents moved here when I was five. It took a while for them to trust me with the shop location information.

I was horrible at keeping secrets at five. I told anyone who would listen that I could do magic.

But, thankfully no one ever believed me, and oddly they couldn't get that rule to stick, but the no magic outside our house rule did stick.

So I would tell people that I was magic folk and I'd tell them all the magic I could do, and they'd ask me to do a magic trick, and I'd tell them I can't because I can only practice in my house.

We never had any house guests because of it.

So of course, they'd think I was a cute little kid pretending when I was actually giving my parents heart attacks."

Cam continues after a brief pause. "They finally took me to all the locations a year ago. One got cleaned out, one is in a shop, and the house one.

They were talking about a house, so I assumed they might just know about that one.

Bruce must know about it because of his wife."

"What was his wife?" I ask.

"A dreamer. She helped my mom a few years ago. She was going to die, and Dannie stopped it from happening." His words bring back the connection between Nikki and Bruce.

It must be the aunt that was blood-related.

"And, you think he only knew about the house one?" I ask.

Cam turns around to look behind us, then spins back to look forward. "Maybe, he specifically mentioned house. He could be keeping the other one secret from the others. But, I don't know if Dannie knew about the other shop or not, and if she had told Bruce."

"Is it normal not to know about the hidden shops?" I ask.

"Very normal. You either knew about shops because they were on SuperData, DataBase, listed on a verified list the Council provided, or because you were personally invited to an illegal one.

Dannie technically wasn't even supposed to marry Bruce, since he's human, but in that circumstance, you also aren't supposed to tell them about the shops.

But, of course, everyone breaks the rules."

"So if all these humans knew about demons before this, why didn't they reveal their existence?" I wonder out loud.

"We prefer supernaturals. Demons are one thing, but supernatural covers everyone." Cam explains.

"Supernaturals then," I confirm.

"Sometimes, they present themselves as the anomaly. Or sometimes, they'll tell them that the Council will kill them if they find out. Or, they were killed; usually by the person who told them." I imagine if Darius had told me, he would have gone with the second one. He attempted the third option.

"Did the Council make them?" I ask vaguely.

Cam turns us around a corner house. "No. Usually, it's buried as necessary damage control, but everyone knows it's more like domestic violence. She tried to leave and promised she wouldn't tell anyone, then he killed her."

"Oh." I sound.

"Sometimes, if they can, they turn their partners.

But, that's also against the law, unless you're rich and influential. Then you can parade around the woman your son turned, by accident, and the Council pardons it." The heavy emphasis on 'by accident' has me thinking that it wasn't an accident.

We turn down a road. I quip, "Supernatural drama of the rich and famous?"

"Yes. It was a scandal. There are all sorts of conspiracy theories about what really happened, but nothing's proven and the Council will never tell. But no one has seen the son in public since it all went down.

Anyway, we're getting close, so we should quiet down."

Cam guides us through a yard to an alley and we get across to the backyard of the house next to Bruce's.

Along the way, I look for the bear but don't see it.

I can't see into the yard where it was from here, so I can't check to see if it's still there.

Rayleen opens the door for us, and we walk inside.

"I bring gifts," Cam announces.

A few people in the kitchen take bags from us. My arms tingle from the pressure relief.

Joy erupts in the room before Cam quickly shuts it down. "Some of the humans found the shop and one of them wants to burn it down. We have to go back before they can do anything."

Leah cuts me off from the rest of the group.

"You can go now." Leah threatens as she glares straight at me.

"Let's go, Rayleen. Hope that helps." I try to be polite.

I get why I'm not welcome.

We leave out the back. I can't help but feel a little bitter, they are throwing us outside to the bear, but I don't know if they know about it or not.

We go around to the front. Each house has a gate, so I don't think the bear would likely barrel through for no reason. Though, we as food is hardly no reason.

The bear is nowhere around the front.

I hurry us through Rayleen's frustrated complaint. "My legs are tired."

"Just a little longer," I say.

"I'm cold." She extends her complaints.

"We'll be warm once we get to the house." I try to reassure her.

She doesn't say another word as we get close.

We go back to the house and in through the front door. Safe again, I think.

People didn't notice anything. They are still looking through the back. We take off our boots and settle on the couch.

I want to make it look like we were never gone.

Chapter 26

His laugh grates on my nerves. The warm feelings brought up by seeing my uncle weeks ago, now have turned sour. I can't help but get annoyed at the sight of him. Uncle Bruce can't breathe without each breath scraping against my brain.

"She's going to betray you. She can't help it." His words echo in my ears.

I had abruptly left our conversation after that, and have been avoiding him since.

It worked until he hooked up a generator to our house, and decided to overstay his welcome by eating our food and telling stories; all while too close to Jaiden.

Uncle Bruce swipes Jaiden's hair back, exactly like he used to do to Auntie.

It twists my stomach.

I have to get her out of there.

I walk in from the doorway I was lurking in. Putting on my customer service voice and smile, I say, "Hey, sorry. I just need to steal Jaiden for a bit."

Jaiden pops up rather quickly. "Sure, excuse me. I'll be right back."

"It might take a while," I inform them. Maybe it'll get Uncle to leave if he knows that Jaiden will be a while.

I can hope.

I lead Jaiden from the living room to the back entry. When I think we're out of hearing, I stop and turn, and she nearly crashes into me.

"Sorry." She apologizes.

"You're not allowed to be alone with Uncle anymore. He's-His-" I swipe her hair like he had done and grimace. "You just have to trust me. He's being inappropriate."

Jaiden stares blankly for a moment. I prepare for her to react negatively.

She checks back towards the way we came. "I used the word creepy." She almost whispers.

It's a bit of a relief that she also felt something was off.

"Oh, so it's not just me?" I jest.

"No. At first, I thought it was just him noticing similarities and reminiscing, but now it seems like he's replacing something." She describes the feeling perfectly.

"Yes!" I agree. "He used to swipe Auntie's hair like that. It was a cute lovey thing they did."

"Gross." She summarizes.

"Ick." A voice calls from the basement. Jaiden and I jump and snap our heads at the noise.

A woman comes out from the basement. She had been in and out earlier, and I assumed she was done with the supplies by now. I should have checked. "Do you want to come on an adventure with me? We can go check on our furry friend. It'll get you away from him, but you'll have to dress warmly."

They seem to know each other well enough; that's good.

"Probably a good idea." Jaiden turns to me. "Gives you a real excuse why you pulled me away."

"Sure. That sounds good. Thank you, ...?" I trail off with a questioning pause.

"Michelle." She fills in the blank space.

"Nikki." I return while pointing at myself.

"He's coming this way," Michelle warns.

Jaiden quickly throws on her jacket. She slows down to a normal speed while putting on her boots.

Uncle Bruce comes through the kitchen doorway, and out to us. "Going somewhere?"

"Yeah, sorry. They need my expertise on something." Jaiden smoothly comes up with.

"What expertise are you providing?" Uncle asks.

"Assorted knowledge. I skipped a couple of grades and had access to a private tutor for years. I've learnt all sorts of things kids in school normally wouldn't. Medical stuff, history and science have all been useful recently."

"Good for you." Uncle Bruce puts his hand on Jaiden's shoulder. "Sounds like you have a good head on your shoulders."

My stomach clenches as his hand squeezes her shoulder. Jaiden doesn't let it affect her smile.

"We should get to it. Nice seeing you." Michelle politely excuses them.

She takes Jaiden's hand to pull her away.

"Let's talk. I feel like I haven't seen much of you lately." Uncle Bruce says after they've gone.

"I've been busy. Lots to do." I brush off.

Maybe I should have invited myself to go with Michelle and Jaiden.

"Never too busy for your Uncle. Especially, after I went to the trouble of getting you a generator." Uncle Bruce, master of manipulation. I knew the generator would come with a price. That price starts with his presence and a requirement to interact with him. "Let's go to the garage. I need something in there and we can talk."

"Sure." I find irony in going off alone with him right after telling Jaiden not to be alone with him. Not that I think he'll do anything to me, but it's still a bit funny.

I put on my boots and jacket, while he does the same. He leads me out to the garage through heavy snowflakes and foggy breath. I pull my hands into my sleeves to keep them warm.

Uncle Bruce pushes hard. The door swings open on the second push. We go inside, and I close the door behind me.

The garage is significantly cooler than the house. Still warmer than outside, but only because there's no breeze in here.

I wait in silence as he shuffles around the garage for a couple of minutes. He fiddles with things here and there, opens and closes drawers, and peeks inside boxes.

"How have you been doing?" He finally says.

"Good. You?" I return.

"Good." Uncle meanders about another minute before he gets to the point of this. "I know you took offence to me telling you Jaiden will betray you.

She seems like a nice girl. You've grown protective of her.

Explain to me, why you would continue to let people think you're the one who has visions?"

I explain my reasoning. "I got kidnapped and tortured because of it. Once I confirmed to them that I had visions and would work with them, the torture stopped. They still think I have visions and could still be after me. And, if they capture me again, it would be better if they still think that. Could keep me alive and not tortured. I don't want Jaiden to have that target on her."

"Would she do the same for you?" His question shocks me.

Why would that matter?

It's my decision. It shouldn't be tied to whether or not she would do the same.

"Doesn't matter," I tell him.

"It does matter" He shouts angrily. "You can't rely on them."

I raise my volume to match his but keep my tone calm. "It doesn't matter. I knew what I was doing before Jaiden came and rescued me here. I didn't even know she was coming after me, I hadn't seen her since the birthday party until she showed up with a bunch of people to rescue me.

So it doesn't matter if she would risk being kidnapped, tortured, and killed for me, because it doesn't matter. She also didn't have to come after me. She saved my life."

Something sharp occurs to me. "Did Auntie betray you somehow?"

Uncle Bruce wags his finger and then points it at me. "Being with someone like that, they're always betraying you. Lying to you. Withholding information. You can't do anything without knowing that they'll find out. The dreams change their actions and personality. Stops them from things because they are scared of one stupid dream."

He no longer yells, but he speaks with vitriol. "Dannie refused to have kids because while we were trying she had a dream of dying in childbirth; of our baby dying too. She couldn't see anything except that outcome, so she refused to have kids.

She wouldn't even wait and try some other time. I've always resented her for making that decision for us.

She wasn't even right all the time. Half the time, I thought she was delusional. She'd say something was supposed to happen, but it didn't."

I interject. "Jaiden isn't Auntie Dannie."

"They're exactly the same." He's pushing his resentment on Jaiden; on everyone.

Auntie decided not to have kids after having a vision of herself dying, and he decided to resent her for the rest of her life.

Blaming supernaturals for it now that she's gone.

To accuse her of being delusional or lying because not every vision came true.

"Then, I'm not you!" I burst out. "If Jaiden has PTSD from an incredibly sad and horrific vision, I'm going to help her, not blame her!"

He shoves his finger at me. "You don't know-"

I leave before he can say more; slamming the door behind me.

This explains some things. He resents his supernatural wife and thought she was delusional. I see now, how he's turned out now.

And, why he could be dangerous.

And, exactly how dangerous he could be.

I should have gone with Jaiden. An adventure to visit a furry friend sounds more fun than whatever family bonding bullshit that was.

Chapter 27

"Close the door!" The resounding shouts have me internally shaking my head. It's become a thing, every time the door is opened a bunch of people shout those words.

"Last time, I promise," I answer back. I remove my boots and winter clothes and set them in their proper places.

Everything and everyone should be set now.

Nothing like moving houses in the middle of a blizzard. A possibly deadly combination of heavy snow, wind and cold hit us hard.

I miss weathermen telling us what the weather is going to be. We could properly prepare for things. We could have had everyone moved before this started.

Our house and the one next door are warm enough from the fire and electric heaters, but beyond that, the rest were starting to get too cold.

We moved most things with the people, but some stuff was left behind. Much of the last half hour was spent with able people grabbing the remaining items.

Now we should be all set.

I take a look at the large crowd huddled in the house, and immediately think there are too many people in here. Hopefully, it's temporary. When the blizzard is done, and we can clear some snow. Going forward, we need to emphasize getting heat to the other houses.

"So this is what it's like to have a generator." The snide comment slides by me the first time, but then he repeats it louder. He wants a reaction, maybe even an interaction.

I look over at him just as an elbow collides with his ribs. "Shut up and be grateful."

"We didn't choose who got the generator. Bruce found it and hooked it up to preserve his house. At least it means you have access to it now, either here or next door. Only because we decided to hide an extension cord in the snow, so we could share the power. It's better than nothing. And, we will keep searching for more generators and solutions after the storm."

I walk by not interested in continuing a fight with them. I've heard many rumblings about favouritism with the generator. And, it's true. But, not the part where we don't care about the supernaturals; just like Bruce.

I walk into the kitchen, hoping to find Dominique. She's exactly right where I last saw her; settled in the booth with her friends, and many others milling about.

I settle in the doorway to the dining room, so I can see either side with a turn of my head.

"But, ultimately what are you going to do?" Stephanie asks Dominique.

"Then I'll eat the meat. I'd prefer not to, but I won't starve to death over it." Dominique says. It's good to know.

We're going to run out of fruit and vegetable cans eventually and true spring could be three or four months away. It would be easier to eat and keep up strength if she would incorporate meat.

I watch the conversations happen, but tune out the noise to be inside my head. It's too loud in here.

I've had about enough conversation by this point. It seems like the only thing to do for fun is to talk to each other, but I've never enjoyed talking to masses of people for long periods.

A memory pops into my head, of my French teacher calling me out as the only person who can go through her class without saying a word. It mortified me at the time, but now I can find the humour in it.

That happened just before all of this. Two months ago; I think. Maybe it's been two and a half months. It's absurd how much has happened.

But, I wouldn't want to go back to the way things were. Forgetting the bigger picture of the supernatural hiding, my personal life was awful.

I don't miss school and certainly not homework.

I don't miss work.

And, I don't miss my family.

I was burnt out from living my daily life. Fifteen years old, and burnt out already. I'd be surprised if I made it through much longer without having to get checked into a hospital.

Life shouldn't have been like that.

I don't know how much better this is. But in some ways, it seems like an improvement.

I have reasons to smile now. Like, I can't wait to make last night's vision come true. The thought itself adjusts the fake smile on my face into a real one.

A thick blanket of snow on the ground provided plenty of ammo for a snowball fight, even if some of the snow wouldn't hold that shape well. I threw some balls that broke apart midair.

A few of us were playing, but I don't know exactly who was hidden beneath the snow gear.

The cerberus bounded through the battle trying to snatch the snowballs. In her excitement, she landed on me and pushed me over. It took a bit for us to right ourselves. I had gotten stuck.

I wonder how they are doing out there. Would they be okay with a big snowstorm like this?

Michelle comes into the dining room and to the cooler for a drink. I take the chance to ask her while I'm thinking about it. She had said they had shelter, but would it hold up on a cold snap?

Walking up to her, I quietly ask, "Do you know how Artemis, Apollo, and Athena are? If they'll be okay in this?"

"I don't know. I wasn't able to get up there with all this, but I'm sure they'll be fine. We can check after the storm is done." She reassures me.

"Okay, thanks," I tell her. Michelle goes back out to the living room and I go back to my leaning spot in the kitchen doorway.

The kitchen conversation has turned to people describing their favourite foods.

I envision the chicken cacciatore mom would only make me for my birthday supper. She refused to make it any other time of the year. She said that it was too much work and that it wouldn't be special anymore if we made it any other time.

"Close the door!" People shout from the living room.

Chapter 28

Rayleen rolls the dice and bumps her token the same number as the dice commands. She cheers a little, "I'm getting so close. I'm going to win!"

Daniel goes next, while I sip my hot chocolate.

Quickly, I pick up the dice on my turn, roll and move my token. Rayleen takes much longer with her turn than Daniel and I included.

This is how it should be. Utter content as we enjoy each other's company.

I dip my dry cookie in my hot chocolate, and Rayleen rushes to copy me.

The wind whistles against the outside. Rayleen looks up worried.

"Just the wind." I remind her.

Something crashes in metal thunder.

A few people rush to look out the window for the cause.

"Is that a bear?"

"Better not be."

Daniel gets up to go look with the others. I stay behind to make sure Rayleen doesn't get scared.

"We'll be okay," I promise to her worried eyes. She scurries up to her feet and rushes to my lap for a hug. I wrap my arms around her tightly and kiss the top of her head.

"What the fuck is that thing?"

"Dogs?"

"Fuck."

"No, it has three heads. Shit."

Three people rush by with weapons to get their boots on. "Help us get it. We're under attack!"

A mess of a hoard gathers in the front entry to put on, at minimum, boots. Weapons are handed out and people exit the house.

I'm frozen in place.

What do they mean by under attack?

Is it just the dog, or are there more?

Did Darius and Sandra come back?

Rayleen breaks out of my arms and rushes to the window to get a good look. This only spurs my legs to follow after her.

In the dark and through heavy snow, we can't see much.

"Stop! It's not attacking. We don't have to kill it!" A male yells. I hear a yelp soon after.

A cold chill runs up my spine and gives my skin bumps. Turning my head, I notice the door wide open. I run to shut it. I contemplate locking it, but that would lock out all the people out there. I doubt a lock would do anything against a three-headed dog.

I get back to Rayleen and the couch to watch.

A wall of snow rises up, blocking the dog from the angry crowd. Some of the dark figures fall on their backs.

The wall comes down and the dog is gone.

Cam comes through the door first. He dashes down the hall. Slipping over the snow attached to his boots. He catches himself so he doesn't fall down.

Angry men slam the door open and stomp through the house. Cursing Cam out. They look for him.

Daniel breaks off from them to come to us.

"What happened?" I ask.

"He stopped it with magic. Told it to go home. Now they want him gone." Daniel says.

I hope Cam left out the back.

"Should we go?" I ask cryptically and quietly.

"No, they're just mad right now. They'll get over it." He looks over to the hall, then back to us.

"But-" I motion to Rayleen.

Daniel hesitates. "Right. We'll see."

Rayleen covers her ears and closes her eyes when the shouts peak. I put my hands over hers.

I hold my breath as a man comes by with Cam hoisted over his shoulder. He carries a backpack with one arm; he must've gone back for that.

With the door still open, the man throws Cam outside the house.

They swear and call him names. Tell him to never come back or they'll kill him.

I look over to Daniel.

"Yeah, maybe." He responds quietly to my previous question.

They slam the door shut. Rayleen jumps. I surround her to give the both of us some comfort.

They continue to holler for twenty minutes before some finally decide to break off. Daniel takes that as an opportunity to move us to the bedroom.

I try to settle Rayleen down for bed, but I doubt anyone will be able to get to sleep any time soon with all the excitement.

Daniel is handed a folded paper by Brad. "What's this?"

"Meeting invitation." Brad moves on to deliver more letters to others before leaving.

He goes quiet as he reads the invitation. He hands it to me after. It reads:

Meeting of the HUMANS.

Tomorrow @ 9AM.

Chapter 29

The snow and cold have shut us all inside, and I don't know how much more I can take.

Or, any of us can take.

People are getting restless and irritable. We've already had to switch some people back and forth between the two houses to avoid more fight breaking out.

One of the bedroom doors is shut; it strikes me as weird.

I open it without knocking. Jaiden squeaks and tries to shut the open window. It's a bit chilly in here, but not bad. I don't think she's had it open for long.

"Sorry. I needed fresh air, but people get mad when you open a door." She says.

"It's okay. Keep it open. Just not for long." I go sit next to her. "I need it too." I take in a deep refreshing breath.

"How are you doing?" She asks.

"I didn't realize how stale the air was," I reveal my thoughts.

"Me neither. It's suffocating; slowly." She puts it exactly how it feels.

Tears draw to my eye but don't fall. "Maybe we should force everyone outside for a few minutes. I didn't realize how depressing it would be to be forced to stay inside so much."

"That's why Christmas was invented. Why all wintery holidays were invented. They bring joy and hope to dreary long winters. Curb a bit of depression, so more people last until spring." Jaiden enlightens.

If that's true, then we need to do something. We don't need people killing each other and we certainly don't need anyone killing themselves.

"Sounds like we need a holiday."

"That's not a horrible idea." She agrees.

"What could we do?" I ask. We could follow all the other holidays. I think Valentine's is next.

"I don't know. Second Christmas?"

I nod and take a mental note. "We didn't really have the first Christmas, so that could work. But, what about the rest of the time? We still have at least four months of snow and cold."

What's something that people could look forward to?

There are all sorts of winter sports, but that's less appealing when you know the chill won't leave you for days after. Maybe we could arrange a winter sports competition for one of the warmer days near spring.

We could try to arrange a feast, but that would be better suited for Christmas. And, I wouldn't want to make a habit of feasts where there's potential for spoiled leftovers and massive food waste.

What could masses of people do inside a house?

Game night is dismissed as fast as it enters my thoughts. Games have tendencies to cause fights, so we can't even try to attempt that until people have spaces to go to calm down.

We have electricity now, so what about a movie night?

"Do you think we have enough power for a movie?" I ask. I have no idea about what wattage or power any of that would need. I don't know how much power we have left on the generators. Someone mentioned they were nearing their max, but I'm not sure how accurate that was.

"I have no idea." Jaiden bites her lips together and looks up. "Maybe just the TV and DVD player, but not the sound system. But, if everyone's willing to trade off a few hours of heat for two hours of movie, we likely could justify it."

I jump up from the bed and leave the room. Excited to look into putting this into motion.

In the living room, I find a very sad movie collection. There aren't many movies to choose from and they are mostly old classics.

Not exactly what I'd want for a first movie night. Especially, when I'm trying to build up morale.

"Does anyone know what the movie collection looks like in the other houses?" I shout above the noise. The immediate room's noise turns to nothing.

"Why?" Calli asks.

"We're planning a movie night to keep up morale," I announce.

"You're planning on wasting energy." A man says.

"Two hours of heaters off traded for two hours of movie entertainment on the odd occasion, so we don't kill each other or ourselves over the next four months; is hardly a waste of resources." I reason. He shrugs and agrees after that.

"There's a movie shelf at our place, but I didn't think to look at it." That seems to be a general consensus among people. No one thought to check out the movies because no one thought they'd be able to watch them.

I hadn't either.

When I was visiting when I was younger, I wasn't allowed on the TV at all while I was here. I was barely allowed to have my phone, while also not being allowed to do much more than text my parents and take pictures. Not that the pictures were any good back in those days. Flip phone cameras sucked.

"Our place has lots of kid's movies. Should have something there for crowd pleasers." A woman says.

"That would be great." Kid's movies might be best. They tend to be more upbeat and have happy endings.

Talking about movie night creates a pleasant buzz around the room.

This is why we need it. Something we can collectively look forward too. Something everyone, no matter who they are, can enjoy.

About Jacey K Dew

Jacey is an author and mom who was raised in Leduc, Alberta by her adoptive family.

She took inspiration from familiar locations to set the scenes. Asking the question, what if supernatural beings took over?

Jacey started writing stories when she was sixteen and continues to have a passion for creating tales. Writing across genres in whichever story needs to be told next.

Jacey can be found at a multitude of social sites under the handle @jaceykdew and her website hub jaceykdew.ca

Her link page can quickly sort you to social sites, merchandise and book shop, blog, fan club, and a few retail stores her books are available at.

You can also sign up for her newsletter on the links page to receive the occasional email about on goings, book releases, bookish news, discounts and freebies.

jaceykdew.ca/about/links

Subscribe to SuperData to immerse yourself in the Three Souls Universe. Choose between free and paid levels to customize your reader experience. Free to access forums, emails, customizable profiles, freebies, discounts, behind the scenes information, and Ask the Author discussions. Or, choose a paid subscription to add physical mailed items.

jaceykdew.ca/superdata

Other Books by This Author

Vacation Romance

Skylar Bryson goes on the vacation of her lifetime. Tasting freedom and stepping out of her comfort zone while meeting interesting new people and gaining a different perspective. Will Skylar find more than adventure in Mexico? Once Skylar returns home her world is turned upside down. Will Skylar find her support system in her new companion, or should well enough have been left alone?

Coming of Age, Life Lessons Novella

Anna's parents had strict rules for life. Suddenly, at eighteen, her parent's deadly accident throws her life into turmoil. She has nothing more than her parent's rules to go by, but she soon learns that maybe her parent's beloved rules may be wrong for her.

Small Town Drama Novella

She never thought she'd have to return to the city in the crux of a mountain. When her mother falls ill, Kara is beckoned home and thrust into the world she left behind.